D0459335

A PRINCE ON PAPER

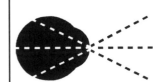

This Large Print Book carries the
Seal of Approval of N.A.V.H.

RELUCTANT ROYALS

A PRINCE ON PAPER

ALYSSA COLE

THORNDIKE PRESS
A part of Gale, a Cengage Company

Farmington Hills, Mich • San Francisco • New York • Waterville, Maine
Meriden, Conn • Mason, Ohio • Chicago

Copyright © 2019 by Alyssa Cole.
Thorndike Press, a part of Gale, a Cengage Company.

Thorndike Press® Large Print African-American.
The text of this Large Print edition is unabridged.
Other aspects of the book may vary from the original edition.
Set in 16 pt. Plantin.

LIBRARY OF CONGRESS CIP DATA ON FILE.
CATALOGUING IN PUBLICATION FOR THIS BOOK
IS AVAILABLE FROM THE LIBRARY OF CONGRESS

ISBN-13: 978-1-4328-6573-3 (hardcover alk. paper)

Published in 2019 by arrangement with Avon, an imprint of HarperCollins Publishers

Printed in Mexico
1 2 3 4 5 6 7 23 22 21 20 19

For all the people who dream too big.

CHAPTER 1

Welcome to the world of One True Prince, where the prince of your dreams might be just around the corner. Are you ready to find true love with a handsome royal? If so, enter your name here, and then the keys to the kingdom are yours! Remember to choose wisely — the royal life isn't all fun and games, and not every prince is who he seems to be!

Nya Jerami returned her obscenely comfortable seat to the upright position, then pushed aside her braids to remove the wireless earplugs from her ears — no amount of relaxing meditation music was going to make her feel better about returning home to Thesolo.

Before leaving to participate in an early childhood development masters program at a university in Manhattan, she'd imagined days spent surrounded by a throng of intrigued peers, and nights being courted by handsome men. She'd had a plan for how things would go: after years of being kept like a caged bird by her father, she would arrive in Manhattan, spread her wings, and soar straight toward her happiness. That was how things happened in the films she had grown up watching, where every timid girl secretly had the heart — and talons — of an eagle.

But in real life, the jostling crowds and tall buildings had made her uneasy, the subway trains had given her motion sickness, and traffic had moved in a wild and frightening way that left her in constant fear of being crushed. She'd sat silently in class, biting back her thoughts, and her peers had barely known she'd existed. Dating had gone no better, a series of uncomfortable and disheartening encounters with creepy men.

The plane bounced over some light turbulence and Nya closed her eyes against an unwelcome thought. Perhaps her father had been right with his constant reminders she should dream smaller, want less — the simple fact was that for Nya, New York had simply been too big.

She'd had plenty of exciting adventures — fighting space pirates, taming a vampire king, being sought after by every senpai in her high school — but those things had taken place in the virtual dating games she played on her phone. In those worlds, she was fearless, always knew the right thing to say, and if one of her dates annoyed her, she could delete him without much guilt.

Now she peered through the window of the private jet of the royal family, the African landscape unrolling beneath her like a familiar but suffocating quilt heralding that her adventure in New York was truly finished. There were no expansion packs available.

Game over.

"We'll be landing in Thesolo in approximately two hours, Miss Jerami," Mariha, the flight attendant, said as she peeked her head into the cabin for the approximately one thousandth time. "You'll be home soon."

"Thank you," Nya said politely, nausea roiling her stomach.

Two hours.

Home.

"Are you all right?" Mariha's face creased with concern, and though Nya should've appreciated it, she hated that expression. People always looked at her like she was a vase perpetually in danger of falling off a

9

shelf. In Thesolo, she had been the finance minister's frail, sickly daughter, too weak to know her own mind. That image had stuck with her well past childhood, and despite having single-handedly rejuvenated the Lek Hemane Orphanage School during her tenure as a teacher, people still patted her on the head and spoke to her like her dance of womanhood hadn't been half a lifetime ago.

They'd taken their cues from her father, who'd spent a lifetime explaining to people that Nya needed his guidance. Even his imprisonment hadn't erased the script that he'd written for her.

"Nya has her little job, yes, but she cannot handle too much work. The stress is dangerous for her, and she prefers being at home."

She'd been guilted and wheedled and talked down to until she was a nonplayer character in the role-playing game of her own life.

Home. Two hours.

Her hands went to her stomach, which was busy twisting itself into anxious balloon animals.

"The flight is a bit bumpy," she said, finally gazing up at Mariha. "Do you have something soothing for the stomach?"

"We have the goddess blend tea, of course.

That has many uses," Mariha said, and then her smile fell as she seemed to remember that Nya's father had used the same tea as a poison, corrupting nature and tradition for his own ends. Mariha blinked rapidly. "I'm sorry. I wasn't — Forgive me, Miss Jerami, I wasn't insinuating! I —"

"It's all right," Nya said. Her father had ruined even the pleasure of tea for her. "I prefer ginger ale."

"Ginger ale. Right away," Mariha replied, her blinks still transmitting apologies in Morse code. "Wi-Fi service has resumed, by the way."

With that, she hurried down the aisle, her low heels thumping on the plane's carpeted floor.

Nya snatched up her phone from the seat beside her, opening her friend messaging app as anxiety feathered over her neck, scrolling back to the conversation just before her flight had taken off.

INTERNATIONAL FRIEND EMPORIUM CHAT

Ledi: If coming back is too over-whelming, just let me know. I want you here, but I also know that this isn't going to be easy for you.

11

Nya: Of course, I'm coming to your wedding! Don't be ridiculous. I'll just ignore the people whispering about how I tricked you into being my friend after my father hurt you. Or debating whether I'm a disgraceful daughter who will visit my father in prison or a disgraceful one who won't.

Portia: Those options don't seem fun. Let me know if you need help dealing with the attention. Johan can help, too. Ask him for some pointers.

Nya: I know Johan is your friend, but that guy is weird.

Portia: 😕 Aren't all of us weird?

Ledi: Thabiso and I found a secret dungeon in the palace (don't ask), and I will gladly jail anyone who upsets you.

Ledi: Just kidding, I'm not a despot. I *will* publicly call them out and embarrass them, though.

Portia: That's worse than a dungeon, as we all know.

Ledi: Yep. 😈

Nya: I'll be fine, thank you. Also, please be careful in the dungeon, or at least send us a map so we know where to search if you and Thabiso disappear.

Ledi: We have cell phone reception down there, and we had new locks put on that can always be opened from the inside. I'm not trying to live that "Cask of Amontillado" life.

Portia: Did you look into those therapists I gave you a list of, Nya?

Nya: Gotta go, flight is boarding! 😬

Portia: Okay I can take a hint. ☹ Tell Johan that I brought him a present.

Nya's brow furrowed. She'd missed that last message and nothing else had followed it because Ledi and Portia were together and could speak to one another.

Nya: What do you mean "tell Johan"?

13

The message went unread — it was before daybreak in Thesolo.

Her phone emitted a ping and she quickly switched apps, a little burst of relief filling her when the load screen for *One True Prince* appeared. OTP was a cute, but immersive, dating simulator game that had developed a cult following — you played the role of new girl at a boarding school full of princes in which one of them was a spy bent on destroying the system of monarchies forever. It was silly fun, but kind of intense: you had to be ready to receive messages at any time, even the middle of the night. Like true love, the game worked on its own schedule; you had to keep up or be rich enough to buy your way out of your mistakes.

She'd romanced all of the princes except for two: Basitho, whom the developers had clearly based on her soon-to-be official cousin-in-law, Thabiso; and Hanjo, a bad-boy prince based on Thabiso's best friend, Johan. She cringed at the idea of romancing even a fictional version of Thabiso, who besides being her cousin's soul mate, was also pretty goofy. As for Hanjo . . .

Johan Maximillian von Braustein was an infamously attractive extrovert, happiest at the center of a party or in front of a camera. He was everything she despised in a man —

self-indulgent, spoiled, expecting everything around him to bend to his wishes.

She hated the ease with which Johan moved through the world. She hated that he always seemed so sure of himself. She hated that when Portia had first introduced them, for the briefest moment Nya'd felt *something* as their gazes met, sparking a wild, ridiculous hope. Then, like most people, Johan had quickly looked past her in search of someone more interesting.

Hanjo Millianmaxi bon Vaustein was a two-dimensional video game character that was the closest Nya would get to the playboy prince of Liechtienbourg paying her any mind. Not that she wanted him to or anything — she was hate-romancing this character. That was it.

ONE TRUE PRINCE, MESSAGE FROM: HANJO

Hello, Nya. I saw that you were having trouble in Advanced Royal History Class. Do you need me to tutor you?

She looked through the available responses.

A. Why would I want help from a carrot

15

head like you?
B. How dare you insinuate I need help!
C. I would love that. I'll bring homemade
   treats! <3

She didn't want to insult him outright since romance was her goal, so A was out. B was rude, too, but C was much too close to what people would expect her to say in real life. She hit B, then put the phone down where she could keep an eye on it.

Mariha returned with the ginger ale, hovering as Nya sipped.

"Do you need anything else? Toast? Tums? A heated pad?" Mariha was smiling, but there was still mild panic in her eyes, as if she worried about insulting the new princess's cousin right before the wedding ceremony . . . or raising the legendary Jerami ire.

Nya had her own anxiety to deal with, though, and Mariha's was fraying her already taut nerves. "I believe I'll go lie down."

It was ridiculous for a plane to have a bedroom, but her body felt heavy with dread, her back was strained from packing up her apartment, and her heart ached at the weight of all her worries. She felt . . . odd, and a voice that sounded like her father

16

whispered, *You are not well, my child. You are frail, like your mother. This is why you must stay home.*

She stood, eager to escape Mariha's nervous attention and the sudden reminder that her body had betrayed her in the past and could do so again.

No. That won't happen now. You're free.

"Lie down?" Mariha tilted her head and drew it back. "Are you quite sure you want to do that?"

There was censure in her tone. In Thesolo, everyone thought Nya couldn't make the simplest decision.

"Why wouldn't I be sure?" Nya asked. "I said I was going to lie down, not parachute from the plane."

Mariha opened her mouth, closed it, then raised a hand awkwardly. "Of course. But —"

Nya held up her own hand. "I'm going to the bedroom. Do not disturb me until we are ready to land. Please."

Mariha's confused expression relaxed into raised brows and . . . what was that grin about?

"Oh. Ohhh. Of *course*, Ms. Jerami." The hovering anxiousness was gone now. "If you need any — ah — anything in particular, check the top drawer in the bedside table."

17

"Wonderful." Nya turned and strode as confidently as she could toward the bedroom as the plane bounced over air currents, walked in, and closed the door behind her.

The room was completely dark.

Where is the light switch?

She slid her palms over the wall beside the door in frustrated panic. She couldn't very well head back out into the cabin and ask for help after her haughty exit. Giving up, she pressed the home button on her cell phone, the dim light from the screen illuminating the edge of the bed.

She shuffled her way toward it and sighed in relief as the soft mattress gave way beneath her palms and her knees. The bed was decadent, as any bed befitting royalty would be, and she allowed her weary body to sink into the swaddling comfort.

Too soft, she thought, then chided herself for her ingratitude.

Now that she was alone in the dark, tears stung at her eyes and her chest felt tight. She would be home, Thesolo home, in less than two hours, and despite all the assurances she'd given to friends and family, she was not prepared.

She thought of how Mariha had said

Jerami like the word was a hot coal on her tongue.

It was a venerated surname in the small but powerful African kingdom — Annie and Makalele Jerami, Nya's grandparents, were respected tribal elders. Naledi Smith née Ajoua, born of a Jerami, was the country's prodigal princess-to-be, whose impending marriage was currently the most anticipated event in Thesolo's history.

The name was also reviled in some quarters now because of the man that made Nya's hands tremble with nerves.

Alehk Jerami the traitor. Alehk Jerami the disgrace of Thesolo.

Alehk Jerami, Nya's father.

He'd committed many crimes against the kingdom of Thesolo, as everyone had discovered two years before — blackmail, treason, fraud — but the worst among these had been the shameful act of poisoning his own kin. Annie and Makalele and Naledi — Ledi, whose parents had fled years before to escape Alehk's threats and died in a land far from their ancestors, leaving their daughter orphaned — had almost lost their lives.

No. Her father had almost taken them.

Unspeakable.

In the aftermath, people spoke of how Alehk harmed everyone closest to him, as if

19

he himself were poison. There were even rumors that his beloved wife hadn't really died in childbirth, though Nya was certain that wasn't true. But his daughter? It seemed that no one thought about mousy little Nya when it came to the crimes of Alehk Jerami, except to pity her or wonder if she'd aided him.

He'd loved her too much to hurt her, everyone thought, but too much love could hurt, too.

Would you leave me, too, Nya? After having taken your mother from me? Answer me, child.

No, Father. I will never leave you.

She sucked in a breath against the panic and pressed her thumbs into the corners of her eyes, as if stopping a leak in a dam. Nya wouldn't cry. She wouldn't, even though she felt more alone than she ever had before. Even though she was certain that being home, which should have made her feel safe, would only make that hollowness inside of her feel even deeper, darker, and more inescapable.

I wish . . . I wish.

The bed suddenly shifted, the tilt of the mattress jarring, and Nya was pulled into a strong, solid embrace. Her nose tickled at the smell of lemon and lavender, citrus and almost abrasive floral, as far from the smell of the eng flower of Thesolo — her father's poison of choice — as she could get. The arms that clamped around her were lean and muscular, and the body it pulled her against was just as fit. The body was warm — so warm and cradling her so perfectly that she relaxed and sighed at how . . . *right* it felt before her fear and common sense kicked in.

She was alone on the plane. But someone was in the bed behind her. *Holding her.* Had her distress been so acute that it had reached Ingoka's ears? Had she conjured this sudden comfort? She knew the folklore of the lesser gods, of those who gave humans what they wanted but always took more than they gave.

No, this is no time for fairy-tale silliness.

She tried to tug herself free from the stranger's arm because, be they god or man, something really fucking weird was going on.

The hold tightened. *"Reste bei mir."*

The sleep-slurred words came out in an exhalation that tickled Nya's ear and made her belly jolt. She pushed at one of the arms from below and the hold loosened as the stranger snorted and began to move. A large hand patted her arm, paused, then pulled away.

21

"What have we here?" The voice was deep and smooth, a European, judging from the strangely accented English. So definitely not a lesser god of Thesolo, and more likely a human — one who might be dangerous.

She jumped up off the bed, listing a bit as the plane dipped and tilted, fumbling with her phone as her hands began to tremble slightly. She was on the plane usually reserved for the royal family of Thesolo. Ledi had made her listen to those true crime podcasts so Nya knew that this could be some depraved assassin.

What kind of assassin snuggles people to death?

Stranger things had happened.

"Who are you and what do you want?" She tried to access the flashlight app, but her thumb was wet from the tears she'd pressed into submission and the fingerprint reader wouldn't work. She pressed the button along the phone's side to take photos instead, no unlocking required, and the bright bursts of the camera's automatic flash revealed the outline of a man stretched out on the bed.

The bed she had just sought out for safety and comfort. A jolt of anger and fear sliced through her as her thumb repetitively pushed the button.

22

"What do you want?" she asked again, stepping back toward the door.

"Hmm. Biscuits?" The lazy response was punctuated by the sound of shuffling on the sheets. "Biscuits would be *super.* I missed the in-flight meal."

Wait. That voice is familiar. And the language . . .

A light suddenly flicked on, and Nya blinked several times, and then kept on blinking even after her eyes had adjusted. Her ears hadn't lied.

Oh! It's him.

"Oh. It's you." Johan Maximillian von Braustein's thick auburn hair was tousled and unruly, his cheeks slightly flushed as if he'd been dreaming of something naughty. His dress shirt was unbuttoned at the collar and rolled up to his elbows, revealing the reddish hair on his chest and dusting his forearms. The shocking blue eyes that routinely stared out from the covers of tabloids? Those were bright and clear, even if the rest of him was still half-asleep.

For a second, she was hit with the same ridiculous certainty she'd had the first time she'd met him — that he was appraising her like a man tallying the pleasure of making her his, and willing to trade them all.

Then he looked away, his features the very

picture of boredom. It had been her imagination running away with her again, fooling her into hoping for wide vistas when her actual view was blinkered at best.

He gathered a lump of tangled bedsheet close to him.

"Ledi's cousin. Naya, is it? I thought you were a pillow," he said before yawning hugely. Then he glanced at her, as if he'd thoroughly forgotten her presence in the time it had taken him to yawn and was now mildly surprised to find her there. "Well? Do you have biscuits?"

"No." She realized she was still holding her phone out defensively and lowered her arm. His gaze on her intensified, and Nya felt the English being knocked from her head by the impact of it. "The bed. I want to be in it."

"I see." That shocking blue gaze warmed beneath long lashes that drooped as if they'd suddenly grown heavy. "Are you here to seduce me, Naya?"

Nya almost dropped her phone at his audacity. He was so calm, so sure that if she was there it must be to fulfill his needs. Her vocabulary returned, reloaded by her anger. "Seduce you? No! I didn't even know you were in here!"

He rolled over onto his side, resting his

head on the mound of bedding he'd gathered, the better to see her. "I know this trick. 'Oh, I'm just a timid little thing who wandered into the lair of the big bad wolf.' " He chuckled and patted the mattress. "Very well, then, Naya. Come to bed and I'll eat you up."

Goddess. He'd gone from ignoring her at every encounter, to not remembering her name, to accusing her of seduction, to offering . . . THAT as easily as the priestesses handed out garlands at the flower festival. She wasn't sure what was more intolerable, his assumption or the amusement in his tone. He was wrong about her intentions but, like everyone else, thought the mere idea of Nya taking what she wanted was laughable.

Even the most docile Jerami wouldn't tolerate this disrespect. She gripped the phone and pointed it at him. "I am pulling no tricks. And my name is *Nya.* You might remember that before inviting me to lower myself with a man like you."

"My mistake," he said lightly, seemingly resistant to shaming, then scooted over. "Well, the bed is big enough to fit two, and I wouldn't mind some company right now."

Nya paused, dropping her hand to her side again. There was *something* in his tone . . .

25

but before she could identify it, he glanced at her sidelong.

"I didn't ask before because I was asleep, I suppose, but do you prefer big spoon or little spoon?" He raised his eyebrows suggestively, underlining the fact that to him this was a joke. But to her . . .

Nya had never been held by a man before Johan had, apparently, mistaken her for a pillow. His arms around her had felt good in that moment before reality had set in, when he might have been a figment of her imagination and not a world-famous fuckboy. And now this jerk who had never bothered to learn her name and would likely forget her existence again as soon as the plane landed, thought to make light of the most intimate experience she'd had thus far?

Of course. Self-indulgent, spoiled . . . he doesn't know what it's like to be alone. For him, spooning a random woman on a plane is just another Tuesday.

"You can be big spoon if you want," he offered when she didn't respond, and Nya sucked her teeth. He really was as appalling as the tabloids made him out to be.

"I will be the *only* spoon. Get out." Her voice trembled and she swallowed hard against the lump forming in her throat. She could still feel his arms around her, holding her close. The heat of his body and his scent surrounding her. For the first time, she'd known what it felt like to be . . . cared for. And it had been this ridiculous man, who cared for no one but himself. This greedy, wanton playboy with his good looks and smooth words, who expected her to bend to his wishes.

Nya was both embarrassed and furious.

Worse, behind her fury, a small lonely voice in the deepest part of her whispered, *Go to him. Isn't this what you dreamed of?*

Johan sat there looking at her with his confident grin, as if he was in cahoots with her traitorous hidden desires.

Nya was lonely, but she had suffered enough humiliation for one lifetime.

She gestured toward the door. "Get. Out."

"I'm quite comfortable," he said, settling in. "And let's not forget that I was here first, Mademoiselle I Want to Be in Bed."

This teasing was so much worse than all those times he had ignored her in New York City because she'd imagined situations just like this, despite her distaste for him. Situations where he couldn't pretend she didn't exist and was hit with the realization that she did and she *mattered* — and perhaps even that he wanted no one but her.

27

Your dreams are too big, girl.

Now he was finally looking right at her and all he saw was a woman to be treated like a joke. That was all anyone would ever see.

Her father had been right.

"I said get out!" Nya had never yelled before. It was strange, how the angry words scraped her throat. How did people do this all the time? No matter. She would shout him to the threshold of Ingoka's abyss if necessary. "You rude, inconsiderate, selfish, arrogant —"

Her words caught on an ugly choking sound and tears spilled down her cheeks, a sudden graceless torrent. She raised her hands to her face.

Apparently, I haven't *been humiliated enough.*

"Ah, *scheisse.*"

She could see the white of Johan's dress shirt and the gray of his pressed slacks through the spaces between her fingers as he moved from the bed and stood before her, but she refused to look up into his face.

"Nya." His voice was gentle now. So, so gentle, wrapping around her like his arms had, which somehow made everything worse.

She shook her head and sniffled against

28

her palm. "I want to be alone." Her voice broke like that of a reedy youth, and she squeezed her eyes shut even harder. She had spent so much of her life never breaking, pretending that everything was all right, and of course it would happen now, in front of *him.*

"Here," he said, and then there was the feel of silky soft material against the back of her hand. "Take it, along with my apology. I've behaved . . . I won't say it was quite out of character, but I know better and shouldn't have spoken to you in that way. I took my bad mood out on you."

"It's fine. I'm used to that," she said miserably as she snatched the handkerchief he offered. If her father had prepared her for anything it was that her happiness was always to be at the whim of some man.

She wiped at her face, inhaling the scent of lemon and lavender that had wrapped around her so comfortingly before.

"Used to it?" Johan's voice was a little sharper now, the lazy, inviting drawl a little more firm. "That doesn't make it right. I was an ass."

She blew her nose, barely listening. She knew that men only apologized when you made them question their own idea of themselves. She would assuage him, so he

29

could feel like a good man again and leave her alone. "It's fine. I accept your apology."

"Don't pardon me so easily." She glanced at him to see that he had one hand on his hip, the other behind his back as he leaned a bit closer to her. "Or pardon me if you want, I suppose, but don't do it because you're *used to* dealing with asses."

"Sorry," she said automatically. With her father, *sorry* had been a magic word to make unpleasant conversations stop.

"For what?" Johan pressed, and the brazen man had the nerve to sound annoyed with *her.*

Nya didn't respond. She was annoyed herself — and confused. Johan had insulted her, then comforted her, and now was defending her from himself? Men were exhausting, truly.

She sniffled.

He made a sound of consternation. "I don't have any more handkerchiefs, but my shirt is quite absorbent if you need a shoulder to cry on. It's made of the finest cotton."

"I have my own shoulders, thank you very much," she said, aware her words didn't quite make sense. "I'm not going to cry all over some disrespectful man."

He rolled his eyes. "Come now. You've read the tabloids, I'm sure. I've been linked to worse bodily fluids than tears."

"What?" She shouldn't have asked — she wanted to be rid of him — but this was all so bizarre that she couldn't suppress her shocked laughter. "Is that gross oversharing supposed to make me feel better?"

"Does it make you feel worse?" He grinned at her, then brushed aside a lock of hair that had fallen in front of his eyes.

She looked at him. "I suppose not."

"Gutt." His gaze flicked to the door and then back to her. "Do you still want me to leave?"

Nya was aware that he was no longer being flippant — that if she wanted him to *stay,* he would do that, too. Her head spun a bit at how quickly Johan could change the tone of the conversation, like a car shifting gears, but then she shook it. This wasn't a game. He wasn't her one true prince. In the end, he was just another tiresome man who wanted something from her.

"No," she said. "You should go."

"Comme tu willst," he said softly. "The light switch is on the console on the bedside table, next to the USB port."

With that he let himself out, taking the bundled-up top sheet with him. She wouldn't conjecture why, given his whole bodily fluids thing. Instead, she flopped

31

down onto the bed, still somewhat in shock.

Maybe it was for the best she was returning home. She would go back to work at the orphanage school, where the children needed her. She would resume visiting her grandparents, who loved her. She would once again be boring, timid Nya, because that's who she was anywhere she went and she might as well stop trying to be someone she wasn't.

Her phone buzzed in her hand.

ONE TRUE PRINCE,
MESSAGE FROM: HANJO

I like a girl with spirit! I'll be in the library tomorrow afternoon, and we can pretend it's a coincidence when you show up and sit beside me.

"Shut up, Hanjo," she muttered.

She was about to put the phone down when she remembered the camera flash she'd used to figure out who the snuggly stowaway was — she had taken photos of him. She shouldn't have felt a gnawing curiosity as she navigated to the camera roll — it was kind of creepy having the photos, even if she hadn't taken them intentionally.

There were several pictures. All were dark

with blurry patches of light, except for one that was as clear as if he'd posed for her. She expected his expression to be sly playboy boredom, but his expression was somber as he looked toward the camera. He looked . . . sad?

No, he looks like a man about to bother you for no reason, because that's what he did, she reminded herself. Then she looked closer.

Was that?

No, it couldn't be.

But it was.

There, poking out from underneath the playboy prince of Liechtienbourg, was the face of a small, ratty, oddly disgruntled-looking teddy bear.

"Oh goddess," she whispered, not quite sure what to feel. He was a *very* weird man — not because he slept with a teddy bear, but because from everything she knew about him, he was the last man who would. He slept with *models,* and drove fancy cars, and . . .

Well, it didn't matter. She doubted she'd see him, or his angry bear, much after the plane landed anyway. He was the loud, in-the-middle-of-the-action type. She was usually safely holding up a wall, looking at those types in admiring scorn. She'd keep his teddy bear secret safe. She would *not* think about how it was rather cute.

She put her phone down and opened the drawer the flight attendant had told her about, where she found a box of luxurious, aloe-infused tissues — along with condoms, lubricant, and a pair of fuzzy handcuffs.

She remembered the flight attendant's smirk when Nya had insisted on going into the bedroom.

Nya slammed the drawer shut, curled up on the bed, and pulled the pillow over her head. It smelled of eng, but faintly, very faintly, of lemon and lavender.

She sighed.

If Mariha was a gossip, the Nya of the fantasy world would once again be much more interesting than the real one.

CHAPTER 2

Where is Jo-Jo? In the days leading up to the darkest day in Liechtienbourgian history, the infamous prince is nowhere to be found! Crown Prince Lukas has been seen out and about more than usual, though. With the upcoming referendum dividing the country, is the reserved young prince ready to step into the spotlight?
— The Liechtienbourg Bugle

Despite what the tabloids said about his reckless behavior, Johan, aka the Tabloid Prince of Liechtienbourg, aka Bad Boy Jo-Jo, had a rigid sense of control. That no one was aware of this was evidence of that. He showed people what he wanted them to see — what they wanted to see, really — because that was what worked best for him. For his family. For everyone.

He didn't think of himself as manipulative, a word that sounded villainous; he preferred cunning — Machiavellian, maybe, but without the immorality and murder. He made sure no one was hurt by his scheming. No one but himself, but that hurt was negligible compared to others he'd suffered.

So it bothered him, as he stretched out in a plush seat in the main cabin of the private jet, that he'd let his control slip.

He'd told himself he was joking when he'd suggested to Nya that he would eat her up, like a cliché of a pervert. *Scheisse,* he cringed just thinking about it. He'd convinced himself the joke had served a purpose — distraction from an untimely discovery of his sleeping partner Bulgom Pamplemousse von Bearstein, who was now stowed away with Johan's carry-on. Everyone knew "Prince" Johan cracked scandalous jokes. Everyone thought he *was* one.

But Johan avoided letting his jokes overlap with his desires. And Nya? He desired her.

It was a problem.

He'd only started watching her because, well, her father had almost killed his best friend's fiancée and tried to foment a coup in his best friend's country. Thabiso and Naledi had apparently overlooked her potential role in the matter, explaining that Nya would *never* hurt anyone, but Johan was a bit more cynical. When he'd traveled to New York for charity events or political summits, he'd kept an eye on her and her lovely, shy smile. Her curves, more luscious each time he'd glimpsed her during visits chez Thabiso over the past year and a half. Her quiet amusement with the small things other people didn't pay attention to.

Somewhere along the line, discreetly watching her out of prudence had changed to discreetly lusting after her. He'd thirsted, he'd considered risking it all, and then he'd done what any intelligent person would do — he'd ignored her with a strength matched only by Europe ignoring migrants and America ignoring creeping fascism.

When she'd glance at him, as if considering starting a conversation, he'd spot someone he desperately needed to talk to across the room. When Portia tried to draw her into their jokes, he'd combat roll away. When Thabiso had told him they'd be sharing a flight, Johan snuck into the private jet's bedroom and cowered in the dark.

Control.

But when he'd asked her to come to bed, his joke had been a need beyond his control, and it hadn't been funny. It had been ungentlemanly, rude, and if another man had done the same in his presence Johan would have decked him, or at least embar-

rassed the hell out of him. He was left feeling a bit disoriented. Bad Boy Jo-Jo was a
persona that he used to protect himself and
those he loved; he didn't like how easily he
had slipped on that mask with Nya, how
reflexively he'd reached for crassness and
ended up hurting her.

Maybe it was the stress. Or maybe he'd
really needed a cuddle right then, and Bulgom Pamplemousse von Bearstein simply
hadn't been enough.

It was *that* day. D-day, and not the Nor-
mandy one. Death Day.

He grabbed a lock of hair and twisted, the
movement a tic he'd never outgrown but
had learned to mask with a seductive sweep
of his fingers through his carefully tousled
mane.

There were few things that upset him —
or rather, there were few things he allowed
himself to be upset about — but even he
couldn't fake cool detachment from something as brutal as this.

Back home, the news would be replaying
snippets from his mother's funeral, and ten
years wasn't nearly enough time to make
reliving that bearable. When, at seventeen,
his life had fallen apart — and the adhesive
that had joined him to his blended family
had been suddenly ripped away — he'd

been told that it would hurt less with time. Even then he'd known it was a lie. You couldn't love someone as much as he'd loved his mother — you couldn't be loved by someone as much as he'd been loved by her — and ever stop hurting at their loss. He managed, but he never moved on.

He'd usually spend this day distracting his brother, Lukas, the actual heir to the Liechtienbourgian crown, who had been only seven when their mother passed away. Johan had dedicated his life to making sure that Lukas was loved as Johan had been loved and was protected how Johan hadn't been. He'd taught Lukas all the ways to be liked and accepted by his peers, how to be the *right* kind of boy, one who didn't cry and prefer books to people. He'd pushed Lukas from under the constant burden of the spotlight shone by voracious royal watchers, taking it onto himself. But Lukas was seventeen now, old enough to make his own plans, and had decided he wanted to hold a memorial for their mother.

Johan wasn't going to display his pain for public consumption ever again, and he couldn't put on his Bad Boy Jo-Jo act at his mother's memorial, so he'd been relieved when Thabiso's wedding festivities had provided him with an out.

In the plane's bedroom, when he'd awoken with the ragged wound of loss gaping within him and the woman he desired in his arms, that infuriatingly needy part of him had decided to shoot its shot in the worst way possible.

He groaned and sank deeper into his seat.

All for the best. He could certainly avoid her over the next few days, but ignoring her would be next to impossible. Repelling her would have to suffice. She'd lashed out at him in anger, but she'd been ready to forgive him, by the end. He'd watched her for long enough to know that she was too good, too gentle, for a man like him.

He knew what could happen to women like that.

I'll be okay, Jo-Jo. It's just a bit of fatigue. All I need is some vitamin C, jah?

He pulled his tablet from the travel bag he'd stashed in an overhead compartment when he'd boarded, then logged into the spreadsheet he shared with Greta, the assistant in charge of handling his jet-setting playboy schedule, his official social media presence, his paparazzi herding — and his charitable enterprises.

Johan's mother hadn't been wealthy; that was what had made her and King Linus's love story such irresistible fodder for high-brow journals and tabloids alike. But between the insurance payout for her untimely death, the money she'd arranged to be bequeathed to him since he wasn't entitled to the royal riches, the allowance given to him by Linus, and a fantastic financial advisor, Johan had more assets than he would ever know what to do with.

Some of that went toward his expensive clothing, personal trainers, and top-of-the-line hair care products, but he received many things for free — he was a *trend disseminator,* which was apparently the "manly" term for influencer.

Most of his money was used to fund the growing network of charitable organizations he contributed to and the employees who helped him with the endeavor, like his assistant Greta. Much of his travel was attending fund-raisers for those charities, but when he was on the front page every week for some new possible scandal, those events were usually seen as PR stunts to make up for his misdeeds. And that was how he preferred it.

We do not do good to be praised for it, Jo-Jo, but because one good deed is like a ripple in the water. You have no idea how far one ripple will spread, or who it will reach.

The familiar anger at the unfairness of his

mother's passing lunged up in him at the memory of her words, at the reality that her ripples had been stilled forever, but he tamped it down with practiced efficiency.

The charities were something he didn't share with the press, and he'd publicly deny any such schmaltzy sentiment behind his link to them, of course, but his mother's words had never left him. He wasn't trying to make her proud, even if she was looking down on him from somewhere. She didn't — hadn't — believed in kindness for the accolades they would bring, and neither did he. He was making ripples for the same reason Mother had: because the world *needed* ripples — in the absence of her kindness, it needed waves — and he would do what he could to create them.

Quietly.

Cunningly.

He scanned the spreadsheet, scrolling down to rows highlighted in red and reviewing information in the Update columns, typing his responses in white font so that Greta would be able to keep track of them. The European Women's Heart Disease Awareness Fund, the first charity he'd supported, had broken fund-raising records that week. Of course it had, with his mother dominating the news and the awful irony of her death commented on again and again with macabre headlines.

The day before his mother's funeral, Johan had marched into the *Liechtienbourg Bugle*'s offices and punched the editor who'd allowed the headline "Queen of Our Hearts Didn't Take Care of Her Own." That had been when Bad Boy Jo-Jo, just a chrysalis of a persona he'd used to fit in at boarding school, had emerged on the front page with flamboyant red wings and a taste for trouble — he'd never left it.

Johan squinted at the screen of his tablet, which needed his attention more than useless memories.

The Liechtienbourg Migrant Health and Home organization, his latest charity interest, had come under attack during debates about the referendum — Milos Arschlocher was the man leading the charge on that, claiming that the royal family was allowing Liechtienbourg to stray from tradition.

Johan tamped out another spurt of anger.

After addressing what he could, he reviewed his dossier on Njaza, the diplomatic visit that he'd arranged to take place after Thabiso's wedding. No Liechtienbourgish official had been to the former colony since Linus's father, decades ago. It hadn't been possible, or rather it hadn't been permitted, until the recent coronation of King Sanyu, and Johan wasn't sure how he would be received. The previous king had banned travelers from Liechtienbourg, with good reason after the Liechtienbourgish rich had squeezed Njaza dry and then left the country in the throes of civil war.

Sanyu, who had been two years ahead of Johan and Thabiso at their elite prep school in the Swiss Alps, had been one of the few who had avoided bullying Johan in those first weeks before he had figured out that the other boys didn't care what he was actually like as long as he would roughhouse, say crass things, and only cry if it was from anger — the only acceptable emotion, it seemed.

The flight attendant walked in carrying a tray that held the kale-carrot-mango protein shake he'd asked her for, and Johan shut down his tablet. As she placed the drink down, she gave him the conspiratorial look she'd been sporting since he'd left the bedroom.

"Is Ms. Jerami still . . . sleeping?" she asked coyly. When he'd first boarded, the woman had gone into the state of nervous shock that overtook lots of people when they met him, even those accustomed to dealing with VIPs. Johan was a bit of an outlier even amongst royalty. He fell into the category of semi-celebrities people thought they *knew,* and now that he'd seemingly lived up to his reputation, the flight attendant felt comfortable enough to basically ask if he'd worn Nya out.

Johan reminded himself about his big bad wolf line — he was hardly the one to pass judgment on this woman for seeing him exactly how he'd taught people to see him. He modulated his voice to vague disinterest. "I hope so. She looked like she could use the rest."

The attendant raised her brows, and Johan inhaled deeply.

"Nothing happened between us," he said on the exhale, his bluntness only slightly softened by the charm he ratcheted up. "She didn't know I was in there because, as you know, I asked for privacy when I boarded. I'd appreciate if you kept any misunderstanding about that to yourself."

"Oh yes! Of course, Your Highness." She executed a little curtsy, but as she straightened, she winked at him. "My lips are sealed."

Scheisse de merde. By tomorrow there could be all kinds of "mile high club" puns screaming from the front page of the tabloids.

"Nothing happened," he reiterated. He almost added that he wasn't "your highness" either. He was the stepson to the King of Liechtienbourg and half brother to the actual prince; he was Liechtienbourg's literal redheaded step-prince. He'd once printed up cards to hand out to people in a fit of youthful pique, but that had gone over like burnt schnitzel with the king.

He sighed, then fluttered his lashes in the flight attendant's direction until he had her full attention. "Mariha — what a beautiful name that is. Now, Mariha, I don't mean to push this, but I must make sure that there are no falsehoods spread about me and the *princess's cousin.* That would be terrible for everyone involved, wouldn't it? If it was discovered royal staff had spread lies that might hurt Ms. Jerami?"

He tried to muster his look of affable pleading underlined with stern threat.

"Right, Your Highness," Mariha said carefully. "I understand. I'll go wake Miss Jerami because we'll be landing soon."

Her gaze lingered on his, as if they now shared a thrilling secret, and then she strode away. Johan groaned and pressed his head back into the headrest. He was off his game. Even though he'd run away from Liechtienbourg and memorials and memories, he

46

couldn't escape the general malaise that came with this anniversary every year.

He pulled out his phone and did a quick check in on Lukas, whom he expected to be in bed given the time difference, but who appeared as ONLINE in their chat app.

Jo: Ça va, petite bruder?

The message was first marked as RECEIVED and then as READ, but no telltale "Baby Bro is typing" appeared as it usually did. After a moment, Lukas's status switched to OFFLINE.

Johan's breath went shallow for a moment but he didn't panic.

There was a perfectly reasonable explanation for his lack of response. Maybe Lukas had noticed he had a message, half-awake, then fallen back to sleep. Or hadn't actually read Johan's message, and would respond in the morning. It wasn't as if his brother, the person he cared about most in the world, would *purposely* avoid him.

He switched to his secret social media handle to check the relentlessly nosy royal watcher accounts that had begun to track Lukas despite Johan's distracting antics.

The first thing to pop up in his feed was a photo of his brother, looking sad and pale as he stood in front of the memorial to their mother, holding a wreath. His mouth was a grim line, but his posture was straight and his expression steely. He looked every inch the image of a handsome, dutiful future king, surrounded by strangers in dark suits, and it made Johan's stomach turn. He'd tried so hard to keep Lukas out of the spotlight, but the comments below the image showed his control over that was slipping as well.

@BougieBourger I never noticed but he's SO HOT. I hope everyone votes YES in the upcoming referendum, but if the NO vote wins and the monarchy is abolished, he can come bunk with me.

@GimmeDatBraustein Oh, the poor leibling. Some woman is going to be a very happy future queen, though, if they make it through. Is it true he's seeing Princess Sadie?

Johan frowned. Of course people thought that a picture of a motherless boy in mourning was a great time to conjecture on his dating life. They'd done it to him at the actual bloody funeral.

@crispincakes Jo-Jo didn't show up! But didn't he freak out at his mother's funeral? It's no wonder —

Super.

Johan stopped reading and put his phone away. He hadn't had to suffer the full indignity of social media dissection when his mother had died, and some newspapers had been respectful enough not to publish the photos of his breakdown. He wasn't going to keep reading to see what people trying to revive his trauma would say about it.

He reached through the starched collar of his shirt for the thin, ornate ring on a chain around his neck and took a deep breath. He reminded himself that feelings were useless, unless they belonged to other people and could be protected or used to his benefit — never both.

Maybe Lukas had learned from him, a bit too well. Johan hadn't done much regarding the upcoming referendum because there was influencing as distraction and influencing as politics, and the latter was not his domain. But the always scheming little voice in the back of his mind felt a bit of pride if his brother had known that his appearance would sway people to a yes vote. The voice of his heart, which reasoned that Johan

49

schemed so Lukas wouldn't have to, wasn't quite as amused.

Nya shuffled down the aisle as he was finishing his smoothie and took her seat across from him. She kept her gaze straight ahead, sphinxlike, and the sun streaming in through the window outlined her profile and her crown of braids in gold. Her burnished silhouette was lovely, and Johan imagined capturing it on a cameo, like the old Liechtienbourger love charms — except he would never have the right to own such an object.

"Hello again, Naya," he said, with a deferential tilt of his head. The plan was to walk the tightrope of annoying her — within reason — so that she would avoid him over the next few days, but not so much that she *really* hated him.

She turned her head slowly, regally.

"Yes, Jo-Jo?" There was the slightest hint of unruffled derision in her tone as she used the tabloid nickname for him.

He was both affronted and delighted.

Could she possibly understand how much he hated that name? No, but she'd assumed that he wouldn't be pleased by it. She was soft and gentle, but not all the time, he was learning.

He fought off a smile, and cleared his throat.

"I'm going to apologize again," he said. "There is nothing humorous about a strange man propositioning a woman trapped on a plane with him, and it's not my style."

He looked up at her through his lashes and grinned, a one-two combo he thought would work best on a generally reserved woman like Nya who wasn't used to being the center of attention. Now she would blush, and stammer, and accept his apology not out of reflex but because he'd charmed her. Then he could go back to ignoring her for both of their own good.

She gazed at him steadily, but didn't say anything for a long while. Johan's jaw began to ache from holding his patented smile in place — it usually worked much more quickly than this.

He was off his game, indeed.

Just when the awkwardness was becoming almost intolerable, she tilted her head back and looked down her nose at him.

"Do you mean it? Or are you just trying to make yourself feel better?" Her voice was firm, with no hint of his charm having worked on her.

"Yes. I mean, no. I'm apologizing because I shouldn't have behaved that way," he responded, surprised to find himself flustered.

"If you take a moment to think *before* saying offensive things to a woman, and then *don't* say them, you'll have nothing to apologize for and she won't have to make you feel better about it." She tapped her index finger thoughtfully against her temple as she looked at him, then reached for a magazine on her tray table and pulled it into her lap, ignoring him.

"What?"

"Keep your apology." She flipped the magazine open.

Oh là. He *was* losing his touch.

This . . . was not how things were supposed to play out. She was supposed to accept his apology with a shy smile. Maybe a giggle.

"I don't understand," he said, more to himself than to her.

She glanced at him from the corner of her eye.

"Weren't you the one who told me I shouldn't excuse you?" she asked. That surprising anger that he'd heard before she'd cried crept into her tone. "I get it. It was a joke to you. But I've had some time to think and I don't want your apology or your protection. I want to not be treated like a sex object or a . . . a *sugar bubble* depending on your mood."

She turned a page decisively.

Oh là là.

Johan tore his gaze from her and tried to wrap his mind around the current situation. Nya — wallflower Nya, barely able to make eye contact Nya — had just soundly put him in his place. For a second time. She was like a feather pillow with a knife hidden in its down, and he kept managing to sit on the pointy end.

He hadn't expected that response from her at all, which was worry enough in itself, but his reaction was even more trouble-some.

He liked it. He *quite* liked it.

Oh là là là là.

He was prepared to sit in silence because he was supposed to be ignoring her, but then he heard a little shuddering sigh emanate from her direction and glanced across the aisle.

Her head was bowed over the magazine but the fingers of one hand tapped the pages nervously. The imperious demeanor she'd sported when putting him in his place had slipped away and she seemed smaller. Sad-der.

"Ahem." He took a moment to recalibrate

his idea of her and what she might need to lift her spirits before speaking. She'd laughed a bit at the body fluids bit, though he sensed that she liked being joked with more than raunch. "What exactly is a sugar bubble, so I can avoid treating you like one?"

"Google it," she said, though the edge of her mouth turned up just a millimeter. So she wasn't entirely immune to his charms, then? He could work with that. All he needed was the slightest crack and he could ease his way in, turn this situation around.

Okay, maybe he *was* manipulative. But he didn't like seeing Nya Jerami cry, nor did he like her sighing and troubled across the aisle from him.

He would distract himself from his worries about Lukas by helping her ease her own. That's all this was.

He picked up his tablet and tapped at the blank screen as he pretended to do a search. "Hmm. 'Sugar bubble is the name for a beautiful opalescent form of dark pearl, hollow with a thin shell. It appears delicate but is actually almost indestructible.' Oh, but this sounds like something good, this sugar bubble."

He looked over and saw her shoulders shake a bit, but her head was still down.

She lifted a page of her magazine but didn't turn it. She was listening.

"This is interesting, too. 'Many people think the Trojan War was started over Helen of Troy, but this is a common misconception as her nickname was Sugar Bubble. The war was actually over the theft of this rare jewel, but fighting over a woman sounded more macho in the history books.' "

Her head swiveled in his direction, a smile on her face that rivaled the sunlight glowing through the window behind her. There was a repressed amusement in her tone when she spoke. "You're lying."

"Ouay." The word came out deep and low because he was flirting, despite his best effort not to.

"This isn't going to make me accept your apology," she said cautiously, but then closed the magazine. "What else does it say?"

Johan worked his bottom lip with his teeth in faux studiousness to suppress his grin.

"Let's see, let's see. Paris stole the famed sugar bubble from Menelaus because the king owed him some money, and Paris really wanted to buy this *sweet* new chariot —"

Nya's giggle mixed with the ping of the PA system, and then the captain's smooth voice filled the cabin. "We will begin making our descent shortly. Please ensure your seat belts are fastened."

When Johan glanced at Nya, the laughter was gone from her eyes. Her frown may as well have been a blaring siren, impossible for him to ignore.

Merde. Telling stories was one thing, but what he wanted to do now was another.

He'd already insulted her. He was likely the last person she wanted to share anything with. But something in him itched to bring the smile back to her face, or at least to smooth away the frown.

He was used to this urgent need to assist; it was his shameful secret. There couldn't be a distressed person within fifty paces without Johan catching wind of it and that urge to fix it almost overwhelming him. He buried those acts by acting a fool every two weeks or so, and occasionally showing his ass — literally. He couldn't bury the fact that this desire to help Nya felt different, with roots in something not at all altruistic.

It's nothing more than a courtesy.

He ran a hand through his hair so that a few locks hung before his eyes, giving him a nonthreatening, shaggy-dog appeal.

"Nya?" She looked at him, and he dropped his shoulders forward, smiled sheepishly, and swept the hair away from his eyes, emphasizing that his attention was entirely on her. He waited, saw the moment when her gaze went a little soft, then spoke. "I didn't make a great first impression, but if you need to talk, I don't gossip and you'll rarely see me again after the wedding, if ever. Perfect, as far as confidants go."

She squinted at him as she considered his offer. "*First* impression? I guess you would make for a good confidant since you forget my existence so easily. That was like the eighth time we've met, but I guess I do tend to blend into the background."

Oh, she was wrong about that, but it wasn't his place to correct her. He raised one shoulder, then dropped it. "Yes. I'll probably forget everything as soon as we step off the plane. I'm careless like that."

"I told Portia you were weird," she said, scrunching her face as she regarded him.

"I hope Portia defended my honor," he said, slightly hurt but also oddly pleased. She'd talked about him with her friends — why?

It doesn't matter.

"Of course she did," Nya said. "And I'm fine. I just have family problems, and returning home means I have to deal with them."

Johan liked to wallow in how frustrating his family was, but none of them had tried to kill anyone or foment a coup, to his knowledge.

She shook her head, as if clearing away bad thoughts. "Are you excited for the wedding?"

"I'm excited for my friend's future," he said, taking her cue to change the subject. He understood complicated families and the aversion to speaking of them, if nothing else. "I don't particularly enjoy weddings, but I think Thabiso's will be good."

Johan loved weddings, but he didn't enjoy them. They were an emotional minefield, and not exactly the best place for a man invested in maintaining an air of aloof disinterest.

She looked at him, and her smile was genuine, though there were still creases of worry around her eyes.

"It will be great. I'm *so* happy for them, even though I've been selfishly focused on my own problems." She pressed her hands together. "The goddess has truly blessed them. It is no small thing, two people coming together."

The genuine warmth in her words was somehow transmitted physically to Johan. He felt it in his body, how deeply she cared for their mutual friends. This was just vicarious emotion; he wondered what it would be like to be the recipient of that care himself.

The plane's descent began in earnest then, and she turned to secure the items on the table in front of her, breaking their eye contact.

Johan held on to his armrests, white knuckled, and not because of the altitude. For the duration of his time in Thesolo, he would stay away from her. He needed to avoid the warmth her kindness kindled in him. He needed to remember that even the brightest flames could be doused in an instant, and he would never be left alone in the darkness again if he could help it.

He turned toward his own window and stared down at the patchwork of green and brown.

Control.

He would only be in Thesolo for a few days. He could hardly get into much trouble in that time, anyway.

CHAPTER 3

ONE TRUE PRINCE,
MESSAGE FROM: HANJO

Nya, are you there? I've got the blue blood blues, but getting to know you makes things a little better. I want to know everything about you, like . . . what are your thoughts on princes? Specifically: would you date one? ☺

Nya's stomach ached and her back hurt and her body felt heavy with fatigue — even floating in the royal spa's oversized hot tub couldn't rid her of the panic that had weighed her down since she'd stepped off of the plane.

Being back home made her feel awful, and feeling awful made the anxious thoughts cycle through her mind even faster.

Could she trust the things she ate and drank? Would someone else try to make her sick, or hurt her? What if her father had been right, and her constitution was just weak? What if her father managed to escape from prison, and she had to see him unprepared?

Everything will be fine.

She could feel Portia and Ledi staring at her from where they perched on the underwater benches around the hot tub's perimeter, and their gazes were an additional weight. This was supposed to be a time for jubilant celebration, but her friends couldn't have fun because they were worried about her. She'd thought she wanted people to worry over her well-being, but now she felt frustrated, like when her father had fawned over her in the name of keeping her safe.

Everything just felt weird and she didn't know how to navigate being in a homeland that no longer felt like home.

When she'd arrived at the palace that morning, her grandparents had greeted her first, pulling her in for tight, bone-cracking hugs with their thin arms. They'd complimented her on her weight gain, with her grandfather going so far as to say that she was as fit as a prize heifer, and she'd felt that unfamiliar anger flare in her. Her grandparents had been the best part of her life, always, but she'd wanted to ask them why they hadn't noticed when she'd looked like a gaunt, sickly heifer. Why they'd made her return to her father after visits with them, even when she had cried and begged to stay. Instead she'd kissed their soft cheeks and told them she'd missed them.

They'd hovered like polite, worried flies too afraid to land on the dung that was her father's current situation. Then Ledi and Thabiso had appeared, also hovering, and then Portia had shown up and been the first to bluntly ask, "Are you okay? About your dad?" Portia's fiancé, Tavish, had given her a quelling nudge with his elbow, and if Nya hadn't already liked the Duke of Edinburgh she would have started to just then.

"I'm fine," Nya had said, because what else could she say the day before the wedding festivities began? The truth — that she felt like goat hide brushed in the wrong direction, and she couldn't pinpoint why — was not happy-celebration appropriate. She'd forced a smile, and kept that forced smile, and now just wanted to float in warm fragrant water and discuss things like dresses and makeup, not the fact that her father was locked up a few kilometers away while she was receiving the royal spa treatment.

"How was the flight with Johan?" Portia asked loudly, her voice traveling through the water surrounding Nya's ears. "Did you guys talk? He's really good at making people feel better."

Nya flailed and began to sink, so she flipped with a splash that sprayed water over Portia, accidentally of course, and took a seat between her two friends on the bench.

"We talked a bit. After I ended up in bed with him," she said, pushing her waterlogged braids behind her ears. She wanted to shock them, and she only felt a little guilty when both of them flailed.

Portia let out a laugh that was caught somewhere between scandalized and impressed. "Nya!"

"Want to run that by us again?" Ledi asked, cupping a hand over her ear.

"Not like that. I didn't know he was on board the jet, in the bedroom, because *someone* sent vague texts instead of just telling me he was going to be traveling with me." She shot a disapproving look at Portia.

"Sorry. But also not sorry because how did you manage not to see him? It's an airplane."

"The jet isn't that big," Ledi agreed. "We're a wealthy kingdom, but my in-laws aren't wasteful enough to buy a jet people can get lost in."

"He might have been keeping a low profile." Portia tilted her head thoughtfully. "Yesterday was . . . you know."

"Oh. Right." Ledi nodded somberly.

Nya didn't understand, but since they didn't share their insider knowledge with her, she continued.

"I went into the bedroom, it was dark, and well, he was there. In the bed. Nothing happened, besides him being weird." She shook her head.

Neither of them had to know that, for the briefest moment, she'd considered his proposition, and that when he'd left the room she'd been unable to stop thinking about what could have happened if he'd been genuine and she'd been fearless. What-ifs only led to trouble, though.

What if Father isn't truly doing anything wrong? Surely it is my imagination. He couldn't do something so awful. I'll give Ledi these pills just in case, instead of causing alarm for no reason.

Ledi held up both her hands. "Wait. Back up. You were in bed with Johan. *Johan* of the wild parties and public nudity. Weirdness could encompass a lot of things in that situation."

"He thought I was a pillow. I jumped out of the bed, surprised. He . . . offered something lewd, I think, and then asked if I wanted to cuddle. I kicked him out." She didn't add how she'd cried in front of him, and how she'd gripped his handkerchief in her fist afterward and tried to ignore the lemon-and-lavender scent of him. "But the flight attendant probably thought we were up to something. Fictional me will have had quite the tryst by the time the gossip makes the rounds."

Portia's expression was serious, her light-hearted curiosity gone. When she spoke, her voice held the concern and willingness to destroy for her friends that had made Nya love her.

"He said something lewd? I know he can be flip, but I don't care how upset he was, he shouldn't have —"

"I handled it," Nya said. She let her arms float in front of her, focusing on how they bobbed in the water instead of her friends' concern, and how it both soothed and aggravated her. "People say things like that sometimes because they think it's entertaining to tease me. You know that. He was just doing what people always do, and once he understood I didn't think it was funny, he stopped. People don't always stop."

"Are you sure you're o—" Ledi began, but Nya gripped the bench with her toes and pushed off, swimming away from the ques-

65

tion people kept asking but didn't want the answer to.

When she got to the other end of the hot tub she hoisted herself up and then plastered on her fake smile before turning toward her friends. She pointed down the hall toward the sauna, gave a thumbs-up, and when they hesitantly returned it, she slap-splashed her way to the dark wooden door.

She grabbed a towel along the way, squeezing the moisture from her braids as she walked, feeling like a sulking child who was ruining everything.

She knew her friends cared, and she felt terrible for the odd resentment that they didn't care in the way she *needed* them to. They loved her, they were trying their best, but she didn't even know what she needed — how could anyone else?

She'd always kept her emotions in check — calm, reasonable Nya, quietly taking care of things while everyone assumed she couldn't even take care of herself — if she'd screamed and acted out maybe that would have gotten people's attention. Maybe then they would have seen what her quiet deference really was, and what her father's bombastic nature really hid — a locked birdcage.

She wrapped the towel around herself and kneaded the small of her back with the knuckles of her left hand. Ledi had told her to visit the masseuse, but even the thought of it made her feel like she was taking too much. It was like this every time she visited the palace — she'd grown up under her father's strange and confusing doctrine, which stated she had to be a good girl to get nice things, but whenever nice things were within her reach she'd been told that no good girl would want them.

It was a hard lesson to unlearn even if she knew it wasn't true. Ledi and Portia told her all the time that she deserved anything her heart desired. Maybe one day she would believe it.

As she pulled the door to the sauna open and was hit by a wall of steam, she somehow knew that *he* was in the small, dimly lit room. One of those flashes of déjà vu that the priestesses called Ingoka's foresight and Naledi explained — something about patterns and synapses.

Again, with the small spaces. Again, with the too-damn-handsome-and-he-knew-it Liechtienbourgian. He was some kind of mythical creature, popping up whenever she was in distress to mess with her even more. Her fairy fuckboy.

Still, she was a bit shocked to find the long, pale expanse of him seated on the upper bench of the sauna, hunched forward and arms stretched so that his fingertips reached toward the bench below.

His head was dropped down, a mass of wild auburn, but it jerked up as the wooden door creakily announced her entry. She was met with ruddy cheeks and a sharp gaze that resonated within her private hollowness, like the sad moan of wind over the mouths of empty glass bottles.

She shivered, despite the heat, and despite the fact that it was only her imagination again. This was Prince Jo-Jo. What she'd read as sadness was probably disappointment that she wasn't some conquest he'd invited for a tryst.

Then something in his gaze shifted as it traveled in two quick flicks, down to her toes and back up to her face. She'd barely made out the motion through the steam, but it passed over her like a flash of blue fire, burning away the confusion that had driven her from her friends and leaving her feeling stripped. He no longer looked somber, as he drew himself back up to a sitting position, and in fact seemed to be smirking.

See? Jo-Jo's gonna Jo-Jo.

She fought the urge to pull her towel

around herself. She'd been raised to be modest, and the hot-pink bikini she'd bought for a trip to Rockaway Beach was anything but — but this was Johan, who frequented nude beaches and wild parties. Her boy-cut bikini bottoms were unlikely to tempt him.

He reached beside him for the wooden bucket, and she heard the slosh of water as he pulled it closer to him, but her eyes were on his torso. If there was any tempting happening, she was the only one feeling it.

Much abs. Very six-pack.

He was all sinewy muscle, and though he moved with a lazy grace as he scooped up a cup of water, she knew that he could move quickly if he wanted to. He had when she'd burst into tears and he'd rushed to offer her his handkerchief.

She noticed a flash of silver at his neck, but the long chain was nestled in the surprisingly thick auburn hair on his chest, and she looked away instead of following the direction it pulled her gaze.

"*Gudde jour,* Nya," he said.

"You remember my name now?" she asked, taking a step into the room. She felt like leaving would be giving in to him somehow, and Nya was tired of being controlled by the whims of spoiled men. He

69

was the one who had behaved strangely on the plane. *He* could leave.

But it had been kind of fun, after the strangeness, when he'd made her laugh. She hadn't expected such silliness from him — she hadn't expected him to acknowledge her at all outside of trying to seduce her. She wouldn't mind if they could talk like that again.

She took another step into the room, letting the door close behind her, and then flipped the hourglass nailed to the wall that would let her know when five minutes had passed. "I thought I was easy to forget."

"I made a mnemonic device. *N-Y-A.*" He ladled water onto the heated stones, sending up a billow of steam. The moist heat enveloped her as she looked up at him.

"What does it stand for?" she asked. "Naughty young . . . antelope?"

He laughed, the dry, bright sound cutting through the steam, and she moved toward it. She allowed herself the pleasure of knowing she'd shocked him a little.

She stepped onto the lower bench, then pulled herself up to the top one, where it was hotter and not just because of the annoying man occupying the other half. She'd sweat away this agitation and anxiety that had settled in her, and Johan wouldn't get in the way of that.

He sat beneath the dim lightbulb, and when she glanced at him she could see the rivulets of sweat that coursed their way over broad shoulders and that strange muscle some people had at the base of their necks.

"Antelope? No." He placed the ladle down and stretched his legs forward, but didn't volunteer anything else about his memory trick.

She tugged her towel under her thighs, protecting the skin from the hot wood. "Well, that's good. I wouldn't appreciate being called an antelope."

"If I was going to give you a nickname it would be Sugar Bubble." There was mischief in his voice, and in the way he glanced at her sidelong, almost like the name was something shared between them and not her flubbing her words. Inside jokes were intimate, like being cradled against his body had been. She wondered what his arms would feel like around her now, him in his tiny speedos and her in bikini. Luckily for Nya, they were in a room made expressly for awkward sweating.

"I guess I have to call you Jo-Jo," she said.

When he spoke again, his words were stilted. "Please don't call me that."

She could barely keep up with this man,

flirting one second and subdued the next, but she remembered the look in his eyes when she'd stepped into the sauna. Whatever had resonated between them then was in his voice now.

"Sorry," she said. "I didn't mean to offend you."

"You didn't," he said, suddenly casual. So sudden she might have imagined that vulnerability in his tone just a moment before.

What was with him?

"That's what my mother used to call me. Now the tabloids use it because they think it's funny, and people at the palace use it because they think I like it. I've grown used to the reminder, but right now is not a good time."

"Oh." Nya remembered Ledi and Portia's cryptic conversation, and — suddenly — what had been playing on the news channel in the lounge of Gate R as she fretted over returning home. A remembrance of Queen Laetitia. It had been ten years since the queen of Liechtienbourg had died of an undetected heart issue — some had said the cruelty of the world she tried so hard to fix had been too much to bear. Others said she'd paid more attention to the health of others than her own.

She hadn't paid attention to the news, but

hours later, Nya had found Johan alone in the darkness clutching a ratty teddy bear. And he'd asked her to hold him.

Oh.

Both in the plane and in this sauna, she'd assumed that he'd blocked her chance to silently brood, when in reality she'd twice interrupted his.

A sudden tenderness filled her, despite how his overconfident presence usually irked her. She knew what it was, to be motherless. She knew the gaping void it created, and she'd never even known her mother, who'd died in childbirth. She'd lived in a shrine to the woman, though, her father's constant vigil over what they'd lost — what had been taken from him. She couldn't imagine that bittersweet effort at keeping her mother's memory alive being broadcast on international news stations. She did know what it felt like to have everyone know and dissect your most private pain, though.

She wouldn't give him pity, since that's what she was fleeing herself. Was that what anyone ever wanted? She sat and breathed and sweated beside him in silence for a long moment.

"I can come up with another nickname for you," she said finally, dabbing her towel at her forehead. "If you want."

The wood bench creaked and she felt the vibration of him shifting to look at her.

"That depends, Sugar Bubble. Is the nickname going to be an insult? If not, then yes, I want."

She hadn't imagined Johan would care about being insulted, because she hadn't thought much about what it was like to be him. Well, she had, but she'd focused on the part where everyone thought he was attractive and funny and he could do whatever he wanted with no fear of retribution. Even as she'd fought her grudging crush on him, she hadn't considered that he was a real person with real feelings and real vulnerabilities.

She was no better than the people who assumed they knew who she was. Okay, she was slightly better because now that she knew, she would do something about it.

She looked at him — really looked at him. At the way his shoulders were tensed despite his grin, and how the nail of his middle finger scraped at the wooden bench in a repetitive motion.

"A nickname is important," she said, pulling her gaze away from him. She stretched her neck to the right and left, loosening the tension. "Let's see. What do I know about you?"

"If this has anything to do with my hair, I'll shave it all off, I swear," he threatened playfully. She was glad that his playfulness had returned.

Nya didn't think a shaved head would detract from his handsomeness, even if his dome was shaped like a mountain range underneath, as the aunties said.

He was mischievous and cunning and had a pointy nose. Sometimes he jumped around ostentatiously. She wouldn't leave out that red hair, no matter what he threatened, and she couldn't forget how lonely he'd looked in the picture she had of him.

Phokojoe, she thought, remembering the traditional tales she'd learned as a child and passed on to her students. *The trickster god.*

"Phoko," she said. "I will call you Phoko."

"Phoko," he said, trying to fit his Liechtienbourger accent over her Thesoloian one and doing a pretty good job. "I don't know what that means, but it doesn't sound like an insult so I like it."

"Excellent. I'm good at making up names. I will add that to my CV."

They chuckled, and Nya inhaled the warm air deeply, feeling her body relax a bit.

"What kind of job are you considering

75

now that you're back in Thesolo?" he asked softly after they'd sat quietly for a couple of minutes. A harmless question, but one she was surprised he bothered to ask.

"Are you asking as my confidant?"

"Yes. I'll forget as soon as I walk out of this sauna."

"I'm not sure," she said. "I thought I would go back to teaching at the orphanage, but they don't really need a teacher with my credentials right now. They say I am overqualified, but I think they don't want the negative association with my father."

"That hardly seems fair."

She smiled at how disgruntled he sounded on her behalf. "It's fine. I . . . I don't think I want to work there anymore. And if I do, I have some connections in high places. I'm sure they'd be willing to hire the princess's cousin if not the criminal's daughter."

He made an absurdly exaggerated gasp. "Nya. Are you implying you would use coercion to get a job? I thought you were sweet."

She smirked at him, not sure it was a compliment. "Sweetness doesn't pay the bills, does it, Phoko?"

He laughed, and she shook her head.

"I'm joking. I can find something on my

own, once I figure out what I want to do."

He threw more water onto the hot rocks. "I wish I could help, but the only thing I know how to do is cause drama and herd paparazzi."

"Those are very useful skills in today's market," she said, index finger on her chin.

"The people of my kingdom don't really think so. My family doesn't either."

"That shows what they know. I just saw a very lucrative offer for a dramatic paparazzi herder on JobSearch.thesolo." She grinned at him. "I applied, though, so you'll have to beat me if you want the position."

She stiffened waiting for him to respond with innuendo and ruin everything, but he shook his head slowly, then slicked his sweat-damp hair back, leaving one palm resting on his head. His other hand gripped the bench. "I cede it to you."

She looked at the hourglass she'd flipped when she'd walked in. She'd already been in the sauna for well past the recommended time period and was starting to feel it. And it'd been a couple of hours since she'd checked her phone. If she didn't hurry, whatever message Hanjo had sent her in *One True Prince* would disappear. If she missed that next message, which was meant to take their relationship from casual flirting to explicit flirting, she'd either have to pay to retrieve it or wait until the next morning to reload the game from a save point.

"I have to go." She made her way down from the bench to the floor, but paused when he grunted in reply. "How long have you been in here?"

He slid down from his seat to the bench below and placed a hand unsteadily on the wall. "Hmm. Not quite sure, actually."

A thread of alarm hemmed her suspicion.

"You should come out and have a cooling soak, then," she said. "Too much heat can be dangerous."

Johan stood, a sheepish grin starting to pull up his mouth and his gaze locked on hers. Then the grin slipped away like the sand in the hourglass, and his eyes went white as the irises rolled up. He started to pitch forward. Nya ran to him, arms scooped ahead of her to catch him under the armpits, but she wasn't prepared for the deadweight of an unconscious playboy.

"Eh, eh, eh!" she called out. She braced with her legs as much as she could, but Johan's bulk brought them both down to the floor. Her braids cushioned her head as it bounced against the warm wood, but then she was stuck under Johan's sweaty, solid mass. The floor was damp with moisture and though Nya was concerned for him, she was also wary of how many bare feet had passed over the planks pressing into her body.

"Phoko!" she said urgently. "Johan!"

He stirred a little, but she was still pinned beneath him. The hot metal of whatever pendant he wore pressed into her rib cage.

"Wake up," she cajoled, wriggling a bit to get away from the heat of it — and him.

His head lifted slowly, slowly, until it was directly above hers.

"Was ist passe?" he asked groggily as his eyes fluttered open. His nose brushed hers, once, twice, three times as he shook his head and blinked.

"Did you eat today?" she asked, trying to move her arms. His whole body was pressed into hers, and she thought she could feel every muscle and every sinew that held him together. *Every* muscle.

She stopped moving.

"I don't think so," he admitted.

Nya sucked in a breath. "You are crushing me, Phoko. Can you roll over? I'll go get a doctor."

"No, no doctor." He braced his palms on the floor and levered himself up, staring down into her face. He looked embarrassed and confused. "I'm sorry. I don't know what came over me."

"It's okay," she said. "It happens all the time in small, hot spaces like this."

A cool breeze cut through the steam, and they both turned their heads to see one of the palace guards standing over them, eyes wide.

"I thought there was danger," the woman said, averting her gaze. "I didn't realize — I didn't mean to interrupt."

Johan was in his tiny swimming trunks. Nya was in her hot-pink bikini and — she glanced down at the newly freed-up space between them — yes, her front-clasp top had failed to constrain her bosom during the fall.

She shimmied her hands up to fix her top, which Johan seemed not to have noticed. "He fainted after sitting in the sauna too long. Can you help us?"

The guard didn't indicate that she believed Nya in the least, but she strode over to them. She made a big show of hoisting Johan up from behind, and Nya made sure the cups of her bikini top were in place.

"Shall I call the royal medic?" the guard asked.

"Yes," Nya said.

"No. Unnecessary," Johan overruled as he

stood with the guard's help.

He was too woozy to see that his rejecting aid made this whole situation even more suspect.

"Please escort him to the dining area of the spa, and get him something to eat and drink," Nya said. "And have a medic check him, just in case."

Ledi and Portia stuck their heads into the doorway, one above the other, like curious kittens. "What happened, Lineo?" Ledi asked.

"I found Prince Johan on top of Ms. Jerami, but it appears he fainted. Similar to His Highness fainting on top of you in the royal dungeon, I suppose," Lineo said without even a trace of a smile.

"No, he really did," Nya insisted as Lineo led Johan away.

Johan looked back over his shoulder at her as he was led out. "Thanks for catching me, Sugar Bubble."

He had the audacity to wink, as if this didn't look bad enough.

Nya crossed her arms over her chest at Ledi and Portia's questioning gazes.

"Is it so hard to believe he just fell on top of me?" she asked.

"Well, no," Ledi said. "But when you add in your admission that you shared a bed on the plane, it is kind of suspicious. If you're only examining the evidence without context."

"Well, please do add the context, then," Nya said sharply.

"The context that Johan is known for his irresistible attractiveness?" Ledi asked.

Nya shot her a dirty look. "No man is irresistible, especially one who spends his time behaving as he does."

"He called you Sugar Bubble," Portia said. "What does that even mean?"

"Google it," Nya bit out.

A knowing smirk lifted one corner of Portia's mouth and she glanced at Ledi.

"He. Fainted," Nya said. "And now I'm covered in whatever fungus lives on this floor."

"Okay, okay," Ledi said. She shot Portia a warning look. "Let's go get you defungified with a body scrub. If you want us to come along, that is."

"Of course, I do," Nya said, then sighed. "I'm sorry I ran away earlier. I don't want to talk about my father. I'm having a lot of feels right now and I don't know what to do with all of them yet."

"I would tell you to talk through them. Ledi would tell you to ignore them," Portia said, picking something from Nya's braids.

"You can decide what feels right for you, and whether or not you want our help with that. We're here for you, whatever you decide."

Nya sighed, glad she had good friends; she knew what life was like without them and she never wanted to go back to that. They were just trying to help. And she needed their help, even if she didn't know exactly how yet.

"Thank you," she said. "I do have to check my phone first."

Fungus could wait. She had a two-bit prince trying to woo her. She would think of the 3-D prince she'd had on top of her later.

CHAPTER 4

Royal Wedding Inspiration?

While most reporters are being denied entry into Thesolo for the royal wedding of Prince Thabiso and soon-to-be Princess Naledi, a source in the kingdom has confirmed that both Prince Jo-Jo and the Duke of Edinburgh are in attendance. Good news comes in threes, so can we expect to hear wedding bells ring for His Grace and his enterprising partner, Portia Hobbs (best friend to the bride)? We might ask the same about Jo-Jo to make three, but we pity the woman who tries to tame him!

— *The Looking Glass Daily,*
Royal Beat

"Hi Lukas, it's your brother, Johan, remember me? I think maybe you've forgotten since all my calls go to voice mail, and you aren't responding to DMs, PMs, or texts. Call me back."

Johan ended the call and then reluctantly scrolled down to *F* to find his stepfather's listing: Forshett Laffel. "Fork Spoon" had started as a joke and settled into a compromise. The king had asked to be called *papp,* but Johan found that difficult when the very laws of the land made it painstakingly clear that he was not and would never be Linus's real son. Forshett Laffel, it was, then.

The phone rang and Johan regarded his nails. Though his father couldn't see his display of nonchalance, it was a habit he'd fallen into when he was nervous or uncomfortable. If you stood around looking like you thought yourself better than everyone, it had a twofold benefit: 1) people left you alone because 2) they assumed you must think that for a reason.

"Hallo, Jo-Jo!" The king sounded surprised. "Have you gotten yourself into trouble again?"

Johan supposed it was strange for him to make a phone call at some odd hour in Liechtienbourg for no reason. But he didn't *only* call to warn of his misadventures before they hit the papers, did he?

"Hallo, Forshett. I'm trouble-free for now, alas," he sighed into the phone. "Give me a few hours, though."

Linus chuckled.

"I'm calling about . . ." Johan found he couldn't bring himself to admit that Lukas was ignoring him. ". . . the referendum. How's it looking?"

"Hmm, not good, *meng fis,* not good." The king sighed. "It seems that more people think the monarchy is a relic of the past and that we are good-for-nothing wastrels sucking at the public teat than I'd imagined."

Johan couldn't *exactly* argue with that. He'd gone from a boy with country roots to living in the palace. Being in forced proximity to the rich and royal had taught him any number of things, primarily that lots of them *were* wastrels. His Prince Jo-Jo act had, in part, started as a sarcastic lampooning of the behavior so many of the rich people around him indulged in. He'd waited for someone to notice and call this out, but instead it had made people who'd avoided him suddenly seek his company and tabloid journalists fight over scraps to report on him.

"Hmm," he said.

The king read that sound as sympathy. "If you believed the opinion section of the papers, the public want us gone. And Milos Arschlocher's rhetoric isn't helping."

"That's a pity," Johan said. "But you do have your kitchenware empire to fall back on. Everyone loves a good spork."

"For the last time, they're not sporks. They are finely crafted utensils that speak to elegant sensibilities!"

"Hmm," Johan said again, but he smiled. Unlike many royals, Linus had work that he believed in, and his silverware business employed people who might not have found work otherwise, like migrants who had crossed the border into the kingdom seeking a safe place to live. "And Lukas? How is he taking this?"

"Lukas is being Lukas," the king said airily.

Johan sighed. "And what does that entail?"

"You know, staring at his phone. Going to soccer practice. Grooming his horse. Teenage prince stuff."

"Okay. And he's not upset? After the . . . event?"

Linus sighed deeply. "No. He's *gutt.*"

"What about you?" Johan asked grudgingly. Part of him, the part that would always be a little boy watching the fairy-tale courtship with dread, still wished his mother had never married Linus. He'd once blamed the man entirely for her death. He now merely mildly resented him every now and

87

then. But his stepfather, who'd never remarried despite many offers and could sometimes be heard having quiet conversations with the photo of Laetitia hanging in the parlor, also needed support. "Are you hanging in there?"

"I'm *gutt*. We're all *gutt*."

Johan didn't know why he bothered asking. Everything was always *gutt* because apparently it had been bred into the royal line not to let pesky things like sorrow and grief get in the way of duty, and Lukas had apparently inherited the stiff, if perhaps a bit thin, upper lip of the von Brausteins.

"*Gutt*," Johan said drily.

"*Gutt*," the king said, a hint of desperation around that last consonant that almost made Johan want to see how long they could keep up the single-word conversation.

"*Ja*," Johan said to break their loop.

"Well. Have fun in Thesolo. Don't start any international incidents when you visit Njaza."

Johan heard footsteps and saw Thabiso approaching. "I doubt I could do anything worse than three hundred years of brutal colonial rule, so no worries there. Bye, *Forshett*."

He disconnected the call as Thabiso reached him, sporting the smile of a contented man in a world full of cause for discontentment.

"I haven't seen you in denim for ages!" Thabiso said, walking in an exaggerated circle around Johan and stroking his beard. He gave a nod of approval. "Looking *très* rugged, *meng ami.*"

Johan felt strange in the stiff blue jeans he was wearing for the day's activities, paired with the official wedding T-shirt he'd found in his room: soft-pink cotton emblazoned with #BisoVelcroLedi in black print, some inside joke between the couple, he assumed. His uniform outside of the gym, beach, and bed was at a minimum an oxford shirt and slacks, designer wear that fed into his playboy persona, but apparently what was in store today would require getting dirty.

Thabiso wore the loose-fitting purple linen tunic that was emblematic of Thesololan royal sporting wear. As the summer sun beat down on Johan, he wished he had opted for the same.

"I thought about doing double denim, but I didn't want to get anyone too hot and bothered," Johan said. "Mostly myself."

Thabiso laughed. "Speaking of that, are you sure you're up for today? It's okay if you need to rest," he said as they walked through the ornately carved wooden front doors of the palace. "The traditional wedding hunt is, well, tradition, but I'd rather not visit the royal hospital ever again."

Johan straightened, puffing his chest a bit. Sometimes he forgot that Thabiso had known him for half his life, before the muscles and the fancy haircuts and the models. Thabiso had met Bad Boy Jo-Jo 1.0, awkwardly posturing as he tried to fit in at a school full of rich boys who had nothing in common with the boys of his childhood except for their ability to sniff out weakness — or emotion, which was the same as weakness to them.

Thabiso had been there in the aftermath of Johan's loss and, though they didn't speak of it often, knew why Johan was out of sorts.

"I'm feeling much better, and I made sure to eat breakfast and hydrate," Johan said as they approached the small cluster of people near the palace's grand fountain, abstract cubes beneath steady flowing water, meant to emulate the breathtaking waterfalls the country was known for. "I should be able to stay upright as long as I steer clear of small, abnormally hot rooms."

He had no idea how long he'd sat in the sauna the day before. After swimming laps with Thabiso, reenacting their swim team years, he'd gone in to sweat out anxiety about Lukas and memories of his mother. He'd fallen deep into thoughts about his family and the future of Liechtienbourg. Then Nya had come in, and leaving hadn't even occurred to him.

Then he'd fainted on top of her.

Super.

"Oh. What does *phoko* mean?" he asked Thabiso. He knew conversational Thesotho, but had never come across the word.

Thabiso stroked his beard. "Rumor? I guess that's the closest translation."

"Oh," Johan said. "That makes sense."

He'd been a bit giddy when Nya had bequeathed him with a nickname, but this felt worse than other insults, though it made sense. That's what came to mind when people thought of him: rumors of his wild and wicked deeds. It was the bed he'd constructed for himself, purposefully and with great dedication, and Nya had simply laid him in it.

"Perhaps you misheard?" Thabiso asked, as if sensing that hadn't been the answer Johan wanted. "There's also *phokojoe*. It means fox. We have children's tales of Phokojoe, a trickster god. He would turn himself into what people desired most in the world to lure them into his mystical lair."

91

Johan grinned and nodded appreciatively. "I see."

That made sense, too.

"It sounds bad, but it's a fairy tale." Thabiso clapped him on the shoulder. "It has a happy ending."

Johan had been obsessed with fairy tales as a child; his mother had given him a big book of them, and he'd read them under her desk in the royal secretary's office, back when she'd been single and her dealings with royalty had been in an official capacity, as an employee. When her time at work had been regulated by workers' rights protections. Queens had no such protections, it turned out.

The stories in that book were why Johan had been terrified when the king had fallen in love with his mother. They were why he'd tried to sabotage their love up to the day of the wedding. Not because King Linus was evil, but because everyone had started to say their love was a fairy tale, and it had seemed to Johan that a curse was being laid down, by tabloids instead of an evil witch.

He'd known how the fairy tales he'd memorized played out — there was unnecessary pain and suffering caused by the human need for love and shelter. And he'd known how they ended — with sadness and longing, and mothers dead and gone.

Thabiso was fond of Disney, though — Johan had been dragged into many a re-watch of childhood classics in Thabiso's dorm room — so Johan didn't give him his TED talk on why fairy tales didn't mean happy endings. He just nodded.

When he glanced at Thabiso, he realized his friend hadn't seen his agreement because he was staring down the long, columned walkway that stretched along the front of the palace. Johan tracked Thabiso's gaze to Naledi. If he looked at his friend very closely, he was sure he could make out little hearts fluttering about Thabiso's head like an InstaPhoto filter. If he looked at himself closely, he could make out the pool of dark-green churning envy that had opened up at his feet.

What would it be like to be able to love like that? Openly, without fear that it would be snatched away? Thabiso had never lost anyone he cared for. Johan didn't wish that for his friend, *ever,* but he couldn't help but be jealous of it.

"Hey, Biso." Ledi stepped joyfully into Thabiso's arms. Naledi *had* lost people she loved, but it'd happened so long ago that she couldn't remember. She could only think about what she'd gained: family, friends, and a people she would help lead.

Johan was happy for them. He didn't want to feel envy. He didn't want to feel *anything* and that's how he went about his life because, as with everything, if Johan did something he did it excessively.

"Why is the boy crying under your desk again, Laetitia?" King Linus asked with concern.

"My Jo-Jo is very sensitive, Your Highness. Some of the boys at school don't understand that —"

"Mamm, don't tell him!" Johan glanced up apprehensively, waiting for Linus to explain that Johan was eight and too old for such behavior, like Johan's teachers did.

His mother's cool fingers brushed against his cheeks, wiping away his tears, and she looked down at him with understanding in her eyes because she always understood these things.

"It is a gift to feel so much, Jo-Jo. It is what makes you special. Don't forget that."

"*Mmoro,* Phoko." When Johan looked down, pulled from his memory, Nya stood before him. She wore a pink head wrap tied into a bow, her bun of braids poking through, and her lips had been swiped with a sparkly nude gloss. Her outfit was the same pink T-shirt he wore, but in a scoop-neck style, paired with curve-hugging blue jeans and pink trainers.

Her clothing accentuated her curves, but it was her wide brown eyes that stopped him. There was a bit of the shyness he'd thought was her most noticeable feature, but there was also playfulness and a kind of probing concern that skewered him. "Are you doing better?"

She'd asked him the same at dinner the evening before, but her grandmother had come and pulled her away, telling her that there were people she had to greet so as not to seem rude.

"Ouay," he answered carefully. There were few people who inquired about his well-being and meant it. Most of them were in his peripheral vision — Thabiso, Tavish, Ledi, and Portia. For some reason, their inquiries didn't make him feel like this. There was something about Nya that pulled at him — a pull he had been fighting successfully for a year and a half but, in the wake of their recent run-ins, was starting to feel like a losing battle.

His control was slipping again.

If he'd only wanted to sleep with Nya, it would have been manageable. Lust was basic and could be ignored. But his attraction swelled each time he saw her, ballooned each time he heard her voice, and because he most definitely would not indulge it, had been all he'd thought of since the plane had landed in Thesolo.

Oh là là.

"Here," she said, and pressed something smooth and rectangular into his hand. "In case you feel woozy again."

He looked down at the juice box he now held, decided the illustration of a dew-speckled peach on the box was not a hidden message, then looked back at her.

This might have been a joke at his expense — fainting wasn't manly after all, and being saved by not one woman but two was even less so. Johan had grown up being told so many of the things he did weren't manly. He'd chosen playboy as his public persona because he could hold a grudge and enjoyed petty revenge as much as the next person.

However, if it wasn't a joke, then that meant Nya, the woman who had captured his attention completely as she stood quietly trying to make herself smaller, and whom he'd been rude to for months, had worried about him. This morning, she'd thought of him and searched out a juice box, specifically to give to him. It was a kindness. It was a connection.

Oh là là là là.

96

He'd been wrong about her, had seen her as some timid woodland creature who might skitter too close to him if she wasn't careful, and get caught in his snare if he wasn't even more careful than her, but in fact she was simply kind. Nothing so benign as nice or pleasant, but *kind.* There was nothing soft or gentle about that trait in a world that specialized in crushing it.

If he were a superhero, a kind woman would be his kryptonite. Good thing he wasn't one; it meant he could fight the urge to say something deliberately cutting and crude just to, figuratively, hurl her into the sun.

"Thanks," he said.

"No problem!" She smiled at him once more, revealing two front teeth that were slightly too large. Johan had seen her teeth before, had never paid particular attention to them, but now he felt a throb in his chest and his brain shouted that those two teeth were somehow *extremely* cute.

Oh là là là là là là.

She walked over to Portia and Tav, who were chatting with a palace guard about his scimitar. Likotsi, Thabiso's assistant, and her wife, Fabiola, had shown up, and apparently neither had received the memo about dressing down, as Likotsi was wearing a linen suit and leather loafers and Fabiola looked like she'd stepped out of a pinup calendar right into a pair of six-inch heels. Each of them pulled Nya into a hug, and they each kept a hand on her arm as they talked to her.

Nya grinned and seemed to fawn over Fabiola's shoes — Johan refused to imagine what those heels would look like on Nya. He slipped the juice box into his backpack and walked over to his friends.

"Let's take a selfie," Portia said, grabbing him and placing him next to Nya, then pulling out her selfie stick. Everyone huddled together, and though Johan mostly avoided impromptu photos unless he had staged them to be impromptu, he moved closer to Nya, resting his hand on her shoulder on one side and his cheek against her braids on the other.

She smelled good, like ylang-ylang and the musk of whatever oils she used on her hair, the same scent he'd gotten a whiff of when he'd awoken on the plane. And she was warm, but not soft — she'd gone stiff at his touch.

"Sorry," he murmured, beginning to move his hand away, but she reached up to stay him. He glanced at her from the corner of his eye, but she was looking at Portia's cell phone, lips slightly parted.

"Say 'hashtag Thesolo forever'!" Portia called out.

Johan didn't say anything because all of his attention was on Nya's hand atop his. It was hard enough tearing his gaze from her to look toward the phone, but he finally did.

"Perfect," Portia said, scrolling through the photos as everyone broke apart.

"Attention guests!" The commanding, unignorable voice of Thabiso's mum, Queen Ramatla, boomed over the small gathering and they all turned to her. She was flanked by her husband the king on one side and Nya's — and Naledi's — grandparents on the other. "We thank you all for making time in your busy schedules to see our beloved Thabiso and Naledi joined before Ingoka and the goddess legion. Now, on this day before the wedding, we will have our traditional wedding hunt."

"And you made fun of my fixation on medieval hunting after I found that book at Mary's," Tav said smugly, grinning at Portia. "Now *my* useless information gets to save the day."

"You know I love all of your useless information, honey," Portia said warmly.

"Enough, you two," Johan said lightly. "Save it for the hunting trail."

Portia raised her hand, as if they were in class. "So by hunting . . ."

"Of course, times have changed, and we will not be asking you to actually harm any animals," the king said.

"Thank goodness," Portia exhaled. She slid her arm through Tavish's and leaned her head on his shoulder.

Johan felt the pool of envy lapping at his toes again and looked away. He flexed his hand, still tingling from Nya's brief touch.

"You are here because you are closest to the hearts of our beloveds," Queen Ramatla said loudly.

"And because we are too old to be bothered with such sport," Makalele added, drawing laughter from the group. He tweaked Naledi's elbow and she beamed at him.

"The tradition used to be that the bosom friends of the beloveds would form hunting parties of two, sent out to bring back meat for the next day's feast. But, as our kitchen is well stocked, the goal is simply to bring back a *living* animal of the type required."

"Wait, we still have to capture live, wild animals?" Portia exclaimed.

"They're domesticated, not wild," Ledi corrected.

"Now, you must break off into pairs," Annie said, ignoring Portia. She raised her hands and surveyed the small crowd. "Well, it appears that is already done. Ledi and Thabiso, Portia and His Grace, Kotsi and Fabiola, and . . ."

Her hands dropped and she fixed Johan with *the look*. The look that said *I've heard about you*. He ran a hand through his hair, scruffing it to make himself look younger and less threatening, and then gave her his most dazzling smile.

She twisted her lips. ". . . Johan and our Nya." She paused. "You, boy. Listen."

Johan pointed at himself innocently. "Me, Auntie?"

Thabiso groaned even though he was the one who had taught Johan the honorific. Annie looked even more suspicious.

"I expect you to behave properly with our precious granddaughter, even though you will be alone, unsupervised, and —"

"I'm a grown woman, *Nkhono*," Nya said, cutting her grandmother off. "I can handle myself, just as I did living alone in one of the biggest cities in the world. And Johan is . . . a friend. You don't have to worry."

Johan wasn't surprised by much, but Nya's use of the word *friend* did just that. He had friends, and even more people who claimed him as such. But after over a year

101

of purposefully ignoring her, then crudely asking her to join him in bed, then collapsing on top of her, she would call him friend?

His heart beat a little bit faster.

"Yes. We're friends," Johan added, hoping to quell any fears, and because he liked saying it out loud.

Since when? Portia mouthed at him, her thin eyebrows drawn together speculatively.

"Only friends." Johan stepped in front of Portia, eclipsing her from Annie's view. "Nya is safe with me."

He glanced at Nya, hoping she felt reassured, too, but she'd pulled out her phone and was staring at it intently, lips screwed up in a way that showed annoyance but was also entirely kissable. He waited for her to look over at him, but apparently whatever was on her phone held her attention.

"You are saying you won't debauch my granddaughter?" Annie asked bluntly, apparently determined to draw this uncomfortable moment out.

"Never," Johan said, placing his hand over his heart. "You have nothing to worry about."

"I would worry a little bit," Makalele said, with a twinkle in his eye, teasing his wife. "He's a handsome lad. He reminds me of that Liechtienbourgish soldier on leave from

Njaza who tried to woo you away from me all those years ago. Doesn't he resemble him?"

Annie shot him a different kind of look. "I have no idea what you mean, as *I* did not consort with colonizers. But if I had to remember, I do believe it was you he was trying to woo, no?" Makalele shrugged sheepishly and Annie looked back at the group, her gaze jumping from Johan to Tavish. "Not that *you* are colonizers. Not currently."

"It's a nasty addiction, that colonizing. Glad we were broken of the habit," Johan said smoothly.

"Okay, I like this boy," Makalele said, shaking his finger in Johan's direction. "Come now, Annie. Relax."

Annie still looked suspicious, but finally nodded. "You will be led to animal-specific 'hunting' grounds, cleared with the landowners, where you will spend the morning finding your quarry. And that's it. No funny business."

She darted a final warning glare at Johan.

"What? I was promised there would be funny business." Fabiola pouted.

"I have an exemption," Likotsi said. "You shall have all the funny business you desire, my lady."

103

"Johan has already made it clear that I'm not the type to inspire debauchery, *Nkhono*," Nya said stiffly, staring at her phone. "It is unnecessary to press the issue."

Johan glanced at Nya and saw a message pop up on her phone:

I got no response to my last message, cherie. Do you not have time for me? I thought we had something special, but perhaps I was wrong.

She angled the phone away from him, frowning as her fingers tapped at the screen, then tucked it into her pocket.

A feeling that Johan hadn't experienced since the moment he'd peered out from under his mother's desk and saw her and Linus staring at each other in starry-eyed wonder gripped him: jealousy. This was different from amorphous envy at his friends' relationships.

He didn't want Nya getting texts from someone calling her *cherie.* Or rather, he wanted her getting them, but only from him.

He was *jealous.*

Johan thought he might faint again.

Nya crossed her arms over her chest and worried her bottom lip, clearly upset.

Anger rose to meet his jealousy and clasp

its hand. He couldn't be with her — he didn't date people who inspired actual emotion in him, and Nya was a veritable muse. Whoever she was dating should treat her with care and kindness, not passive-aggressive texts in the middle of a wedding celebration.

"If anyone doesn't find their, um, quarry, it's fine," Ledi said. "This is just for fun and we're happy you're here celebrating with us."

She looked anxiously over at her grandparents, who grudgingly nodded.

"Yes, just for fun," Annie said. "Though I will add that my best friend wrestled an antelope for me and Makalele and I have been married since —"

"Eighteen seventy-three," Makalele cut in, then struck a pose. "Melanin, the greatest beauty secret."

Everyone broke into laughter, except Nya.

"Let's go, *friend*," she said, then sauntered off after the crowd moving toward the stable.

"Hmm," Johan said, then followed her.

CHAPTER 5

ONE TRUE PRINCE,
GROUP CHAT MODE

Basitho: What did you do to upset Nya, Hanjo!?

Hanjo: I didn't do anything. Maybe she's just intimidated by my ethereal beauty.

Basitho: She's been pretty quiet today. You better not have made her angry with your weird talk about the monarchy.

Hanjo: I would never upset Nya. I don't upset people I like. What would be the fun in that?

Nya had never ridden a horse. The animals were an integral part of Thesolo's culture, but her father had denied her pleas to be allowed to take riding lessons during primary school.

A horse can tell when its rider does not possess a strong will. You are already sick, do you want a broken leg, too? Or worse?

The lessons were compulsory, but he was a Jerami and a royal minister, so the teachers had accepted his decree without question. She'd helped teachers grade exams instead because she was a good, dutiful girl. Now she was wondering if her father had been right, as she sat perched atop her horse, which had stopped in the middle of a clearing and was refusing to move.

"Please. Just work with me." She tugged the reins. "Come on. Who's a good horse?"

The horse raised one hoof and Nya thought she'd finally gotten through to it, but then it stamped the ground and firmly shook its head, tossing its blond mane.

Johan led his horse in a tight circle around Nya and pulled up beside her, but she refused to look at him. She was still under the dark cloud of humiliation from his announcement in front of her family and closest friends that they need not worry because he certainly wouldn't be tempted by *her*.

She wasn't owed anyone's affection or desire — she knew that. She simply wished he hadn't said it like it was so obvious, like it was beyond the realm of possibility. Especially after the spark she'd felt when he'd stood next to her during the selfie. She'd been very aware of his body pressed along her side, and the weight of his hand on her shoulder, and the press of his cheek against her head. His nearness had shaken her, because he certainly hadn't confused her with a pillow this time, and of course her imagination had run away with her again. As usual, reality had clotheslined it.

She supposed it wasn't his fault. Everyone treated her like a silly girl instead of a woman. At a certain point she had to consider that maybe they were right.

Plus she'd missed an important message from Hanjo while she was sleeping. Now the character was in passive-aggressive mode and she'd have to spend the rest of the day placating him, evidence that the game developers were indeed men. She didn't even have reception in the grassy plain where they'd been dropped off. Her mood was decidedly not good, and Johan sitting smugly beside her with his perfect face and his perfectly behaved horse didn't help.

He adjusted the hat, woven from rushes, that he'd been given by the stableman who had helped them select their horses. The man who had said Nya's horse had a sweet and docile temperament to match her own, as if that was a compliment.

"Do you know how to ride?" Johan asked when he got tired of waiting for her to acknowledge him. Nya wasn't sure if there really was laughing condescension in the question or if his words were being filtered through her mood, and she didn't quite care.

"Not everyone grows up participating in international polo competitions," she responded curtly.

"You're right." He absentmindedly scratched his horse behind the ears.

Johan seemed to be ignoring her annoyance, which annoyed her even more.

"I certainly didn't," he continued. "I learned to ride a horse alongside my younger brother, to make sure he was safe. The polo came later. I'm not very good at it, but my pants are usually tight enough to distract everyone from that. My personal trainer is really into glute definition."

Her eye twitched but she willed herself not to look down at his jeans-clad bottom. "No, I don't know how to ride, but it can't be that hard if you can do it. My horse is defective."

109

She turned to glare at him head-on, her chin lifted toward the summit of the mountain range in the distance, and found him looking at her with amusement.

"Horses can't be defective," he said. "But they can pick up on the mood of the rider."

"Oh, so I'm defective, then?" she snapped, perilously close to tears. "Perfect. Great."

His brow furrowed. "That's not what I said. Humans can't be defective either, and *you* could never be thought to be so."

"Mmm-hmm." She wouldn't fall for his smooth talking.

"You're upset about something, and your horse is picking up on that. I certainly am."

Nya's eyes went wide. *Something.* He wasn't even aware that announcing that she was undesirable in a public setting could be that *something.*

She sighed and slumped in her saddle, feeling defeated. Everyone else had a preset partner for this excursion, someone who loved them. Who wanted them. Before she'd been embarrassed in quick succession by her grandmother and then Johan, she'd been excited by the possibility the day held. A morning alone with Johan, who was weird and full of himself, but whom she actually enjoyed talking to, for some reason. The fantasy that lurked under her eye rolling at his behavior had bobbed to the surface. Maybe he would look at her under the bright summer sun and suddenly see what everyone else seemed to miss: she was a woman, with hopes and dreams and desires. Maybe he'd look at her and fall in love.

Bah.

She wished she could stop dreaming, as her father had demanded. It always made the inevitable disappointment of reality that much worse.

"Sugar Bubble?" Johan's voice was cajoling. "Maybe this is the result of a lover's quarrel? I saw you texting and then your mood changed. If you want to talk . . . your confidant is at your service."

The tightness in her face loosened as her glare shifted into pleased shock. He thought she was upset because of a lovers' quarrel? He thought she *had* a lover?

"I don't mean to pry," he added quickly. "If you don't want to talk, I understand, but since we are friends . . ."

He smiled at her then, and though she'd seen hundreds of photos of him over the years, she'd never seen this particular smile. It was tentative and somehow soft, though his stance in his saddle and the way he gripped his reins were not. His gaze was searching.

He wanted to help her.

With her love life.

Her bad mood faded, and a warm happy feeling bloomed in her chest. She tried to find a name for this feeling, that wasn't infatuation, and she realized it was quite simply the thing she'd been annoyed about to begin with: friendship. This was not the brief romantic fantasy that had played out in her head, but she liked this, too. A shy, smiling Johan offering her his expertise because he wanted to make her happy.

She chuckled and shook her head. "I don't need to talk, but thank you for offering."

His horse huffed.

"Look, I accidentally saw that text you got," he said. "Anyone who would send you a message designed to distract you from your friends is not worth your time. And *cherie*? Really?"

Text?

Nya bit her lip. Johan had seen her message from the *One True Prince* game. And now he was offering advice on how to deal with some game writer's idea of what *he* would be like to date.

She couldn't help it — she burst out laughing. Her life was truly ridiculous.

Her horse made a sound of complaint,

and she covered her mouth as she composed herself.

"Ah yes," she said. "Him. He needs to be reassured a lot, but he's actually very sweet as you get to know him. So I've heard."

"Hmm." Johan pressed his lips together disapprovingly. "Well, I'm here if you need to discuss anything. Don't sell yourself short, though. You're . . ." He looked off into the distance, squinting into the sun. "You deserve someone who adores you, Sugar Bubble. Don't accept anything less."

The sun was beating down on them, but that wasn't what made her cheeks flame. Johan had managed to make her feel like an unwanted castoff and a cherished gift in the space of a morning. She was not the type of woman that men adored, and Johan probably knew that, but he still thought it was what she deserved.

Her hands tightened on her reins.

"Thank you, Phoko," she said softly. "You're very nice, you know that?"

"Nice?" His lips pursed dubiously.

She wanted to debate him, but startled as her horse lurched into motion beneath her and began to walk. Nya tightened her thighs as she swayed in the saddle, then glanced at Johan as a startled laugh bubbled up in her.

"It's working!" she yipped. "Yay!"

113

He grinned and adjusted his hat like a cowboy in the old Westerns she'd watched with her grandfather.

Friendship, she reminded herself as her breath caught.

"Let's go catch this goat," he said. "Our friends' happiness depends on it."

"Actually," she said, cheeks warm again. "Um, this tradition has a specific purpose. Bringing back delicious food for the couple to eat gives them strength in the marriage bed after the wedding feast."

Johan sputtered out a laugh — he looked almost boyish when he was caught off guard.

"I think my statement stands that their happiness depends on it. Or happy ending at least." He closed his eyes, feigning solemnity, and placed his hand over his heart. "Far be it from me to leave Thabiso even symbolically undernourished on his wedding night." He peeked at her from beneath his lashes, a smirk undermining his serious expression. "Let's go catch us a sex goat."

Nya laughed, and he laughed, too, their gazes brushing warmly as his horse fell into step beside hers.

Goats were surprisingly hard to catch. They were stubborn and willful and did not submit easily. After the fourth goat they'd ambled toward — after being given permission from the shepherds — had pranced away, Nya was ready to make one out of sticks and underbrush and call it a day.

Finally, after laughing at their struggles, a group of children left a goat tied up in their path, giggling as they watched from the tall dry grass. They cheered heartily when Nya managed to undo the knot on the rope.

The children took Nya and Johan to meet their father, Semii, who invited them to tour his grazing land. As they marched through the thicket surrounding the shepherd's home, Nya pointed out the flora she'd grown up reading about in her *Encyclopedia of Thesoloian Plants.* Makalele had sometimes taken her out with him as he did his weekend rounds of the village, when her father was busy in the capital and couldn't complain, and he'd helped her pick them out and compare plants to the printed images.

She'd loved those times, though now she wondered why her grandfather had never mentioned it to her father.

Because he'd known that Father would not want you doing such things. He'd known . . .

Semii spoke with reverence for the land his family had protected for generations, and about how each season brought new troubles, but also new delights. To her surprise, Johan spoke to the man in passable Thesotho. Semii beamed and encouraged him, and then they went back to the family home, where his wife and her father had prepared lunch for everyone.

After lunch, Nya and Johan had started their trek back, talking about things like their favorite films, and whether or not Portia and Tavish had managed to capture a cow. He'd also talked about his brother, briefly but enough to make clear how much he adored the boy. Nya had thought how nice it must be for him, having a sibling he cared for — he wouldn't know what it was like to be lonely.

"Today was a good day," she declared as their horses picked their way over the open shrubland on the route back to the palace. "It gives me hope that being back home won't be so bad."

Perhaps it was sharing too much, but she was full of delicious food and drunk on fun conversation. Her head buzzed a bit from happiness. This was the feeling she'd had when spending time with Ledi and Portia in New York when she hadn't been afraid, and what she worried would not be possible in Thesolo.

Will this good feeling last when the wedding festivities are over?

"Do you miss New York yet?" Johan asked.

"I don't, to be honest. It was . . . too big, I think," she said, surprised he wanted to know anything about her time in New York given how he'd avoided her there.

He looked at her. "Too big?"

His expression was curious, and it hit her then that Johan traveled all over the world, having exciting adventures. Right now, he was dressed in down-to-earth sexy cowboy cosplay, but everything about his usual persona was the embodiment of "too big."

Everything? Nya's cheeks warmed.

"Um. Yes. I could never feel comfortable there. I guess that makes me provincial." She shrugged. "I did well at school —"

"You were doing an education program, no?"

Nya almost asked how he knew, and figured Portia or Thabiso must have mentioned something.

"Yes. I just wish I'd done so much more, both in school and in everyday life."

"What did you want to do that you didn't?" he asked.

Nya was starting to wonder whether Semii had sprinkled magic dust in their food that made Johan suddenly interested in her

117

— then that thought left her cold because she knew some people did put things in your food and the results were generally much worse than a handsome man becoming interested in you.

She glanced at Johan, wary, but then she remembered they were friends now. You could tell friends things and they wouldn't make fun of you too much.

"I wanted excitement and romance and fun. I thought I would move to New York and be swept up into this glamorous city life." She sighed. "I wasn't. To be fair, Ledi did warn me that there was nothing glamorous about grad school."

"Glamorous New York City life is overrated, unless you enjoy going to boring parties and being talked at by people on cocaine," Johan declared.

"Oh!" Nya said. "That doesn't sound fun."

"It really isn't." He patted his horse encouragingly. "Did you eat bagels?"

"Yes."

"Go to a Broadway show?"

"Once a month! They were all so good!"

His lips curved up. "Did you have fun with Ledi and Portia and Thabiso?"

"Of course!"

"Then it sounds like you did have a

glamorous New York City experience, just not the one you see in movies."

Nya let his words sink in. "You're right, but I wanted the movie experience. I wanted to be someone other than the person my father had told me I had to be. I felt so trapped here — not by my country, but by what everyone assumed about me because of my father."

"I know this feeling," Johan said. "When people think they already know who you are and what you're capable of."

"Yes!" Nya adjusted herself on her saddle, having slipped in her excitement at being understood. "I wanted to shock people, to show them that I wasn't the silly girl they thought me to be, and New York had become this symbol of freedom. But then I got there, and I was still the same old me."

"There's nothing wrong with being you," he said without hesitation. He sounded kind of annoyed with her, like he had when she'd apologized on the plane.

People always said stuff like this to her, like the motivational memes posted on social media. It was easy to say such things when you were Johan, and people thought you handsome and daring no matter what you did. But he was trying to help, so she didn't correct him or allow his ease with himself to bother her as it once had.

"You *are* nice," she responded.

"I'm really not," he said more firmly. "You can ask our friends when we get back. I lie, frequently, and not to make people feel better about themselves. I avoid giving compliments like I dodge Liechtienbourger wasps in summer. I wasn't speaking generally — there's nothing wrong with being *you*. Nya. More people should be Nyas, to be quite honest."

He looked at her, eyes dark with challenge, telling her that he was as stubborn as the goats that had evaded capture. He wouldn't let her argue with him on this.

"Nya, my child, you are far too weak, in body and mind, to leave home for university."

"But Johannesburg is not very far, Father. I can do it."

"And who do you know in Johannesburg who will take care of you when you fall ill, or when you become frightened by silly things?"

"I don't get frightened by things, Father."

"Yes, you do, my child. Or you would if I wasn't here to keep you safe."

"But —"

"Would you leave me, too? After taking your mother from me?"

"No."

"Good. Then I will let the local university

know you'll start there, and that you won't be needing a dormitory."

Tears gathered in her eyes at the memory. Her father had always made her feel small; she wasn't used to how easily Johan made her feel big.

"Thank you." Her voice was quiet — the words had just squeaked by the lump of emotion in her throat.

"It's a basic truth, no need to thank me for stating it," he said.

She couldn't quite accept Johan's statement as truth, so she settled on the fact that it wasn't a lie. It was a not-lie that Johan seemed to feel very strongly about, and his insistence on her worth made her feel happy even as she spoke of unhappy things.

"Everyone doesn't see me as you do." She knew that was presumptuous, but Johan had already clearly stated what he thought of her and she wasn't going to be rude enough to second-guess him. "Everyone has it in their heads that I need to be protected. They think *being me* is a problem. You saw my grandmother."

That poked at the bruise to her ego left by his reassurances that she was completely safe with him, but that was fine. She had a surprising new friend and that was enough for her.

121

Johan sighed. "Yes. She was being a bit overbearing, which is why I had to lie to her."

When she glanced at him, he was looking straight ahead, his expression serene but unreadable.

"You said you didn't lie to make people feel better."

He shrugged. "I didn't lie to make her feel better. I lied so that we could continue to be partners and get on with our day."

Nya didn't take her eyes from him. "What was the lie? Exactly?"

"That I would never debauch you." He still had that bland look on his face, and even casually scratched his horse behind its ears.

"Wut?" The word came out like a lake toad's croak.

"I don't *intend* to debauch you," Johan said, his voice even and cool, but not dismissive. "It would be a terrible idea, as ideas go, because, well, I'm *me.* But."

"But?" Another croak.

He did look at her then, and though his words were cool, his gaze was warm — not from the summer sun, but from some inner source of heat that Nya could not bring herself to imagine, despite her propensity for dreaming impossible dreams. "If debauchery was what you wanted from me? I would do it. Thoroughly."

That last word wasn't one she'd used often when speaking English, and as she watched the way his mouth handled it — his tongue licking toward the roof of his mouth, the way his teeth pressed against his bottom lip — she wondered if it was on the list of world's sexiest words, because she was suddenly thinking things she should not be. Like how it would feel for him to form those same three syllables against her lips. Or elsewhere.

Come to bed, and I'll eat you up.

She stared at him, her mouth sealed shut by desire and possibility and delight, and he gave her that mischievous grin. "See? Not nice. Remember that, Sugar Bubble."

There was a noise in the distance and they turned to see Likotsi and Fabiola on one horse, riding to catch up with them as they approached the palace.

"We got our pig!" Fabiola called out, pointing to the small — and now that they grew closer, squealing — creature she held in her arms as Likotsi handled the reins from behind.

"We got our sex goat!" Johan jiggled the rope tied to his saddle.

"Huh?" Fabiola asked, looking at Nya.

123

"Pardon?" Likotsi looked to Nya for explanation, too. "Sex? Goat?"

"You can explain," Johan said to Nya, then trotted off toward the palace gate with their quarry.

He wasn't nice.

And he'd offered up his debauching services. For a second time, if she counted their run-in on the plane.

Her mind had always been a fertile planting ground for fantasies, but she reluctantly salted that earth. She'd spent one nice day with Johan, but, on every other day, he was the type of man she had vowed to avoid. Yes, he was charming and likable and knew what to say, but she knew full well how those traits could be used against her.

Besides, what if her fantasy did become reality? She would just be a plaything for a man like Johan, and that wasn't what she wanted or needed.

Friendship is enough, she reminded herself. She had so few friends. She would ignore the heat that had been in his gaze, and had pooled reciprocally in her belly.

Her horse stamped impatiently and turned its head to give her serious side-eye.

"Sorry," she said, patting the horse's neck gingerly.

Johan was a playboy, and offering to

debauch women was what playboys did. She wouldn't think about it again.

"Ignore him," she said to Kotsi and Fabiola. "He's just being weird."

CHAPTER 6

The wedding of Prince Thabiso and Princess Naledi is today (check out our live feed and cover story), and our source in Thesolo claims that love is in the air! While Prince Lukas has been misbehaving back home, calling his future leadership abilities into question, rumors are circulating about Jo-Jo and a mystery woman being found in a compromising position — more than once! There is speculation that the woman is Nya Jerami (photo; back left; credit: InstaPhoto of Portia Hobbs), cousin of the bride! Could this reportedly demure former schoolteacher really be the woman to capture Jo-Jo's heart?

— *The Looking Glass Daily,*
Royal Beat

Johan tried to shake his strange mood as he prepared for the wedding ceremony in the private chamber in the temple. The last wedding he'd attended that he'd actually had some stake in had been Mamm's. He was happy for his friends, but also fought thin tendrils of anxiety that bound his cheer.

"Are you nervous? Ball. Chain. Etcetera."

"Why? We're already married," Thabiso said, adjusting the collar of his traditional jacket in the mirror. Outside, in the larger chamber, the other members of Thabiso's wedding party laughed and talked amongst themselves. "We're already living happily ever after, mate. This is just an excuse to rub it in everyone's faces."

"Have you not noticed that the prince is a bit overconfident?" Likotsi asked as she brushed Thabiso's hands aside and adjusted the collar herself.

"Yes, but now you'll be *very* married," Johan said, not quite sure what he was getting at. He lifted his chin as Likotsi shifted her attention to him, making sure the suit he'd been gifted — slightly less ornate than Thabiso's, and a blend of traditional tuxedo and modern Thesolo style — was in proper order.

"I *want* to be very married," Thabiso said, then raised a brow at Johan. "Not everyone can live the eternal bachelor life. Even Likotsi has settled down."

She shot him an annoyed look.

"I pride myself on doing what the average man can't," Johan said with a flippancy he didn't really feel.

Now Likotsi's pointed look was transferred to Johan, her eyes telling him that his hijinks weren't appreciated.

"I'm glad you both have found happiness, *meng ami.*" Johan said before they left the room to be caught up in the whirlwind of a royal wedding. "Let's go get you married again."

Love was for brave fools and Johan was entirely too clever and too cowardly to succumb to it. Loneliness wasn't exactly a jaunt down the Riviera, but at least he was in control of it. He didn't allow himself to become attached to many people, which kept the fear of them being snatched away from him at manageable levels.

It was a perfectly reasonable way to live. It was necessary.

Still . . . he hadn't stopped thinking of Nya's pleasant shock when he'd admitted what he should not have admitted ever — that he would do anything she wished, including debauchery.

Especially debauchery.

He was off his game and his control had slipped, yet again; he was starting to worry that Nya emitted some kind of antibullshit wave that stripped him of his power of persuasion.

Kryptonite, indeed.

He'd enjoyed their day together. He was no stranger to physical attraction, *clearly.* That was one aspect of his persona that wasn't made-up; even though Jo-Jo still felt like the introverted boy teased endlessly by his peers, he now presented a package that attracted a very different kind of teasing. He'd grown to appreciate how women and men responded to the idea of him, even if no one ever really saw past the surface. He liked sex, and he liked the people he had sex with, but he always returned to his solitary life of jet-setting and charities and, above all, watching out for Lukas.

But he'd wanted to stay out on that goat hunt with Nya. He'd wanted to listen to her talk about the genus and species of flowers, and he didn't give a damn about flowers. He'd wanted to see her laugh and play with the shepherd children, and pick up tender chunks of roast goat and suck the juices from her fingers. He hadn't wanted the day to end, and that was not a good thing.

Control.

Johan didn't do attachment. He had his close friends, and his brother, and his stepfather. But there was a built-in distance

129

with those people, no matter how dearly he loved them. He could pop in and see them, satisfy his selfish desire to be in their presence and see their smiling faces, and then run off without explanation because that was what they now expected from him.

Nya was different. Something about her made his whole body feel light and fluffy like *buchtel,* as if her sweetness was somehow transferred to him. Johan had never cared much for sweets before, but he suddenly had an insatiable craving, and it frightened him.

The wedding ceremony itself was a splashy affair, a melding of traditions from America and Thesolo. Portia had been ordained somewhere online and performed the American portion of the ceremony, funny and moving and full of all the love she felt for her friends, because Portia didn't hide those things.

Johan was unable to stop glancing at Nya across the aisle from him, dressed in simple white linen that contrasted Naledi's bright yellow gown. Tears streamed down her full cheeks, appled from her wide smile, and the joy radiating from her was palpable, as it had been when she'd spoken of the wedding on the jet. She caught his eye as she laughed at a joke Portia cracked about food delivery services, and Johan was struck by a thought that almost made him topple over in front of the audience: *Is this how she would look at me as we exchanged vows?*

No. He didn't wonder things like that. He didn't *want* things like that.

The rest of the ceremony had passed in a blur of affection and readings and dancing priestesses and joy. And now Johan was at the reception, drinking wine and wondering why Nya's joyful face and shining eyes wouldn't leave his mind.

He reminded himself of that again as he stood beside a dignitary from Zamunda, the wedding reception whirling around them. The twenty-piece band on the stage, with at least ten of those pieces being rhythm instruments, played a bass-heavy cover of a pop song that had been popular a couple of years before, and Johan tapped his foot in time.

"It is lovely, yes? This wedding?" Mawa, the Zamundan diplomat, asked. "Almost as lovely as the union of our king and queen all those years ago."

"Quite lovely," he said. "I hear the wedding of Njaza's king last month was lovely as well."

Mawa said nothing and when he looked at her she was nodding nervously. "Ah. Yes.

Yes. Quite. Er . . . the bride was lovely! She's from Thesolo, so Sanyu made a good match for his people."

Njaza had a bit of a reputation, but Mawa's reaction did not bode well for his upcoming visit, or Sanyu's union.

"Did they seem happy?"

"Oh, look, there is my friend, the ambassador from Druk. I have not seen him in ages. Please excuse me!" Mawa executed a quick bow and rushed away toward the man dressed in the saffron robes of a monk.

That wasn't suspicious at all.

He sidled closer to the next conversation, the group of men he'd been keeping an eye on since they'd settled in the space next to him and the ambassador. He'd found that when you offered the elite free drink, they usually talked about things that they shouldn't. Johan had a feeling that's why the rich were always celebrating something or someone with an open bar.

The group of men in the traditional garments of tribal elders sipped their drinks and spoke animatedly in Thesotho. The way they huddled together said they were speaking of things they didn't want shared.

Johan wasn't fluent by any means, but he made out "Alehk Jerami" and "bastard" and a few other curse words, which was good.

132

No coups were being fomented in this corner of the ballroom. Then he heard "Nya" and "offense to Ingoka," which was not good.

"She should not be here," one man said, switching to English as the upper class in many countries often did. "It is said that she knew of his actions and did nothing."

"How would she know?" The man next to him raised his dark gray brows. "She is simple, they say. That's why he hid her away for so long, no?"

"I heard he kept her in a plastic bubble," added another man.

"That was a film," the first man said, rolling his eyes. "She worked at the orphanage in Lek Hemane."

"Even if she wasn't weak as a fledgling and silly as a fainting goat, no man would ruin himself with a traitor's daughter," the second man said, mouth pulled into a grimace.

Johan fumed as he considered all of the ways he could insert himself into the situation and defend her but causing a scene at Thabiso's wedding was beyond the pale even for Bad Boy Jo-Jo — even if he wanted to kick each one of the men in the back of the knee for their rudeness.

Nya had told him how people thought of

133

her, but Johan hadn't realized the traits he liked in her could be seen through such a negative lens. She wasn't weak or silly, but these men spoke as if it were a fact. He supposed to them it was one — that was how things worked. Someone said something with confidence, and then everyone assumed it to be true, and then it *was* true. That was how he'd become the playboy prince.

His phone vibrated in his pocket, and he pulled it out quickly, hoping it was Lukas, but it was his stepfather. He made his way into a plant-lined alcove and accepted the call.

He hadn't heard from his brother in days, and the nagging feeling that something was wrong and he didn't know had been assailing him since he'd stepped off the plane.

"Is everything *gutt,* Forshett?" he asked, pulling at his collar, which seemed to tighten as the low-level panic that he'd been suppressing ballooned inside of him.

He hoped for the usual *gutt* from his stepfather to allay his fears, but the king sighed.

"It's your brother," Linus said gravely.

Johan's knees almost gave out, and he leaned back against the wall as casually as he could muster. The corrugations of a reed tapestry pressed into his back, but he couldn't force his body to move just yet.

"What happened?" he asked, his voice strained, a million awful scenarios of how Lukas could be lost to him running through his mind. The part of his brain that was always thinking ahead was going through contingencies for escaping the ballroom while in a full-blown panic, and coming up blank.

"He's developed a bit of a wild streak," Linus said, with normal levels of fatherly aggravation. "I just got a call from his school because he got into a fight with one of those American tech heirs."

Johan waited, chest tight, then asked, "Does he have a concussion? What hospital is he at? Was he *shot*?"

The king made a startled noise. "What? No. He's here at the castle, and not allowed to leave his quarters."

Relief and annoyance danced through Johan's veins and he slowly straightened. The fabric of his shirt stretched around his chest as he inhaled deeply. "He's all right?"

"Well, I wouldn't call this all right," Linus said.

"Forshett —" Johan slammed his mouth shut against the harshness of his tone, not allowing the fear still flowing through him to make him say something rash. He swallowed, though his mouth had gone dry. "You made me think he was hurt. Or worse."

"I did no such thing," the king said evenly. "I said, 'It's your brother.' Be sensible, Jo-Jo. I thought you'd outgrown these outbursts."

Johan almost threw his phone down to the ground. Did Linus really not remember? Because Johan did. He'd been in his dorm room, packing his weekend bag for his visit home with a knot of worry in his stomach when his cell phone had rang. *C'est ihre mamm,* Linus had said gravely.

He knew from experience that explaining to Linus how three words could send him spiraling into a panic would do no good, so he moved on.

"Why was he fighting?" Johan asked, grabbing at a lock of hair and twisting. All of his fights had been defensive, started by other boys who picked up on Johan's perceived weakness — emotion. But Lukas wasn't like Johan — Johan had made sure of that. He was sporty and well liked and didn't spend all his time sighing about the state of the world and crying over imaginary people.

"It doesn't matter why. We're in the middle of a referendum and *now* he does

136

this? Von Brausteins are known for strength, dexterity, and victory in battle, but this is boarding school, not war." Linus sighed. "Have you spoken to him recently?"

"I've been busy," Johan lied. If Linus didn't know that Lukas was avoiding him, he wasn't going to tell him. Handling his brother was one of the few things Linus saw as useful about Johan. It was one of the few things he saw as useful about himself. "I'll try to reach him, but I'll be home in a few days."

"Yes, always gallivanting about," Linus said.

"I'm an ambassador," Johan replied stiffly. "Gallivanting is my job."

Linus didn't say anything.

"Has the press picked anything up about Lukas's fight?" Johan didn't feel like arguing, and was already figuring out how he could help spin this.

"I don't think so," Linus said, then paused. Johan heard the recalibration in that brief silence, and when his stepfather spoke again there was insinuation in his tone. "They *have* picked up some news about you in Thesolo, though. News that could be helpful."

"What's that?" Johan asked, already knowing he wouldn't like the answer. Linus was using his "cool dad" tone.

"This woman you are flirting with. Nya Jerami?"

Johan had been pacing back and forth in the alcove, but he stopped and pressed his phone closer to his ear.

"Nya is the cousin to the Princess of Thesolo, who is the wife of my best friend," he said carefully. "I have not been flirting."

Not *really.* Offering to debauch someone was a three at most on his ten-point flirtation scale.

"There's a story in the *Looking Glass* about the Duke of Edinburgh attending the wedding, and a group photo in which you are most definitely giving this Nya woman a *look*. The article mentioned that you've been turning your charms on her and found yourselves in some . . . situations."

The cool dad tone had leveled up to "totally cool dad" tone, which was more than anyone should have to tolerate.

"Do you believe everything you read in these rags? You know most of the stories aren't true."

"I don't believe it, but the public apparently does. After that story ran, the royal PR team noticed that our approval rating in the referendum jumped up and talk on social media was more favorable."

A dull anger throbbed in Johan's jaw from clenching his teeth so hard. "Forshett. Don't," he warned.

"This is your brother's future at stake, Jo-Jo. He has been raised to be a king. What will he do without a kingdom?"

"Get a job?" Johan wasn't thrilled about the referendum, or the people who were pushing for the end of the monarchy — those like this Arschlocher guy who were tired of having their greed leashed by rules that prevented Liechtienbourg from becoming a tax haven like other small countries. But it was a constitutional monarchy; the people would vote, and what the people wanted mattered more than even his brother. If the worst came to pass, Johan would be there for Lukas as he always had been.

"I have not asked anything from you in a long time," the king said, his voice no longer jovial. "You do what you want, when you want, and we deal with the bad press. But the referendum is in a couple of weeks. Can you not manage to date this woman until then?"

"She's not some plaything for me to parade around for points," Johan said. "She's kind and intelligent, and I will not —"

"Oh!" Linus said. "You like her. *Gutt, gutt.* I thought I would have to persuade you, but I see I was worried for nothing. Have fun at the wedding. Talk to your brother. Date this woman you like. Bring her back home with you. See you soon, son."

The line disconnected; his stepfather had hung up.

Johan stood in the alcove, furious — at what King Linus had asked of him, and at what the man had so easily discerned. Linus thought that Johan liking Nya made everything easier, when in fact it made it harder. So much harder. Panic welled in him at the possibility of what would happen if he didn't crush this attraction he'd been harboring immediately, but he calmed himself with the fact that he'd be leaving in two days' time. Depending on what she decided to do with her life, he might never see her again.

Reassurance had never felt so shitty.

"You all right, mate?" Tavish strode up in a fine kilt, two plates of food in hand. "You look ready to smash that phone, which I obviously endorse."

"I'm fine," he said.

Tav raised his brows. "Want to talk? You're into that talking-about-your-feelings shite. And it helps, I'll give you that."

Tav had it all wrong. Johan was into talking about *other* people's feelings. Talking about his own was about as fun as licking sandpaper.

Johan shook his head and plastered on his most convincing smile. "Just my brother acting out. You know how it is."

Tav had a younger brother, and indeed knew how it was, which is why Johan had purposely focused on that aspect of his troubles. Besides, he couldn't exactly share the crude suggestion his stepfather had made. Crude, and much too tempting.

Date this woman you like. Bring her back home with you.

Tav shook his head. "He's what, seventeen? *Pfft,* good luck with that, mate."

"Thanks," Johan said. He followed Tav to the VIP table on the stage, where their friend group had been seated, though he hadn't been there for most of the night. He'd been schmoozing and doing ambassadorial stuff and avoiding Nya.

She was talking intently with Portia, who was describing something excitedly, waving her hands around. Portia reached out and linked arms with Tavish as he sat, using her free hand to continue gesticulating. Nya laughed and nodded, but her gaze kept flitting to her phone.

Johan narrowed his eyes, wondering what kind of games this boyfriend of hers was playing this time to have her so anxiously awaiting his message. Or maybe they'd already made up, and she was hovering over her phone because she was awaiting something sweet from him. He shouldn't be upset; if anything, he should be glad that she was proving the men he'd eavesdropped on wrong. Someone was obviously very interested in a traitor's daughter. Someone besides him.

Control.

He approached the table, and the empty seat beside Nya, and sat down. Her phone lit up with a message.

My mission is a lonely one, Nya. I wish I could be with you right now. Do you want to be with me, too?

Johan grimaced as she glanced at her phone and smiled with what seemed like relief.

He cleared his throat.

"*Ça geet et,* Sugar Bubble?" he asked with deliberate lazy ease. He did not feel at ease at all. The bodice of the white linen gown she wore had a deep V, revealing the curved mounds of her breasts and the shadowed valley between them. Her makeup had been touched up since her crying during the wedding, and her eyes were lined in kohl and sparkling teal. Her lips had a natural look again, just the lightest sheen of gloss to accentuate their fullness.

Johan fidgeted in his seat and then wrapped his hands around his sweating water glass. She turned to him, somehow curling in shyly even as she swayed in his direction.

"Hi, Phoko," she said, and his body had the most ridiculous reaction. He leaned closer to her, almost a lurch it was so abrupt, and he suddenly understood the "moth to a flame" cliché. This attraction was absurd, and dangerous. *She* was dangerous, there in her beautiful bright warmth. Flying closer would surely lead to his demise. Moths who flew into flames weren't exactly role model material, but then again, constant fiery death hadn't stopped them after millennia of existence.

Johan leaned even closer.

"Phoko?" Portia asked from across the table. His gaze jumped to hers with a quelling look and she pinned him with a speculative glare. "Now you both have pet names for each other? That's cute. Cute and interesting."

He rolled his eyes at Portia's relentless curiosity, aka nosiness, sure she was scheming how to get information out of one or both of them, and turned his attention back to Nya.

"Is your evening going well?"

It might go slightly less well when he told her she'd been linked to him in the tabloids, especially with the fertile gossip fodder that was her father. Maybe Nya's text buddy wouldn't like it either — maybe he'd be jealous. Johan tried not to take pleasure in that, and failed.

There was the slightest hesitation before she nodded, the briefest delay before she forced her lips up into a smile. Now that he was really looking at her, he could see that the joy radiating from her earlier in the night had been tempered. There was an uneasiness in her wide eyes and nerves in the way her hand reflexively sought out her phone.

"Is he giving you trouble again?" he asked.

"He?"

Johan glanced at her phone, somewhat smug in the fact that she had forgotten the existence of whoever this mystery man was, at least for the moment.

"Oh! No. It's not that. Some people are not happy that I am here," she said quietly.

Her gaze darted out to the crowd near the stage, and he understood how this was working even before he saw the cluster of people glancing up at her with cruel smiles — in sitting at a table of honor, she was also being put on display for those who had not forgiven her father, like the men he'd eavesdropped on.

Rage mingled with a sudden intense desire to shield her from their blatant insults. They were trying to make her feel unwanted, at the wedding of her cousin, at an event meant to celebrate love. He was used to this aspect of life among the rich and wealthy, which was magnified in small kingdoms like Liechtienbourg and Thesolo. Some people enjoyed looking down on others and making them feel less than — he knew that truth in his bones.

"Hey," Portia said, snapping to get his attention. He understood then why they were eating with linked arms — they were blocking Nya from the gossips' line of sight. "Are you trying to murder those people with your brain? Please tell me you can. I've been trying with no success and Tav won't let me use the sword I made as a wedding present."

"It's okay," Nya said. Her hands dropped into her lap and her gaze followed them. "It is to be expected after my father's crimes."

"It's *not* okay, Nya," Johan said. "You did nothing wrong. You're not your father."

"The man knows what he's talking about," Tavish said, waving his fork.

Nya sighed. "Thank you, everyone. I'm not feeling well, though. I'm going to lie down for a bit, but I'll be back."

"The reception will probably go on until morning, there's plenty of time for a power nap," Portia said reassuringly. "Do you want me to come with you?"

"No. Stay and enjoy yourself." She was trying to keep her voice light and cheerful, but it rang false to Johan, as did the way she wouldn't meet anyone's eye. He remembered then, why he had first started watching Nya — because she *had* done something wrong in trying to counter Ledi's poisoning instead of stopping it.

What must she feel like now, at this wedding of people she loved but had hurt by her inaction, where half the guests thought her evil and the other half thought her foolish? Thabiso and Ledi had forgiven Nya, but she'd sat and taken the abuse of strangers because she thought she deserved it.

I'm used to it.

"Text if you need me," Portia called out. "It might take me eighty-four years to get

146

to the guest wing, with these long-ass hallways, but I'll be there."

Nya nodded and turned to leave the dais. Johan's gaze trailed after her as he searched for an excuse to follow, catching on something that was a more-than-valid reason. He'd wanted to shield her, and now he would.

He stood smoothly from his seat and sidled up behind her, so close that he was almost touching. It was the practiced move of a playboy on the prowl, which was at least somewhat less attention grabbing than him wildly flailing up to her. She made to turn and face him, but he placed his hand on her waist, holding her in place while trying not to touch her any more than necessary before explaining.

"What are you doing, Phoko?" she asked, looking back over her shoulder, brows knit in annoyance.

"You have something on the back of your dress," he said. She shook her head and turned to walk away, so he decided to be more direct. "It's a *monthly* something, tied to the moons and tides? I'll walk behind you so no one sees."

People were already being cruel to her; he wouldn't allow them anything else to hold over her.

"Oh no." She stiffened beneath his light hold, her shoulders hunching. She shook her head. "I haven't had . . . I can't remember the last time I . . ."

"It's fine," he said, in his best carefree-prince tone, even though the shame in her voice made him want to hold her close — closer, rather.

"You don't have to . . ." Her voice faded into a humiliated whisper and she tried to step away from him. "Your suit might be ruined if you come too close."

He tightened his hold on her waist with one hand, then took her hand delicately in his other one, something he'd learned in the dance lessons required at his boarding school.

"I've already told you that bodily fluids don't scare me," he said near the exposed shell of her ear. It was true, though not because he was a playboy as he'd led her to believe. Johan had been visiting hospital wards since he was a child, at his mother's side and long after she was gone. "Come, Sugar Bubble. You should know by now that I don't do anything because I *have to.* I do what I want, and right now, I want what you want. Do you want me to shield you?"

He couldn't see her face but knew she stared at the ground because the column of her neck was exposed to him. Her fingertips closed more tightly around his hand and she nodded.

"Then I will," he said and began moving them along the edge of the crowd. He followed in her footsteps carefully, trying to stay close enough to block her but also leaving enough room to prevent any . . . friction.

He hadn't realized how far away the door was when he'd impulsively jumped behind her. And he'd thought there might be some chatter, but not the invisible spotlight that seemed to make everyone's head swivel to look at them.

Some guests stopped to stare, others tapped the people nearest to them and pointed. It seemed that, despite his attempt at inconspicuousness, they were making a scene. That was fine with Johan — scenes were his specialty.

"Smile," Johan said, leaning his mouth down near her ear again. "Pretend I'm whispering dirty things to you. Absolutely filthy."

"What? Why?" she squawked, stopping abruptly so that he almost crashed into her.

"You said you wanted to shock people, remember? I think we can multitask here." Johan glanced around the crowd. "If you don't want excitement, speak now or forever hold your peace."

Her shoulder blades pressed into his chest as she inhaled, and he could feel her shaking from nerves. "Sure. Why not? I can't stop people from talking about me anyway, and each day brings some new embarrassment. Let's do this."

"Comme tu willst," he said in a low voice, slipping his arm fully around her waist.

She started walking again, head held high, and he followed. When they reached the dance floor, he changed the rhythm of his steps to match the thrumming drumbeat, and his hips swayed of their own accord.

"Hello! Excellent party. Yes, we love this song! This is our jam!" Johan called out to the people they passed, pumping one fist in the air as he stepped fully into his role of fun-loving prince. Then he turned his mouth toward Nya's ear. "You're supposed to be pretending I'm seducing you."

"I'm trying to!" she snapped. "And besides, everyone will laugh at the idea of you. And me. Together."

She was right — anyone with common sense would wonder why someone like Nya would even talk to Johan, let alone be within seduction range of him.

"Fine, I'll have to actually talk dirty to

you," he warned, then cleared his throat dramatically as she stiffened in apprehension. He imbued his voice with a husky lewdness. "Three-day-old lasagna pan that has not been soaked in the kitchen sink. Welcome mat at a pig farmer's house. Sweaty socks that have been worn for thirty consecutive days."

Her belly undulated against his forearm before laughter burst out of her mouth in a wild, high peel that was much louder than anything he expected from her. They were so close to the door now, navigating around large gowns and dancing guests, but everyone in the vicinity looked in their direction again.

"The deep fryer at a shady schnitzel shop," he drawled. "The last stall in a bus station bathroom."

"Enough!" she cried through a fit of giggles, and just like that they were at the entrance to the hall. Thabiso gave him a quizzical look as he passed through the doors, and Johan raised his eyebrows mischievously because, as he'd said, he wasn't nice. If you were going to cause drama, you had to go all the way.

As they swept into the hallway, he spotted the guard who had helped him from the sauna, whose wide-eyed expression showed just what a scene he was causing. "Excuse me, Lineo, was it? Can you have a shuttle cart swing by the entrance to the summer garden and wait there? Thank you, *merci,* I will tell the prince and princess about your excellent service to the palace."

He slowed down his pace now, though he still held Nya close to him as they left the air-conditioned coolness of the palace. They strolled past milling guests smoking out front or taking a break from dancing, until they reached the nearest garden. He released her as they stepped onto the vetiver-lined pathway, not enjoying how empty his arms felt when she moved away from him.

"Here we are," he said, slightly out of breath. "You can wait here, and I'll let you know when the shuttle cart arrives to take you to your room."

Away from him, and the thoughts running wild in his head after having her so close to him.

She placed her hands on her hips and looked up at him. "Seriously, Phoko?"

He tried not to stare at the rapid rise and fall of her chest.

"What?" he asked innocently, making his eyes wide.

"Why did you do that? I appreciate it, thank you, but everyone will be talking about us now!"

Her expression was somewhere between frustration and giddiness — creased forehead but bright eyes and a mouth that didn't know whether to smile or frown. This was the perfect time to tell her that everyone, or at least certain journalists with access to printing presses and large readerships, was already talking about them.

"It was the first thing that came to mind," he said instead. "I told you causing drama is one of the few skills I possess."

He shucked off his suit jacket, something he should have thought of before dancing her through a room packed with the elite of Thesolo and several other nations.

"I also wasn't a fan of the idea that you had to sit there and accept people's cruelty as punishment for something that hurt you, too."

Her mouth opened and closed, and there was something about how her lips pressed together with apprehension but her eyes pleaded for understanding that made Johan forget that she was a dangerous flame.

He took a step forward with his jacket hanging from one hand by one sleeve and reached behind her to pull the other sleeve around her waist. "If anyone is going to gossip about you today, they should be saying

153

that you were so breathtaking that you were whisked away by an infamous playboy. That he was so overcome with longing that he couldn't wait for the festivities to end to get you alone."

"Well, if they're going to spread lies, I guess that one is as good as any other." Her gaze searched his, and he could easily see her confusion. A breeze blew, making the palm fronds behind her dip, dancing across her back and shoulders as if they, too, were swayed by the desire to touch her.

She shivered at their caress, and Johan found himself jealous of flora. He wanted to make her shiver, wanted to know how she liked to be kissed and touched and pleased.

"I don't lie to make people feel better about themselves." Johan pulled one sleeve through the other and tightened slowly. Slowly. Her breath caught as the knot came together at her waist. He should have let go then, should have stepped away, but she gasped at the cinch of the fabric as he tied the sleeves — it was a gasp of pleasure.

He tugged the knotted sleeves, bringing her a step closer to him. "And I don't lie to you."

"Phoko." Her eyes were huge, but there was no fear in them. Curiosity. Puzzlement. *Heat.* That last one was the problem, because it seemed to require a response, one that Johan felt more than qualified to give her.

Although he knew that this was bad, bad, very bad, his head started to dip down toward hers.

His stepfather's words echoed in his mind. *Can't you date this woman for a bit?*

Linus misunderstood the problem. Johan could see much further than "a bit" when he looked into Nya's eyes. He saw the bait that was laid down for the foolish protagonist in every fairy tale. Love. Shelter. Kindness. He saw it and he wanted it — wanted *her* — even though he knew the bait was inside a cage of eventual despair.

Despair seemed worth it, just then.

His mouth was so close to hers now, her stuttering breath a staccato whisper against his lips. A heady rush of possibility surged through him in anticipation of learning the feel of her, and the taste of her, making his head spin. When he inhaled, the scent of ylang-ylang tickled his nose.

Her eyes fluttered closed and she leaned forward to meet his kiss . . . and then the palm fronds parted and the face of a disgruntled grandmother pushed through them.

"Eh, eh! What are you doing?" Annie

Jerami snapped as Nya and Johan jumped apart.

The fronds rustled a bit more and Makalele stuck his head through. "Probably the same thing we were doing, love," he said with a grin.

Panic swept over Nya's face, then embarrassment.

"Nya said she needed some air, as the ballroom had become a bit stifling," Johan said with a calm he didn't feel. Nya's grandparents had saved him from making a terrible mistake, but his body wasn't quite as thankful as his brain was. "I was escorting her to make sure she would be safe."

"Safe from what?" Annie asked, dropping a hand onto her hip as she looked him up and down.

"The peacocks have been very aggressive lately," Nya added solemnly, surprising him.

"Right. You two can protect her from the dangerous peacocks —"

Makalele giggled, and Annie rolled her eyes at him.

"— and I'll go see about transportation for you, Nya," Johan said, then turned and jogged off.

He'd been millimeters away from kissing Nya, who had managed to drill through all of his defenses without even seemingly wanting to or trying.

Running away was the only logical action.

CHAPTER 7

ONE TRUE PRINCE, TEXT MESSAGE MODE

Hanjo: I've never met anyone like you before, Nya.

Nya: (B) There's nothing special about me. Besides, you barely know me!

Hanjo: Let's change that. I have an idea that might be a little wild . . . but then again, all of my ideas are a little wild.

The morning following the wedding, Nya lay in bed with a heating pad under her back and the blankets pulled over her head. She didn't want to face this day, or the embarrassing memories that her duvet couldn't block out.

After returning to her room from the

gardens, she'd showered, left the voluminous linen dress to soak in cool water, and rummaged through the bathroom cabinet, coming up with a menstrual cup, which she'd had to look up instructions on how to use. Her period had always been irregular due to her health issues — the issues that had mostly disappeared once her father had gone to prison. This humiliation was another thing that could be blamed on him.

She'd put on a new dress, refreshed her makeup, and then climbed into bed, too embarrassed and confused to return to the reception. Johan's intentions had been good. He'd been convincing, too, trying to make her feel better with his jokes and his smile and his looking at her like she was the juiciest lamb shank at the feast.

She wasn't foolish enough to think it had meant anything to him, though, beyond a kind gesture. It shouldn't have meant anything to her. But then the thought of going back into the ballroom and seeing him laugh and flirt with others, or worse, having him admit that he'd only done it to make her feel better, had flattened her out on her bed.

He's nothing but a frivolous fuckboy, she reminded herself. But somewhere in the last few days, that frivolous fuckboy had become

159

her friend. The part of her mind that had daydreamed about him for months, despite her distaste, wished it was possible for him to be more.

Foolish girl, her father's voice had chided. *Your dreams are too big.*

She'd attributed the tears that sheened in her eyes to hormones, and had fallen asleep with the memory of Johan's face moving toward hers playing on a loop.

"Nya?" Portia's voice sounded outside the door, paired with a firm, efficient knock that had to be Ledi.

Nya took a deep steadying breath. She was sad and listless, her back felt like it was being punched by tiny goblins, and her stomach seemed ready to betray her, but she'd already lost hours of quality time with her friends by wallowing in her embarrassment. She rolled to her side and called out, "Come in!"

Ledi and Portia entered looking radiant, in part because of the sunlight pouring through the door behind them. She glanced at her window to see that the heavy, light-blocking curtains were still drawn.

"What time is it?" she asked, sitting up.

"Time for the reception brunch," Ledi said, coming to sit at the foot of her bed. Portia sat on the other side, and they each leaned back against a bamboo bedpost. "Are you feeling okay?"

She'd texted them what had happened when she'd awoken to an alarm to check *One True Prince,* and told them not to worry.

"I am embarrassed," she said, flopping back onto her pillows.

"Don't worry, no one saw your dress. Not a peep on social media so far. And even if they had, so what? It's natural." Portia's resolute tone indicated she would kneecap anyone who bothered Nya about it.

"Not because of that. Because of Johan." Nya pulled the sheet up to her chin. "He must think I'm ridiculous, not even knowing my own courses. But I almost never have them! I thought it was just the stress of returning home making me feel strange."

"Have you been to a doctor about that?" Ledi asked, always the professional. "Irregular periods are fairly common, and they can put you on birth control to regulate it. You should also make sure it's not something serious."

"I will do that," she said, then took a deep breath. "I was scared to go before because I was worried they would ask why a woman almost thirty from a nation with universal health care had never had such troubles looked at before."

"So. Like. Why is that?" Ledi asked quietly.

Nya's stomach roiled, and she wasn't sure if it was with upset or because she was about to say something she'd never told anyone before. Ledi had always questioned her about her health, and Nya had always evaded, but now . . .

She looked down, and so she was able to see both Portia and Ledi's hands as they reached for hers and squeezed.

"Until you came to Thesolo, I was always sick. My childhood doctors assumed it was just my *frail nature,* as my father constantly told them, because there was no pattern and seemingly no cause, and I'd accepted that. But I've had time to think, without my father always telling me what was true and what wasn't. He knew how to use the traditional plants to do many things, and —" Tears filled her eyes. She tried to say more but the words choked in her throat, blocked there like the warnings she'd wanted to give Ledi when Alehk Jerami had pressured her to drink more tea.

"And then he went to prison for poisoning me and suddenly you're looking like a snack and getting your period," Ledi finished angrily. "I had my suspicions and I didn't want to push, but *that motherfucker!*"

Both of her friends squeezed Nya's hands more tightly, holding on to her as if they were in a stormy sea together and they wouldn't let her sink. She swallowed thickly.

"That *asshole*," Portia said. "And he has the nerve to pull this now, after what he put you through?"

"Portia," Ledi said in a quelling tone that made Nya's head snap up. She drew her hands away and laced her fingers together.

"What do you mean 'now'?" she asked, dread icing her from her feet to her scalp.

"Your father heard you were back," Ledi said, and though her voice was calm her face was taut with anger. "He's been demanding to see you. And he says that he will not share the extent of his dealings — of the danger he put Thesolo in — until you pay him a visit."

Nya hugged her arms around herself. "No. I can't. I'm sorry, but I cannot. I will not."

She couldn't explain the sickness rising in her throat, or why she started to shake. Her father had never laid a hand on her, except to give her a loving pat. Never raised his voice, except to run off people he thought might harm her. He'd treated her like a fragile teacup that needed to be wrapped in bubble wrap and stored in a dark cupboard to keep it safe.

He'd told her everything he did was out of love. And, even if they hadn't realized it, so had everyone else, by smiling and re- marking what a good father he was, by absorbing his belief that she needed to be treated with care and following suit.

She wasn't certain what would happen if she sat in front of him and looked into that face she both loved and hated. If he opened his mouth and spoke those words that had kept her under his control for so many years.

You took your mother from me. Would you leave me, too?

She'd fled without telling him, but even after her time in New York, she worried that her answer would be what he'd programmed her to say. *No father. Never.*

"You don't have to do anything you don't want to," Ledi said fiercely. "Sorry, but fuck this motherfucker. You don't owe him anything. But it also isn't right to keep this from you, because you're a grown woman and you can make your own decisions."

Nya nodded, though she wished someone would tell her what she could do to make the pain stop.

"Hey," Portia said, coming to kneel beside Nya and rub her back. "Why don't you take a hot shower, relax, and then come eat with us?"

"Yes. I'll be fine. I just hate that he would use me like this," Nya said on a shuddering breath. "It's just how he is, though. A zebra cannot change its stripes."

"We can kill him, right, Ledi?" Portia asked hopefully.

"I'll look into it," Ledi said, stroking her chin in a very Thabiso-like fashion.

Nya wasn't sure how to tell them that death threats weren't helping, but then someone cleared their throat and they turned to see a wide-eyed palace staff member in the doorway.

"Good morning, Indira," Ledi said, inclining her head toward the woman.

"Excuse me, Your Highness and esteemed guests. Good morning. I am here to clean but I can come back if I am interrupting a matter of import," the middle-aged woman said. She glanced at Nya, then down to the ground.

"No, nothing of import," Nya said, trying to surreptitiously wipe at her face.

"Can I be of assistance to you?" Indira asked.

"Can you please take the item that's soaking in the bathroom to be washed?" Nya said politely. "Oh, and please take Prince Johan's suit jacket and have it cleaned and returned to him, too. Thank you."

She pointed at the jacket hanging from the bathroom door and tried not to remember the look in his eyes when he'd tied it around her.

Indira glanced at the jacket. "Yes. I will do that."

"Thank you," Ledi said warmly.

"It is my pleasure to serve," she said, then disappeared into the bathroom.

"Ugh, why does this have to hurt?" Nya complained, talking about both her period and life in general. "It really isn't fair."

"Did you take any pills?" Portia pulled a bottle of over-the-counter painkillers from some hidden pocket.

"I'll take one," Nya said, ignoring her instinct not to take any medicine at all. Portia wouldn't harm her.

There was a splashing of water and then a sharp gasp, and when Indira came out from the bathroom with the dripping bundle of linen she looked stricken. Nya was awash in embarrassment, which she was starting to think had become her perpetual state. She had tried to scrub the dress, but apparently hadn't done a good enough job.

"Ms. Jerami, I — Are you all right? Do you need any unguents, poultices, or herbal remedies?"

Nya relaxed. The woman was just worried

about her well-being.

"I appreciate your offer," Nya said. "I am in pain, but it's not that bad. Nothing uncommon given the situation."

Indira nodded sharply. "Yes, it is exactly that, Ms. Jerami. Blessings of Ingoka upon you, and her wrath on those who have caused you any distress."

The woman marched toward the door, came back to snatch the suit jacket up, then marched out again.

"What was that about?" Portia asked.

"Maybe she heard about my father," Nya said, then sighed. "Okay, go to the brunch. I'll be there soon."

Her friends hesitated.

"I swear on my stash of dating games."

They each hugged her before they left, and she made her way into the bathroom, feeling both heavier and lighter. She decided not to think of visiting her father. She was good at pretending everything was okay, after years of practice. She would smile and laugh and not let anyone know that her father could still hurt her, even from behind bars.

The brunch was still going strong when Nya arrived clad in one of the rompers she'd bought when she planned on running wild in New York City, but had never dared to wear. She'd chosen the outfit because the red silky material was stretchy and comfortable and the brunch was outdoors in the summer garden, but as she'd stared in the mirror and dabbed at her red lipstick, she'd thought of Johan. Johan who was suddenly a friend, but a friend who she wanted to appreciate how nice her legs looked in heels and how her melanin popped.

She'd also thought of her father, who'd only allowed her to wear drab, dark, loose-fitting clothing because "men were like dogs."

Do you really want to wear that outfit, child? What will people say?

If someone was giving him information about her, he should know that his daughter was wearing bright colors, showing skin, and inviting the dogs to feast their eyes on her.

Okay, she only had one particular dog in mind. A fox, to be more precise, and one whose mouth had been so close to hers the night before that their noses had brushed.

As soon as she walked into the gated-off area of the garden where the brunch was being held, her gaze landed on him. Everyone was laughing and talking but he sat staring at his *jollof* like the meaning of life could be found in the grains. He looked up suddenly, his gaze locking right on to hers, and she wobbled in her Mary Jane stilettos even though she knew how to navigate grass in high heels. Ledi had taught her in Central Park, outside the royal town house.

"Cousiiiiiin!" Thabiso called out happily, seemingly having indulged in the apricot mimosas that were on the brunch menu. "Come, we saved you a seat!"

He pointed to the seat across from him — next to Johan. She was starting to wonder whether the goddess wasn't testing her. In the many visits to New York he'd made, he hadn't spoken a word to her, but now she couldn't seem to escape him. She'd comforted herself with the fact that he was a spoiled jerk who she didn't want to talk to anyway, but she'd been wrong on that front. She wanted to talk to him, about anything and everything, even if he was exactly the last man in the world she should get ideas about.

He was looking at her curiously, and she wondered if she'd made the wrong fashion choice. Maybe red had been the wrong color to wear the day after her incident.

She slid into the seat, aware that Johan was still looking at her oddly. Maybe he'd been drunk the day before and had forgotten what passed between them. Maybe he was disgusted. Maybe he thought she was shameless, strutting in with her skin exposed and —

No, that was her father, not Johan. She was fairly certain her Phoko had no idea the word *shameless* existed.

"Gutten jour," he said, his voice husky. She wondered if he'd stayed up late partying, and that was why he sounded like a sexy Franco-Germanic vampire. He would make a good Rognath the Vampire Lord, especially if he kept staring at her like he was capable of eating her — which he had already offered to do.

Which I might not turn down next time.

Heat rushed to her face at that thought.

"Mmoro," she replied, turning from him so he couldn't guess what she was thinking. Across the expanse of grass beyond the tables, a few of the royal guards stood overlooking the small gathering. Lineo, who had definitely seen Nya's breasts in the sauna *and* witnessed her weird exit from the reception with Johan, gazed at her, then at Johan, then back at Nya. She said something to the woman beside her — was that Indira, the palace staff woman? Nya cringed; they were probably talking about how weird she was, running from the reception and

ruining expensive fabric.

Nya grabbed a pear tart, biting into the pastry and sighing with delight. She hadn't been allowed to have sweets very often before — her father had told her that her stomach couldn't tolerate them.

While she was in the hospital, recovering from the shock of her father's crime and detoxing from the awful evidence of her father's love, she'd raided the vending machine and eaten the sweets she always eyed at the market. She'd figured if what her father said was true, the hospital was the best place to test it. Nothing had happened besides a wild sugar rush and, a few days later, an acne outbreak.

She'd decided to take Ledi's advice and go to New York immediately after.

"I have to talk to you about something," Johan said as she chewed. "When you're done eating."

She glanced at him, took in his nervous state. "Are you all right? Are you worried about the referendum?"

He startled. "You know about that?"

His gaze dropped to her mouth and she wondered if she had smeared her lipstick.

"There's this invention called the internet," she said with a little more attitude than was necessary.

171

"Right. Sorry. A lot of people don't even know Liechtienbourg exists," he said. "Outside of royal watchers. But no, it's not that. Not directly at least."

"Are you worried about your trip to Njaza?" Thabiso called across the table. "Even I don't really mess about with that Sanyu. His father was mean, and they say he's meaner."

"It's just one day," Johan said in that stiff aristocratic way he spoke in sometimes. He didn't speak like that when they were alone, Nya realized. "Besides, how intimidating can a man whose first name is Stanley be?"

"May the goddess protect Johan tomorrow, especially if he calls Stanley Sanyu by his first name," Thabiso said solemnly, hands clasped. Then he reached out and grabbed one of the goat meat pastries from the middle of the table with a gleam in his eyes.

"Tomorrow?" Nya felt panic stir in her. The wedding obviously wouldn't last forever — three days was short for a Thesoloian wedding celebration, but it'd been adapted to fit the modern schedules of the guests. But it seemed much too fast, and she was shocked to find that she was sad that she wouldn't see Johan anymore. Sad like she had been when Portia had left for Scotland,

and Ledi and Thabiso had gone back to Thesolo.

She'd be alone again, alone with the decision of what job to take, where to live, and whether or not to see her father.

"Oh," she said.

She ate quietly after that, unable to shake the sadness that had descended upon her while the conversation continued around her. Guests began to leave the table eventually. Likotsi was taking Tavish and Portia to the palace guard museum, and Fabiola had to go call her cousin and aunt. Ledi and Thabiso started making lovey-dovey eyes at one another, and Nya stood.

"I'm going to go for a walk," she said, and then sped away before anyone could stop her.

She hated the feeling rising in her. The wedding had been difficult and full of strange events, but her friends had all been together. They'd talked and laughed and had fun, despite the worries pressing in at her from all sides. Now they would leave, paired off and happy. Portia had her new life coaching business and Tavish had peerage duties. Ledi and Thabiso would be occupied with royal duties, and Ledi's STEM program for young girls would be launching in the coming weeks. Likotsi and Fabiola had their own lives to attend to. Johan had his own life to go back to, as well, and because she was a girl who didn't crush her dreams when they were small enough, now she would miss him.

He wouldn't give her a second thought — it had only been a few days, and their interactions had been forced by the wedding. It wasn't as if he'd sought her out. She'd taken a few coincidences and blown them up into something more. He'd find some beautiful Njazan woman who didn't make a mess of herself and have fun with her.

Ugh. Why did it hurt to think of that? Nya followed the gossip columns, and read about the people Johan was alleged to be dating. She wasn't sure she'd be able to do that anymore.

Foolish girl.

She found what she was looking for — the gazebo where she had gotten to know Naledi during her recovery in the royal hospital. It was surrounded by honeysuckle plants, the air sweet with their scent, and she took a seat on her favorite bench so she could feel sorry for herself without standing on four-inch heels.

"Nya?"

His voice was outside the gazebo; she was

hidden by the greenery wrapping itself around the wooden posts, and she stayed quiet. She wanted to see him but also wanted to be alone with her loneliness, to not have to put on a smile and reassure someone that she was okay when she wasn't. She wanted to sit with the knowledge that she was a silly girl who would miss a man she barely knew.

Just then her phone chimed in her hand.

Hanjo: Have you heard the news? Someone graffitied DOWN WITH THE MONARCHY over the entry to the palace. The royal guards saw no one. I'm shocked to say the least.

Nya:

A. Oh no, how horrible!
B. Good! The monarchy needs to be destroyed.
C. Do you know who did it?

"Dammit, Hanjo!" she muttered, tapping C without really reading and then putting the phone beside her on the bench. She was turning off the sound when the response popped up.

Hanjo: It would have to be someone with access to the palace and who knew the guard schedule . . .

She heard the creak of Johan's footsteps on the wooden boards of the gazebo, but kept her eyes on her phone. When the black wing tips were in her line of sight, Nya looked up into Johan's eyes. They were an impossible shade of blue, and his lashes were long and thick, and goddess, why did he have to look like a sim dating hero come to life?

It wasn't fair, wanting and never having. She was tired of it.

"There you are," he said in the voice he used when they were alone. The one that wasn't cloaked in sarcasm and dry wit.

She blurted out the first thing that came to mind as she stared up at him. Anything that would drive away the looming embarrassment of what had happened between them the previous evening, and the crushing reality that she didn't want him to leave, and probably not just because he was her friend.

"Do you use Jamaican Black Castor Oil?" she asked, pointing to her own lashes.

"Pardon?" His auburn brows rose in very reasonable confusion.

"Your lashes. They're very . . . lustrous."

He blinked a few times, inadvertently showing them off.

Embarrassment flamed through her — this was one reason she stuck to the dating sims when it came to talking to men. Choosing a pithy response from a list was easier than coming up with conversation on your own.

"Thank you?" His deep, accented voice was tinged with amusement. "I'm glad my lashes please you."

Oh goddess.

"I should go," she said, standing to move past him before more silliness flew from her mouth.

"Nya."

He didn't reach out to stop her, but the beckoning in his voice was as good as his fingers curling around her wrist. She looked back at him over her shoulder.

His gaze was warm and inviting and if Nya didn't know better, she might imagine that the Tabloid Prince of Liechtienbourg fancied plain boring her.

You dream too big, girl.

His full lips pulled up into a grin. "You should stay."

"Why?" she asked, her voice sounding high and girlish and exactly how people

177

would expect she'd sound while alone with a handsome man. She reminded herself that she had been alone with him several times. There was no need to act like anything had changed, apart from him offering to debauch her, and parading her through the reception, and almost kissing her.

"You're upset." He held up a hand, miming for her to wait, then pulled open his pocket, pretending to take out a small square. Nya squinted at him, amused, as he pretended to unfold the square into a larger rectangle, which he then hung from an invisible hook near his head. "Confidant services are now open."

He pointed encouragingly at the invisible sign, brows raised, and she laughed, shaking her head. Some of the tension that had ratcheted itself up in her dissipated. This was Johan. Who always encouraged her and secretly slept with an angry teddy bear.

"Oh, if only your fans knew you'd hidden your sexiest skill — miming."

"Miming is a respected art in Liechtienbourg," he said, then pointed to his invisible sign. "What's wrong?"

"My father wants to see me." It was easy to tell him, now that he'd reminded her that they were friends. "He's making threats about what he'll do if I don't come to the prison."

Johan's lips pressed together into a tight line, and he folded his arms across his chest, shifting from mime mode to something like a stern bodyguard. "Do you want to see him?"

"Maybe I will one day," she said. "But not now, and definitely not because he forced my hand. I'm trying to figure out what I want to do once everyone leaves and I'm alone again."

"I see." He uncrossed his arms and made a big show of taking down his imaginary sign and refolding it, glancing up to see if she was pleased. After he'd crammed it into the pocket of his slacks, he beckoned her. "Come. Let's sit down."

She moved to walk toward him, but the heel of her shoe had found a comfy resting place in a knothole in the gazebo's wood floor. Nya went sprawling forward, arms windmilling as she searched for something to hold on to before face planting.

Her fingertips brushed something metal and smooth as her hand slapped against Johan's chest. She grasped his shirt and he caught her beneath her armpits and righted her.

"There we go. Now we're even," he said,

looking at her with amusement. "You caught me, and now I've caught you."

He didn't let her go, and his gaze didn't leave her face. She watched as his eyes seemed to darken a shade, as his tongue darted out to run over his lips.

"Nya." He shifted his hold on her and there was a distinct metallic clink on the wood. She looked down and saw his silver chain in a puddle at his feet between them.

"*Scheisse,* no!" Johan usually spoke with some level of smooth refinement, but there was ragged panic in his tone before he released her and lunged toward something rolling away from them across the floor of the gazebo. Whatever it was threw off light as it bounced along the planks, like he was chasing one of Ingoka's sprites, and then his palm closed over it, flattening it to the ground.

He dropped his head in relief where he kneeled.

Nya clenched her fists, frustrated that her clumsiness was the reason Johan had completely lost his cool.

"I'm sorry!" She tried to go to him, but her heel was still firmly stuck and she was strapped into the shoe.

He was quiet for a moment, and when he turned around his expression was somber,

as it had been in the photo she'd accidentally snapped of him on the plane. He
moved toward her, still on his knees as if he
wasn't thinking of his expensive slacks at
all.

"It's all right. And I didn't mean to curse
— it was an accident." He reached her and
held up his hand, a ring pinched between
thumb and forefinger. It had a thin band of
silver, and a small blue garnet in the center
with even smaller diamonds nestled on
either side. "This was my mother's. I never
take it off, and I was just a bit shocked to
see it making a run for it."

She could only imagine the fear that must
have surged through him as he watched it
roll away. She'd been allowed to touch very
few of her mother's things as a child, as her
father had wanted to keep them in their
original state. She remembered how it had
felt to lose access to even the few things
she'd cherished.

"It's beautiful," she said, reaching toward
it.

A voice sounded from outside the gazebo.
"Here they are, Elder Jerami!"

Nya swiveled to find Annie walking toward
them, shaking her head and wearing an
expression so foreboding that Nya had never
seen it, even when her grandmother had

dealt with hecklers at town meetings in Lek Hemane.

"Ah, so here you are, Granddaughter." Something in Annie's tone made Nya's jaw clench.

"Is something wrong, Grandmother?"

Annie looked past her to glare at Johan. "You said you wouldn't debauch her. You lied."

"That's technically true," Johan responded casually, dusting his knees as he stood. "I don't see how it's any business of yours."

"Eh! Speak respectfully to your elders, Phoko!" Nya chided, her upbringing warring with her confusion at her grandmother's behavior.

"I apologize for my rudeness," he said to her and not her grandmother.

Annie shook her head. "I do not want the apologies of a jackal who would seduce a helpless woman on a plane, like Lineo's sister Mariha witnessed. Then throw himself on her in the sauna, like Lineo herself witnessed. Then take her virginity and discard her, like Lineo's cousin Indira discovered when she gathered the laundry this morning and overheard Nya being comforted. You could not wash away the evidence of her maidenhead!"

The words resonated through the gazebo.

"Oh my goddess! Seriously? Please just kill me now," Nya blurted out. This was too much — this would be the humiliation that broke the camel's back. "Lineo, bring that scimitar over here."

"Hmm." Johan calmly brushed back the hair that had fallen over his eyes. "I think there's been a misunderstanding."

"Like a zebra misunderstands that a hippo is more dangerous than a lion?" Annie asked.

"I — I'm not familiar with that phrase," Johan said, still calm.

Nya's humiliation was pushed away by anger — she was *not* calm.

"*Nkhono,* I love you very much, but you dishonor me right now with this talk of debauchery and maidenheads," she said, angry tears stinging her eyes. Her grandparents and Ledi were all she had left of her family, and now her grandmother was just another person who thought she had no sense. "This is completely inappropriate."

"Dishonor? You should have thought about dishonor before letting this man seduce you. Do you read the papers, my child? He has no morals and no taste, on the arm of a different man or woman every night."

Johan cleared his throat and raised his

183

hand. "That's a bit harsh, and an exaggeration. I have exquisite taste. That said —"

Nya cut her hand through the air, waving his jokes away. This wasn't the time.

"And what if he did seduce me? Ingoka does not believe that desire is a sin," Nya reminded her grandmother. "Did you chastise Naledi for being with Thabiso? Or is everyone else allowed to find happiness except me?"

Her grandmother looked like she'd been slapped, and though she had just chastised Johan for his disrespect, Nya didn't care as much as she should have. She was tired of swallowing her anger like stinging nettles, cutting herself on the way down so she wouldn't harm others.

"They have experience," Annie explained in the same voice Nya had used with the youngest children at the orphanage. "Others are not easily influenced like you, especially now that you have no one to look after you."

Nya grit her teeth, her ears ringing from an anger that threatened to overwhelm her. She tried to walk toward her grandmother, but her shoe was still stuck — *she* was stuck, and she hated it. "Eh! If you're so concerned about me, you might have paid more attention twenty years ago. My whole life! You were perfectly happy to turn a blind eye to a father who treated me like a prisoner instead of a daughter, who purposely made me ill! And *now* you care about my well-being?"

There was a sudden unnatural silence in the gazebo, apart from Nya's heartbeat pounding in her ears and her breath coming in shallow gasps.

No. She hadn't meant to say that.

"What? What are you saying, child? Alehk has made many . . . mistakes. He has hurt many people. But he loves you. Everyone knows that." Annie raised her hand to her chest, and Nya remembered that, though she was tough, her grandmother was old.

She remembered the few times she had spoken back to her father when she was younger. Sometimes she would get sick right after, ending the discussion. Other times, her father would leave for a day and come back with medicine from the doctor for himself, saying that he'd been warned he would die of a broken heart if she didn't listen to him.

You must be a good, obedient girl, Nya. Or do you want to be in this world alone?

That threat had lost its potency over time, partly because of age and common sense and partly because she hadn't thought it possible to feel more alone.

"Nya? What are you saying?" Annie asked again, pulling her from her thoughts.

"Nothing," she said, wringing her hands and looking down. She hadn't swallowed her anger this time, but it seemed those nettles stung her when she spat them out, too. "I'm sorry. I've behaved very improperly toward you. But you are mistaken. I am not . . . no one wants . . . there is nothing between Johan and me."

Annie was still silent, but Lineo would not be deterred. "If that is true, then why did we catch him down on one knee with a ring held out to you, Ms. Jerami?"

"Because sometimes the goddess needs a laugh?" Nya whispered, fighting scalding tears of humiliation.

"Because I was proposing, actually," Johan said. He was speaking in the strange tone again, and she recognized what it reminded her of. It was how she imagined Phokojoe the trickster god would sound as he lured hapless humans to his lair.

He looked at her, and his gaze was unreadable as he took her hand in his.

"If you accept, you can come with me to Njaza, and then to Liechtienbourg. There's no pressure, and you can return home whenever you want." He leaned closer to her and whispered, "I expect nothing of you if you say yes, and it is fine to say no."

Her head was spinning. Arguing with Annie. Accused by Lineo. A proposal from Johan. "I need to sit down," she said.

"Hold on." Johan knelt again and fiddled with the clasp on the strap of her shoe, a band of sunlight highlighting the orange and gold of his hair. When he spoke, it was still quiet enough not to reach the others. "You should know that my stepfather asked me to bring you home because a newspaper article suggesting we were dating made the royal family gain points in the referendum polling. That's what I was going to tell you. I'm not asking you *this* because of *that,* but you should know what I stand to gain before you make a decision."

He tapped her ankle when he was finished, and the brush of his fingertips jolted her back into reality. A reality in which Johan, Tabloid Prince of Liechtienbourg and renowned fuckboy, had just asked her to be his fake fiancée, and then told her a truth he could have kept to himself without her ever knowing.

People always thought she couldn't handle the truth, but he'd given her information she needed to make a decision that should have been NO. But really, what he was offering was no different than what Hanjo and Rognath and all of her sim dating heroes had — a brief adventure, with all of the highs and lows of love, but none of the risk. Johan wouldn't smother her or try to hold her in place when she wanted to be free. He wouldn't treat her like she was nothing but a weak extension of her father. She could end this arrangement as easily as tapping "no" when asked if she'd like to continue playing in *One True Prince.*

She stepped out of her shoe, but instead of heading for the bench to sit, she turned to him. Her friend who would help her like this, because he opted for the most dramatic route whenever possible. She ran her fingers through his hair, the silky auburn locks sliding over her fingers as he stared up at her, eyes intense. She might have thought it mattered to him, whether she said yes or no.

"I accept," she said, and he grinned. He took her shaking hand in his and slid the silver band onto her ring finger, where it fit exactly right. The stone was the same blue as Johan's eyes, and they were both twinkling in the sunlight that slanted through the gazebo.

Oh goddess.

She looked at her grandmother, chin raised to hide the panic in her eyes.

"Nya?" Annie's voice quavered a bit, and it reminded her of her father.

Would you leave me, too?

There was a noise above them — a sudden summer rain peppering the roof of the gazebo. It came down hard and unrelenting, blurring the colorful flowers outside the gazebo behind a wall of liquid gray.

"Praise Ingoka, bestower of blessings!" Annie said in a steadier voice, raising her hands and clapping. " 'The goddess cries when good tidings arise.' "

Nya was confused at the sudden shift in the mood in the gazebo. "Wait —"

"I was worried, but this is a good omen. Your grandfather will be so happy! Both of our granddaughters have found their true love match!" Annie let out a joyous ululation, her anger apparently having been washed away by Ingoka's tears.

Nya sighed. She hadn't been wrong about the goddess getting a good laugh from her life.

"Not quite the reaction I expected," Johan said from beside her. His hand slid over hers and she was certain he would remove the ring. Instead, he ran his thumb over it absently, then over the sensitive skin on the back of her hand.

She shivered; the brush of such a small,

inane patch of skin shouldn't have made her whole body tense in anticipation.

Of what?

She looked up at Johan, at the muted sunlight filtering through his long lashes and the contented look on his face. He glanced at her, and the side of his mouth that was in her line of sight curled upward. "We'll just have to try harder to shock them. If you wish."

His thumb brushed her hand again, somehow both a threat and a promise of what shocking things they could do. Together.

This was just an act. This was just a dating simulation in three dimensions. She would live this fake happily-ever-after until the end credits rolled, because even if her dreams were too big, they were hers.

She wasn't going to let this one be a disappointment.

"Yes. Let's shock everyone," she said, and she meant it.

CHAPTER 8

Last night, when I tucked Johan in bed after the wedding rehearsal dinner, he was quieter than usual. When I asked him what was wrong, he said that he was worried. Worried that he would lose me, now that I was going to be wife to a king and queen to our people, and worried that his jealousy meant he was a bad boy. I will never stop marveling at how much this boy *feels,* and how he pays attention to those feelings. I told him that he would never lose me, no matter what. Then he asked me why I had to marry Linus anyway and I tried not to laugh. I just told him that one day, he'd meet someone special, and he'd have his answer then.

— From the journal of
Queen Laetitia von Braustein,
Private Collection of the
Castle von Braustein Library

191

"What's the script, mate?" Tavish asked before taking a sip of his beer. He and Thabiso had stopped by Johan's room after the subdued engagement celebration — a big party would take away from the wedding they'd just attended. Nya and Johan didn't want to be *those* wedding guests, and besides, having a real party for a fake engagement seemed a bridge too far, even for Johan.

"Yeah." Thabiso had been looking at Johan strangely since he'd arrived back from the gazebo, with Nya wearing his mother's ring and Annie shouting the good news to everyone. "How did this situation arise? Because you've never paid her any mind, from what I could tell. And she thought you were weird."

Johan transferred a crisply folded oxford shirt into his suitcase, laying it deftly over the disgruntled face of Bulgom Pamplemousse, who had been safely stowed away before his friends had come into the room.

Thabiso was one of the people that Johan didn't lie to. Not really. But he couldn't reveal that he was just as confused as everyone else. He'd spent the whole evening trying to pinpoint the exact moment when his last shred of control had been carried off by a passing bird or gust of wind.

When exactly he'd lost his damn mind.

He'd intended to find Nya in the garden, tell her about the annoying article in the paper, say he'd enjoyed their time together, then bid her farewell. He'd *considered* what Linus had asked of him, but had ruled it out because, well, he did like Nya. And he really didn't want to. He'd been so close to making a clean getaway, but when he'd stepped into the gazebo and found her sitting beneath a trellis festooned with flowers and the sunlight pouring over her, he'd been unable to resist the fairy-tale bait.

He'd *mimed* for her, for God's sake. He kept all photos from his miming phase in a lockbox, but he'd happily busted some moves for her without a second thought.

Now he could only await the despair.

"Weren't you just telling me I couldn't be a bachelor forever?" he asked, deflecting.

"I did say that." Thabiso pushed off the wall and strode over to where Johan was packing, casually flipping the suitcase closed. "But I didn't expect you to jump on the first vulnerable woman you encountered and ask for her hand in marriage."

Ouch. Johan hadn't expected Thabiso to be supportive, exactly, but was this how his best friend saw him?

"We already told you how this happened,"

he said blandly, tucking away that bit of hurt. "It's not real."

"That makes it worse," Thabiso said. "Nya's not a woman to be dated and disposed of, like you usually do."

Johan tucked his boxer briefs into a corner of the suitcase with four sharp jabs before allowing himself to speak.

"Are you saying that you don't trust my intentions or you don't trust Nya's ability to make her own decisions?" He asked this carefully, though a cascade of unexpected anger at his friend rushed through him. Even if Thabiso didn't know everything, he should know *Johan.* "And before you answer that, *meng ami,* remember that you have quite the colorful dating history *and* you met your wife while lying about your identity."

Tav tensed beside them, as if worried he'd have to break up a fight.

Thabiso stared at Johan hard for a long moment, and then sighed, relaxing. "Dammit. It appears my alpha persona only works Naledi." He stroked his beard and gazed at Johan, worry still in his eyes. "Look, you're one of my best friends. She's my family now. I know you have a hastily constructed plan, but let me tell you, those don't always work out. I don't want either of you getting hurt."

"I won't hurt her. And she *can't* hurt me," Johan said flippantly, mustering his best frivolous Tabloid Prince smirk.

Thabiso shot Tavish a look. Tavish whipped his head toward Johan, widened his eyes, blew out a puff of air through pursed lips. "Mate. *Mate.*"

"It's a PR stunt." Johan shoved the bags of apricot candy Lukas was obsessed with into the front pocket of his suitcase. "You know how I am. I don't do relationships, love, or any of that nonsense. We're friends and we both agreed to this, and when its effectiveness is over we'll part ways. It's as simple as that."

"Simple?" Tav chortled, pulled out a chair, turned it so the back faced Johan, and straddled it. "That sounds like a recipe for a fucking mess."

Johan closed his eyes and pressed his thumb to the bridge of his nose. He deeply regretted ever having convinced Tav that sharing your feelings was a good thing. Now his friend was going all Maestro Tav, like Johan was one of the students in Tav's European Martial Arts classes.

"And what did the priestess have to say?" Thabiso pressed.

Annie had called in the head priestess from the temple to bless the engagement, even if there could be no huge celebration. The woman had sat privately with Johan and Nya, stared at them for several long moments, and declared that they would have a long and fruitful relationship if they were truthful with themselves and the world.

Nya had gasped, and Johan had been startled, but he'd reminded himself that all it took to forecast someone's future was a bit of insight into human emotion. He shocked people the same way all the time, and Ingoka wasn't working through him. He knew better than to say that, though. He was a skeptic, not a jerk.

"She said whatever she thought sounded good."

"Mmm-hmm." Thabiso placed his hand on Johan's shoulder, lightly. "Please do not hurt Nya. She is hurting already. And do not hurt yourself. You can say what you want, but how many years have I known you?"

"Not long enough to know that math is my worst subject, apparently."

Thabiso wouldn't be deterred. "I've known you since before the fast cars and late nights and flashing cameras, yeah? I've watched you grow and change, and I maybe notice the things you think you hide by fluttering those lashes at people."

Anxiety clawed its way up Johan's back. Johan played a role, and usually Thabiso played one, too: the friend who put up with Johan's jaded outlook on the world and talked him out of doing anything too ridiculous. But now Thabiso was tugging at Johan's mask, the one he wore even around friends. The one that he'd slipped on while standing over his mother's grave, eyes dry and heart flooded with tears.

Thabiso released him, as if he'd felt Johan's muscles bunch beneath his grip. "I'll back off. But don't think that those walls you've put up to protect yourself will hold. Some people are wrecking balls, you know. Ask my wife."

Johan was really beginning to understand the term *smug marrieds*.

"Okay, okay, Biso Ray Cyrus." Johan dropped back onto the bed, his hands behind his head and his face schooled into nonchalance. "It's not like we're in love or anything."

And that was true. Whatever it was that Johan felt for Nya wasn't anything like love. It was just a swelling sensation in the middle of his chest whenever he saw her or thought of her, and the desire to be around her as much as possible.

Besides, everyone was acting like Nya was

some complete innocent, when she had someone texting her love messages all the time. When he'd asked if the man would be upset about their arrangement, Nya had become all flustered and said it wasn't serious so it didn't matter.

"It's just for fun," Johan said with finality.

Tav burst out laughing. "Good luck, mate."

Johan sighed. He was going to need it.

"You know what we're gonna ask," Portia said.

Nya, Ledi, and Portia were seated in the small lounge area of Nya's room. Pajamas were on, head scarves were tied, and a nineties rom-com was streaming on the flat screen. Nya sat cross-legged on the floor, applying an oil mix to her scalp and braids. The scent was calming, and massaging it in was something to focus on apart from her decidedly strange reality.

"What?"

"How did you go from 'that guy is weird' to 'I'm going to pretend to be engaged to him'?" Ledi asked. "I'm not judging — you know I want you to embrace your freedom. I'm just confused."

Nya was quite sure that Ledi was judging, at least a little, but she couldn't blame her.

It had come out of nowhere — to anyone who had never been privy to Nya's more fantastical daydreams.

"I was gonna ask if they'd shagged, but your question is more tactful," Portia said, reaching for a handful of popcorn.

Ledi took an unpopped kernel and threw it at Portia. "You and your fake Scottish accent need to chill."

"It's called 'phonetic accommodation,' ya knob, and I get teased enough in the tabloids, so shut it," Portia drawled, eyes narrowed in Ledi's direction as she loaded a whole handful of popcorn. Ledi trained another kernel in Portia's direction, as if looking down a sniper's scope, and after a stare down they both lowered their fluffy weapons. Portia glanced at Nya. "And tabloids are something you're going to have to deal with, too. Even if you only plan on doing this for a few weeks, it can be really, really intense."

Nya felt a stirring of panic at that — freedom wasn't the only reason she had run from Thesolo. Some of the less professional journalists had tried all manner of ways of approaching her — stalking her in the palace gardens and even sneaking into her hospital room.

She'd thought she would be left behind

once everyone returned to their daily lives, but now she was about to set out on an adventure that would thrust her into the spotlight. She wouldn't be alone, but perhaps she wasn't as prepared as she needed to be.

"I'm aware of the risks, but I think I must go." She held up her hand and looked at the ring Johan had slipped onto her finger. The ring she knew meant so much to him, but that he still had trusted her enough to let her wear. "I'm like Frodo."

Ledi rolled her eyes. "That's a horrible comparison. You're definitely more of a Samwise."

"Oh my goddess," Nya said, hand to her chest. "That's so nice of you!"

Portia did let her popcorn fly this time, pelting both of them. "Can we be serious for a second? Like, I'm in the paper a lot with speculation about whether Tavish and I will get married and what kind of duchess I'll be if we do and whether I'm good enough. And Tav, while I think he's the hottest man alive, is in the paper a fraction of the amount that Johan is. So be prepared."

"Speaking of that." Naledi reached down and handed over a small travel bag. "Condoms, travel size lube, plan B, zip ties — don't look at me like that — and more condoms."

Nya tried pushing the pouch back to her. "No, it's not like that," she said, though she remembered the heat in Johan's eyes. She remembered him saying he would debauch her if she wanted, and how close his lips had come to hers the night of the wedding.

Ledi shook her head. "Girl, look. We've all read this fanfic. You've *sent me* this fanfic. I'm not saying this is going to last forever, but I would be remiss in my duties as your friend if I didn't send you out equipped."

"Aw, you're like the fairy godmother of safe sex, Ledi," Portia said with real affection. "And you never know, Nya. Maybe you'll meet some other dashing man on your adventure and fall in love for real. Better to be prepared."

"No!" Nya said. "Well. That is. I don't think I can feel that way about a man without knowing him for some time."

"You've only known Johan for a few days." Ledi dropped the pouch into Nya's lap and gave it a firm pat. "You never really talked to him before, right?"

"He didn't talk to me," Nya corrected. She didn't add that though she hadn't spoken, she'd watched. She'd fantasized, despite her odd resentment of him. She felt like she knew him, even as she was learning that he wasn't quite the man the tabloids made him out to be — or the man he tried to convince everyone he was.

"That's not better," Ledi said with an eye roll. "And didn't you tell me that you were done with spoiled, demanding men when I asked if you had feelings for Thabiso way back when?"

"Yes. But I think maybe Johan's not really like that?" Nya was starting to feel unsure of herself. Was her father right? Was she just a foolish girl getting herself into trouble?

Ledi and Portia shot each other worried glances.

"I think he's great," Portia said. "But —"

"This isn't about him," Nya said firmly. Her friends were crossing the line from caring into coddling, exactly what she wanted to escape. "*I* want to be exciting, and glamorous. I want to do things without people worrying over me like I'm a child riding a bike without training wheels. Both of you already have love and freedom and respect, so you wouldn't understand."

Neither of them could know what it was like, coveting adventure so badly after being trained to believe that wanting *anything* other than being a good girl made her a bad one.

"I was too scared to live freely in New

York," she said. "That's why I didn't go out much, or make friends, or live the life I thought I wanted. But now, maybe I won't be scared."

Portia pressed her lips together, then moved to sit beside Nya, wrapping her in a hug. "Sorry. We're just looking out for you. But you're grown and sexy, and you deserve some fun. Just let us know what we can do to facilitate your adventuring. I, obviously, can hook you up with a sword. Finest quality Scottish steel, love."

Nya hugged Portia back, hard.

"My dungeon is always available if he hurts you," Ledi said. "And I can lose the key if need be."

"I love you both," Nya said, throat tight. She paused for a moment, a sudden choking happiness making her catch her breath. She had friends. Real friends, who loved her more than her imaginary childhood companions — constricted by the bounds of Nya's imagination — ever had. "But I think this is one of those quests where I have to find my own tools."

After they helped Nya pack, laughing and talking about highlights of the reception, like the king and queen being caught kissing behind a giant floral arrangement, Ledi and Portia went back to their own rooms.

Nya sorted through the correspondences in the basket beneath a slot on her door, an old-fashioned holdover at the mostly technologically advanced palace. There was one from a fellow teacher at the orphanage, asking Nya to stop by and chat.

Ah well, maybe when I get back.

The next envelope had her name in familiar flowing handwriting.

No.

She opened it, even though she knew nothing good awaited her.

My obedient daughter,

Have you truly forsaken me? Do you not understand that everything I have done, I have done for you? Every night, I sit in the silence of my cell and I speak to your mother. I tell her that what I always feared has come to pass — that our child has left me — and that I will soon join her and the ancestors because my heart cannot take such a blow.

Nya stopped reading, even though several more paragraphs followed, crumpling the paper into a ball as she fought the waves of panic rippling through her. She dropped the paper to the floor and curled up on her bed, heart thudding in her chest and nausea roiling her stomach.

She was ready to leave for Njaza. *Now.* Thabiso had warned that King Sanyu was frightening, but nothing scared her more than the effect her father's words had on her.

The unfamiliar coolness of the ring Johan had slipped onto her finger grazed her face as she pressed at her cheeks, and she allowed it to calm her.

She already had the first tool she'd need for her quest, and she wouldn't let her father hold her back any longer. She was going to travel, have fun, and not regret a damn minute of it.

CHAPTER 9

Jo-Jo Single No-Mo?

We're hearing reports that Johan is leaving Thesolo an engaged man!! We're waiting for confirmation from Castle von Braustein before breaking hearts around the world, though popping the question at someone else's wedding sounds par for the course for a scene stealer like Jo-Jo. The globe-trotting prince is scheduled to visit Njaza next. Sign up for our *Royal Watchers* app to get updates about the trip in real time!

— *The Looking Glass Daily,*
Royal Beat

Johan had spent most of the night in Thesolo, and their plane ride northeast across the Continent to Njaza, telling himself that this wasn't perhaps the worst miscalculation he'd ever made. It wasn't that he regretted this — oh no, he didn't, and that was the problem.

He already felt despair pressing in at him each time Nya gave him a sweet smile or excitedly pointed something out as their car rolled toward the Njazan royal compound. She was so . . . open. He'd suited up, but she'd dropped whatever figurative armor she'd worn, as if his ring had cast off some evil sorcerer's spell.

As if this was real.

If, when he'd first met her, she'd been the bud of a plant, curled in on herself, now she was unfurling, spreading her leaves. He wasn't sure what he would do when she began to bloom in earnest, especially if it was for him.

"Look at how beautiful it is! On the news, they only show bad things from Njaza," she said. "But this is just a place like any other."

She sat with her face turned toward the window, her long braids spilling down her back. The tips of the bow she'd tied on her head wrap peeking up like cat's ears. Her dress was a subdued Ankara print dress in orange and green, with capped sleeves and a skirt that went past her knees. A conservative "visiting royalty" dress that shouldn't have made his heart hammer like it did.

"Sugar Bubble."

"Yes?" She turned to look at him, her eyes sparkling with excitement.

Johan's emotions splashed up, a storm surge that was met with the barrier of his resolution that he wouldn't feel more for her.

"We should discuss how to handle this relationship. Since it's fake." There, it was out in the open again, that reminder that she shouldn't expect too much from him. He thought the sparkle would leave her eyes, but instead she grinned.

"Yes! I've been thinking about this. It's going to be so much fun!"

It bothered him, how she always seemed to defy his expectations, but it delighted him, too.

"And how do you suppose we handle this fun?" he asked, trying to keep his expression neutral.

Her face scrunched a bit, something she did when turning a thought over in her mind, he'd noticed. "We just have to do what we've been doing. Being friends. Isn't that what a relationship is? Friendship?"

Merde. She was so goddamn earnest. She was looking up at him with those big brown eyes, proudly declaring herself as his friend, a direct hit to the barriers Johan had thought almost invulnerable. Then her gaze dropped from his eyes to his lips and she made a small sound in her throat. "I guess there are other things."

His whole body went tight.

"What other things?" he asked, his voice suddenly deeper. He wanted to hear her say them. He wanted a whole list, spoken in that sweet unassuming voice of hers.

"You can hold my hand sometimes," she ventured, tangling her fingers together in her lap. "Kiss my temple, gently, if you think that's okay. When things get tense, you can do a wall slam. Oh, and you can threaten to kill anyone who looks at me!" She scowled menacingly after that, as if giving him instruction.

"Pardon?" Johan cocked a brow.

"This is how people show romantic affection for one another in my . . . experience. And we can look at each other like this."

Her chin lifted and she narrowed her eyes, then ran her gaze up and down his body. The pink tip of her tongue darted out over full dusky lips, and oh god, Johan had been wrong again. *He* was the one who didn't want this to be fake. He wanted to know how soft those lips were, to feel that tongue slip against his.

Oh là là là là là là là là.

The air in the backseat of the Rolls-Royce

was suddenly stifling, and sweat beaded beneath the hair at the nape of his neck.

"How?" The word came out as a squawk and he cleared his throat. "How exactly does one re-create that look?"

The sultry expression dropped away, replaced by her sunny smile. "I was just thinking about the comments I'd read about you on social media. 'I would climb him like a redwood!' and 'I would lick him like an orange Creamsicle!' You know, sexy things." Her smile wavered and her head dipped with uncertainty. "Was it convincing?"

Yes. The answer was a resounding yes. He could have just nodded and looked away.

But.

Johan's control was gone, and there was nothing to leash him.

He slid across the leather seat, closer to her, just shy of crowding her, and stared down into her eyes.

"You did great. Maybe something like this would work, too," he said. He imagined taking her face in his hands, kissing her deeply. Wondered whether the same curiosity she showed in everyday life would follow her into their bed.

Their bed? What?

"What are you thinking about?" she asked

quietly. "It's very effective."

You, he wanted to say. He *couldn't* think of anything else. He was submerged in the warm brown depths of her irises. His nose was filled with the sweet scent of her, and he wanted to taste her, to sip at the nectar of her gentle kindness, as alluring as gingerbread houses and poisoned apples.

"Schnitzel," he replied, sliding back to his side of the seat. "A really tender, delicious schnitzel."

"I'll have to try this schnitzel when we get to Liechtienbourg if it can make you look like that. Oh, there's the palace!" She turned and pressed her face closer to the window again as they approached the structure, which looked like an exercise in East African gothic design.

Johan pressed a fingertip to the bridge of his nose. He needed to focus. He was an ambassador, and this meeting was important. He threw back his shoulders and lifted his chin as Nya looked back at him

"Can I admit something?" she asked quietly.

"Yes," he said. "You can tell me anything. Confidant, remember?"

He pointed to his imaginary sign, which was apparently always hung at his side now.

"I'm really nervous." Her eyes were huge

and round. "I'm trying to be brave, but I tried to be brave in Manhattan, too, and I failed."

She trusted him enough to tell him her fears. Johan tried not to let that affect him, but it did, the warm sensation slipping into the cold and lonely passages of his soul.

She sighed. "I don't want to fail again, especially since you're going to all this trouble —"

"Spending time with you is *not* any trouble," he said firmly. Not in the way she thought it was, at least. "And this isn't some test. What is 'failure' here?"

She paused. "I make mistakes and embarrass myself, and you. I prove everyone right who says that I am a silly girl who should have just stayed at home."

Johan had the feeling that "everyone" was her father. "Look. Only you get to decide how much a mistake embarrasses you, or what failure means. It's normal not to feel brave. I never do."

"Really?" Her mouth quirked and one brow rose. "But you always know what to do. You never look worried."

"That's bullshitting, not bravery, Sugar Bubble. It's okay to be nervous. But you're smart and engaging, and it shines through even when you try to hide yourself away."

He almost didn't say the next thing, but even if she always surprised him, she was still human and he knew what she needed to hear. Maybe because he needed to hear it, too. "Besides, we're in this together."

"We are," she said, the fear leaving her eyes. "Thanks, Phoko."

"What is the Phokojoe tale, by the way?" he asked, memory sparked by the name. "Thabiso mentioned it to me."

"Oh." She smiled softly. "Phokojoe was a fox god — demigod, really. A trickster with the ability to shape-shift. He could change himself into whatever the humans he encountered desired most."

He knew she wasn't being unkind. She was unaware that she'd so deftly summed up his essential nature. This was why he both loved and hated fairy tales; they told you things about yourself you didn't want to acknowledge.

"Why?" he asked. "Does he eat them?"

He cringingly remembered that he'd offered to do the same to her on the plane. That she was in Njaza with him, willingly, was some kind of miracle. Or maybe like the priestesses had implied, it was fate.

"No! Phokojoe wasn't bad. He was just lonely, and tricking people into liking him was easier than admitting that," she said, head tilted. "At least that's how I read it. But you know, everyone interprets stories differently."

Johan bristled, feeling as if she'd stripped him down in the backseat, and not in an enjoyable way.

Mercifully, the car pulled to a stop then, and the door was opened by a serious-looking young man dressed in a long black robe.

"Njaza welcomes you," the young man said, bowing his head so that Johan could see the intricate patterns in his braids. The man glanced up at Nya, then quickly back down again. "And your betrothed."

"Thank you for having us," Johan said, bowing as well.

"Yes, thank you," Nya said, stepping out of the car and matching the man's low bow. "Your hairstyle is very becoming."

When they both straightened, the man was smiling — he wasn't immune to Nya's sweetness either, it seemed. "Thank you. I am Lumu, advisor to the king. You can both come with me."

They strode through the palace's front door, a huge oval port with doors of what appeared to be gold. Images of warriors in battle stood in relief on the doors, a reminder to all that entered that Njaza was a land that had been feared for its fierceness, even when under the control of colonial forces.

The hallways featured huge wooden statues in the same theme, and the ceilings were painted with images of their war gods, elegantly slaughtering invaders in baroque frescoes.

"I see you brought me a gift," Sanyu said grandiosely as they entered the receiving room, his gaze trained on Nya's bow-tied head wrap.

Johan could see why people deferred to Sanyu's wish not to be called Stanley. He was even more massive than he had been as a teenager, taller, with a thick, muscular body — Johan considered asking him who his personal trainer was because his thighs were like damn tree trunks. His hair was shaved around the sides and at a slightly asymmetrical angle, and his goatee was styled in a similar fashion. His mouth was pressed into a line of bored amusement.

"Does my present have a name?" Sanyu asked in his commanding voice, once again eyeing Nya.

I'll kill you for looking at her, Johan stopped himself from growling, and then marveled that Nya had been right about this relationship stuff, though he wasn't faking that sentiment.

He took her hand.

Johan had prepared himself to put up with a certain amount of well-deserved shit from the newly installed king, but not this.

"This is Nya, my fiancée, but very much her own woman."

Nya executed a curtsy, but her voice was colder than usual when she responded. "A pleasure to meet you, King Sanyu."

"It is a shame that she does not *belong* to you," Sanyu said, meeting Johan's gaze. "I thought I might take something precious and irreplaceable from you and then offer you a trifle in return, since you said you wanted to learn more about the historic relationship between our countries."

Johan said nothing, because the king was right on some level but was also about to get decked if he mentioned Nya one more time, thick thighs or not.

Sanyu began to laugh, a belly laugh that held no mirth. "I am joking. I have a beautiful bride of my own, and unlike the Liechtienbourgers, I do not take things just because I have the strength to do so."

"I'd heard that the new king of Njaza was a man to be respected," Nya said, surprising Johan. "Your bride hails from my kingdom, so I hope that this is the truth. I understand the point you seek to make, Your Highness, but treating me as an object does not deepen my regard for you or relations between our three countries."

Johan was a bit taken aback by her formal iciness but then he remembered that, sheltered as she had been, Nya was the granddaughter of respected elders and the daughter of a royal minister. She likely knew how to play at aristocratic brinkmanship, even if it wasn't her forte.

Sanyu stared at her, and then he nodded his deference. "I apologize, Nya, granddaughter of Annie and Makalele, daughter of Alehk. I see that you have inherited the Jerami pride, though I hope certain other traits skip a generation."

He motioned to an aide who took away a steaming cup of tea from the table beside him, then turned his gaze back to her.

Nya gave him as hard a look as Johan had ever seen on her face, but then her gaze moved past him and softened.

"Shanti!" she exclaimed, dropping both the aristocratic pretense and Johan's hand as she hurried over to the dark-skinned woman in a yellow tunic dress who had entered the room. Johan noticed two things about the woman, immediately: she was both beautiful and enormously unhappy. Her surprise as Nya ran to her, the way her eyes filled with tears that she blinked away as Nya began speaking in Thesotho — Johan looked away to give them privacy.

"My wife," Sanyu said, watching with a closed-off expression as Shanti slowly became more animated, picking up on Nya's enthusiasm.

Sanyu was unhappy, too.

Hmm.

"I again extend my hearty congratulations on your coronation and nuptials, and King Linus and Prince Lukas send theirs as well," he said. He thought about what he knew of Sanyu. The new king of an unstable kingdom, raised by a father considered cruel and formidable. "Your father, and now you, have done and continue to do the actual work of rebuilding your country. I'm happy to discuss how Liechtienbourg contributed to the problems of this region, and what we can contribute to make it right. I'm not happy to let you insult my fiancée, though. Don't do it again."

Sanyu smirked.

"Your African fiancée, acquired just in time for a visit to a former colony? Do you think I was born this morning? I'm sure you've already alerted the paparazzi. What a great photo opportunity! The benevolent European prince and his African betrothed, washing away the sins of the past." Sanyu spread his hands as if shaping a rainbow, then dropped them into his lap and gave Johan an unamused look.

"I hadn't thought of that angle," Johan said, ruffling his hair. "That would play really well with the referendum crowd. 'Prince Jo-Jo Solves Racism' would be one of my better headlines. My stepfather could actually put that one on the fridge."

Sanyu looked at him for a long moment, again, and then allowed himself a chuckle. It wasn't his boisterous laugh, but it was authentic and slightly less filled with malice.

He clapped once. "Well. Since you have solved racism, you can come meet the children. Perhaps you can solve their problems as well."

When they shuffled into the modern hospital, which looked like a giant alien duck had laid a metallic egg alongside a beautiful lake, Johan felt at ease for the first time since his arrival.

There was a certain lack of surety when it came to fake fiancées and angry kings and their silent wives, but talking to children was something Johan was good at. It was something he enjoyed — his mother had brought him with her on her travels, and she always made sure to talk to children, and more importantly to listen to them, just as she had listened to him when he was a boy. He made hospital visits often, but those were usually private and those that weren't were considered PR to cover his ass for *not* covering his ass.

"Do you know anything about the civil war in Njaza?" Sanyu asked, looking down at Johan. There was a carefully controlled grace to his movements, though he was a large man. Behind them Shanti, willowy and with doleful eyes, spoke quietly with Nya, and a retinue of three royal guards and two advisors hovered behind them all.

Johan almost said "of course" but it wasn't a matter of course. He'd had to research on his own because Liechtienbourg's treatment of Njaza had all but been written out of their history books. His country had done a great many good things in the past, and it seemed that this was the shame they preferred to overlook. "I've read about the various factions that struggled for power after independence was won, but I always welcome more information," he said.

Sanyu came to a stop and Johan followed suit, peering into a room with several

children playing — no, they weren't playing. Well, not *just* playing. It was physical
therapy: several of them were wearing
prosthetic limbs, and some raced around in
wheelchairs.

"I can give you information, but only one
thing is currently relevant. *Land mines.*
Land mines lie in the earth of Njaza and,
like much of history, one wrong move sets
off a powder keg." Sanyu gestured to the
children, and his expression was lined with
fatigue. "After Njaza won its freedom by
force, we were blacklisted. Strapped down
with sanctions and boxed out by tariffs."

Johan breathed deeply and blinked. As
always, the unfairness of the world was
something that cut into him quick and deep.

*I know it's not fair, my Jo-Jo. We cannot right
every wrong, but we can't be crushed by that
tact. We help where we can, liebling. Others
help, too. And it makes a difference even
when it doesn't feel like enough.*

"My father was a proud man. He responded to the shunning by doubling down,
by telling the world we didn't need their
help and turning away the aid of even our
neighboring countries." Sanyu exhaled
deeply, like a bodybuilder readjusting his
hold on the overloaded barbell he was
charged with lifting. "I have been away for a

221

few years, and now that I'm back I'm working on many, many things, but my country has been cut off from assistance for years. I'm tired of seeing my people injured, von Braustein. You spoke of making things right when you contacted me? I don't give a damn if this is just good publicity for you. If you want to help, this is where it starts."

Johan gazed at the children, then nodded. "Okay."

Sanyu glanced at him sidelong. "That's it? You'll just wave your magic wand?"

"Well, no, we have a lot to talk about and set up, but that will take some time. I am saying okay, I am committed to helping, no matter what happens during the referendum, and I believe King Linus and Prince Lukas will also pledge their aid." He made a silly face at a boy who was giving him a puzzled look through the glass. "Some of the children are pointing at me and laughing, so I think we should go say hello."

"I believe I will go help plan the evening meal," Shanti said woodenly, turning and walking away before anyone could reply.

"Let's go in," Sanyu said, a frown on his face as he pulled the door open. The children crowded toward them, ignoring their therapists as they moved toward the door.

Johan sat down on a chair so he was closer

to eye level with the children. This was one thing he didn't have to worry about faking. A bold little girl with two afro puffs walked up to him.

"Are you from Liechtienbourg?" she asked.

"Yes," Johan said. "But I came to visit my friend Sanyu, and he brought me here because he said you were the coolest people in Njaza."

The girl crossed her arms. "My mother says never to trust a Liechtienbourger because they'll steal your land from you while handing you a lollipop."

Sanyu laughed and Johan grinned while patting at his pockets.

"Your mother is very smart. I ran out of lollipops, though, so your land is safe." He waggled his fingers to show empty hands and the girl smiled.

Nya came and knelt beside him. "What's your name?" she asked the girl.

"Angela. And yours is Nya." Angela patted Nya's leg. "We saw it on the news. They say that you will be a princess!"

"She'd make a very beautiful princess, don't you think?" Johan cut in, seeing Nya's surprise and hesitation.

"Yes!" Angela cried out. Nya settled on the ground beside him and they passed the next half hour that way, playing with the children, before being escorted to visit with other older patients and to talk with hospital staff.

At the end of the long day, they shared dinner together.

Shanti bowed her head after everyone had been seated. "I hope everyone enjoys the selection. I cooked it myself to honor both the newfound relationship forming between Liechtienbourg and Njaza, and to welcome the sister of my land and to . . . congratulate her."

"Super," Johan said, keeping his tone from being overly warm. "We appreciate your kindness and your hospitality."

"Yes," Nya added. "Oh, you made goat stew! Thank you!"

"Thank you, Wife," Sanyu said, but as he lifted a spoon to taste, one of the aides behind his chair, who had followed him everywhere throughout the day, stepped forward.

"Taste test, Your Highness."

Sanyu grudgingly held out the spoon. The man sipped at the broth, spit it into a napkin, and shook his head. Another aide surged from behind him to pull the plate away. "It does not meet royal standards. The meal from the royal chef will be brought out."

Sanyu sighed, and Shanti placed her own fork down.

"Well, I think it's delicious," Nya said brusquely. "And I bet you worked very hard, Shanti. Thank you."

She shot Sanyu a pointed look.

"Yes, Wife. Thank you," Sanyu said in his gravelly voice.

Shanti nodded, but kept her gaze down as she excused herself from the table.

Sanyu continued the conversation smoothly, and Johan went along with it as they discussed other possible ventures Sanyu had planned. Sanyu couldn't hide how he glanced at the empty seat, and Johan felt a bit of pity for the man.

Love really could be terrible. Good thing he was an expert at avoiding it.

CHAPTER 10

The bedroom prepared for Nya and Johan was luxurious bordering on excessive, but then Sanyu's father had been *very* into visual displays of power. He hadn't started charities for children and pressed for help reentering the national stage in order to gain allies and help shore up his country's infrastructure, as Sanyu had discussed over dinner.

As Johan sprawled on the bed, large enough to hold a football scrimmage on, he was dismayed to find that he might actually be growing to like Sanyu. He was really going to have to stop this liking people business.

Nya came out from the shower, sporting a plush-looking bathrobe that was much too large and threatened to slip off her shoulders. Johan didn't want it to — if he was given the chance to see her body, he wanted it to be her decision. The robe, not caring

226

about what Johan wanted, suddenly slid down, revealing the thin spaghetti strap of her nightgown and the smooth curve of her shoulder.

"Fuck," he muttered.

"What?" she asked.

"Druk. A Himalayan kingdom and Njaza's main trade partner," he said. "Are you glad you got to see your friend?"

She stretched out on the other end of the much too large bed. She wasn't even within arm's reach, which was perhaps why she had flopped down without trepidation. That and she was probably exhausted.

All of this had started with sharing a bed, on the private jet, and an accidental cuddle. When she'd listed the scope of their relationship, cuddling hadn't been included, which was disappointing but probably for the best.

"Shanti? We weren't friends before, though I hope we are now. I didn't have any, really, and I don't think she did either. All I know of her is that her family was determined that she would marry royalty and she spent most of her life training to be the perfect political wife." Nya sighed. "That, and the fact that Ledi threw up on her during her illness."

"Hmm." Shanti had seemed more like the perfect Stepford wife, but he considered that he might be misunderstanding some cultural aspect of her behavior.

"She's miserable," Nya said.

No, he'd understood perfectly.

"What do you make of Sanyu?" he asked.

She pursed her lips in concentration and Johan looked away from them. "I think Sanyu will make a good king one day," she said diplomatically. "I'm not sure if he'll ever make a good husband."

Johan sighed. "This is why I don't believe in marriage."

"You don't either?" Nya asked sleepily, surprising him. "At least Shanti can leave the marriage at the end of the Njazan wedding trial if she wants. Not everyone is so lucky."

"Wait. You were the most emotional guest at Thabiso and Naledi's wedding. Every time I looked —" It wouldn't be good to reveal how often he had looked at her over the course of that night. "You seemed very into it."

"I am *into it*. For other people," she said. "I spent my whole life cooking and cleaning and doing what I was told, and that's what most marriages seem to be. I see no reason to willingly trap myself in such a situation."

Her voice turned hard, like when she'd kicked him out of the jet's private bedroom or when she'd stood up to her grandmother. Her kindness made it easy for him to forget that she'd had a difficult life. When someone was so open, it was easier to think that they'd never gone through hardship, because if they could come through it in that way, why couldn't other people?

Why couldn't he?

Johan had taken his kindness and buried it beneath parties and suits and reams of tabloid covers. He felt a kind of awe that Nya had gone through something so difficult she could barely speak of it but hadn't let it harden her. He felt a perplexed joy that she had shared even a little bit of that pain with him.

"If you want to talk about your father, my confidant services sign is always flipped to Open for you."

She rolled to her side so that her back was to him. "I don't want to talk. Right now I want to pretend that he doesn't exist. And I want to pretend the guilt I feel over wanting that doesn't exist either."

"All right," he said. "I'm a good listener, but I'm even better at ignoring inconvenient feelings."

"How do you do that?" she asked.

"Focus on other, more cheerful things," he instructed. "Like the inevitable extinction of the sun, and the supervolcanoes lurking beneath the surface of the earth waiting to blow."

"Phoko." She looked back at him with those huge brown eyes and Johan wished, not for the first time, or even the second, that their game was real. That he could show her how he felt with his lips and his hands, but mostly that he could *hold* her.

"You did great today," he said. "You shouldn't be nervous. You stood up to one of the most feared royals in the world twice."

Nya shook her head. "That wasn't standing up to him. I just pointed out when he was impolite."

"Nya, the man has people trailing him all day whose express purpose is to kiss up to him. Pointing out the old king's impoliteness had some people thrown in prison."

Nya's eyes went glossy and Johan realized what he'd said.

"Sorry."

"It's okay."

He reached out and brushed his fingertips over the back of her hand. "You should get some sleep before our flight tomorrow. Try counting sex goats if counting sheep doesn't work."

She giggled and rolled back in his direction, reaching out and thumping the empty space on the bed between them playfully, her worries seemingly gone. "Good night, Phoko."

"Good night, Sugar Bubble," he said.

He reached for his tablet to catch up on work, then remembered he wasn't alone. That realization shouldn't have warmed him as it did.

"Do you need me to turn off the light?" he asked, but she was already asleep, arm still stretched toward him.

His mother's ring glinted on her finger, a reminder of all the reasons he didn't want a partner, no matter how good it felt in the moment. This was only temporary, and then they would go their separate ways. If they stayed together, they'd eventually have to go their separate ways in a more permanent fashion. Johan was aware that his worry wasn't normal, but he didn't think allowing yourself to just *love* without thinking of where it inevitably led was normal either. *Till death do us part* — just the thought of it made anxiety tickle his scalp.

He looked back to his tablet and opened the spreadsheet Greta had updated, created a new cell for the Njazan Land Mine Recovery Organization, and began adding the information he'd learned that day.

He then began drafting an email to Thabiso, discussing the situation overall in Njaza and wondering if his friend had any thoughts.

His email inbox was full of initiatives he had to approve, and he tackled those next.

He had work to do, work that would be there waiting after Nya had gone.

He got to it.

CHAPTER 11

ONE TRUE PRINCE, TEXT MESSAGE MODE

Hanjo: Nya, I dreamed about you last night.

Nya: (A) About me? How odd! What happened?

Hanjo: I'm not sure I can tell you without scandalizing you . . . besides, I'd rather show you.

The mattress was soft — almost too soft — and Nya awoke from a dream that the marshmallow man she'd seen in a film as a child was trying to chew her with his soft teeth. She'd been frightened, but embarrassingly, it had also felt kind of good.

Her phone vibrated in the sheets beside her — likely a message from Hanjo.

Across the bed, Johan was still awake. He sat with his back propped against the dark wood headboard, legs crossed to support his tablet.

He was scanning the screen and typing on the thin keyboard attached to it, focused and intent, a pair of black-framed reading glasses perched on his nose. He was *working,* which was not something she'd ever imagined really. He was Bad Boy Jo-Jo; his job was supposed to be spending his days lounging and his nights living to excess, but here he sat in blue sweatpants and a white tank top, looking studious. After a day of engaging in charitable endeavors with small children.

She wondered what his fans would think if they saw this side of him, hair wild and lips pursed in concentration, scrolling screen reflected in his lenses. She'd never found him to be more attractive, which was a problem given that they were sharing a bed.

He took off his glasses to rub his eyes, and then stretched.

"What are you working on?" she whispered, reaching for her phone. He paused with his hands high above his head and his back arched, musculature on full display, and tilted his head to look down at her.

"Did I wake you?" He finished his stretch and dropped his arms. "Sorry."

"No. The bed was trying to eat me," she said. His brows knit in confusion, and she shook her head. "And I have a message."

She squinted at the screen.

Hanjo: My dearest Nya, whenever you're close to me, I don't think of royalty and rebellion. I think of this strange ache in my chest.

Nya:

A. You should get that heartburn checked out.
B. Ache? What does that mean?
C. The rebellion is the most important thing right now.

She selected B because she was asking herself the same thing, and then put the phone down and looked at Johan. "You didn't tell me what you're working on."

"Just a hobby of mine," he said. He laid his glasses on the bedside table and then dropped back onto his pillow.

"What kind of hobby?" she asked.

He shrugged. "It's a bit hard to explain."

"Try me. You might be surprised what I'm

able to understand," she said, slightly an-noyed. That was something people had always said to her, unable to imagine she could grasp complex ideas. Even at the orphanage, her suggestions for growth and expansion and bettering the lives of the children had been questioned, and then eventually reworded by others who took the credit.

"No, it's not that," he said. "I know you'll *understand.* It's just . . . my hobby is fund-ing charities. Boring stuff. Hard to explain." He shrugged, but it wasn't as nonchalant as usual.

She leaned up on her elbow, fascinated. "Funding charities? So that's why you were asking so many questions about the opera-tions of the land mine retrieval group to-day?"

He nodded, but didn't look at her, as if he hoped her questions would stop if he didn't make eye contact.

"How many charities does this hobby of yours involve?" she pressed.

"Not very many. Forty-nine? Fifty after today, I suppose."

"Phoko." She reached her arm out across the bed, scooching forward so she could poke him in the side. "Are you going all pink in the cheeks because I've discovered that you're a secret philanthropist?"

"I'm not a philanthropist. I just give some of my money to organizations that help people in need of assistance," he said.

"Mmm-hmm," she replied, her smile so wide that the air-conditioning in the room chilled her teeth.

"And it's not a secret," he said grumpily. "It's just not discussed very openly, and I use a variety of techniques to prevent people from finding out about it."

She felt suddenly warm, talking with him like this. It was the middle of the night and he was telling her about his work. About what he valued. It felt . . . intimate.

"Wow." She shook her head. "Now that I think of it, I've seen *so* many photos of you at charity events. I just assumed you were there for —"

"For the alcohol?" Johan cut in drily.

"For the, ah, admirers," she admitted.

His gaze dropped away from hers. "See? I don't even have to hide it, really. People's assumptions do the work for me."

Nya realized something. "Why did you tell me? You could have said you were looking at social media."

Those long lashes fluttered up as he met her gaze again. "Because you asked me. The alternative would have been lying, and I don't do that with you."

The way he said "with you" made it seem as if he was happy to lie to others, maybe even to everyone. Everyone but her.

This was probably not a good trait in a man, but Nya couldn't help but feel pleased. He owed her nothing after all, because she wasn't really his fiancée, but he would give her the truth, which was usually all she wanted in life.

"I knew you were nice."

"Nice is not a compliment," he said. "It's what you say to people with no other redeeming qualities."

He leaned back atop the overstuffed pillows, his hands folded behind his head. Nya's gaze traced the shadows of his muscled biceps down to the dark auburn hair under his arms.

"Do you want compliments?" She assumed he got them all the time, but he had been so hesitant even when she'd wanted to give him a nickname. So sure she was going to insult him.

He glanced at her warily. "You've already complimented my eyelashes. That's enough."

"You're very good with children," she said. "You made them laugh today, and didn't mind when they made fun of you."

He nodded. "True. Though I didn't appreciate the boy who said I looked like a yam."

"You treat me as an equal," she pressed on. "And I'm comfortable with you. I've never slept in a bed with a man before, and I should be nervous right now, but I know that you're my friend and you won't hurt me. I slept more soundly than I have in a very long time."

The wariness didn't leave his gaze, but he made a flustered exhalation that shifted the locks that had fallen over his eyes.

"I told you I wouldn't debauch you unless you wanted me to. That's baseline normal behavior, Nya. Honestly."

Nya understood that his words weren't meant to be seductive, weren't a declaration of anything more than his role as a playboy prince, but she'd decided that in this dating simulation, she was a brave and adventurous girl. One who asked questions that might lead to more, and one who wondered —

"What would you do? If I *was* interested in being debauched?"

Just like that the wary amusement fled his eyes, burnt away by blue flash fire. It seemed he was thinking of schnitzel again.

"That depends," he said, and he must

have wanted schnitzel very badly because there was *hunger* in his tone, making his voice deep and sexy. "Have you ever been debauched before?"

"No," she whispered, shifting under the duvet. "A man kissed me on one of my dates in New York, but I didn't like it very much. It was . . . slimy. Like badly cooked okra."

He shuddered. "You have quite a way with words."

She laughed, though she hadn't laughed after that kiss. She'd gone home, brushed her teeth for a very long time, and then deleted the dating app from her phone, freeing up more storage room for her games.

He looked down at her hand, and then at her face.

"Hmm," he said. "In that case, I might . . ." He pierced her with his hungry look again as his hand hovered over hers on the bed between them. "May I?"

She nodded. She most certainly couldn't speak. She hadn't thought he would really —

"In that case, I might start with light debauchery." Johan ran his fingertips over the back of her hand, a light caress that sent shivers racing up her arm, to her breasts, to her belly. He caressed again, this time tracing to the tips of her fingers before lacing his own through hers and lifting so their palms pressed together.

His heavy-lidded gaze was fixed on her as he softly kissed the pad of her pinky, and then her ring finger, his full lips warm and gentle. It should have been an innocent gesture, but paired with his cobalt stare, each touch of his mouth was like an electric shock. She was warm, so warm, and her breaths came slow and cautious, like one sudden gasp might distract him from the amazing things he was doing to her with his mouth.

He kissed his way to the whorl on her thumb, his mouth lingering there, then parting as he sucked gently — just enough to send a wave of scandalized pleasure through her body.

Oh goddess.

The next kiss landed on the palm of her hand, his breath hot and ticklish, and when his lips grazed her wrist she gasped, unable to contain it. He didn't startle; he grinned. His stubble rasped against her skin as he did, and she pressed her thighs together against the sudden throb at their juncture.

Johan dragged his mouth down her forearm, so slowly that she thought he might stop at any moment, and her body teetered on the edge of panic that the pleasure might end.

He didn't stop, though.

He edged closer to her on the bed, the better to debauch her, and when his lips landed on the bend of her elbow, he *licked.* It was a strong, sure motion, that lick. It told her many things at once, reminded her that he wasn't a man who hesitated once he acted on his impulses.

"Oh my," she breathed. Now she knew what that seemingly useless patch of skin had been made for — Johan's mouth.

He was at her biceps now, tongue lightly tracing over her trembling muscles.

My whole body is trembling, she thought. *He might lick me everywhere.*

Her breath caught, and it seemed that he heard it because his torturously slow motions sped up a bit, intensified, as he charted a course for her throat. When he reached the curve of her shoulder, she felt the light graze of his teeth there, and then the sharp drag of enamel against her collarbone and up, deepening when he reached the notch where her neck and shoulder met and *oh goddess* she hadn't known what she was asking for. If this was light debauchery, then she would surely die at mild.

He made a sound that was almost a groan

as he lingered there. "You smell good, Sugar Bubble. Like dessert."

She was trying to keep still despite the riot of sensation charging through her, but her hand flexed in his at those words that sounded so, so naughty when spoken against her skin, and Johan's motion up her body stopped. He kissed her neck where his teeth had been, then exhaled, his breath cool against the heat left by his mouth.

"Do you want me to stop? Remember, I want to do what you wish, and if your wish is for me to stop, I will."

Something occurred to her then.

"Do *you* want to? Do this? You don't have to just because I asked." She suddenly felt ashamed, wondering if she'd forced him with her silly question. Just because debauching was his *thing* didn't mean he wanted to do it to her.

He squeezed her hand, which was still entwined with his, and ran his nose up the column of her neck, and Nya was almost offended that even that part of his body could make her skin prick with need.

"Thank you for asking, but I wasn't clear if you think I don't want to touch you. Or taste you. I'm not a demigod seeking to grant you your every desire — I'm a man who *wants* to."

His eyes were still dark and hot, and she realized in that moment that there was no schnitzel. Or rather, *she was the schnitzel.* He wanted her, not for forever, but that was fine. He was her friend, and for right now, he would be her lover. It felt natural, like in her games when one response in the multiple choice was so obvious that you'd be a fool not to select it.

"Don't stop," she said, and if there had been any doubt in her mind that he was doing this out of pity, it was dispelled by the wicked grin that spread across his face. She expected him to say something witty then, like he always did, but instead his other hand came up to cup her face, and he kissed her.

Nya's okra kiss had been bumbling and messy, a sneak attack when she'd politely leaned in for a hug after meeting a date for coffee. She now realized that what'd happened before hadn't been a kiss, it had been a travesty, and one that Johan was doing his best to thoroughly erase from her memory.

His mouth was warm, and his lips soft as they caught hers — that was the only way to describe the motion, like she'd been in free fall until his lips pressed hungrily against hers, holding her in place with the sheer force of his want.

He wants me. That thrilled her as much as his touch, the realization sending gossamer threads of desire through her body.

His fingers flexed, against her face and her hand, and his tongue sought out hers, the movement sleek and innate.

She pressed closer to him, her other hand grasping at the neckline of his tank top as she pulled him forward, pulled him until he rolled on top of her, their lips and tongues still seeking each other out.

His weight drove her into the mattress and she slid her arms around his neck. His weird shoulder-neck muscles flexed beneath her forearms as he rested his elbows on either side of her face and dipped his head to hers. And his hips . . . they'd briefly moved against her before, during their dramatic escape from the wedding reception, but now she could feel the hard length of him through his sweatpants, so close to the need between her thighs. His motions were slowly pushing her sleeping gown up, and she knew what she wanted from him. She wasn't sure enough of herself to go too far, and didn't want to just yet, but she could do this over the clothing exploration.

She leaned up to meet his kiss, and her hands slid down to his hips, gripping them as she positioned the V between her legs against his erection. There was the fabric of her underwear and his sweatpants between her mound and the thick, shocking outline of him.

Johan groaned a lascivious sound into her mouth, and it was as satisfying as a purloined sweet.

"*Oh là là,* Nya." His voice was low, so low that it vibrated through her body, like he could give her pleasure with that, too. "That's not light debauchery. Are you sure?"

"I'm requesting the upgrade," she whispered. "Mild debauchery, please."

"*Comme tu willst,*" he growled. One of his hands slipped behind her head, lifting and tilting it back before his lips skimmed her neck. His hips coiled and released as he ground into her, slowly but not at all sweetly. They were both fully clothed, but she felt deliciously exposed as pleasure cocooned her body.

She'd seen as much porn as the next woman, had touched herself before, and knew what her body liked. She'd never seen much need for any help with this particular aspect of life, and none of the men she'd dated before had inspired her to think otherwise. Dating had always felt like something to do just because she was free to do it once she'd left Thesolo — because she was supposed to. Nya had never really been attracted to the men she matched with on the apps, and without that attraction, no pressing need for more than a polite good-night hug had ever developed.

Sexual touching had seemed like a mildly interesting activity she might enjoy but was probably better in fantasy, like hiking in the Catskills. This was different from how she'd imagined it would be — the weight of Johan, his lemon-and-lavender-tinged-with-sweat scent, the way he looked into her eyes, slowing down or increasing the pressure as he read what she needed from him.

There, with her body feeling both light and heavy with desire, her hips twisting to press her clit harder against Johan's erection, she realized she wanted more than friendship from him. More than touch.

She pushed the thought away, focused only on the pleasure spiraling through her body and Johan's labored breathing, his flushed cheeks and the way he stared so hard that she might combust from the magnifying glass heat of his gaze alone.

"Is this good for you?" he asked, his voice rough. His hips were moving slower now, but more emphatically, and she changed her tempo to match his. The new simmering pleasure forced her head back into the pillow.

"Yes. You feel so good."

Johan made an ungainly sound and he somehow grew harder against her. She opened her eyes to see that his eyes were closed, his expression almost one of pain. She remembered him teasing her about talking dirty as he'd guided her out of the reception; maybe he hadn't been entirely joking.

Maybe that was what *he* liked. What *he* wanted for himself.

"Do you like when I tell you how it feels, Phoko? Do you want me to, um" — her voice trembled on the next whispered two words — "talk dirty?"

He dragged in a breath. *"Ouay."*

She felt it all through her body, the power in that word and how he was handing it to her. She felt his need, too, and surprisingly, she felt her own. She wanted to give him pleasure. She wanted to make him groan like that, again and again.

The only problem was she had never spoken dirty before.

"I like the sensation of you on top of me. You are heavy and strong and your weight feels good. Your muscles are very firm."

Oh god, what kind of dirty talk is this?

She expected him to burst out laughing, but he kissed her temples, her ears, her hair as he allowed a bit more of his weight to press down on her. As he ground against her, sending a shock of pleasure through her that made her toes splay.

She slid one of her hands down his muscled back, then up into his disheveled hair, and tugged lightly. His eyes squeezed shut more tightly as he growled and thrust harder against her, then they opened, storm dark and hot and pleading.

"Your thing . . ." It seemed she could still feel embarrassment even as pleasure tingled through her and her heart hammered in her chest. She couldn't say the word she wanted to, but she kept talking. "You feel so good moving against me. Your . . . eggplant emoji is hot and hard and long."

He released a muffled mixture of laughter and pleasure.

"Nya. Are you trying to kill me?" His grip on her tightened, and his grinding sped up. A thin sheen of sweat covered her body, and his hair was damp and curling beneath her palm.

"Yes." She moaned as he rubbed against her with just the right pressure. "Johan, I've imagined you touching me, and the reality is *so* much better. Goddess."

He didn't say anything, but his hand tightened on the back of her head, repositioning her face so that his greedy mouth found hers easily. Now he moved with a bucking, thrusting motion that mirrored what they could have been doing if they were naked and she was ready.

This is what he wants to do to you.

The thought sent her over the edge. She moaned into his mouth, once quick and low, then longer, then a yip that broke sharply into a surprised shout as an orgasm surged through her, sending tingling pleasure from her head to her toes.

Johan went rigid above her, all but his hips, which thrust a few more times before a tremor ran through his body and he collapsed on top of her, his face nestled into her braids.

His breathing was harsh when, after a long moment, he rasped out, "Why do I feel like *I'm* the one who's been debauched? Thank you, Sugar Bubble."

Nya didn't know what she was supposed to do at this point, so she did what she wanted.

"You're welcome. I think we both did well." She lightly punched his arm. "Way to go."

He laughed into her neck and kissed her

there, sending a fresh spark of pleasure through her. She ran her hand through his hair.

Friends, she reminded herself. *With benefits.*

Eventually they broke apart to visit their respective bathrooms, and she arrived back to the bed before he did. She picked up her phone.

ONE TRUE PRINCE, TEXT MESSAGE FROM: HANJO

What does the ache in my chest mean? Love, Nya. I think it means love.

She put the phone down on the bedside table.

Johan walked in, shirtless, hair tousled and damp, and came over to her side of the giant bed. His gaze skipped to her phone just before the screen went dark, then back to her, before he slid under the duvet beside her.

"You never answered my question on the jet," he said, voice almost hesitant. She was confused, and then she smiled and pushed him to his side, throwing an arm over his shoulder as she curled around him from behind.

"Big spoon," she said, and then they fell asleep.

CHAPTER 12

Although there has been no official confirmation from Castle von Braustein yet, Jo-Jo has indeed returned home in the lead-up to the historic vote for Liechtienbourg's future with a woman on his arm. Not much is known about Nya Jerami, but former classmates and coworkers describe her as "shy," "a good girl," and "way too good for that kind of man." What's known about her father, who currently resides in Thesolo's maximum security prison, is a different matter (click **here** for more). She arrived at Liechtienbourg Airport in Sommetstaad, the country's capital, looking quite happy at Jo-Jo's side.

— *The Looking Glass Daily,*
Royal Beat

The country of Liechtienbourg was often described as a town masquerading as a kingdom, and the traditional response from

Liechtienbourgers was *e blade deguisee als bottermesser* — "a blade disguised as a butter knife." As they sat in the king's royal parlor, Johan couldn't help but think the same of Nya. Her deceptive softness could mask desire so sharp that he was still bleeding from just a graze of it. All he'd been able to think about on their flight from Njaza was making her cry out again, but there were no bedrooms on the commercial flight they'd taken, and they'd both slept most of the way there.

A fire crackled in the fireplace, the room filled with the familiar smoky scent of winter in the castle, and outside the large old windows, snow fluttered from the gray sky to melt on the cobblestones.

King Linus listened intently as Nya regaled him with tales of Ledi and Thabiso's wedding, including a dramatic recounting of Johan passing out in the sauna.

Had he really thought she was shy before the wedding? Had she changed, or had his perception of her shifted? Maybe both, though he'd always known there was danger in the flutter of her lashes and bells chiming in her sweet laughter.

Scheisse, he was a mess. It was bad enough that he couldn't stop thinking of her, but now his thoughts were florid enough to impress Likotsi.

Linus ate the last bit of his pastry and then clapped his hands to his knees. "I'd wondered why Jo-Jo never brought anyone home with him before," he said in English, his accent smoother than Johan's because he'd been taught the language alongside his mother tongue as a child, like most of the aristocracy. "Now I see he was just waiting for this marvelous woman seated across from me. You're lucky I'm not a few years younger, Jo-Jo."

Nya giggled and bowed her head, which was a normal reaction to the weird cool dad compliment. Johan's reaction wasn't normal at all.

He reached out and took Nya's hand in his. "She's *mine*."

Linus's eyes went wide, his chuckle fading away to discomfort.

Johan let out a laugh that was a bit too loud and loosened his grip on her hand — though he didn't let it go. "Ha-ha. Yes. That's what a possessive weirdo would say, *non*? I'm joking. I'm glad you think Nya is as wonderful as I do."

He glanced at her, grinned, hoped she was believing this terrible lie. He was so hung up on her that he couldn't even prevaricate correctly anymore.

Scheisse de merde.

She winked at him, more of a clumsy blink really, and he called back her ideas for how he could pretend to show affection. She thought that he was faking this reaction, even after she'd brought his defenses down like a house of straw. Johan sighed with relief, then dragged his thumb slowly over the back of her hand because if she gave him a centimeter he'd take two kilometers.

He turned back to Linus, who looked pleased as punch, likely thinking about how this would help the referendum. "Where is Lukas, Forshett?" he asked. His brother usually came running to meet him when he returned home, but was mysteriously absent.

"Ach, who knows? I thought your brother was a good boy, but it seems he's hit his rebellious streak. Fighting, missing appointments, talking back to his tutors. He slammed a door in my face!" Linus shook his head. "Laetitia would know what to do about this. She would have known what to do with you, too."

Johan hated when Linus spoke of his mother like this, as if her death had been an unavoidable accident like a trip down a flight of stairs. The doctors had told her to slow down until they figured out what was causing her fainting spells. Johan had begged her. Linus had let her do as she wished, working herself to her limits for strangers, and here they all were now — except for her, and her heart condition that had been discovered too late.

"Well, she's dead." Johan didn't realize how hard his tone was until Nya's hand went stiff in his. He waited for her to pull her hand away, but slowly, one finger at a time, her grip tightened around his. Not to stay him — to give to him. Strength. Support. He took a deep breath. "So that means he needs us, his father and his brother, to make sure he's okay. Has he been going to the therapist?"

"Ouay," Linus said, without animation. He was hurt by Johan's words. Because Johan had let his emotions rise to the surface.

A surge of guilt made Johan's tie feel too tight. He tugged at the knot. He knew the king hadn't *really* caused his mother's death. He knew Linus still grieved, too. He should apologize.

He didn't.

"Teenage boys are often a handful," Nya said, breaking their awful silence. "At the orphanage, where I taught, they could sometimes seem to change overnight, even older boys who had always behaved. We

257

called it 'pants short, head strong syndrome.' "

Linus managed a smile. "Is there a cure for this?"

"Time and patience." As she talked, she flipped her hand that was in Johan's, so that his was on the bottom, and rubbed his knuckles with her thumb. She didn't look at him — he wasn't even sure if she knew she was doing it, which hit him that much harder. What they'd done in their bed in Njaza was one thing, but this kind of absent-minded comfort was a different intimacy than he was used to.

"It will help if you stop treating him like a child," Nya said. "Or rather, treating him in what he feels is a controlling way. Right now he's searching for his place in the world, and the reminder of his mother's passing has surely brought some unresolved issues to the surface."

Hearing Nya speak calmly and profession-ally in an effort to help his brother was too much. He couldn't look at her without risk-ing saying or doing something he would regret. She was kind *and* competent, and he was utterly done for.

Nya continued. "You don't have to let him run wild, but give him *gentle* reminders that his behavior is something only he can control. Let him know that if he needs to talk, you'll be there."

"Well, you see who he has as a role model," Linus said jovially, gesturing toward Johan with his teacup. "It's a wonder this behavior didn't start earlier."

Johan froze again, waiting for Nya to agree with Linus, for them to both laugh knowingly. He'd played the role of clownish playboy for so long that his muscles shouldn't have been tensed in awful anticipation — after all, that was the reaction Prince Jo-Jo was designed to elicit. A bright, ridiculous distraction.

"If he follows in Johan's footsteps, then you have nothing to worry about. My fiancé is a nice man." That edge had returned to her voice, her singsong accent more pronounced as she lifted her chin in challenge. Suddenly, Johan didn't mind being called nice. Suddenly, it seemed like the highest compliment because to Nya, it *was.*

Linus didn't speak for a moment, his gaze shifting back and forth between Nya and Johan. *"Une fra avec des couteaux für die pieds,"* he said slowly, nodding. "You chose well, Jo-Jo."

"What does that mean?" Nya asked, face scrunched with puzzlement. Johan prepared to translate but then she continued. "A woman with knives for feet?"

"You speak Liechtienbourgish?" Johan hadn't even thought to ask, given the country's tiny population.

"I speak a little of several languages. Practicing gave me something to do when I was stuck at home." She shrugged. "It's just a mix of French and German, right?"

Johan raised a hand to his mouth in horror. "Please never say that in public, unless you want to be pelted with waffles by angry Liechtienbourgers."

"I like waffles." She winked.

"Not when they're flying at you like cars on the Autobahn."

"And if I say it in private?" she asked with a cheerful brazenness. Johan felt the blood rush to his cheeks. She'd managed to scandalize him in front of his stepfather, who hadn't seemed to notice the innuendo in her words.

"It means a woman who will do anything for her man," Linus interrupted helpfully, bringing the conversation back to his country's strange colloquialisms.

"Like 'The Little Mermaid,' " Johan added, taking a sip of cool water. "The fairy tale, not the film."

"I see," Nya said. "Is there a term for a

man who would do anything for his partner?"

"I'd never thought of that," Linus said. "No."

Nya twisted her lips. "I was imagining something much cooler than regular old patriarchy. Lady Knife Feet sounds much more interesting."

Johan laughed, unable to resist her serious contemplation of the phrase.

"I haven't heard you laugh like this in years," Linus said, looking just a bit awestruck.

Johan sobered and straightened in his seat, pretending not to see Nya glancing curiously at him.

"About the referendum," Johan said, steering the topic away from himself. "Any news?"

"The opposition has ramped up their attacks, with Arshlocher saying our remembrance of your mother was an attempt at manipulation and not a painful coincidence. They've tried to insinuate we live off the public teat, even though that's what they want for themselves, but our side has been doing a good job at showing the revenue from my businesses. It's been a good way to share my elegant silverware design."

He glanced meaningfully at the lumpy

spoon Nya was stirring her tea with.

"Ohhh, I wondered where this lovely item had come from," she said. "It's unique and eye-catching."

Linus nodded approvingly, and Johan wondered if perhaps Nya was better at lying than he was.

"I've seen the attacks about refugee resettlement programs as well, and some rumblings about my trip to Njaza," Johan added. "I've been emailing with the PR company. I was thinking about a campaign featuring stories from the last Great War, reminding our citizens that many of them are descended from refugees who came here from across Europe. The royal family has always protected those in need."

"Oh, that's good! We need to be seen out and about in the lead up to the vote, showing why we deserve to maintain our position," Linus added.

"Why do you deserve that?" Nya asked, stirring demurely.

Linus didn't hesitate. "Tradition. Stability. Monarchy is the only form of government this country has known."

She placed the spoon down on the edge of her saucer, ignoring it as the misshapen thing tilted over onto the table with a clunk. "Did you know my father is in prison?"

Linus didn't flinch, years of diplomacy keeping his expression bland and light. He nodded once. "I saw something mentioned about that, but thought it better not to bring up such unpleasantness."

"Well, that unpleasantness happened because he wanted to uphold tradition. He wanted power, to create stability, but stability as he knew it — stability that benefited him. He thought he knew best." Nya's voice was even, serious, with none of her usual cheer. "Have you asked yourself whether what's best for you, the status quo, is not what's best for your people? I have to ask because I'm part of this, too, now, and your actions reflect on me just as mine will on you."

Johan expected Linus to get flustered, but the king drew his shoulders back — not an act of defense or offense, but a sign that he was taking Nya's questions seriously.

"I believe with all of my heart that this is the right system for this country. I have studied countless other types of government and run through all of the possibilities, but given our size, the surrounding powers, and, yes, our traditions, I do not think a complete change is what is best. I will step down without hesitation if the people think otherwise, I want them to make their own informed decision and not be swayed by false propaganda."

"Like a fake engagement?" Nya asked quietly.

Linus looked confused. "How fake is it if Johan likes —"

The door to the parlor opened, cutting off whatever embarrassing thing his stepfather was about to reveal. Johan turned, and what he saw so shocked him that he sprayed his mouthful of tea over his carefully pressed pants. "Lukas?"

His brother, who generally wore preppy khakis and polo shirts, had on a tight-fitting, fuchsia, long-sleeved T-shirt with a white skull on the front, white skinny jeans, and black calf-high combat boots. His thumbs poked out of holes in the sleeves of the shirt . . . and his hair!

The curly blond locks Johan had taught him to maintain had been shaved along both sides; the remainder had been dyed a violent shade of pink to match his shirt — and his nail polish, because the tips of his fingers now sported blunt pink nails.

The look was the norm for some teenagers, but not for his brother, who Johan constantly guided in all things, including fashion.

Anger and a desperate panic clamped

around Johan. This was what bullies looked for, when seeking out their victims. This was what would make the paparazzi descend on Lukas without mercy. Johan couldn't protect Lukas from this.

He emitted a garbled sound, that was some approximation of "What the —"

"Hi. I'm Nya." She stood, releasing Johan's hand. "You must be Lukas. I'm so happy to meet you."

"Hi. Yes. It is my pleasure," Lukas said. He walked over to Nya, took her hand, and bowed over it, the epitome of politeness, then slouched into the seat next to Linus without even looking at Johan. He tapped his index finger along the wooden armrest, as if drawing attention to the polish.

Johan had been worried over his brother's well-being for the last few days, but now he was ready to strangle him. He'd spent years showering the boy with love and attention, hiding him from the prying eyes of the paparazzi, protecting him the pitfalls of boarding school bullies, and now he was being repaid for his troubles with this neon nightmare.

The stocky boy held up Johan's bear which should have been safely in his backpack. "You want me to return it? Why don't you go cry to your mamm?"

"Your hair —" Johan started, frustration choking him.

"— looks amazing!" Nya finished. "Did you dye it yourself?"

She leaned forward, elbows on her knees, giving Lukas all her attention.

"Jah," Lukas said, his shoulders rising toward his ears, then dropping into a defiant slouch. "I cut it, too."

"Good job! The style is very striking. The asymmetrical look is very popular right now."

Johan knew he should follow Nya's lead, and her advice not to treat Lukas like a child, but this was all too much.

"Have you gone mad?" he asked, his hand tightening over one of his knees. "Do you know what will happen when the first picture of this gets out? Do you know what people will *say*?"

Lukas cut him a hard look, the expression unfamiliar and terrifying. "Worried you won't be the center of attention anymore?"

"No. I'm worried about you making a fool of yourself," Johan replied, his voice ice-cold, a freezing barrier to counter the scalding shock of his brother's sudden change in temperament. Lukas had always looked up to Johan, admired him — the real him — but now glared at him like he was a stranger.

266

A stranger he didn't like at all.

"If being myself means people think I'm a fool, then *people* can go fuck themselves."

He said the last two words with such a pointed vehemence and narrowing of his eyes that there was no mistaking who they were meant for. Johan. Those words were meant for Johan. It was Johan who could go fuck himself.

An actual physical pain boomeranged through him at the anger in Lukas's voice. What had happened to his sweet little boy? Yes, Lukas had mentioned maybe dyeing his hair, but Johan had thought it was simply a passing fancy and Lukas hadn't seemed upset when Johan had vetoed the idea. He'd looked at nail polishes months back, but Johan had remembered how he was teased for painting his pinky nail a cheerful yellow once and had talked his brother out of it. Lukas talked about the usual things teenagers these days talked about, and Johan always subtly reminded him that he wasn't just any teenager, that he always, always had to think of what people would say. Then they'd watch a film or play video games or go for a walk, and everything would be fine.

This sudden, brash upending of everything Johan thought he knew about Lukas — and had tried to protect — was like a punch to the kidney.

"You can't be serious," Johan said. He didn't want it to come out sounding nasty and derisive, but this was the first time Lukas had ever hurt him, and his go-to defense was nasty derisiveness, it seemed. "The referendum is days away, people are looking for any reason to strip you of your title, and you think now is the time to make trouble?"

Lukas's shoulders slumped and he turned his head away with a jerking motion, as if he'd been slapped.

"Eh! Excuse me?" When he looked at Nya she was leaning away from him but fixing him with an incredulous stare. "This is the brother you told me you love so much, and that's how you talk to him?"

For the briefest instant he wanted to tell her she had no clue what she was on about, could never know because she'd never put all her energy into looking after someone and had it thrown in her face. He wouldn't say that to her, though, no matter how angry he was. First, because from even the little bit he knew of her relationship with her father, that would have been incorrect, and second, she was trying to help — and she was right.

"I'm sorry, Lukas," he said, struggling to sound normal even though he felt like he'd just been pushed off the esplanade surrounding the Old City. "I was just surprised. This is very unlike you."

Lukas stood and glared at him. "Unlike me? You don't even know me!" he shouted, then looked at Linus. "Neither of you do!"

Johan didn't know what to say in the ringing silence that followed. It was as if he was watching a film and could only sit there as the scene played out.

He remembered helping his mother change Lukas's diaper. He remembered giving him piggyback rides. He remembered teaching him to ride a bike, and showing him how to make crepes because their mother hadn't been around to do it. He remembered sneaking into Lukas's room in the middle of the night, on too many nights, overcome with the need to make sure the boy was still breathing. But maybe his brother was right. Maybe Johan didn't know anything.

"I guess I don't," he mumbled.

Lukas marched over to Nya and bowed over her hand again, the picture of politeness. "It was a pleasure to meet you. You seem like a good person, so you should know that Johan lies all the time and doesn't

269

care about anything but appearances. Think about that before marrying him."

He glared at Johan once more for good measure.

He left.

"Welcome to the family," Linus said, raising his teacup in Nya's direction before downing the liquid and rising to go track down his son.

Johan sat still, not wanting to look at Nya, or to see the judgment in her eyes. Not wanting her to see the pain in his. He'd become so good at hiding his emotions, burying them under shirtless selfies and snarky remarks — and, yes, lies — that until recently he'd forgotten just how deeply they could affect him. She could say he was nice all she wanted, but if she knew how weak he was, how *oversensitive,* she'd leave him, too.

She is *going to leave. This isn't real.*

He heard her sigh beside him, and then he felt her fingers sift through his hair, her nails gently grazing his scalp.

"Phokojoe, you seem to have forgotten how to lure people to your lair," she whispered, teasing.

"No kidding." He inhaled, leaned his head toward her hand and accepted her comfort, though he didn't deserve it. "I didn't handle that well at all. I wasn't prepared."

"I don't see why you had to be prepared," she said carefully. "Your brother just showed you something about himself. I think he was probably frightened of how you would react. And you showed him he was right to be frightened."

"Fuck," Johan muttered, guilt hunching his back. He should know better. He was supposed to know what people wanted.

"Sometimes children go through things, and it can be hard for the people who care for them to go along with them. But please . . ."

"What?" he asked, glancing at her.

Her expression was pensive and she worried her bottom lip with her teeth.

"Remember that he is your brother, but he's also his own person. You should not try to bend him to your idea of who he should be."

Johan recalled what she had said to her grandmother in the gazebo.

"Is that what your father did to you?" he asked.

"Mmm-hmm," she said. "Whenever I tried to express myself in any way he would tell me 'You don't want to do that. A good girl wouldn't want that.' And then I would get ill, or he would, and that would solve that problem of my wanting."

Her hand stopped moving in his hair and Johan turned his head toward her, pressing a kiss against her wrist. She was staring off into the distance, but she smiled faintly at the pressure of his mouth.

"My offer still stands," he said. "If you want to talk or —"

"I don't want to talk about it, confidant," she said.

"What do you want?" he asked. A sudden desperate desire to ease her burden, to free her from the sadness that her memories had opened up for her, seized him.

"I don't know," she said. "That's a question I was never allowed to answer and now when people ask, I come up blank."

She sounded so lost — a woman who'd come to the end of the breadcrumb trail and didn't know where to go next. The needy, selfish part of Johan thought it wouldn't hurt to guide her toward him in the meantime. "Will a kiss do until you figure it out?"

That coaxed a smile from her, and chipped away at some of the pain from the argument with Lukas.

"Yes. I would like that. Thank you."

Politeness was suddenly so damn sexy. His gaze traced her profile and the curve of her sweet mouth as something twisted hard in his chest. It was painful, what he felt just looking at her.

He froze, the ache in him both familiar and something entirely new. He was scared of what could happen if he kissed her again because in doing so he'd be biting into the poisoned apple, selling his soul to the sea witch — and he'd gladly take on whatever cursed despair came of it for just another taste of her.

"Johan? Kiss me," she urged, and though her voice was gentle, it was a command, which was even sexier than her politeness.

He leaned over in his seat and pressed his mouth to hers, kissing her as thoroughly as he could manage in the awkward position. Her soft lips molded to his, slick with gloss that tasted of strawberry.

She made a soft sound of surprise, but then her grip in his hair tightened, holding him as she met the stroke of his tongue with her own. A tremor ran down Johan's spine as she tugged at his strands, her eagerness nourishing some insatiable part of him.

He licked into her mouth, greedy for the delicacy of her exhalations. He would give her anything, but he would take, too. Take the sweetness of her mouth, and the rare happiness that settled over him because she was near. Take the illusion of love and belonging that flared in him like the heat and light of the last match in an ice storm.

A cold wind whirled around him, waiting for that light to burn out, as all flames did. He ignored it as she moaned into his mouth. He ran his hand over the textured delineations of her braids, then the silky smooth of her skin. His hand cradled the back of her neck and he kissed her, slow and luxuriantly, like he was awakening from a cursed slumber.

Control? What was that? Something that existed in some other faraway kingdom, maybe. But not the one he was building with Nya.

His hands slid down around her pliant curves, and he tugged her into his lap, holding her as he kissed her without thought of ever stopping.

She gasped and sighed, teasing his desire to give her pleasure because that was what gave *him* pleasure. And while Johan enjoyed pleasing others in general, the insatiable need that fed on her moans and her writhing was *très, très spezifisch.*

He unbuttoned the top two buttons of her shirt, slipping a hand inside to palm her breast through the thin silk of her bra. He brushed the heel of his hand over her nipple and she curved away from his touch, giggling.

"That tickles."

He was glad she trusted him enough to tell him what felt good and what didn't. He grew harder against her bottom and felt her gasp as he pressed into her. He pulled his hand out of her shirt, then lowered it, circling his fingertips around her stockinged knee, then her inner thigh, the circles growing concentrically as his hand moved up beneath her skirt.

"Yes, this is better," she said. "You can move your hand higher toward my . . . peach emoji. If you want to do that."

Her expression was somewhere between brazen and bewildered, with a heavy dose of plain embarrassment, and it was the sexiest thing Johan had ever seen. It wasn't her inexperience; it was how she was figuring out what she wanted, despite it. How hard she worked to say what she wanted even though she had been taught to feel ashamed for just that. Still . . .

"Peach emoji? That is advanced debauchery."

"Isn't it, um, you know? A vagina?" She whispered the last word.

Johan tried so hard not to laugh, but he had to a little. "Maybe in your circles, but

275

in mine, it's a . . . *derriere.* I'm perfectly happy to debauch you in that way, but it requires a bit more preparation and —"

"Oh goddess!" Nya covered her eyes with one hand. "This is what I get for being unclear."

She pulled her hand away from her face and placed it atop his through the fabric of her skirt, determination in her eyes.

"I want you to touch me. *There.*" She pulled his hand up. "Now. Please."

The silky slide of her stockings under his palm as she guided his hand was nice, but he wished it was her soft skin instead. He cupped his hand over her mound, kissing away her gasp as he pressed two firm fingers into her clit.

"Comme tu willst," he murmured against her lips.

"Yes," she whispered, her voice thready. "Your hands are so strong. Do you play piano? Because they are —"

Johan switched up his pace from fast and shallow to slow and deep, and she stopped her ridiculous yet arousing dirty talk then, arching in his lap. Her eyes and mouth and everything in her expression were squeezed hard, but her hips moved in his lap, teasing him.

"Mmph." Her shoe fell off as one of her

legs kicked up seemingly of its own accord, and then she turned her head into the lapel of his jacket, letting out a moan that vibrated through him at the same frequency she shuddered against him. Then she was suddenly limp, curled up in his lap with her face still pressed into her chest. Her warm breath passed through his jacket and shirt as she calmed herself.

"Um. Good work. Thank you." She tilted her head up and kissed him on his chin.

He heard the door opening, somewhere behind the roar of his own want.

"*Hallo,* Jo — Oh! Pardon me, pardon me," Greta said, pink rising beneath the golden apples of her cheeks. She raised her tablet to block her view of them. "I assume this is your 'fiancée'? Congratulations to you both, and I must say that you're really going the extra mile to keep up appearances."

Nya's hands pressed against his chest as she jumped out of his lap, and Johan held on to her fingertips as she toddled to her feet, reluctant to let her go.

"Greta, you know if I'm going to play a role, I play it well," he said, straightening his collar and then standing up beside Nya.

"Yes, a regular Daniel Day-Lewis," she said, clapping her hands together. "I've come to discuss the Njaza organization?"

Nya didn't look at him, but nodded toward Greta. "I'm Nya Jerami. It is a pleasure to meet you, though I would've preferred less embarrassing circumstances."

"No worries. I work very closely with Johan, so it would take a lot to shock me," Greta said.

"I see," Nya said. "Yes, I imagine you're used to this kind of behavior."

She let go of his hand, and clasped her own.

"I actually have to go check my phone, I'm expecting a message," she said. "I'll leave you to your business."

"Nya," Johan said, and she stopped midrush to the door. He wanted to ask if the message she was expecting was from her mystery man, but that would be absurd. It would make it seem like she owed him the information, when she didn't owe him anything.

"Do you know how to get to my room?" he asked instead.

"Yes," she said. "It's next door to mine. Which is where I'll be. Have a good meeting."

"Do you like the opera, Ms. Jerami?" Greta asked, and Nya paused again. "The last showing of *Rusalka* at the Royal Liechtienbourg Theater is in two weeks. It's a lovely performance, and it would make an excellent official engagement outing, just before the referendum."

Johan grimaced against the sudden jet of anxiety at the idea of watching *Rusalka* with Nya. "I'd rather not."

Greta looked perplexed. "It's your favorite. Don't you think it would be odd if you missed the performance? Everyone already expects you to attend. Is there some reason you don't want to go?"

He glanced at Nya. She was standing stiffly and looking at the ground, her demeanor drastically different from moments ago. "It's fine, if you do not want to fuel any more gossip."

"No, it's not that." He couldn't very well tell her what his problem was.

"Jah, Johan loves fueling gossip, so it must be something else."

Johan glared at Greta.

"It's nothing," he said, straightening the lapels of his jacket. Besides, I'll be giving Nya a tour of the city later today and we'll be making the rounds before next week. Plenty of gossip will be fueled."

Nya tried to smile, but her eyes held a wariness that Johan hated.

"Jo-Jo. As your assistant I have to tell you that it will reflect badly on the family if you skip this prereferendum event."

"You're right." Johan grimaced. "Save the Royal Box for us then."

"Excellent," Greta said.

"Great," Nya added, and now she was the one using the Phokojoe voice she'd teased him over. She didn't sound enthused at all.

"Perfect," Greta said, oblivious. "You will need a dress for the opera, so I'll make an appointment with the modiste for tomorrow. There hasn't been a woman in the palace for some time, so I know she'll be quite excited to meet you."

"Thank you," Nya said, and rushed out the door before they could stop her again.

"Not your usual type," Greta remarked as soon as the door shut.

"What's that supposed to mean?" Johan asked irritably.

"You actually seem to like her. That's *gutt, ja*?"

"Not at all," Johan said, rubbing his temples. "Not in the slightest."

Greta looked at him for a moment then shrugged. "Right. Okay, I'm going to need some more information about the land mine detection systems you linked me to."

Johan could deal with that. Helping to get rid of a legacy of tragedy would take his mind off of Nya, and the fact that she would be gone soon, which would be a different kind of tragedy but only for him.

"Let's get to work," he said.

CHAPTER 13

ONE TRUE PRINCE,
MESSAGE FROM: HANJO

I can't stop thinking of you, even while plotting the downfall of the monarchy. I have to be careful, so as not to raise suspicions, or else I would come to you right now. Are you thinking of me, too? Give me a sign!

Nya sighed and closed out of the game without responding. Hanjo was annoying her with his neediness, in part because Johan was annoying her with his Johan-ness.

They were faking this engagement. They'd told the people most important to them that they were faking it, and that was part of the fun for her — it was a virtual dating game come to life. That was what she had wanted! But did he have to be so cavalier about it?

It hadn't felt fake, the way he'd kissed her,

touched her . . . she was inexperienced, not insensible. The way he'd leaned into her caress, the desire to please her in his eyes before he'd pulled her into his lap — that had been real. But so had his talk of playing roles, and his dismay at the idea of appearing at the opera with her. The truth was she'd only had one bad kiss before him. Maybe Johan kissed everyone like that.

Johan lies all the time and doesn't care about anything but appearances, Lukas had warned her. Johan had admitted as much to her himself. Still, her inner compass that had always pointed away from Thesolo and toward a place that would make her happy had stopped spinning wildly and was pointed at an annoying playboy prince. Because she was a dreamer, and a fool.

Why did being foolish feel so good?

She dropped back onto her bed in the guest room attached to Johan's suite, which was as hard as the bed in Njaza had been soft, probably something to do with the country's obsession with toughing things out. She unlocked her phone to check the messages from her friends.

Portia: Nya! Welcome to Europe! How is Liechtienbourg?!

Nya: It's cold. The king said I have knife legs and the crown prince dyed his hair pink.

Portia: O . . . kay? Sounds legit. Anything else?

Nya: Johan is a good kisser. 😊

Ledi: 👀

Portia: ☺

Nya: I may have fallen victim to one of the classic blunders.

Ledi: I'm assuming you didn't start a land war in Asia or cross a Sicilian. Nya, are you catching real feels? It's only been a few days!

Nya: I know. But Johan is so . . . nice.

Ledi: Nice?! Are we talking about the same Johan?

284

Nya: It's hard to explain. I can feel that he is, even when he tells me he isn't.

Portia: I warned you. Fuckboy with a heart of gold. She didn't stand a chance, really.

Ledi: Look, I like Johan a lot. He's great, he's funny, and he helped me when I was setting up my STEM nonprofit. But he doesn't exactly have a sterling track record when it comes to dating.

Nya: Right. I have to remember that this situation is like my games. I've been training for this! We're just playing through a romance. It will end, and that will be fine.

Ledi: Nya, it's okay to feel something. This isn't a game.

Portia: I don't want to stick my nose into your business

Ledi: BUT

Portia: but

Ledi: hahaha

Portia: 😊 BUT it's possible that Johan likes you, too. I saw him sneaking peeks at you all through the ceremony. Even Tav noticed, and that takes a lot.

Nya: Oh, I don't know. I think Johan is like that with everyone.

Portia: That's why he's had so many fake engagements before? 😒 Nya, do you know how many PR people have begged and pleaded for the same thing he offered you? He turned them all down.

Ledi: She has a point. And my dungeon is still available in case he does anything out of pocket.

Portia: Just be yourself, don't put up with nonsense, and don't hide what you feel. And don't forget you can leave at any point. Or if you need me I can come to you. We're on the same continent!

Nya: Thanks guys. 😭

Nya: Has there been any word from my father?

Ledi: There have been a few, actually.

Nya: Does he know about the engagement?

Ledi: Oh yeah.

Nya: Is he mad?

Ledi: BIG MAD

Nya: Good.

Nya flopped onto her bed and stared at the high ceiling, with its ornate molding, so very different from the palace at Thesolo. The Moshoeshoe Palace was warm somehow, while this place felt . . . cool. She really did feel like she was living a *One True Prince* fantasy. She sighed, picking up her phone again and opening the game. A chibi version of Johan with round cheeks and wide eyes stared expectantly at her from the screen, and her responses hovered below.

A. Of course, I miss you. Have fun destroying the monarchy!

   B. I have a life of my own, Hanjo, but maybe I miss you a little.

   C. I'm reporting you to the authorities for treason.

There was a knock at her door, and she stumbled from the bed and opened the front door to the room before realizing it was coming from the door connecting her room to Johan's, since she was staying in his suite.

She marched over and cracked it open, willing herself to be cool and confident — willing herself not to care too much. Not to remember his mouth so hot against hers and how she'd shuddered in his lap.

"Hi." Johan often had a carefully casual, easygoing way about him, but he looked tense. His hair was disheveled, and the knot of his tie was loosened. And in his wide, deep blue eyes there was that uncertainty and need again, the need that made her want to reach out to him.

She shoved her hands into the pockets of her skirt.

"Hello," she said.

He took a step closer to her, but he didn't reach out either. Instead, he began adjusting his tie. Nya's gaze tracked how his long fingers tugged at the length of silky black and pushed up at the knot. His hands slowed and stopped, and when she looked at him he was staring at her, the faintest flush spreading over his sharp cheekbones to match his full, rosy lips.

Her skin prickled along the path his mouth had traced, from her fingertips up to her neck.

"Hrim," Johan said.

Was this some kind of Liechtienbourger greeting?

"Hrim," she mimicked, inclining her head toward him.

Johan seemed confused, then shook his head.

"I wondered if you wanted to go for that walk. I can show you around Sommet-staad."

"Is it time to pretend?" she asked. She tried to sound excited — pretending was all she should expect with a man like him.

"Pretend?" Johan leaned against the door frame. Behind him she could see his room: white walls, dark wood furniture, and no trace of the Phoko she knew. You could draw no conclusion about the occupant of that room . . . perhaps it *did* match the Phoko she knew, after all.

"I'd prepared to lie to you," he said. "And

tell you that we have to go out and be seen by the citizens to churn up some goodwill for the referendum. But."

"But?" Nya's expectations leapt past *should*.

"But I want to take a walk with you. That's all. I want to show you where I'm from."

His expression was so earnest, so vulnerable — and she saw the precise moment when he slipped his careless rogue mask back on.

"We can put on disguises to avoid the press if you want," he said, grinning. "I have lots of them. My favorite is a sea captain's hat and a pipe. I also have a merman tail and —"

"Phoko." She said the word quietly, but he stopped speaking because he always seemed to be listening for her voice. She thought about the advice Ledi and Portia had given her. She thought about what she wanted, and the role she had assigned herself in this live action dating role play.

Nya took her hands from her pockets and lightly grasped his tie. She slid her fingers up toward the knot, adjusting it because he had left it slightly askew. "You don't have to pretend with me, you know. Even if we pretend with everyone else, even if this ring is only on my finger temporarily, you can be yourself with me. You're not the only one capable of being a confidant."

Johan stared at her, and she patted the knot, her fingertips grazing his throat as she pulled her hands away.

"Hrim," he said again.

"Hrim?" she replied.

He made another guttural sound, one she couldn't replicate if she tried. It sounded like a wounded animal. "I'm not sure I know how to do that. Be myself."

Nya took a deep breath, because bravery required oxygen. "I like you, Phoko. I like you very much. I don't expect you to feel the same way, but I think it only fair to tell you if we're going to be ourselves."

She smiled up at him, despite her pounding heart, despite her father's voice telling her she was a wanton fool who deserved whatever the fallout of her forwardness would be.

Johan's face was contorted by complete and utter horror before it snapped back into something resembling normal.

Ooookay. Maybe she should've kept her feelings to herself. *Sorry* was on the tip of her tongue, but Johan had told her not to apologize without reason and he'd been right.

"It's that easy for you?" There was wonder in his voice as he reached out and stroked her cheek. He leaned in close and examined her face, her eyes. "Being open like that? Revealing your softest parts without fear I'll skewer you?"

"Your people really need to find some nonpointy-metal ways of expressing your emotions," she said, laughing from sheer relief. "Of course I'm afraid. But I've always been afraid. Why not be afraid and maybe enjoy myself, too?"

His hand cupped her cheek and then he leaned down to kiss her forehead. "Do you want the captain's hat or the mermaid tail?" he asked.

"Neither," she said. *I want you,* she didn't say. "I want to go see your country and meet your people."

"You don't have to do this," he reminded her. "If you want to just hang out in the palace and not help with the referendum, that's fine."

"I know. But you forget I have my own goals. My father thinks we are engaged. People are giving him information about me. I want him to see me in the newspapers, on the arm of a handsome man that I like very much, and I want him to suffer."

Johan tipped her head back and looked at

her, his brow creased. "He hurt you more than you've let anyone know," he said quietly. "Because for *you* to want someone to suffer . . ." He shook his head, and when he looked at her again he was as charming as ever. "If making you happy will hurt him, then he's in for a world of pain."

Something warm and soft, and yet more dangerous than the blades the Liechtienbourgers were obsessed with, unfurled in her chest. Johan hadn't said he liked her. But he was holding her close and brushing his thumb tenderly across her cheek. Even if he was pretending, as long as he didn't break the spell, she would keep living like her dreams were attainable.

And when their charade ended and it was time to let this dream go? Who knew? Maybe she would find even loftier ones.

CHAPTER 14

LIECHTIENBOURG FREEDOM ALLIANCE FORUM

Jo-Jo's surprise fiancée seems to be sweet as quetschentaart, but her father is a bad apple. The man is currently imprisoned for crimes against their kingdom. Is Bad Boy Jo-Jo's whirlwind love affair another Jerami family coup? Does he care enough about his own kingdom to find out? I think we all know the answer to that.

"It's cold!" Nya slipped her arm through Johan's as they stepped out of the castle's secret exit, which opened into a mews between some of the city's oldest buildings. The exit wasn't entirely secret — the media and the street's inhabitants just all mutually agreed to pretend not to see Johan or Lukas when they suddenly appeared from the door in the wall. Johan had thought it exciting when he'd first seen it, like the entryways to fairy worlds in his books. But like most worlds you accessed through a secret door, the price of entry had been higher than expected.

Nya pressed against him, and though he knew her coat was of the finest, thickest wool, he was sure he could feel her body heat through the fabric. Either that, or just being near her made him warm.

Scheisse, he was pathetic. And she liked him despite that.

They walked out into the darkening afternoon, the low heels of her boots clicking on the cobblestones. The castle was on the highest level of the tiered capital city, with the old towne spreading out below like a quilt of quaint old European houses.

"It's not so different from Lek Hemane, but looks like something from a movie," Nya said. "Like small, furry creatures should live in these houses."

"I'm sure furry creatures live in at least some of the houses," he said drily, and tried not to sigh when she laughed and tightened her hold on his arm.

"What was it like growing up here?" she asked as they turned onto the main street, full of people heading home from work or school. He'd tucked his telltale red hair up into a blue knit hat, but still drew gazes. Some people stared and a few of them suddenly had urgent business to take care of on their phones — which were conveniently pointed in Johan and Nya's direction — but no one approached them.

He wondered if he shouldn't have gotten them a security escort. Photos were fine, but what if someone tried something? He rarely used one when he was alone, but he wasn't alone anymore. Not for the next few days at least. And if anything happened to Nya . . . his scalp suddenly pricked with sweat, despite the cold and he stood taller, gazing around at the crowd for possible threats. Liechtienbourg was one of the safest countries in Europe, and had been for ages, but he still held Nya closer to him.

"Growing up here? It was okay," he said, leaning forward to peer around a parked van. "I wandered around this area alone a lot while Mamm was working for Linus."

"I bet you got into a lot of trouble back then," she said, grinning up at him, clearly trying to lift his mood. He could have spun her a tale of himself as a mischievous, free-spirited scamp, but that would've been a lie.

"No. I was a quiet child. I spent all my time reading. Lots of it in here." He jutted his chin toward the compact medieval building they were passing. "Sommetstaad Library. I didn't have many friends. Or I guess I did, if you counted the books."

He'd tried to make friends outside of the pages, but young boys could be cruel to one another. Once they'd learned how easy it was to make Johan cry, it'd become their hobby. The friends he'd had slowly drifted away, not wanting to be targeted. Johan had told no one, not even his mother. He hadn't wanted to worry her, and eventually he'd decided she was the only friend he needed.

He waited for Nya to say how hard that was to believe, to brush off his childhood woes because it had all turned out fine for him now that he was a strapping playboy.

"I can imagine that," she said quietly. "Little Phoko with his big pile of books. There's a solitude beneath all of . . . this." She waved her hand around to encompass his body. "You are shy, I think."

Johan scoffed. "Hardly. We can stop by the newsstand and the tabloids will tell you otherwise."

"But that's not *you.* I've read all about this Prince Jo-Jo." She looked up at him, somehow both timid and defiant. "I told you that I liked you. Well, I have for some time. I would read about you in the papers and on the blogs, and imagine you as a wild bachelor, with no worries, free to do whatever his heart desired. And I wished I could live like that. But — I watched you, when you came to visit Thabiso, too."

Johan's throat went tight as they approached the esplanade that looked out over the lower levels of Sommetstaad and out toward the rural towns.

"You watched me," he said.

"Yes."

I watched you, too.

He didn't tell her, though. Simply kept walking. It was bad enough that she felt anything for him. If she knew that *like* was not enough to describe what she meant to him, his reputation would be forever ruined.

Johan wanted to be ruined by her. He wanted to know how it felt to stop pretending, to stop guarding his emotions like a dragon watching over its hoard. But treasures were guarded for a reason — the world took and took, and he wouldn't gain something so precious as Nya only to lose her.

"What did you see?" he asked. "When you watched."

"It was hard to see you sometimes. You're kind of like the sun, you know." She laughed and shook her head.

"Red, fiery, *et gaseous*?" he drawled.

"No. Incredibly hot." She reached up to tap her gloved finger against the tip of his nose, and Johan's face mottled with heat. "You made me sweat and feel dizzy if I was in your presence for too long."

"Hmm." Johan's heart was beating fast. "You might want to get that looked at."

She rolled her eyes.

"But sometimes, when everyone else was talking, you would look so happy to be there. You looked how I felt, now that I think about it, so pleased for these friends when I'd never had them before. So maybe I should've known we were the same in this way. I was a lonely child, too. And I was a lonely adult. Naledi was the first person who made me feel not lonely."

"But you only met her two years ago," he said before he could stop himself. "Were you lonely all that time?"

"I had my father," she said softly. "And he told me that I should be happy to have him, since I'd taken my mother from him. He told me I must stay home, like a good girl at first, and then like a good woman — like my mother was. Because if I left I would have taken everything from him."

Anger and pity crashed together in Johan's chest, and disgust — with her father and with himself for understanding exactly how and why the man had done such things. It was simple manipulation really, but taken to an extreme and abusive level. It was what he feared he was capable of, made manifest.

"Nya."

"It's okay. I didn't really understand how bad it was until I met Naledi. It seemed normal, and no one else told me that it wasn't." She inhaled deeply, her gaze still darting around and landing on things that caught her interest as they walked. "People think my father poisoned her because he wanted to hurt Thabiso politically, or he wanted me to be Thabiso's bride, but I think he saw something dangerous in the way she'd befriended me. It scared him. But people think he would never hurt me. They know he did terrible things to everyone else, but they still think the way he treated me was love. Oh! Look at this view!"

Johan didn't need to look at the view. He had seen it for years, at every time of day, in every season. At this time of year, the late afternoon sky would be darkening to a frosty midnight blue, with streaks of orange and pink huddled at the horizon like a comfortable blanket before being turned down to reveal the starry pattern beneath.

He looked at Nya instead. At her bright

eyes and wide smile, and the joy that should have been crushed in her so long ago. It wasn't just that Nya wasn't soft — she was strong. Stronger than Johan had imagined. Resilient. She didn't flinch away from her pain, and she didn't even wait to receive the proper amount of pity before she was moving on to pure bliss at something so simple as a sunset.

Sunsets happened every day. Nya Jeramis did not.

His chest hurt from the beauty of her smile, the sudden upward curve of her mouth sharply cutting away the revelation of her painful past.

"How do you do this?" he asked.

"What?" she asked, brows raised.

"How do you not let your pain take away your joy?"

Her brow scrunched and her mouth pursed as she thought of a reply. "Well, what would be the use of that? I'm angry at my father. I'm not sure I ever want to see him again. But he kept me caged for most of my life, in a way. If I spent all my time being angry, I would just be in a new cage of my own making. That would be silly, no?"

Johan stepped forward and pulled her into his arms. It wasn't desire he felt for her in that moment — it was admiration. It was . . .

devotion. It was the resounding crack as every one of the rules he'd constructed to keep people away broke beneath the weight of his feelings.

Basically, it was his downfall.

This was temporary, however deeply the emotion coursed in him. It would end, and Johan didn't handle endings very well. He avoided them at all costs. He was already dealing with Lukas, the person he loved most in the world, pushing him away — he wouldn't be able to take another loss.

Still, he held her close, as the wintry air whipped around them and the last traces of sunlight faded away. Other people walked by, tourists and locals enjoying the view; he was supposed to be out shaking hands and smiling and hoping people would vote to keep his brat of a brother in the castle, but he kept his gaze fixed out over the railing at the cliff's edge.

"Why is the city on two levels?" she asked, turning her head and resting her cheek on his chest as she looked out over the late afternoon lights of the rows of houses below, broken up with patches of darker forest green. She didn't move away from him; in fact, she settled in quite comfortably.

Johan had held a lover before, but not like this. Or maybe he had, and they just hadn't fit so perfectly against him.

"We are a kingdom built on a natural fortress," he said. "Invaders would come from all over, they could swarm and lay ruin to the towns below, but here, the heart of the city and the country is . . ." He forgot the word in English, so he shrugged and pulled her closer. "They couldn't get up the sheer rock walls. It is how we survived changing boundaries and war, and then more war."

"It's beautiful," she said. "Beautiful but insurmountable."

"Ah, that's the word. *Insurmountable.*" He sighed and rubbed his hand over her back.

"It's nice, being here with you like this," she said. "I like the kissing, but I like this, too."

It was so easy to forget that this was new to her. She was not naive, but she was inexperienced.

He should never have slipped that ring on her finger. He would have to take it back from her soon, send her on her way. Some other man would put a ring on her finger, not as an impulsive gesture but after having thought long and hard about wanting to spend his life with her. Nya would accept, and move on, and Johan would still be alone in his fortress city.

He really hated living in a fairy-tale metaphor sometimes.

"Is it called spooning if we hug while we're standing?" she asked suddenly, her voice playful again. "Or forking?"

She started to chuckle and then gasped as her gaze jumped up to meet his. "No, I didn't mean, that is —"

He leaned closer, cleared his suddenly dry throat. "Sporking. It's called sporking."

She grinned. He didn't know why, since what he'd said made no sense really, but he was grinning, too, now.

"Isn't that your brother?" someone said in Liechtienbourgish, and Johan shifted his head just enough to catch a flash of bright pink. Lukas, walking toward them with a teenage boy that Johan didn't know. The boy's hair was brown and his clothing trendy, unlike the aristocratic boys Lukas usually hung out with. Johan knew all of Lukas's friends, and this one, who coincided with his brother's descent into rebellion, was not one of them.

"*Jah,* I'm his brother," Johan said, relaxing his hold on Nya. "Who are you?"

"This is my drug dealer, Lars," Lukas said, expression perfectly serene. He even smiled a bit, as if he truly enjoyed tormenting Johan.

Lars elbowed him. "Not funny, Luk."

"Lukas," Johan bit out. "Please. Can we talk somewhere?"

"No. You're busy with your fiancée and I have royal duties to attend to," Lukas said. "Come on."

He tugged at his friend's sleeve, and Lars adjusted his hold on his backpack and looked back over his shoulder apologetically as Lukas strutted away.

"Where is your bodyguard?" Johan called after him.

"Probably wherever yours is," Lukas shouted without looking back.

"Lukas!"

Lukas raised one fist in the air, unfurled his pinkie, and twisted his wrist. Johan let out a string of curses.

"What was that?" Nya asked, replicating the movement. Johan cupped his hands around hers to stop her.

"It is the most offensive gesture in our culture," he explained through his teeth. "It means 'sit on a short blade and spin.' "

"Oh dear," Nya exclaimed, then let out a peal of laughter. Johan didn't see what was funny. "Your people are so violent! Honestly! Knife legs and blade sitting and all of this. Don't you have any nice, nonweapons-oriented phrases?"

She blinked a few times, and he could almost feel it physically — her willing him to calm down.

He took her hand and started walking, slowly, in the opposite direction of where Lukas had gone.

"We have some very lovely terms of endearment," he said after letting the cold breeze whipping up the cliff whisk away his anger.

"Like what? And I hope they are better than *Sugar Bubble.*"

Johan paused, trying not to be hurt. He knew what it was like being called a name you hated. "You don't like Sugar Bubble? I can stop, if it bothers you."

"No! I was just trying to be cool," she said awkwardly. "I like it when you call me that."

"Well, I like it when you call me Phoko," he said, feeling warmth at his cheeks. "Here are some other nonweapon-related names you can choose from: *schneckelein, mausezähnchen, zuckermaus, hasenfürzchen.*"

"And, what are those?"

"Little snail, little mouse tooth, sugar mouse, sweet little rabbit fart."

She burst out laughing and leaned into him. "I think I will stick with Sugar Bubble."

"Okay. Sugar Bubble-Fürzchen, it is."

She swatted at him with her free hand, but her other hand held his tightly.

"Hey. With your brother. You helped raise him after your mother died, yes?"

"Ouay," Johan replied morosely.

"I think you should talk to him again," she said. "Talk *with* him."

"He's been going to the best therapists in Europe since he was a child," Johan said.

"You think he needs a therapist more than he needs a brother?" she asked.

"I'm saying . . ." Johan huffed out a cloud of condensation. "I'm saying that I'm worried that he *doesn't* need me. That if I try to talk to him, it will only get worse. He's been distant since before I left for Thesolo, but I hoped it would just . . . go away?"

"He wants to talk to you," Nya said confidently.

"How do you know?"

"No one tries this hard to get a reaction out of someone they don't want to talk to."

"Hmm," he said.

"Hrim!" she grunted, then looked up at him. "What does that mean, by the way? The word you said earlier? I like the feel of this word. Hrim!"

Johan was still worried about his brother, but he couldn't resist the laughter that bubbled up in him, obstructing his stress.

"It means this," he said, and then he leaned down and pressed his mouth against hers. "Hrimmm," he groaned into her mouth as she gasped, their lips catching softly once, twice, three times.

Her cold fingertips came up to his face and stroked his cheek before she pulled away.

"Oh." She looked a bit dazed, and though the kiss had been brief, it left bright stars circling around Johan's head. No, not stars. Camera flashes.

Johan had allowed himself to forget that this was his life. Parading around for paparazzi. He was used to it, but this felt wrong. This thing with Nya wasn't real, but it wasn't staged like him happening to wander out of the palace without a shirt. The photographers hadn't been invited here.

"That's enough," Johan said as the three men advanced with their cameras. Phillipe, Hans, and Krebs, the local photographers who made their living from photos of Johan, not the foreigners who showed up when their papers needed some Jo-Jo *jus.* Being a tabloid prince was like running a *mamm*-and-*papp* business in a way; people depended on him to make a living at this point. He didn't want to put anyone out of work, but he wouldn't expose Nya to an ambush. "You got your photos, so you can leave now."

"Aw, come on, Jo-Jo. Why did you call us here if not to take photos?"

"I didn't call you," Johan gritted out.

"Well, there're already photogs from London and Paris here trying to break the story, especially with the news out of Thesolo. Wouldn't you prefer it to be some-one you trust?"

Nya stiffened in his arms. "What news?"

Her voice shook, and her body shook, and not from the cold.

"Oh." Phillipe looked at Hans.

Hans looked at Phillipe. "She doesn't know?"

"Your father is on a hunger strike," Krebs supplied helpfully. "He says he has no reason to live if his daughter won't speak to him."

"What?"

Hans and Phillipe rushed over, glaring at Krebs before turning gentler expressions on Nya.

"It's not so bad. They're giving him fluids," Hans said.

"Humans can last for weeks without food," Phillippe added.

That was when the tears slipped down her

cheeks. Krebs started to raise his camera, but Hans blocked it with his forearm.

There was a series of flashes from further down the esplanade, though, and then a figure in the distance turned and ran off.

Johan took a step toward the figure, but instead wrapped a protective arm around Nya.

"I bet it was that *putaine* from the *Looking Glass*," Phillipe said with a grimace of distaste as he looked after the figure. "He used to be a sprinter on the British Olympic team and he puts the skill to use."

"We're going to go back to the castle," Johan said, unease settling in his stomach. His life had only looked completely spontaneous before — even his most impulsive behaviors had some reason behind them, and some level of calculated control. Something was off and he didn't like how the reins were being slowly tugged from his grip.

"Are you all right?" he asked Nya as they walked quickly back to the palace's back entry.

"I suppose," she said. "I have to be all right. My alternative is to run back to Thesolo and admit defeat."

"Is this a battle?" Johan asked, and her head snapped up, gaze hard as it locked on his.

"Of course, it is," she said. That anger that he had first heard on the plane was in her voice again. "Why else would I be here?"

Johan drew himself up. She wouldn't realize that her words had been as brutal as a blow from the woodsman's ax. They shouldn't have been. They were simply the truth. He was the one who had offered her this escape — why should he be hurt by the reminder of it?

Because she said she liked you.

"Right," he said. "And I was just the weapon closest to hand."

"What?" she sniffled.

They turned into the mews, and he realized he was being selfish. She'd just received a shock and didn't need him adding to her problems by expecting her to take care of his hurt feelings, too.

"Nothing," he said, then looked above the entrance. "But that's not nothing."

Above the secret door to the castle, spray painted in bright yellow, were the words *Democracy Now, Monarchy Never!* with a matching *X* sprayed over the door. Nothing remotely secret about it now.

"Well. This has been eventful walk," he said. And he had a feeling things would get even more interesting in the days to come. Underestimating the importance of the referendum had been an error on his part, but hopefully it wouldn't bite him on the ass too hard.

CHAPTER 15

INTERNATIONAL FRIEND EMPORIUM CHAT

Portia: Tav just gave me the paper. What did Johan do to make you cry? 🥟 ⚒

Nya: Oh god, it's in the Looking Glass? There's a nice photo of us in the newspaper here. I used your tips for the perfect photo and pretended I was saying strudel.

Portia: The article says that skeletons from his past have come back to ruin your relationship. "A source" says that a love child has emerged. There's another tabloid saying you were crying because the king was mean to you.

Nya: No, the king is my buddy. And there is no love child — to my knowledge. One of the photographers told me about my father's hunger strike. I had to learn about it from a stranger.

Ledi: Dammit. Okay, that was wrong. But you seemed so . . . free. I didn't want you to come back because of your father's manipulative tactics.

Nya: I wouldn't have come back.

Ledi: I didn't know that. But it was wrong of me to assume. I keep doing that.

Nya: ☹

Ledi: I saw the smiling photos of you two online, saying that Johan was easing the pain of your father's behavior.

Nya: Well, that's somewhat close to the truth.

Ledi: And that *you* were carrying the love child.

Nya: No, we haven't even

Nya: 😐

Portia: 😖

Ledi: That's fine. You don't have to do anything you don't want. If you do decide to do anything, you have your fanny pack.

There was a chiming sound, a doorbell, Nya realized. She ended the conversation and hurried over to the front door of her room, then steeled herself.

What if it's Johan? What if he wants to finish what we started in the parlor yesterday?

Her cheeks burned, as they had last night when she'd slipped into bed and stared at the door separating their rooms, wondering what would happen if she was brave enough to walk over and knock. She had wanted to, so badly, but hadn't.

When she pulled the front door open there was a short, stout woman with silver hair and round rosy cheeks.

"Mrs. Potts?" Nya asked before she could stop herself.

"*Non.* I am Madame Flemard, the modiste?" The woman's arms were wrapped around several items of clothing and her eyes scanned Nya's body. "Yes, yes, yes.

315

Perfection!"

"Pardon me?" Nya stepped back into the room as Madame Flemard stalked toward her, eyes narrowed. "Wasn't I supposed to come to you?"

"I was here at the castle and brought a couple of things I wanted you to try." She was already laying a few pieces on the couch in the room. "I have just the thing. I still follow the trends, you know, and I was given this beautiful print last time the delegation from Thesolo was here. I made this outfit, but there is no one here to wear it! It's not like it can fit —" Madame Flemard pressed her lips together and looked around. "Ahem. Yes. Would you like to try on a dress? I will not be offended if you don't like it, and I have other dresses. We can have pants tailored, anything you wish."

"I do love trying on dresses, and I have nothing to wear to the opera," Nya said. "I need to look . . . I need to *feel* very sure of myself. Like, you know, in the films when the heroine gets a makeover? And the hero falls deeply in love with her?"

"*Jah?*" Madame Flemard nodded.

"I want to look like that, except I want to be my own hero. I want to look in the mirror and think, *Damn girl!* and then show up under my own window sticking out of the sunroof of a limousine."

Madame Flemard laughed with delight.

"I like this spirit. I like it, *jah*. You are a modiste's delight."

"Merci," Nya said, feeling a bit braver.

The woman began rifling through the assorted items and gently pulled out two things: a cropped top with teal and purple flowers and a long matching skirt. Something in Nya's heart jumped at the sight of them.

"How about this?" Madame Flemard asked, as she walked over and held the fabric against Nya's arm. "So lovely."

Nya took the skirt and top, the stiff wax print fabric a reminder of home. A reminder of the simple black and brown items that had made up most of her wardrobe, despite such a rich variety of patterns in their traditional clothing, patterns she hadn't been allowed to wear so that she didn't call attention to herself. She'd had the money to buy her own clothes, but acquiescing to her father had been second nature to her. Her unhappiness had been shrouded in brown and black and gray, and this outfit was like a bright pop of color, demanding all eyes turn to her.

"I think this is perfect," she said.

Madame Flemard helped her try it on,

telling Nya she would take the top to let it out a bit at the chest.

Nya shifted her leg so that it was exposed by the surprising slit that went to her thigh, then fluffed the ruffles around the off-the-shoulder top, and placed a hand over her bare stomach. She liked the soft curve of it now, so different from her years of gauntness.

"Do you have anything I can wear today? We have some kind of winter market to go to. If I'm going to be followed by photographers, I want to make a statement."

"Good idea," the modiste said. "Also perhaps some waterproof makeup, in case there are more tears?"

She eyed Nya's belly speculatively.

"There will be no more tears," Nya said firmly, hands on her hips, and the woman nodded.

Nya tried on a couple of dresses before a bright, sunflower-yellow fabric that caught her eye.

"Oh, what's this?"

"That's one of Jo-Jo's shirts that I mended for him," Madame Flemard said. "He'd lost some buttons."

Nya ignored the part of her brain that speculated on how those buttons had been lost and pulled the shirt on. It loosely hugged her curves, and though too long to be worn as a shirt, it was the perfect length to wear as a dress. "I have a nice brown belt that can go with this and matches my brown boots."

Madame Flemard had tugged at her arm and carefully rolled up Nya's sleeves, cooing the whole time. "I wouldn't have thought of this, but yes, *oui, jah.*"

She shuffled through her suitcase and pulled out the dark brown belt and her nude brown stockings, blushing as she remembered Johan's hand running up her thigh in the royal parlor. She liked wearing his shirt, and the dual sensation of being possessed and possessing.

That gave her pause — her father thinking of her as his to control was what had driven her away from Thesolo. Even now he was trying to exert that control over her, using his own possible death as a winch on the emotions that still tied her to him. But Johan had never claimed any possession over her, except for that joke with the king. She was free to leave when she wanted and, even if she didn't want to, would have to leave soon.

Perhaps she cared too much for him. Perhaps this was a mistake. She hadn't made many mistakes in life because she had never had the opportunity. She would do what she wanted to do, and she wouldn't be ashamed if nothing came of it, because what was the shame in wanting? What was the shame in dreaming?

She tightened the belt and looked at the modiste.

"I'll keep this." She promised to visit Madame Flemard's shop the next day to try on more things and to get her top.

As she was ushering the woman out, Lukas showed up at her door. He was dressed in a dark blue suit with a matching pink tie, his blond-again hair pulled back into a queue. His nail polish had been removed, and he looked like any handsome young aristocrat, except for the frown on his face.

"Oh, hello, my *liebling.* You look wonderful today," Madame Flemard said. She adjusted the dresses on her arm to smooth Lukas's hair. "I have some things for you that I'll leave in your room."

"*Merci,* Flemie," Lukas said, kissing the modiste on both cheeks, then looking expectantly at Nya.

"Hi," she said. "Do you want to come in? I have to do my makeup, but I can still talk."

Lukas stepped in awkwardly, all traces of the defiant teen who told his brother to sit and spin gone.

"Your hair is different," she said as he stepped into the room.

"*Jah.* That was just a colored hair wax," he said. "Can you imagine if it'd been permanent? Johan might have held me down and shaved my head."

"I don't think so," she said.

"You're right," Lukas said. "He would have just told me what a disappointment I was and harped about my responsibility until I shaved it myself." He shrugged. "I just wanted to see how your time here has been going. I saw some talk about Johan's love child online and was worried."

"Which love child? The one I'm carrying or the one that made me cry?" she asked as she sat at the dressing table mirror. She'd already moisturized in nine steps because Licchtienbourg in the winter was asking for ashiness, and now she dabbed on a bit of concealer. She'd spent enough time practicing YouTube video looks in her apartment to do her makeup quickly and efficiently. She decided to go with a simple but eye-catching bronze shadow, brown winged liner, and sheer pink lip gloss.

Lukas laughed nervously. "You're not really pregnant, are you?"

She gave him her best quelling look with

the eye she wasn't spreading eye shadow on.

"Sorry," he said. His gaze lingered on her makeup bag.

"No. The love child story seems to have been entirely made up by journalists."

"Oh," he said, lips thinning. He looked a lot like his brother when he was uncomfortable.

"What about you?" she asked.

"I don't have any children yet, but producing heirs is part of my job so I suppose I will one day," he said with a grimace.

"I meant how are you doing with all of the attention from the referendum?" She didn't know him and would be gone soon, but he was a kid and had obviously come to her room for something.

"Oh! I've been better," he said airily. "Before I just assumed I was going to be king and that was that. Now I've had to think of what will happen if the people vote us out. It's scary, but also kind of exciting."

"I can't quite relate," she said. "But I'm about to go out on my first publicity event. What happens if I trip? What if my stockings get a tear? What if someone says something mean? It must be hard having this attention on you all the time."

"Johan will help you," Lukas said, then

tried to backtrack. "He's a spoiled jerk, but he isn't completely awful. Besides, if you fall, just make it seem like the only thing that could have happened was you falling, and everyone will go along with that."

"Did your brother teach you that?" she asked before smearing on some of the sparkly translucent lip gloss. Lukas was staring at her mouth covetously, but not in the way Johan did. She recognized that look. She'd been in his shoes before, watching others get glammed up while she stood in her black loose-fitting dress and makeup-free face.

This was lust, but not for her.

This moment was important. She was a stranger, though he thought she was his future sister-in-law, but her next words could still leave a lasting impact.

She held up the fancy gloss tube with the golden screw top. "Want to try it?"

"No! Of course I wouldn't! Why would I —" He huffed, then grabbed it from her, losing his stiff royal bearing and reverting to excited teenager. "It's been sold out for weeks and Lars was trying to get it, and —"

Lukas stopped and looked at her, shock and fear in his eyes.

Nya just kept doing her makeup, smiling just enough to let him know that he had nothing to be afraid of from her. "Go ahead.

My friend Portia gave me two tubes because she got sent a bunch to talk about on social media. This one fits your coloring better, so you can have it."

"Really?" Lukas smiled, the most genuine she'd seen from him, before dabbing the applicator at his lips and leaving behind a gloss that looked like crushed diamonds.

"It looks so good on you," she said.

"Thank you," Lukas said, checking himself out in the mirror from behind her. His gaze met hers in the reflection and there was a tension in his eyes. "Oh my god, you really are too good for my brother. How did he trick you into agreeing to marry him?"

Now that she thought about it, Johan hadn't exactly tricked her, but she had been under duress when he'd proposed his plan. She didn't regret saying yes, but she couldn't help but think of the Phokojoe tale again.

She decided to change the subject. "Are you coming with us to the opera Greta was so excited about?"

"I wasn't invited," he said. He studied his reflection, pursing his lips then regarding himself from several angles. The smile that had pulled up his wide mouth slowly relaxed into a frown, and he grabbed a tissue and held it between two fingers.

"That's probably because your brother thinks you hate him," she said, gently taking the tissue from between his fingers and replacing it with a sheer highlighting stick. "Because you're kind of acting like you do."

Lukas shook his head and began dabbing angrily along his temple. "Johan doesn't care. About any of that feelings stuff. He's always so busy worrying about what people think, and what I have to do to make them think certain things. It's exhausting. Even if I did hate him, he'd probably just say something like, 'Oh, how devastating. Now I won't have to waste my time looking after you.' "

Nya sucked in a breath. Though that *had* been a very good impersonation of Jo-Jo, it was a terrible one of Johan. She'd seen the hurt on Johan's face when his brother had cursed at him. She'd seen his frustration when Lukas had run off. And she had seen his hidden pain, snapped in an accidental photo and when she'd walked into the sauna. She'd felt his gentleness with her, and not just when he kissed her. Johan cared about feelings stuff. But he'd have to show his brother that himself.

"I think that you and your brother are having a communication problem," she said diplomatically.

"You have no idea," Lukas said with a deep sigh, then glanced at her. "Do you think he meant what he said the other day? About me looking foolish?"

Nya finished dusting on her setting powder, and then looked at Lukas. Really looked at him. His hunched shoulders and the bluish circles beneath his eyes.

She had her own family problems to worry about. Or to not worry about. If she took a moment to really think about her father starving himself . . . the man had always been stubborn, but now it was clear that he would go to any length to maintain his hold on her.

She shouldn't interfere with this von Braustein issue when she couldn't even deal with her own family, but she also couldn't just let Lukas think the worst.

"No. I think your brother was hurt because he expected you to confide in him, and instead of saying he was hurt, he hurt you back. Redirecting. Projecting. Stuff like that. In the short time I've known him he's only spoken about you from a place of love. Intense love. He's a good liar but that can't be faked."

Lukas regarded her suspiciously.

"Are you a therapist?"

"Just an observer." She would have said

326

she was a teacher, but she was unemployed. Another aspect of reality that loomed ahead of her.

There was a knock at the door connecting her room to Johan's. Lukas quickly gabbed another tissue and wiped off the lip gloss, then slipped the tube in his pocket.

She grabbed her coat and they walked over to the door together.

"Look who I found!" Nya said cheerily as she ushered Lukas out in front of her.

Johan's cool gaze took in Lukas's change in appearance from the day before, but he apparently decided not to make any comment. "Hallo, *bruder.*"

"Hey," Lukas said bleakly.

"You both look very nice," she said, sliding her arm through Johan's then placing the other on Lukas's shoulder so he would feel included, too.

"I always look nice," Johan said jokingly, and Lukas humphed. To be fair, the joke didn't really seem like Johan . . . the Johan she'd gotten to know. He may as well have been miming, performing the act of untroubled older brother.

"Let's go," she said. She hoped they figured out their issue because as much as she liked Johan and was coming to like Lukas, she couldn't fix it for them.

■ ■ ■

They left through the palace's main entrance this time, and there were more than three photographers waiting. The street was lined with cameras, the lenses all turning toward Nya, Johan, and Lukas, with the photographers behind them calling for their attention.

Nya had a brief flashback of a lone journalist in Thesolo who'd snuck into the hospital room where she'd recovered from her breakdown after her father's arrest — and where she'd first discovered that the mystery illness that had plagued her for most of her life had been another of her father's means of controlling her. She'd awoken to the journalist going through her chart, and when he'd noticed she was awake he'd demanded to know whether she'd helped her father with his crimes.

Nya had thrown a pitcher of water at him, and he was arrested after the nurses came to see what the noise was.

She hadn't thought about that in some time, but in the face of all those journalists, the memory froze her for a moment.

"*Ça geet et,* Sugar Bubble?"

She glanced up at Johan, whose voice

called her back to the present.

"Sorry, just got a little overwhelmed," she said.

"Why are you apologizing?" His voice was harsh but his gaze was intent. It was a question and an inside joke — and a reminder that Johan would protect her from anyone, even himself.

"Not sorry," she said, her tension loosening.

He raised his hand, cradling her face in the soft warmth of his leather gloves. "We don't have to do this. I didn't bring you here to overwhelm you."

No. He hadn't, and Nya hadn't come to be overwhelmed either. She'd come to shock everyone, and Johan would help her do that.

"I'm fine," she said, then placed her palms on his chest, pushed up gently on her toes, and kissed him. It was a soft kiss, an innocent press of lips, but . . . Johan was a performer. His hand cupping her cheek held her face in place while his other hand slipped behind her back, pulling her close. Then he was kissing her deeply and passionately and, goddess, she hoped *this* wasn't a performance, too.

The desire in his eyes before they fluttered closed, the urgency of his tongue pressing into her mouth, the devilish groan that vibrated against her lips . . . all of that was real. It had to be.

He pulled away, eyes unfocused and expression dazed as he looked into her eyes.

"All better, then?"

"Hrim!" she replied, not quite able to speak yet, and his features creased as laughter burst from him.

Laughter and whistles from the crowd of journalists and onlookers reminded her that they weren't alone.

"Can we go?" Lukas asked sullenly.

"Sorry," Johan said.

"Not sorry," Nya added, feeling frisky. "But we will keep the PDA to a minimum. Sorry, Lukas."

The journalists kept a respectful distance as they followed their stroll to the nearby market. The stalls all looked similar from afar — wooden posts and red fabric awnings beneath strings of light. As they approached, she could see each vendor sold something different.

Homemade soaps, scary marionettes with yarn for hair, cheeses of all kinds, meats and stationery and cell phone accessories. Their fellow shoppers looked at them, though most pretended not to see them or the group of photographers following them.

The vendors made sure to hold their wares up at an angle that would have made Portia proud.

Johan held her hand on one side, and Lukas strolled quietly on the other. She noticed how Johan's gaze flicked to his brother — and those around his brother — even as he made jokes to break the tension. How he guided both of them around raised cobblestones and away from anyone who looked poised to approach them, despite the fact that guards from the castle tailed them, all while maintaining a carefree demeanor. She knew what it was, to pretend that everything was fine when it was not, but Johan had mastered the art of careless vigilance.

Lukas began to thaw as they walked, though he didn't seem to notice how Johan was attuned to his every move. Nya had seen similar behavior in siblings who came to live at the orphanage — the obsession with making sure no one else they loved came to harm. The social workers had a protocol in place to mitigate the overwhelming fear and guilt the protective siblings felt. It was clear that no one had ever stepped in to do the same for Johan.

She wanted to gather him to her, to tell him he could stop pretending and stop protecting. She squeezed his hand and smiled up at him instead, hoping her eyes radiated the message she'd never received.

I know things are not fine. You aren't in this alone.

Lukas stopped at the marionette stall to explain the history of the creepy dolls to her, which she supposed was his way of bonding, and the vendor let him operate one with flaxen hair.

He worked the strings with ease, smiling as the doll shimmied and kicked across a clear space on the table.

"Johan used to put on shows for me," Lukas said as he settled the doll back in with the others. "He'd make a little stage out in the garden and use marionettes our mother had brought for me."

There was something wistful in the boy's voice.

"Jah," Johan said. His relief that his brother had finally addressed him was almost palpable. "When he got older, we would dress up and act out plays. He makes a very fine Miranda."

"It was fun." Lukas gathered his ponytail in his palm, smoothing the hair as he slid his hand down it. "I used to think he just liked spending time with me. But like everything else, it was just preparation for all of this."

Lukas gestured to the paparazzi surrounding them, and maybe more. Nya thought he might mean all of Liechtienbourg.

"That's what everything comes down to with Johan. Putting on an act. Do you like acting, Nya?"

Johan went stiff at her side.

"I'm not very good at it," Nya said. "Though I think it's necessary sometimes."

"Let's go get a mulled wine," Johan said, pretending the conversation wasn't happening.

"Isn't it a bit early for that?" she asked.

"Never." He took her hand again. "The reason we're a fortress city is that all of the surrounding fiefdoms and countries were always trying to steal our secret recipe."

She glanced up at him, his face the very picture of carefree prince as he scanned the stalls in the opposite direction of his brother, and she squeezed his hand. His mouth twitched, but he squeezed back, and then there was an uproar to the left of them.

Johan pushed Nya and Lukas behind him with one swing of his long arm.

"Jo-Jo!" a female voice called out crisp and clear.

A woman stepping from between the awnings with a bundle in her arms. The security detail that had quietly shadowed them rushed toward her, but she flipped back some of the cloth in her arms, revealing . . . a baby. A redheaded baby.

Nya's stomach lurched.

"Oh, come on," Johan muttered. *"Vraiment?"*

"Does she want you to kiss it or something?" Lukas asked, jostling Nya a little as he peered around his brother's bulk. "Oh. Ohhh. Is this the love child?"

The journalists went wild at that, and Johan glared at his brother. "There is no love child!"

Lukas and Johan began to bicker, and it was only Nya who noticed that the woman had disappeared from the marketplace while everyone buzzed about the baby.

"Is she your former lover?" one of the photographers asked.

"Will you claim responsibility for your child?"

"What does this mean for your engagement?"

"What does it mean for the referendum?"

Johan ran a hand through his hair, and regarded the flashing cameras with a confident grin. "I've never seen that woman before in my life. I have no children — I am certain of that. I know some of you are ready to sell any story, but there are a couple of redheads there in the press pool and if you're going to start assuming paternity by the color of a child's hair, you should get in line."

He said it so calmly that there was no way it was a lie. But . . . Johan was a very effective liar. He could make people believe anything.

Just like your father. The realization hit her like a blow to the diaphragm, making her slightly nauseated.

No. No way. He wasn't at all like her father . . . except Alehk Jerami had always been able to fool people into believing what he believed. He'd even made Nya think that she was weak, helpless, and could never leave him.

No.

Johan has always been up-front with who he is, she reminded herself. *Father never admitted to lying. He never admitted to* anything *he did.*

And now he's starving himself . . .

A female journalist shouldered her way to the front. "Nya! Ms. Jerami! Do you have any comment?"

All eyes turned to her and she summoned her Jerami pride to keep her expression and voice unconcerned. "Comment? I think that child was adorable. Much too cute to be related to Johan. Have you seen baby photos of this man?"

Laughter spread through the journalists.

"I've only been in Liechtienbourg for a short time and I'm still getting my bearings. I think I need to head back to the castle now." She looked at Lukas and Johan. "Shall we?"

Johan took her hand, leading her away as the reporters were held back by security guards. "You're learning fast," he said.

She pulled her hand away, pretending to hold the collar of her coat against the cold breeze. "I come from a family of politicians, Johan, and my father was a criminal one at that. You're not the only one who knows about manipulation."

Her words were curt, and Johan's expression flickered.

"I thought you didn't have a nefarious bone in your body." He stared at her as they walked. "That you do shouldn't be sexy, and yet —"

She sighed aloud and shook her head, glancing back to see Lukas lagging behind them. She tried not to think about the woman and the baby. She tried not to believe that Johan's lies might mean he was a bad person. It didn't matter anyway.

This is a game.

337

CHAPTER 16

It seems that the rumors are true! Johan's heart has been claimed, if the images coming out of Liechtienbourg are any indication. Our boy seems totally smitten, and though we should all be jealous, this is too cute to hate on. We stan a besotted bad boy! Protect #JoNy at all costs!
— Jo-Jo Lovers Unite Blog

That night Johan paced back and forth in his room, unable to sleep. He was too preoccupied with Lukas's behavior, Nya's presence in his life, the referendum, and the bad feeling he had about the events of the past two days.

Greta had been keeping him up-to-date — there had been illegal postering, raucous town hall meetings, and even some small-scale vandalism like graffiti. That was unsettling, given how calm the country usually was, but Johan figured that if people needed to express themselves, there were worse ways for them to do it.

But the things that had been happening since he'd returned seemed personal. The graffiti over the "secret" doorway, the mystery woman trying to cause a stir. The head of the opposition, Arschlocher, was known for playing dirty when it came to business, and Johan didn't doubt he was involved in this somehow.

He'd gone down an internet rabbit hole, finding himself in a pro-Arschlocher forum where people speculated about Liechtienbourg being taken over by foreigners, insisted that Johan was part of the Illuminati, and much, much worse. There was even a conspiracy thread devoted to the death of his mother, but he hadn't clicked through to see that garbage.

He'd heard her doctors tell her to take it easy until they figured out the limits of her heart condition and watched as she tried to help just one more person, and one more, and one more. He knew why she had died: because she cared too much. He didn't need anyone's enraging speculation on the matter.

He'd looked at the formation dates of several of the tamer threads, the ones speculating on the validity of the monarchy,

whether Johan was a pox on Liechtienbourg, and what kind of government would
be best for the kingdom. And they'd all been
started a couple of months ago. It hadn't
taken very long to notice that the most
virulent detractor on this forum was an account named FloupGelee, who seemed
determined to convince everyone that the
von Brausteins were the worst thing that
could have happened to the country. This
person hated Johan, but attacked Lukas just
as viciously, which was surprising. There
was a thread about the fight Lukas had gotten into at school, with several people coming forward with descriptions of behaviors
that seemed nothing at all like his brother,
but very much like someone who shouldn't
be king.

Johan had a stable of private investigators,
and he reached out to one of them, and to
a friend who claimed she was as good as
any PI he knew, just in case.

Hi Portia,
I know you're busy with the new business, but I think you mentioned tracking
down someone using just their username
for your sister? Can you check out this
FloupGelee person if you have the time?
The link is below.

He'd also sent the link to Greta to ask her to look into it. He was a little surprised that she hadn't seen this sooner — she was usually on top of this kind of thing.

Not having any control over the situation was what had Johan wide-awake in the middle of the night and pacing. If he didn't know where the threat was coming from, he couldn't lie or charm to neutralize it.

There was a chiming sound through the door. Nya's phone.

He was already annoyed, but an uncharacteristic anger bloomed at the sound, which he'd also heard the night before. He hadn't asked her about her mysterious text lover since they'd agreed to the fake engagement, but he'd seen her checking her phone in their bed in Njaza, and each time that chime went off, she scrambled for the phone, angling it away from him.

Johan tugged at his hair, reminding himself he had no claim on her and that policing her use of her phone was crossing several lines. Then he walked over to her door and knocked, wiping the frustration from his face.

There was the sound of her getting out of the bed and then of the door unlocking. She wore a silky-looking black scarf around her braids, which were up in a bun, and black

341

gym shorts with a plain white tank top.

She was beautiful.

"Hi," she said.

Johan understood he couldn't very well demand to know what she was doing on her phone, and that he *shouldn't.*

"I couldn't sleep and thought I heard you moving around," he said, casually leaning against the door.

She looked sheepish — or was that guilt?

She has nothing to be guilty about.

"Oh sorry. I was playing a game. I had the chime up loud so I'd receive the notification." She ran a thumb under the strap of her tank top, which had twisted as she slept.

"Hmm." His gaze followed her thumb's arc over her shoulder because he didn't want to look at her face and see if she was lying to him when she had no reason to. He lied all the time, so he was the last person to judge, but he didn't lie to her. If she'd lied to him — that would hurt, even if she wasn't really his.

He nudged his suspicion aside.

"Want to come in?" he asked. "I feel like we haven't had much time to talk with everything going on."

Her gaze brightened. "Are we going to spoon again?"

Johan's body went taut at her enthusiasm.

"Do you . . . want to?"

"I think it could be nice. It's a bit drafty with these high ceilings."

Ah. So he was going to be a living blanket. That worked for him, as long as he got to hold her. "Then yes. Come spoon with me."

She stepped over the threshold, and then past him as he moved out of her way.

She climbed into the bed and looked at him expectantly, and he walked over slowly, moving around the bed to the other side. She rolled over to look at him.

"I liked when we shared the bed in Njaza, and this one is much more comfortable than that one. And the one in my room. Not too hard, not too soft." She pulled the duvet over her shoulder.

Johan couldn't help himself — he reached over and tucked the blankets around her.

Her hand snaked out from beneath the blanket and caught his forearm gently as he pulled away. "Phoko . . . about that woman. Were you telling the truth?"

It was a valid question, but it still hurt, especially when his senses told him that she was hiding something from him.

"I wouldn't abandon a child," he said. "And I have no idea who she was other than someone trying to make me look bad for voters. I don't know if you've read much

343

about it, but the opposition has promised ridiculous tax breaks to the wealthy if we're voted out. There's incentive for Arschlocher and others not to play nice."

She nodded. "I'm sorry. I keep remembering things about my father. And today I thought about how he was also a good liar, and it scared me."

"I told you that I wouldn't lie to you," he said because it was the only thing he could give her.

"That's why I asked you," she said, the barest of smiles on those lips he'd gone too long without tasting. "Maybe I should be more cynical, but I believe you. Because you're a good liar, but you're also a good man. My father isn't, and I shouldn't compare you. It's also kind of creepy thinking of you like that."

He stretched out beside her, wanting to run his hand down her bare arm but restraining himself as if a sword lay in the bed between them.

"It's not creepy to try to figure out if you're attracted to me or to a pattern that you were caught up in and had no control over. You do have control now and you're trying to protect yourself."

"See?"

"What?"

She was looking at him all wide-eyed, and he shook his head.

"Oh no, I'm not *nice.* That's common sense."

"Whatever you say." Her eyes were still bright with pleasure. How could he think she was hiding anything?

"Have you heard any news? About the hunger strike thing?" he asked gently.

She shook her head, her expression flattening.

"I know you don't like talking about this, but you should know that whatever happens to him as a result of this isn't your fault."

"I know," she said quietly. "Well, my brain knows. My heart doesn't. And also . . . this is terrible. I hate that I even think things like this." She turned her face into the pillow.

"Like what?" He still didn't reach for her.

"I'm worried for him, but I don't want to be." Her voice was muffled by the pillow. "Even behind bars, he's still able to make me feel like a bad daughter."

"You're not a bad daughter," he said gently, and she turned her head toward him, sorrow in her eyes.

"Maybe I am. I'm also angry because I want to be the one to hurt him." This came out in a pained whisper. "I wanted to hurt him, to shock him, to make him realize that he has no power over me. And now he's taken even that away by hurting himself. It's terrible, but I hate that he's taken this one weapon I had and turned it against me."

God, she was right. Johan saw now how her father had strung her like the marionettes at the market. Even when she thought she was free, there was yet another string she'd have to saw through.

"I don't know if you can ever really hurt a man like that," he said carefully. "He will take anything you do and make it about him instead of wondering why you're doing it."

Johan thought of how he'd behaved with Lukas and felt a stab of shame. How was what he'd done any better?

"This is how I know you're different," she said, her voice a little wobbly. "I see how you are with your brother. I see how he hurts you. You care about him, not just whether he does what you say."

Johan tried to force a laugh, as if she hadn't just assuaged his fear. "Tell *him* that."

"You tell him. And then it will get better," she said. "Most people have a rebellious stage. I mean, look at me! I'm so much older than him, and I'm still trying to shock my family. I should ask him for some of that pink hair wax."

Johan laughed, and he didn't have to force it this time. Talking with Nya like this made everything seem easier somehow. She'd called him a friend, and even though they pretended to be more — even though in his fantasies they truly were more — he imagined this was what true friendship was: chatting in the middle of the night about those problems you thought you couldn't share with anyone.

"But people do rebel for a reason," she added quietly. "You should let Lukas know that, whatever that reason is, you'll be there for him."

"Do you want to be big spoon or little spoon this time?" he asked as he watched her blink rapidly, trying to fight sleep.

"Little spoon. Please."

He slid under the duvet and they met in the middle of his bed. He gathered her in his arms, ylang-ylang scented and luscious as she curled against him. Her shoulder blades slotted into place against his pectorals, and her thighs and calves nestled against his, like a warm breathing puzzle piece.

She sighed and the tension seemed to drain out of her as she relaxed fully against him. It did something to him, more than making her shudder in his arms had —

though he'd enjoyed that and wanted to make her cry out again and again. There was a deep trust in letting go of your worries in someone's arms, in going soft and pliant not from arousal, but because you felt safe.

He leaned back to hit the light switch, and then wrapped his arm around her again.

"Phoko."

"Hmm?" He was already slipping into sleep. She wasn't the only one who felt safer this way.

"Just so you know . . . you are not the weapon."

"Sie parles de waat?" He couldn't quite hold on to his English as he sank into dark slumber, but he knew that what she said pleased him.

"I keep saying I want to hurt my father, and to shock the world. That's one part of it, but I like just being here with you, too."

Johan was already half-asleep but he hugged her close as peace descended on him.

"Johan."

He squeezed the warmth in his arms, nestled against it. Rubbed against it.

Mine.

Wait.

"Phoko!"

He blinked awake to his room awash in morning light. He was holding Nya very tightly and, given his state, he'd also likely been dreaming about her.

"*Scheisse,* I'm sorry," he said, groggily rolling away from her and adjusting himself so that the elastic of his sweatpants controlled the outward projectory of his erection.

"It's all right. I only woke you because you were, um, poking my peach emoji. Like, poke, poke, poke!"

She poked his back with her index finger, and embarrassed heat rushed to his face. He was a grown man, but this had to be a high school nightmare.

"Is that normal? Can you make it move like that at will?" she asked through her laughter. "It was a funny way to wake up."

"Funny? Excuse me, I'm going to go jump off the esplanade now." He threw his cover off dramatically and tried to hop out of the bed, and she grabbed hold of his arm.

"Phoko."

"Sorry for . . . my eggplant emoji's behavior, and thus mine."

"It's okay. I thought it was something both of us should be awake for. Which is why I woke you." She looked up at him with a shyness that was almost brazen because she held his gaze in spite of it.

"You have my attention," he said, flopping back down into the bed on his stomach, his arms around his pillow and his gaze on Nya.

"I was thinking . . ."

"Thoughts are magnificent," he said in a low voice. "Share them. All of them."

"I was thinking that maybe we could try some morning debauchery. Above-the-underwear debauchery, still. Are you interested?"

Heat flared in him, and that admiration he had for her. From what he'd discerned, Nya was a woman unused to asking for what she wanted, but here she was, asking for him of all things.

"Very much so." He sat up, his back to his heavy wood headboard, and stretched his legs out before him.

"Come here," he said, and she grinned so sweetly in anticipation of his touch that Johan groaned. She moved toward him on hands and knees, climbing onto his lap to straddle him, but he took her by the waist and guided her to turn so that her back was against his chest and her ass was pressed against his cock as she settled between his legs.

She turned her head back to meet his

gaze, her eyes wide with uncertainty.

"One order of over-the-underwear debauchery coming up," he said, then angled his head to kiss her. How had he ever even pretended to ignore this mouth? It was lush and warm and perfectly shaped, and now that he'd felt it pressed against his own without the slightest hint of hesitation he didn't think he could ever settle for another.

He pulled his mouth away and nudged her cheek with his nose so that she was facing forward. "Look over there."

"A mirror," she whispered after turning her head. Johan dropped his mouth to her neck, licking and kissing at the same time his grip tightened on her hips and he ground his hips up.

"Is this your sex mirror?" she asked with just the slightest hitch in her voice.

Johan chuckled at the real curiosity in her voice. "No. You're the only one who's ever been in this bed, so the mirror has led a single-function existence until now."

She looked back at him, tearing her eyes away from the sight of the two of them. "This is a new bed? No wonder it's so comfortable."

"Not new." He nipped her ear, and his hands began sliding up her waist and taking her shirt with them. "Do you like the mirror?"

"It's very nice," she said uncertainly, facing forward again.

"Do you like watching us in it?" His hands cupped her breasts beneath her shirt, his knuckles pressing through the fabric.

"Oh. Well, right now there's not much to see," she replied, gyrating her hips so that she rubbed against him. "Ask me in a few minutes."

Johan knew a challenge when he heard one. He kissed her earlobe, then the junction where her neck met her jaw, and when she exhaled hard he grazed her with his teeth.

Her breasts were smooth and warm and heavy, overflowing his hands, and he stroked them gently, watching her face from over her shoulder. He stroked under her breasts, avoiding the areola that had tickled her last time even though the hard peaks of her nipples poked through the fabric of her shirt.

She arched her back, pushing her chest forward.

"You can touch them," she said, her gaze on his in the mirror. "Maybe I'll like it this time."

He nodded, lifting her shirt to expose her

completely. She raised her arms and he lifted the shirt up and tossed it onto the bed, then cupped her breasts again. He ran his palms over her nipples, then his thumbs, brushing back and forth.

Her hands were on his thighs, and her fingers pressed into the muscles there as her hips rolled. She let out a shuddering sigh and a tight nod.

He took one hard peak between the thumb and forefinger of each hand, rolling gently, and watched her face in the mirror. Her teeth grazed her bottom lip as her head knocked back into his shoulder with a sudden jerk.

"It feels good this time," she said. She rolled her hips against him harder, then turned her head to the side to drop a kiss onto his bare shoulder. It was such a simple, innocent gesture, but Johan shuddered with need, his cock swelling against her.

"Good." He kissed her hair, the side of her face, any part of her within reach of his mouth as he kept his gaze locked on them in the mirror. Then he pinched, gently.

"Oh goddess, yes." Her voice was low with passion, and she reached up and back with both hands, gripping his hair and tugging so that she held him in place as inextricably as he held her. A hot surge of pleasure pulsed in him at the slight pain, and at the way she had opened herself to his touch.

He hardly recognized himself in the mirror, his flushed face and the dark, possessive focus in his eyes. And her . . .

Her gaze was soft with passion and her mouth slightly agape as she made sweet sounds of pleasure. He raised a hand to her mouth, running his thumb over her plump lower lip. Her tongue darted out and licked at the pad of his finger and Johan groaned, taking her chin with thumb and forefinger and tilting her head to the side.

She met his kiss with a moan and he greedily swallowed it. His tongue slid over hers, thrusting into her mouth in a hot, ungainly clash. She pulled away as she trembled against him and her hips worked in his lap, and then she clutched one of his hands.

He thought she was pulling it away, but no — she was guiding him. They both watched in the mirror as she led his hand over her belly and pressed it against the crotch of her shorts. He could feel the repressed spring of her curls through two thin layers of fabric, could delineate the folds of her pussy.

Nya held his gaze in the mirror as she lifted her hips, as if offering herself to him, and he pressed down on her clit. He rubbed slowly, relentlessly, watching the pleasure build in her. The mirror revealed everything to him: how the muscles of her stomach undulated, how her feet pushed down into the mattress, and how her expression contorted as sensation overtook sense.

He gave her nipple a final squeeze before sliding his arm across her chest, holding her close as she bucked beneath the circle and flex of his fingers on her clit. His own cock was so hard that it was painful, but his attention was fixated on the way her eyes fluttered, how she gasped for breath, the press of her fingertips into his forearm as she held on with both hands — pushing and pulling as if she couldn't decide what she wanted from him except his hand on her.

"Johan. Yes. *Yes*."

Her eyes squeezed — he already knew this tell of hers — and when she let out a harsh yelp and shivered in his arms, he slowed, but didn't stop.

She met his gaze in the mirror.

"Oh goddess, I think you could make me come again just looking at me like that."

Her words pulsed through him as if she'd taken his cock in her hand. It seemed her orgasm had helped her get rid of some of her shyness. Johan wondered what a second one would do.

"That's going to be inconvenient," he said, rubbing her hard again. "Because every time I look at you, I'm going to think of how sexy you look right now and I don't think I'll be able to help it."

She turned to kiss him again — he wouldn't have to wonder long. Her second orgasm hit her harder, longer, and made him glad they were the only two in this wing because it seemed his quiet Nya was not always quiet. She keened into his mouth as she rode his hand, and Johan thought one more errant rub of her ass might send him over the edge, too.

He held her as she slumped back against him. In the mirror, her lips were turned up in a sated smile and her eyes were shut as if she was going back to sleep.

"That was fast," she murmured. "You have magic hands."

"Yes. I was cursed by a witch with an 'orgasm hands' spell," he said blithely, though his cock was still hard and he desperately wanted to know what her hands felt like on his body, and how tightly she would fit around his cock. He could live without knowing, though. He wouldn't rush her into anything.

"Maybe I was cursed, too," she said, looking up at him as she nestled down against his erection. "Let's find out."

Johan dearly, dearly wanted to find out, but then his phone rang. People rarely called him, so when they did he always expected bad news.

He kissed her temple and reached for the phone.

"You're up early," Greta said when he answered.

"What's wrong?" He didn't like suspense.

"I was wondering why you locked the shared document so I couldn't make any changes. I need to add more information about the Njaza land mine organization."

The bad feeling that'd had Johan pacing in the middle of the night returned with a vengeance. "I haven't accessed the doc in two days, and I certainly didn't lock you out of it."

"Are you sure?"

Nya sat up, looking at him with worry in her eyes.

"Positive. I'm going to go change my passwords and then you can go in and compare the current docs with our backups to see if anything has been changed."

"Do you think someone hacked it? How?"

Johan had every possible password protection protocol. If someone had accessed the

357

accounts it had to be a high-level hacker. He didn't want to think about the other possibility.

He eased from the bed and grabbed his tablet. "We'll discuss that later. I'll call you in a few minutes."

"What's going on?" Nya asked.

"Just . . . stuff. Work stuff. Referendum stuff. Sorry, I have to handle it immediately."

"Can I do anything?" she asked.

He was going to say no, but if he did, that meant she would leave, and Johan wanted her to stay even if there were to be no further mirror adventures. "Want to make us some coffee?"

She quietly prepared them two cups from the small contraption on a side table, and he filled her in on what he'd discovered the previous night and what had happened that morning.

"Why would someone try this hard to hurt you?" she asked.

"I'm starting to understand just what some people will do for money. They want the royal family gone," he said. Johan smiled at the irony. How many times had he wished for the same thing? But these people were messing with Lukas's future. It was one thing if the citizens voted to get rid of the monarchy; it was another if someone was trying to tip the scales against them.

Nya ran a hand through his hair, the scratch of her nails calming his whirring thoughts. "What are you going to do?"

"I'll have to talk to Linus. I'll see if he's awake now." As he looked up at her, he realized that both the referendum and his personal life were starting to get messier than anticipated. He'd imagined that he could handle both a large-scale social change and Nya with his usual distance, but he'd been wrong, and now one might endanger the other.

"If you don't want to deal with . . . *this* anymore, I understand. I'm not quite sure what's happening or what these people will do — I'm not sure if you'll become a target, too. You set up your web security stuff the night before we left, right?"

"Yes, though I doubt anyone would want to hack my stuff — they wouldn't find anything besides my video game back-ups if they did. And while I am concerned, if I go home it's to a father starving himself to death to punish me, so not exactly an upgrade."

He was glad she didn't want to leave, so he stood up and kissed her, the only way he had of showing her that, because it wasn't like he could just *tell* her.

"Lukas will go with you to the breakfast this morning, if that's okay," he murmured against her lips, planting a kiss every few words.

"Okay, I'll go get ready," she said, giving him a final kiss. When she walked through the door back to her room, Johan felt an inexplicable loneliness. She was literally a few meters away and that seemed much too far. What would he do when she left?

He really was pathetic. And he had accounts to secure. He could deal with his ridiculous determination to balance his heart on the point of a blade later.

CHAPTER 17

ONE TRUE PRINCE,
HANJO STORY MODE

Nya: I was perfectly happy with my boring normal life before you got me involved in this mess!

Hanjo: Were you happy, though?

Nya: . . . No.

Hanjo: And what about now?

Nya: I'm happy when you kiss me, I suppose.

Hanjo: Well, then, I'll keep kissing you. And I won't stop.

It felt strange to be at an event without Johan. Oddly, Nya didn't feel as nervous as she'd been while in Thesolo, even though someone was trying to influence the referendum and wasn't afraid to play dirty.

In a way, once Johan had told her what was going on, she'd felt something click into place. Her grandparents had always instilled in her that Ingoka didn't make mistakes — Nya had hated that expression. To her, it had backed up all the things her father told her, had made it clear that being kept safe in her gilded cage was the proper path of her life.

But now here she was in another small kingdom in the throes of change, dealing with another person or people who wanted to influence the future of a country through trickery and deception. And this time she wasn't related to the possible villains. When the priestess had said fate had brought her and Johan together, Nya had hoped she was talking about love. But maybe it had been this. Maybe Nya could help.

Johan had showed her care and gentleness. He'd made her feel beautiful and strong. She wasn't sure she could do anything at all with just a few days to go until the referendum, but she would pay attention. She would smile wide so people thought her harmless. She would do what she had always done once people forgot her presence — she would watch and listen. Maybe she would stop these people as she hadn't stopped her father.

"I hope you're hungry," Lukas said from beside her. His hair was slicked back into its queue, a bright blue elastic band matching his tie, but his lips were bare. The only color on his face was the dark circles under his eyes. "I asked for Belgian waffles, which offended the chef, but Liechtienbourgish waffles just aren't fluffy enough."

Nya felt a little sad for the boy. He could have been out having breakfast with friends, or going to the mall, or whatever it was that teenagers did for fun. All of the things she'd longed to do instead of helping her father practice his speeches or escaping from her own life through films. But Lukas would be king, and his life was even more regimented than hers had been. And though she'd experienced some scrutiny from the press, his whole life had been spent hiding from the intensity of it.

"I'm sure the chef doesn't mind," she said. There was an awkward silence as they ate, both likely scrambling for something to talk about that wasn't Johan.

"You're graduating this year?" Nya asked.

"Yes. I have to study for the *BAC,* then I'll go to a Grand École in Paris, even though I

363

really wanted to go to California." He shrugged. *"C'est la leiben."*

"Maybe you can do that instead! California would be fun. I dreamed of visiting while I was in the US, but . . ." She trailed off. "You should talk to your father. He seems reasonable."

"There's no reasoning with tradition," he said. "I love my father, but when he looks at me all he sees is his legacy. I think it's the one thing that makes him happy, since mother died, knowing I will be king."

When he glanced at her, there was an anguish in his eyes that almost made her drop her fork.

Oh.

"Lukas. It's okay to disappoint people, you know. This is your life, and not your father's. Not your brother's either. I don't think either of them would want you to be unhappy."

"I don't know if it's possible to be a happy king," he said, pushing bits of waffle around on his plate. "Honestly, this is the weirdest job ever. You're born into it, and people have already decided who you should be and how you should act."

Nya knew that feeling well, and she asked what no one had ever asked her, after her father had told everyone she wanted to be a

364

teacher, like her mother.

"What would you want to do with your life if the referendum decides to abolish the monarchy?"

"Maybe become a pilot," he said. "I was also thinking of studying game development."

"Do you like video games?" she asked excitedly.

"Does an ax cut wood?" he replied, and Nya figured that it was yet another Liechtienbourger turn of phrase.

"What are your favorites? Mine are *Taken by Ragnoth the Vampire Lord* and *Byronic Rogues from Mars.*"

Lukas grew more animated. "Yes! I also love *Senpai High* and *Chicken, My Love.*"

Nya giggled. "I haven't played the chicken game yet. Is it actually good?"

"Yes! I'm playing it now, and there's actually a really interesting plot about a chicken rebellion. I'm romancing the alpha hen, who takes no nonsense and pecks out the eyes of her enemies." They compared games for the rest of the breakfast, talking about the best routes to follow in particular games and the sites they read to find them. Nya recommended *Girls with Glasses,* Portia's sister's site, but Lukas said he usually got his

recommendations from friends in online fo-
rums.

"I imagine you haven't played *One True Prince,*" she said, and watched as the joy of talking about games left his face.

"No. A bit too close to home," he said with a grimace.

Yes, playing a game in which your brother was a character was probably not very fun. Especially when you were the actual crown prince and he wasn't.

Oh. She wondered if that had some part in Lukas's acting out. Johan had taken the spotlight to protect his brother, but maybe Lukas saw it differently. Living in your brother's handsome playboy shadow didn't seem like it would be very much fun.

"Maybe they'll add you to the expansion pack. Prince Saluk," she joked, hoping to cheer him, but received a look of horror instead.

"What's wrong?" she asked, but then Lukas's gaze shifted from her to up and over her shoulder, his face going ashen.

A hand came to rest on the back of her chair, and when she looked up a strange man was staring down at her. *Glaring* was a more accurate description for the look on the tall, thin man's serious face. He was dressed in a suit and had been seated with a group of what looked like businessmen when they'd walked in, but now he was alone.

"Where's the playboy prince? Too busy with one of his other women to do his royal duty?" the man asked, his gaze passing nastily over Nya's body. Nya sat frozen with fear, as she had in that first moment when she'd awoken to find the reporter in her hospital room.

"Arschlocher," she heard Lukas choke out. The man's glare didn't move from Nya.

"I don't know what Jo-Jo has told you, but if you think you're going to show up here and start living on our citizens' tax money, you're wrong. In a few days, the von Brausteins will be erased from history, and you'll be sent back where you came from."

Nya wanted to yell at the man, or to run away, but she just blinked back tears of anger and shame. The man shifted his glare to Lukas. "And you —"

His sentence was cut off by the fist smashing into his mouth. Johan's fist.

The man turned and raised his hands, maybe to fight back, maybe to block another blow, but Johan tackled him to the ground as the restaurant broke into an uproar.

The sound of chairs screeching, customers exclaiming, and photographers rushing in with their cameras flashing filled the previously sedate restaurant as Johan punched Arschlocher again. Nya jumped from her seat, but the security guards were already pulling Johan back and restraining the man.

Johan's handsome face was contorted by rage — he looked like he would kill the man, who had a split lip and a bruise forming on his cheekbone. He looked like he would kill him and not feel an ounce of remorse. Arschlocher's eyes were wide with shock, his bravado gone, and he glanced at Nya and Lukas.

"Don't even look at them," Johan commanded as he adjusted the lines of his suit, and Arschlocher dropped his gaze to the ground as he was led away.

"I didn't do anything," he said to the photographers, a sudden pathetic tone in his voice, as if he hadn't come up to Nya and said disgusting things that made her stomach turn. "I was going to engage in polite debate. Can the monarchy do as they please? Do they not have to follow laws?"

Johan stalked over to Nya and his brother, his intensely focused gaze flitting back and forth over them as if checking them for signs of harm. He was breathing heavy and his expression was murderous, but that wasn't what caught Nya's attention as she looked at him.

Fear.

There was fear in his eyes, a fear that even he, so skilled at hiding his emotions, couldn't mask.

She stood and put a hand on his chest; his heart was beating so fast that it worried her. "We're all right," she said gently. "It's okay. He didn't hurt us, Phoko."

Johan's breathing began to slow and he placed his hand over hers.

"And you thought pink hair would have people talking?" Lukas asked from where he still sat at the table, looking up from under his blond lashes. He seemed an entirely different boy from the one who had laughed and joked with her over waffles, and from the one who had been so excited by a tube of lip gloss. "You just attacked the head of the opposition party."

"I don't care who he was," Johan said. "He looked like he was going to hurt you."

Lukas wiped his mouth and stood. "Well, thank goodness you saved the day. But since you are always thinking of appearances, you have to know that the referendum voters aren't going to look kindly on this. Oh well."

He left, flanked by two security guards.

"It's okay, Phoko," Nya said because she

couldn't say anything else. There was something between the brothers that they needed to work out themselves, and maybe something more than a misunderstanding.

Johan was still quiet.

"Are you hungry?" She reached toward the table with one hand and lifted a waffle, making it dance enticingly in front of his face.

Finally, the hardness left his face and he smiled. Shook his head.

"You're really okay?" he asked.

"I'm not the one punching things. I'm guessing your hand isn't feeling too hot right now."

He sighed heavily, brushing his hair back from his face, twisting it around his finger as he did. "I've made a mess again."

Well, Nya couldn't deny that but she couldn't exactly hold it against him. The man had frightened her. If he'd had a weapon other than gross assumption, things could have turned out much differently. "I think you should call Greta and cancel this morning's events. Let's go somewhere."

"Where?"

"A place where none of this matters. There will be trouble whether you address it now or this evening, right?"

"Right."

"So. Let's go."

CHAPTER 18

@OlafJungstrum Is this the face Liechtienbourg wants to present to the world? Brawling von Brausteins?

@oodlesofstreudel Come on, I mean. It was kind of hot, non? He was defending his people.

@Sneks Defending against what? Arschlocher said he was just trying to have a conversation and got punched out of nowhere. Shouldn't civility be of prime importance?

@JoJoStanAccount Liechtienbourgers love talking about how they're from warrior stock but look at this reaction. I don't like violence, but remember that time some dude broke into the castle to hug the queen? Johan is probably traumatized.

"I thought you would have a nicer car," Nya said as his old Vauxhall crossed the bridge into the idyllic farming village of Schweinsteiger. Johan hadn't traveled to the farther reaches of the kingdom in a few months, but during the drive he'd realized that his love of fairy tales had surely been influenced by the backdrop of his youth. In the summer, the forest would be lush and verdant, but now the trees and small stone houses were nestled in drifts of snow, resembling a frosted ice kingdom.

"Are you making fun of my car?" Johan asked, caressing the leather dash. "Don't listen to her, Hansel."

"No! Just, in the magazines they always show you driving BMWs and fancy things. This feels more like you, though."

He glanced in the rearview, where two bodyguards followed in an SUV, though he didn't think he'd need them. His reaction this morning had been a bit over-the-top, but when he'd walked into the restaurant and found the man hovering menacingly over Nya and Lukas, and seen her sitting frozen with fear? His only thought had been that two people he cared for more than he

373

should might be snatched away from him, and he had to prevent that outcome.

"Are you an expert on me now?" he asked lightly.

"Yes. I've added it to my CV," she said.

Johan was warmed and then cooled by dual realizations — that because he'd shared more with her than anyone, she likely *was* an expert on him, and that she was only half joking about her CV because there was life after this fake engagement for her. The referendum would pass, or her need to shock her father would, and then she would go.

Yes, she liked him, but Nya liked everyone, didn't she?

He wouldn't think about it. He lived by the impulse, and now he would die by the impulse, because thinking about a long-term relationship with a woman he'd only been close to for a short time was ridiculous.

"Where are we going again?" Nya asked, looking around in awe. "It's so pretty here."

"This area of Liechtienbourg is an anti-monarchist stronghold," Johan said. "We're going to see if they hate the von Brausteins less than Arschlocher's party. And to meet my grandmother."

"What!" Nya snapped to attention in her seat.

She pulled down the sun visor in front of the passenger seat and checked her reflection in the mirror there, though she already looked lovely. She always looked lovely.

"Why didn't you tell me this before we left?" She was digging in her handbag for her lip gloss.

The joking lie was on the tip of his tongue, but the truth somehow slipped ahead of it. "I was nervous. I've never taken a woman to meet my grandmother."

She glanced at him from the corner of her eye as she dabbed the gloss onto her mouth. "Oh."

Don't get any ideas, he wanted to add. *It's not because I really like you.*

He more than really liked her, which was as far as his brain would let him follow that line of thought.

"I find that speaking with her helps me see more clearly when things get too monarchied up," he added.

"She's an anchor for you," she said. "Something away from all the Phokojoe performing and royalty business. I get that."

Johan wondered if she got that she was becoming the same for him. An anchor.

"She's not racist, is she?" Nya asked suddenly.

"Hmm. I would say no, though I guess

I've never *asked* her. She's not some sweet grandma type, but she's never said anything weird and she loves Thabiso."

"So she likes at least one fellow Thesoloian. Good to know."

"She hates most royalty, so it's something."

"Even Lukas?" Nya asked.

"Well, she's my papp's mamm, so she's not related to him, but she doesn't hate him." He glanced at her. "It's complicated. And my papp is . . . somewhere. Neither of us know. The best thing I can say for him is that he didn't come crawling back trying to get fame or money."

The car bounced as they traveled up the long, rutted road toward his grandmother's small house. Johan had always seen it as a witch's house, tucked away in the woods, at first because his grandmother was a bit mean, and then because he understood that witches were smart to live alone away from the rest of humanity.

"And before you ask, I've tried to get her a new house or at the very least new furniture and appliances, but she refuses. She's stubborn."

The wooden door in the small stone house opened and his grandmother stepped out, dusting her hands on the apron that covered her jeans and skimmed the top of her insulated boots. She had always looked like this, except now her flame-red hair had ceded entirely to silver, she was shorter and more wrinkled, and her motions were stiffer.

She didn't smile or wave, but she didn't slam the door shut.

Johan got out and walked over to Nya's side, helping her out just in time for an inquisitive pig to trot over and sniff her boot.

"Grand-mère, have you been giving the pigs free range again?" he asked.

"The pigs live here," she replied in a clipped tone. "You two are guests. Be respectful."

"Hallo," Nya said. "*Je bin* Nya."

His grandmother stared and then shifted into her slow, heavily accented English. "Are you my new granddaughter? I am too old to learn new names. I told Johan not to bring any woman here unless he was keeping her forever, so I assume you are wed?"

"Um, not yet?" Nya glanced at Johan, eyes wide.

"Well, you will be soon. I see the way my Jo-Jo is standing there like he just gave me a gift and is scared I won't like it." She looked at Johan and gave him something like a smile. "I like her. Relax, okay? Come eat. And Nya, you can call me Grand-mère."

She turned and went back into the house and Nya looked at him, a question in her eyes that he didn't know how to answer.

"Let's go," he said, ushering her into the warmth. When they were settled inside at the table in the small cozy dining room, his grandmother began bringing out dish after dish, pickles and cabbage and meats piled onto matching plates ringed with tiny painted flowers. Johan nodded toward a framed photo on a wooden side table.

"I was a very cute baby, thank you very much."

"That's why you brought me here, isn't it?" Nya asked, turning to look at the photo of him in a long white gown and surrounded by pillows, his big head crowned in flaming red wisps of hair.

"You besmirched my cuteness in front of everyone."

"You know I think you're cute." She booped his nose as if he were a kitten, and he scowled, pretending he didn't like it.

"Are you why people were asking me if I was expecting a great-grandchild?" his grandmother asked as she finally took her seat at the table, placing a tray with country bread, ham, and cheese on the table next to a plate of delicate cookies. She seemed to squint in the direction of Nya's stomach.

"Johan can explain," Nya said, reaching for a cookie, and then taking a bite. "This is delicious . . . Grand-mère."

The woman nodded but didn't smile. She was busy looking expectantly at Johan.

Johan heaved a sigh. "It appears that someone is trying to make people think badly of me, and by extension the royal family. To influence the referendum."

Grand-mère rolled her eyes. "Referendum. I am too old for this. I'm not fond of the von Brausteins, but what will they replace the monarchy with? It's all shit, whatever you call it, because I doubt we're heading for socialism with all these capitalist *kotzbrockens* funding the referendum."

Johan sipped his tea and glanced at Nya. "Grand-mère is a bit of an anarchist."

"Jah. We didn't have referendums in my day. If you didn't like a government, you toppled it. But kids these days, what can you expect?" She shook her head. "As long as they leave me and my *schweinne* in peace, I don't care."

"Are you saying you've toppled governments?" Nya asked.

"I said no such thing. I am but a humble farm girl." Her eyes twinkled. "But I have to say, Jo-Jo, I was talking to Herr Wagner before you arrived, and he was impressed with you."

"With me?" Johan looked at Nya and explained, "Herr Wagner is the neighbor who keeps Grand-mère updated on my exploits and how much he disapproves of them. My bad behavior is judged on the Wagner scale around here."

"Well, he was all set to vote no in the referendum, but he said he appreciates a royal who wasn't afraid to roll up his sleeves and get his fists bruised. He's reconsidering now."

"Really?" Johan ran a hand through his hair. "It's not as if I'm even part of the monarchy. I'm just —"

Grand-mère waved her hand through the air over the cookies, as if waving away an annoying insect.

"Enough of this, Johan. When people think of Liechtienbourg they think of two people first — your mother and then you. Stop doing her memory a disservice by saying you are not a part of the family she created, and acting like you don't carry on her legacy." She shook her head. "Just like your father, you know that? Always acting like he was some outsider who didn't fit in, when if he paid attention he would have seen —"

She slammed her mouth shut, shaking her head in annoyance as she rocked back and forth in her seat.

"Let me get a snowpack for your hand," she said suddenly, which seemed to mean she wasn't mad anymore but also regretted having shown emotion in front of guests and was searching for an excuse to leave.

"I'm fine, Grand-mère. Thank you." He bit into one of the gingerbread cookies she'd baked. "Well, I'm not exactly proud of my outburst but I guess it hasn't completely ruined everything."

Grand-mère scowled at his knuckles as he reached for a slice of ham. "Why did you do it?"

"I thought Nya and Lukas were in danger," he said.

"Nya and Lukas?" She looked at Nya and her features softened. "When is the wedding?"

"She seemed to like me," Nya said on the ride back. It was afternoon, but beginning to darken in this more wooded mountainous area.

"Better than your grandmother liked me," he said, expecting Nya to smile. But she looked deep in thought, as she had been since they'd left.

"Our grandparents think we're really engaged," she said quietly. "I hate knowing how upset they'll be if they find out we lied."

Johan had been thinking the same. He didn't lie to people he cared about, but he'd let Grand-mère believe Nya was really his. It had felt too good, too real. He could have taken Nya anywhere, but he'd wanted his grandmother to meet her, had wanted Nya to see this one part of his life that had nothing to do with being a tabloid prince. He'd wanted them to get along, and they'd spent a lunch laughing and talking, not even needing Johan to keep the conversation going.

It had felt like . . . a happy ending. And it had been a lie.

"Then don't let them find out," he said. His voice was all prickly wit, no gentleness — he could feel her need for comfort, for something more, but there was no way for him to safely respond without revealing too much.

Because underneath their happy meeting with Grand-mère was the unpleasant fact that he couldn't stop thinking of the heart-stopping fear that had lanced him when he saw Arschlocher looming over Nya. A million awful scenarios had flashed in his mind, each ending with loss.

Johan didn't think his heart could take that loss. He *knew* it couldn't. It was why he'd run from Nya from the start, and why he needed to run again.

"Okay," she said.

He focused on the road in front of him, on the clutch and the stick, anything but the unignorable fact that he didn't want to lose her, and yet he would.

"What will you do if the people vote you out?" she asked, somehow undeterred by his behavior.

"Well, I've had several offers to join those celebrity bachelor shows, and they pay well," he said flippantly. This was the moment where she learned he wasn't nice after all, despite her insistence. Where he picked up the kryptonite that was his affection for her and finally hurled it toward the sun. "It seems like a perfect match for my skill set."

"Yes. Very popular, those shows." This wasn't her normal cheeriness. It was forced. "You would bring in many ratings. And you are quite good at pretending to care for people."

"That I am." Johan wished that the opposition leader he'd fought earlier had gotten a punch in because he deserved one.

They'd gone from laughing comfortably in his grandmother's small dining room to this stifling tension in the car. This was why he didn't do love. This was why he shouldn't have followed her to that gazebo.

"I suppose I'll find a teaching job some-where," she said. "Maybe in America, or one of those other countries where the educational system is being torn down."

"Do you really want to teach?" he asked. "You won't shock very many people with that."

"Not as much as you want to be sur-rounded by women vying for your . . . eggplant emoji!" Nya turned so that she was facing out of the window, away from him. "What is your problem?"

Her anger was sudden and knocked his legs from under him like one of his grand-mère's rampaging pigs.

"I'm an ass," he said, then sighed. "I don't know what I'll do. My main priority is Lukas, and that's hard for me to talk about right now so I just —"

"You just used me as a target for anger that has nothing to do with me. Don't be mean to me because you are upset," she said, her voice harsh. "It's not fair to make other people pay for your emotions."

Johan was glad that his driving skills were impeccable; otherwise he might have skid-ded off the road.

He prided himself on being honest with those he didn't lie to, but he hadn't been honest with himself either. He wasn't being

384

fair to Nya; he hadn't tricked her into coming with him, but he'd certainly used their predicament to his advantage. He hadn't forced her to like him, but every time he sensed his own affection growing too much he tried to push her away. He'd told her that they would be friends with each other. He wasn't being a good friend, at the very least.

"I think you'd make a great teacher," he said. "I also have lots of connections at non-profits all over the world. Lots of them deal with education. I can ask around if you want."

She didn't respond and because he knew her, he knew why.

"I apologize. I promise never to take my anger or fear out on you again," he said, then reconsidered. "I guess that's extreme, since I'm human. I promise to try my hardest not to use the defense mechanisms I've usually relied on in relationships."

"Defense mechanisms? So relationships are a battle?" She was mimicking his question from the first night in Liechtienbourg.

"The most dangerous battle," he said, shifting gears as they approached a winding road. "Losing land or power or riches is nothing compared to some losses."

Her hand came to rest on top of his on

the gearshift. "You're a lot more like your brother than I'd realized. Both of you can be real jerks when you're scared."

He smiled faintly. "You know, you might be on to something."

"I told you. Official Johan Expert, at your service."

They drove on in silence, and though tension still lingered in the car, mostly it was because they both seemed absorbed in their own thoughts. As the castle rose up in the distance, Johan wondered about the man who had approached Nya and Lukas. Why was Arschlocher even there? What had he wanted, if he wasn't trying to hurt them, which would have been a terrible political move?

Now, with only the sound of the tires on the road, Johan again felt that nudge that something wasn't quite right about this. He wondered if he would figure it out before everything fell apart.

CHAPTER 19

Nya knew what the envelope, delivered express Royal Thesolo Mail to her door in Liechtienbourg, would contain.

She was already irritable after a night spent tossing and turning alone in her bed, trying not to think about the lie she was living with Johan and his words in the car the previous day.

She should have ripped up the letter without reading and mailed back the pieces. Instead, she opened it, some part of her curious to see what new low her father had sunk to and another simply too silly to stop loving the man, no matter how much he'd hurt her.

My Dear Daughter,

I am still hurt beyond measure over the betrayal you have perpetrated. You know that when a child's soul is in the clutches of evil, it disturbs the rest of those on the ancestral plain. If you do not care about hurting me, that is fine. But would you disturb the eternal rest of your own mother? Would you not grant her peace?

Your mother was a good traditional woman. She knew to listen to her husband, to put the wishes of her family first, and I do not understand how such an unfeeling, unnatural child could truly be hers. One who would do as she wishes with no care for her parents, living or dead. One who publicly debases herself with a man who would use her and discard her, while everyone laughs at her foolishness.

Come home, my daughter. Make things right. I would see you before I die, and I would know that you have stopped shaming your mother and me.

Nya stared at the letter. She calmly put it down and took a photo of it, then sent it to her group chat. She saw Ledi's response, This motherfucker, before she ran to the bathroom. She wasn't sick, though she thought she would be. Her skin felt clammy and she wanted to cry but sat on the floor fighting nausea instead. She was supposed to be getting ready for a solo excursion in

Liechtienbourg, to an artisans' village, but she considered canceling. It didn't matter anyway — this was all just pretend, wasn't it?

Unnatural child. Everyone laughs at her.

She didn't know why she was so upset. She'd wanted a reaction from her father and she'd gotten one — the truth that she was a silly, useless girl who brought shame to her family.

She gripped her head in her hands and tried to remember that her father was a liar and he'd spent years passing his lies on to her. These weren't her thoughts battering her so hard that she couldn't get up. They were the hooks her father had embedded in her heart over the course of her life, waiting until he had opportunity to tug at them to reel her back in.

Her phone rang and she jumped, certain it was her father, then remembered he was in prison and she had any numbers originating from that facility blocked.

When she reached the phone, she saw it was Naledi.

"Hey."

She waited for Naledi to ask if she was okay, but she didn't.

"Look, I think you know not to believe your father, but I did want to point something out because, to be blunt, he's fucked with your head for your whole life and there are some things you might not be up to speed on."

Nya took a deep breath and fought back tears — not at Naledi's words, but at the fact that someone had finally said them out loud. Her father had fucked with her head her entire life. It was okay if she sometimes got reeled back in.

"Like what?" Nya asked, voice shaking.

"Like, this bullshit about your mom being some demure, respectable woman," Ledi said, clearly incensed. "Look, do you know how our moms and Ramatla met?"

"No, actually," Nya said, sitting on the edge of her bed. Outside the window, snow was starting to fall over the slanted roofs and spires of the old town. "I thought they met in school."

"Yeah. They met in high school. Apparently your mom noticed Alehk being a jerk to my mom after school one day and threw an apricot at him."

"What?" Nya sat down on the office chair.

"Yeah. Hit him right upside the head, and hard, because she was the captain of the cricket team."

"She was?" Nya grabbed a pillow and held it to herself.

"Apparently, she told him he was a bully and basically to go kick rocks, and your dad fell in love," Ledi said. "From what Ramatla told me, your mother was always outgoing and he'd been totally head over heels because of it."

Ledi paused. "I'm not excusing him, but even the queen seemed to agree that her death changed him for the worse. So all of this 'your mom was a meek and traditional woman and would be ashamed' stuff is bullshit."

"But . . . he always told me that she was good and respectful and listened when he spoke." He'd always used her mother's goodness to contrast whatever she'd done that he'd considered bad. "He told me all the time. All the time."

The room spun around Nya a little and she sat on the floor again.

"Maybe he thinks that. It's been thirty years, and maybe he's completely forgotten what she was like." Ledi sighed. "Maybe it hurts to remember. But the bottom line is that he's wrong. Even if he wasn't wrong, you aren't your mother. What she was like has nothing to do with who you are now."

"He completely erased her," Nya said. "He created this fake version of her just so he could manipulate me."

It struck her then, the true heinousness of her father's crimes against her. It wasn't just that he'd manipulated her, poisoned her, made her think she was weak — he'd stolen her mother from her. He'd turned his wife's memory into the same fragile, hollow figurine of a saint that he'd wanted to nest his daughter inside of.

Anger surged in her. Nya would shatter that false idol.

"I hope — I hope he does die! I hope he dies alone and that when he passes on, Mother's spirit denies him and he is forever alone!" She squeezed her eyes shut against her tears, her face frozen in a grimace. Her words were miserable and phlegmy but she wasn't ashamed because she knew Ledi understood. Ledi was the first person who had reached out a hand through the bars of her cage. And though Nya had grown tired of people asking her if she was okay, Ledi was the first person who had asked and hadn't simply gone along with her when she said she was fine.

"It's okay," Ledi said. "You've earned the right to be angry. Just remember this anytime he tries to fuck with you, okay? He's a damn liar."

"Yes," Nya said softly. It was the same thing Lukas had warned her about with Johan, and the same title Johan had proudly claimed.

Johan had pushed her away yesterday with his talk of the dating reality show — like her father, he was an expert at finding the soft spots where even the most glancing blows would hurt like hell. But unlike her father, he seemed determined to please her. To make sure that no one hurt her, including himself.

Still, she would have to be careful. She'd started this with the idea that she was playing a real-life dating simulation game, but it was more than that now. He'd been right about relationships being a battle, and hers was mostly with herself. Could she trust her instincts? Was she just moving from one man who would control her with his lies to another?

She didn't think so, but part of her own battle was being sure that she didn't fall into any traps, even if they were ones laid by her own past.

She hurriedly got ready and then left to meet up with Greta, who would be taking her to the artisan village.

When she got to the lobby of the castle, Lukas was there instead. He was dressed in a peacoat over his conventional suit, but his lips had a diamond glint to them.

"Hallo." He waved a little shyly.

"Hey," she replied. "Where is Greta?"

"She apparently has to look into some threats? Which is kind of frightening. But I'm to go with you instead, if that's okay."

"Are you sure you'll be safe? If there are threats, maybe we should hold off." She gave Lukas a measured look. "After all, your brother won't be there to help this time, though you didn't seem to appreciate it."

"I don't think the threats are physical," Lukas said. "And besides, we'll have bodyguards. Also —" he shifted from one foot to another "— I kind of need to get out of the castle. I've been pretty much on lockdown since I was brought home from school, and yesterday I couldn't even leave my wing because of the Arschlocher incident. I go back soon, until the referendum, but I thought it would be nice if we could take this trip today? Together?"

Nya was still calming herself from her father's letter, but she liked the boy, and she wasn't the only one in turmoil.

"That would be fun," she said. "It will be good to have someone I know with me, and I like spending time with you."

"Really?" Lukas blushed a bit as he opened the door for her to pass through. "Even though I steal your makeup and yell at my brother?"

They hopped into the backseat of the car and the driver pulled off.

"Well, I gave you that makeup, and I think maybe that's related to why you've been yelling at your brother."

Lukas's expression was completely calm, except for his eyes — he wasn't as good at this as Johan. Nya had remembered something one of her fellow students at her grad school program had told her and decided to put it to use. She didn't want to meddle, but she didn't want Lukas to think she'd forgotten what he'd told her by accepting the lip gloss.

"By the way, not to be awkward, but my pronouns are she/her. In case you were wondering." She pulled her phone out from her pocket to check the time, giving Lukas space to answer but not pressure.

"Interesting," Lukas said. "Actually. Now that you've awkwardly mentioned it. I got into a fight at school. There was this smug American kid, Jaden, and he kept going on and on in our gender studies class about how pronouns other than *she* and *he* were fake news, or something. And I disagreed. And after class he kept getting on my case about why I even cared so much, so I punched him."

"Well, violence is not in good taste, but sometimes punch is what's on the menu."

Lukas burst out laughing at her terrible joke, and Nya could feel the relief in his laughter. "It was really cool because after I punched him, my teacher asked if I'd been so upset because *I* wanted to go by *they.* And I said yes."

Lukas glanced at her.

"Okay. So they/them?"

Lukas's eyes were wide and they gave a hard nod.

Nya smiled. "Done. Do you want me to share that with others or . . . ?"

"No! No, it's fine if at home I go by *he.*"

Nya took a deep breath, remembering when Johan had called her Naya and how it had upset her. This was very different, and she was sure more hurtful than Lukas was letting on. "It's fine if you say it's fine, but you might feel better being called what you want to be called."

They waved their hand. "I'll tell my father and Johan soon. When the time is right."

Then the car pulled up to the artisan village and Lukas jumped out to run around the car to open Nya's door. "Seriously. Please don't tell Johan."

Stress lines had formed around their eyes and they gazed at her intensely, as if wondering whether she could be trusted.

"I won't," she said. "But I think that when you do, you might be surprised at how he responds. He's not close-minded."

"You saw what happened the other day," Lukas said. "He was so *mad*. He's never been mad at me before."

"Have you ever yelled at him before?" she asked gently.

"No." Lukas's mouth was pulled down in a frown and she could see the slightest tremble of their lips. They were still a child, really, and they were facing pressures she could never imagine.

Nya stepped out of the car and placed a hand on their shoulder. Lukas sighed at her touch. "I'm sorry. I know what it's like not wanting to disappoint your family. But . . . if you tell Johan outright and he still gets mad? He's not the man I think he is. And that will be his problem, not yours. Now let's go look at clay pots."

Lukas seemed relieved at the change in subject, and Nya made sure to keep them entertained during the visit. When they'd both made their rounds and been photographed by Hans, Phillippe, and Krebs, Nya even managed to get Lukas to take a selfie.

"Can you AirDrop it to me?" they asked when they were safely back in the car, and

Nya handed the phone over without even pretending to know how to use the AirDrop function.

She wondered what Johan was doing. She hadn't texted him all day, and he'd only told her that his day would be busy. It didn't matter, she supposed, but she didn't look forward to spending another night alone.

"I hope my brother is as good as you think he is," Lukas said as they handed back the phone.

"Do you really think he's not?" Nya asked.

"I think . . . sometimes he forgets that he's not Jo-Jo. And that not everyone wants to be a Jo-Jo. I feel like he's stopped being Johan, even with me," Lukas said quietly. "Maybe it's different with you. I hope so."

Nya wasn't sure what she hoped anymore. So instead of hoping, she pulled up Portia's Instagram account and showed Lukas the new eyeshadow Portia had been sent to try out, and promised she'd get Portia to send them a sample packet at school.

CHAPTER 20

Phokojoe the trickster god was observant,
in the way of foxes. He had great big ears
to hear all, and eyes that saw in darkness
or in light. He would watch the people of
the village near his lair from afar. He
watched as the village grew, and more
humans arrived. He watched them for
many moons, creeping closer every night.
They intrigued him; he had been alone for
so very long. One evening, he saw a man
walking on the road that led through the
village, and stepped out in front of the human, hoping to become friends with one
of the strange creatures he'd grown so
fond of. The man shouted and waved his
walking stick, telling Phokojoe to leave
him. This happened again and again,
every time he encountered one of the
humans, until one day, Phokojoe asked,
"What is it that you desire most in the
world?" The human stopped yelling. He

answered, "A fine hat." Phokojoe turned himself into a hat, and the man forgot his fear as he picked up the hat from the road. Phokojoe understood then that the only way to end his loneliness would be to change himself without cease.

— From Phokojoe the Trickster God

After a day spent making the rounds with journalists to explain his fight and an evening in meetings with Greta and the royal security team, Johan showered and collapsed into bed. His public displays of Jo-Jo-ness were usually short-lived, but he'd been on a charm offensive for days, and his outburst and scuffle had taken more out of him than he'd realized — and so had not spending time with Nya. He'd felt off all day, and then he'd received an ominous email from Portia.

Hey!

Glad to hear Nya is being treated well. Keep it up! You seem a decent friend, and I'd hate to kill you. I checked out this FloupGelee person and the IP address is coming from Lukas's school. I'm guessing it's some kid he doesn't get along with? Maybe the kid he got into a fight with? I guess you can look into it more, but that's as much info as I could get. A few of the other accounts had the same IP address, so they were probably sock puppets for this same loser.

That comforted Johan a bit, knowing it was just some teenage brat, but something about it still bothered him.

There was a knock at the door connecting his and Nya's rooms and he rolled onto his back, trying to muster up another burst of suave playboy prince.

He came up empty.

"Come in," he croaked. He'd been planning on going to her, but frankly, his head was a mess and he'd been worried what he'd say, since the only thing he could think of when it came to her was *I want you so badly it hurts,* which for him could easily turn into *I want you so badly but I won't be hurt again.* Not exactly casual and low-key to match the current tone of their fake engagement with benefits. He'd also wondered if maybe she wouldn't want to see him; she'd stayed in her room the past two nights, the chimes of her phone going off.

The door swung open harder than usual, slamming into the wall.

"Sorry," she said, cringing a bit as she

closed it slowly, as if to compensate for her entrance. And what an entrance; instead of her usual T-shirt and shorts, she was wearing a silky knee-length black negligee with lacy bits at the décolletage.

She stood against the door after shutting it, apprehensive.

Johan brushed his hair from his eyes, the better to see what she needed from him. Her chin was up and her hands were on her hips, as if she were presenting herself to him for inspection, the desire for validation as transparent as the lace on her lingerie. He ran his gaze over her body appreciatively before letting out a low whistle.

"Madame Flemard?" he asked.

"Ouay," she replied with a curtsy, and Johan grinned.

She came to the side of his bed, holding on to one of the wooden posts instead of sliding under the sheets.

"How was your day?" he asked.

"It was good. I talked to my grandparents. Got in contact with some people about jobs."

Something inside of him crumpled, but he flashed her a blinding smile. "Oh. Good! Good. *Jah.*"

"I'm tired of things being weird," she said. "I don't like being mad at you."

"I don't like it either," he said. "So I'll stop acting like an ass and making you mad. Problem solved."

She smiled, a tentative tilt of her mouth that wasn't what he'd grown accustomed to, but was a start.

"Do you want company tonight?" she asked.

Johan lay back on the bed. "Well, that depends. Is it you, or is a reporter waiting on the other side of the door to ask me about the fight for the hundredth time?"

"Silly. It's me. Just me." The soft lamplight cupped the curves of her body, and the curve of her shy smile, and Johan felt that lurching pain in his chest once again. For an instant he considered telling her no, telling her this was all over.

He didn't bother. He was already going to be hurt; anything that he told himself otherwise was simply damage control, an inability to comprehend the depth of the hole she would leave in his life.

Ridiculous. He'd spent so long running from love at full tilt that when he'd finally tripped and fell, his momentum made it swift and unstoppable. She was right. It *was* her. Just her.

"I'll go," Nya said and began to turn away from the bed. Johan had been so caught up

403

in his thoughts he'd never responded to her.

"Wait!" He sat up and held his arms out to her. "Sorry, I'm a bit out of it. I want your company tonight and I wanted it the last two nights, too. Come here."

He beckoned with both of his hands.

Her teeth showed as relief shaped her mouth into a smile, and then her knees were on the mattress, then her hands, that lacy décolletage cupping her swaying breasts and reminding Johan that he should have moved closer to her instead of making her crawl across the bed to him.

There was a particularly determined look on her face as she approached, and finally the negligee and her shyness and her heated looks clicked for him.

Oh là là.

"Are you here to seduce me, Nya?"

She gave him the look she'd practiced in the back of the car in Njaza, the one that meant *I want to climb you like a redwood. "Ouay."*

Johan was only able to get out a deep "hrim," and then she sat up quickly and tugged down the top of her negligee, revealing the beautiful globes of her breasts.

He swallowed hard. "Nya?"

"We've only been focusing on me during our time together. I'm not going to look a gift fox in the mouth, and I appreciate you taking things slowly, but . . ."

Her hands went to cup her breasts, and he thought she was hiding them, but no. She teased her own nipples as she arched her back, as if in offering, and desire slammed down onto him like an anvil dropped from the sky.

She'd been sure of what she liked and didn't like from the first time he'd touched her, but this was a new directness in her.

She gave him that smoldering look as she lay back down and began shimmying to tug up the negligee, but then her hands stopped moving and she threw back her head, giggling.

"This played out much more seductively in my head. I don't really know what I'm doing," she said, tears of helpless laughter in her eyes. "This always goes so much more smoothly in films. I feel kind of ridiculous."

The sound of her laughter wound around Johan's heart, and his cock, too, and squeezed. There was no fear in her — a bit of awkwardness, yes, but she met his eye as if she knew that he would never make fun of her. That he would share in the moment with her.

She trusted him, as she had from the start.

"You're doing just fine," he said, his grin

405

wide and real despite his fatigue.

"I'd be doing better if you helped me," she said, and Johan didn't need any further prodding.

"What do you want me to do?" He asked because he needed to know, and because he was selfish and what *he* wanted was to hear her say naughty things.

Her gaze dropped to the bulge outlined by his sweatpants. "I've only felt you. I want to see you. Hold you."

Oh là là là là.

"We'll get to that."

He reached out and gripped her leg just above the knee, then smoothed his hand up her thigh. When he reached the hem of her negligee, he pushed up, gathering it with a hook of his thumb and carrying it up as his hand splayed on her stomach.

He could feel the flutter of her quick breaths against his palm and her heartbeat against his fingertips, but in her eyes there was nothing but certainty — and he'd give her nothing but pleasure.

It struck him then, that he'd never told her something.

"You're beautiful, Nya." He let his other hand trace over the negligee, then up through the valley between her breasts, seeing how she shivered as they grazed her neck before cupping her face. "I don't think I've said that before because, well, sometimes I forget to say things that are obvious."

The certainty in her eyes dimmed and she looked away, but then quickly met his gaze again. "Thanks. And you're nice."

This was why he'd made the biggest mistake of his life in inviting her this close to him. He'd expected her to talk about his looks, too, if she returned his compliment. It was easy for people, the go-to, and she clearly thought he was attractive, but that wasn't why she was in his bed. She thought he was *nice,* and she wouldn't let him or anyone else think otherwise.

"I can be," he admitted. "To people I care about."

Her eyes widened and before she could ask him anything he leaned down and kissed her. He licked into her mint-sweet mouth, his right hand sliding down from her stomach to the V of curls and his middle finger seeking out her slick clit. She gasped as he began to rub, her hands coming up to his shoulders and gripping him hard and her hips lifting upward.

She shifted her body a bit, sliding up on the bed, and he gentled his touch until she had repositioned herself beneath his hand, exactly where she wanted him to touch her. She was a woman who knew what she wanted.

She wants you.

He increased the pressure, massaging deep circles over her clit as her fingernails dug into his shoulders and her moans feathered his lips.

"That feels good," she whispered. "You know exactly how to touch me. Can you — can you feel how wet I am?"

Johan almost came right then because he knew she was saying these things for him. She'd asked him what he liked before, and she'd remembered, and now each time they came together she pushed herself further from her comfort zone.

She was slick beneath his hand, and he adjusted it to slide his ring finger into her hot opening, groaning as she squeezed around him.

"Yes. You're wet and hot and tight, Nya."

She shuddered and thrust her hips up hard — she pushed herself because she liked dirty talk, too.

He moved his mouth, kissing along her jawline and scraping his teeth along her neck. When one of her hands left his shoulder he barely noticed — until it slipped into the waistband of his sweatpants and gripped his cock lightly.

"Does this feel good?" she asked as she began stroking him, her hand soft and warm.

"Yes," he choked out.

"Tell me what you want me to do." She nipped his ear — something he'd done to her before — and Johan shuddered hard.

"Squeeze me as you stroke."

Her fingers flexed and then her grip firmed around his shaft. Her movement was jerky but there was no hesitation. "Like this?"

"Yes, like that. Just like that, Nya." His hips bucked as pleasure shot up his spine.

"Oh goddess," she moaned, her hand still-ing as her back arched up off the bed and her channel clenched his fingers.

Then her other hand came down to tug at the sweatpants, pushing them down to his knees. He leaned back a bit to give her space, and so he saw the way her gaze locked onto his erection.

A slow smile spread across her face. "And now is where I will tell you that *you* are beautiful."

Johan felt himself actually flush at the compliment, and he made to retort but it was cut off by a groan as she resumed her motion without the impediment of fabric and elastic, her palm gliding smoothly up and down from the base to the head, her rhythm matching that of his own hand against her.

After that, she didn't talk anymore and neither did he. He couldn't — all of his energy was focused on fighting the churning pressure for release in his balls and urging her toward her own orgasm.

He pushed another finger inside of her, twisting his wrist as he thrust into her so that his thumb could massage her clit, and she broke without warning, her inner walls quaking around his fingers and her pleasure flowing over his knuckles.

Her cries of pleasure bounced around the walls and high ceiling of his room, and her teeth pressed into his palm as she turned her mouth into his hand to muffle them, but Johan observed these things from a distance as his own orgasm smashed into him, hunching him over as he thrust into her hand.

He collapsed onto the bed beside her, sweatpants still around his knees, cheeks hot, and hand tingling from where her teeth had grazed him. He'd always thought of her teeth as cute, endearing, but now each time she smiled he would remember the pleasant sharpness of them and her muffled cries.

She stretched, making a sound suspiciously close to "hrim" as she did it, then nestled down against him. He looked at her, negligee bunched around her waist and braids fanned out on the pillow behind her.

"You should sleep in my bed from now on," he said because that was the first coherent thought that came to him. "You don't have to knock or ask me. I want you here."

From now on. That sounded like a long time — it sounded like the future — but she was leaving and soon.

She nodded.

"It's a very comfortable bed." Her hand began to slip down his chest and over his abs. "How is your shower? Can we try that, too?"

He scooped her up and was on his feet in what had to be some kind of record time.

"Comme tu willst," he said, kissing her temple just before he nudged the bathroom door open with his toe. He didn't think about how his heart felt too large or his whole body ached for her. He focused on *her* body, and what he would do to give her pleasure again and again.

For now, because now was the only time he was granting himself with her.

She stretched, making a sound deliciously close to 'Brrrr' as she ran a... then
turned and smiled at his He slid... up...

CHAPTER 21

Nya could feel people's eyes on her as she
walked through the lobby of the castle
toward the car waiting to bring her to the
crèche for a photo op with some children. It
was the fifth school she'd visited after having grown tired of sitting around the castle
— as much as she enjoyed the laughter,
caresses, and caring that marked her time
with Johan, she'd wanted to escape her
father for a reason. She wouldn't become
an extension of or accessory for any man,
even while pretending to be his fiancée.

It was odd, how she'd grown used to life
in Liechtienbourg so quickly. She liked the
food. She liked the people she met in the
street. She even liked the sound of the
language, now that she'd heard it day in and
day out for the past two weeks. The city was
just small enough to make her feel comfortable, and not so large that she ever panicked
and felt lost in a crowd. She felt . . . good.

She felt just right, even now, without Johan at her side.

Before she would have shrank away from the way people stared, but she met their gazes with a smile and a nod. She didn't have to remind herself to hold her chin high or not to be afraid and it wasn't just because of the two bodyguards flanking her or Greta at her side. Her clipped wings had started to grow back, and at least a few of the feathers were fire bright.

She wondered if Johan passed her some of his over-confidence when he kissed her and touched her each night when she went to his bed. As much as she loved his hands and his mouth on her body, she enjoyed the actual sleeping just as much.

Johan hugged her tightly as they slept, as if she were his protection from the evils of the world, and sometimes she woke up holding him in the same way. She'd never slept more soundly, and it hurt to think of what an empty bed would feel like once they called off their engagement, so she tried not to.

She thought of the sun blinking out instead.

Ahead of her, in the lobby of the crèche, a group of small children were assembled. As in the previous schools she'd visited, the children came from all ethnic backgrounds, the results of Liechtienbourg's welcoming of refugees as well as its imperialist history.

The three kids in the center, boys with skin from golden tan to dark brown, held up a sign with *WËLLKOMM* written in rainbow letters and the small handprints of the class's children pressed around it on the white poster board.

"Oh, aren't they adorable?" Nya asked.

"I suppose," Greta said cheerily. "If you enjoy small cute animals that leave chaos in their wake."

Nya laughed. She knew the woman didn't mean it in a bad way.

"Wëllkomm!" the children called out, and she responded in the same way. She'd been practicing basic Liechtienbourgish in order to avoid being pelted by waffles, and because some part of her felt a connection to this weird little country that was so different from but also so similar to her own.

She went about the routine that she had at every school — she took a tour of the classroom while chatting with the teachers and their support staff, then read a book to the children with her best Liechtienbourger accent. She read the same story every time, one she'd taken from Johan's bedside bookshelf to practice her language. It was about an evil witch who learns to love the deer who keeps eating the medicinal herbs she plants in her garden.

At the end of the reading, the children crowded around to take a photo, and Nya handed her phone to Greta. "Can you take a few for me?"

Greta snapped the photos, and as Nya hugged the children goodbye, a little girl with skin the same dark brown as Nya's own held on for much longer than the others. She said something, but too low and with the gap-toothed lisp of a child, making it difficult for Nya to understand.

Her teacher grinned. "She says that she asked her mamm if she can wear her hair in braids, too, because princesses have braids."

"Oh." Nya's heart filled with an unexpected joy, but also sadness. She hadn't thought of this aspect of her and Johan's soon-to-be breakup, which would make the headlines. She hadn't thought of it really because, technically, Johan wasn't a prince. But no one paid that much mind at this point — his reign as playboy prince was something so many people saw as just as valid as any other type of royalty. How many girls looked at Nya and saw their own princess potential in her? How many would be disappointed by this game she'd decided to play?

"Well, whatever hairstyle you wear can be a princess hairstyle, because anyone can be a princess," Nya said, knowing it was a bad reply, but completely at a loss for how to respond. Giving the child an affirmative was further into the realm of lying than she was willing to go.

The girl just smiled, tightening the clamp of guilt around Nya.

She patted the girl's head and then stood, walking over to Greta.

"Here you go," Greta said as she handed back her phone. "We should get back to the castle."

She was giving Nya a strange look and when Nya looked at the phone, there was a message from Portia in view on the screen.

Portia: Guys, I have to tell you about this new face mask I'm using. The main ingredient is SNAIL SLIME okay I know that sounds gross and I feel bad for the snails who died so my skin could glow, but my face is SO SOFT.

"Oh, please excuse my friend," she said. "Friend? What friend, I didn't see anything." Greta smiled but it looked forced. She appreciated the assistant's lie, but she was clearly upset. Maybe Greta was a vegan?

"Shall we return?"

"We shall."

The rest of the ride back was spent in frigid silence from Greta, who apparently was a lover of all creatures great and small and now thought Nya was friends with unrepentant snail killers and would hold it against her.

Nya frowned, then unlocked her phone to see if Johan had sent a message from the meeting he'd attended with Linus to make amends for punching the opposition leader. He hadn't texted, but Hanjo had.

The time for freedom from this outdated institution is near. I know you've doubted if what I'm doing is right, but I'm so lucky to have you by my side as I work to dismantle this oppressive system.<3

She'd missed the message and would have to restart from the previous save point.

This was the biggest difficulty of the game, which was relatively straightforward apart from the timing of the messages. It operated in the same way a real relationship did. How much time were you willing to put into it? How anxiously were you await-ing calls and texts from your beloved?

This would be the fourth time she'd had to restart the game since she'd arrived. Once she'd started sleeping with Johan, she'd found it rude to creep off in the middle of the night to flirt with a virtual version of him. But she'd already spent too much money buying the ability to respond to old messages, and she simply didn't have the desire to play anymore. It wasn't that she didn't want to keep playing her games, but this one felt creepy now. It felt like cheating.

She closed the app without answering. She was done with *One True Prince* — she wouldn't like it if Johan had some virtual version of the real-life her that he carried in his pocket. Maybe she would revisit Rog-nath instead.

"Have you heard from Johan?" she asked Greta. She couldn't help but remember his reaction when Greta had mentioned the opera that first day, and wondered if he was still unsure about going. It couldn't be because he didn't want to be seen with her, could it? Not after the last two weeks?

"No." The woman didn't look at her.

"Is there some reason you're behaving rudely?" She had tolerated quite enough rudeness in her life.

"Am I?" Greta asked. "I just didn't want to talk to you, so I didn't."

"Oh, um. I get that," Nya said.

"If you'd like me to talk, I can ask, what are your intentions toward Johan?"

Nya paused. "I'm not sure that's any of your business."

"No, I suppose not. But I've been his assistant for years and I've never seen him like this. Ever."

Nya's heart swelled in her chest. Maybe her dreams weren't so foolish after all. Maybe —

"I don't want to think badly of you, and I'm not going to invade your privacy, but I have to tell you that he shouldn't have his heart broken. It wouldn't be fair, after all he's been through. So you wanted to talk? Consider this a warning if you're up to something, stop being up to something." Greta's serious expression faded then, and she sat back in the seat with relief. "Ah, I'm so glad you asked me to talk. It's good to have things in the open, *jah*? I've been working on this in counseling with my boyfriend, but it helps on the job, too!"

"I don't know why you think I would hurt him, but I appreciate you looking after his well-being," Nya said. She didn't know whether to be pissed off or elated or both.

Greta's phone rang then.

"Oh, it's Jo-Jo."

Nya looked at her phone and wondered why he hadn't texted.

"Hallo? Ah. Vraiment?" Greta had her serious expression on again, and for the next couple of minutes listened and nodded, then responded in rapid-fire Liechtienbourgish.

Her gaze slid to Nya. "It seems that the evening papers are alleging that Johan has been embezzling money into an offshore account."

Nya frowned. "Johan wouldn't do such a thing."

She didn't think Johan was capable of anything so nefarious, but then again, her father had been doing the same. People would do a lot for money and power.

Even participate in a fake romance to get people to vote for their family in a referendum.

No.

Nya felt anxiety swell in her chest, not at the idea of Johan using her, but at the possibility that she'd never be able to believe he wasn't, he or any other man.

"Of course, he wouldn't," Greta said.

"Someone is clearly trying to smear his name."

"What will we do?"

"We?" Greta raised a brow. "The plans for tonight have changed. Instead of the pre-show PR meeting with you and Johan posing for photos, there will be a press conference where he explains what's going on. No press for you tonight, since we can't control what people will ask."

"That's fine. I just want his name cleared."

"Right," Greta said flatly, turning her attention to her phone. She hopped out of the car when they pulled up to the palace and Nya made her way back to her room to get ready for the opera.

Something was nagging her about this situation. It was the same feeling she'd had when her father had been so kind and solicitous to Ledi, trying to win her to his side while plying her with tea he knew would hurt her. Nya hadn't known for sure, but she'd suspected — and she'd been right.

Nya had protected her cousin as best she could then, and she was stronger now. She would try to figure this out and protect Johan, too. It may have been nothing, and Nya wasn't always sure what worries were real and which were plain fear after being told to ignore her own thoughts for her entire life, but she knew there was something more to this. She would think on it, and in the meantime, she would make sure Johan had a good night.

CHAPTER 22

As word spread, all of the other villagers sought Phokojoe out. He would turn into what they desired, and then lure them into his lair, but he found something even sadder than being lonely — that not just any human would do. Some spoke too much, or too little. Some made wild demands, and others hurled curses at him. He always released them after two weeks, and was always glad to see them go. There was one maiden in the village whom Phokojoe had rarely seen. She was kept locked up in the house of her father, who treated her like a rare and fragile flower. On the day she finally came to him, he waited to hear her desire, but instead she laid down a bowl of freshly cooked stew for him and then scurried back home. Phokojoe looked after her, sniffing the food warily. When he tasted it, it was the finest offering he'd ever received.

— From *Phokojoe the Trickster God*

The last time Johan had given a press conference of this scope was when pictures of his bare ass had shown up in newspapers. He'd explained how it was a private moment, and how he had shamed the people of Liechtienbourg with his bad decisions.

Of course, he'd known a paparazzo was there. Why else would he be walking around bottomless? It was around Lukas's thirteenth birthday, when the press had started to get more insistent about prying into the boy's privacy. So Johan had given up his. And he felt more exposed now, forced to provide the information he'd managed to keep secret for so long.

It was just more evidence that in this world of vultures, everything eventually became carrion.

"Are you ready?" Greta whispered beside him, looking tense. She'd been acting a bit strangely since she'd returned from the school with Nya, but he assumed she was out of sorts from having someone rifling through their business affairs.

Directly after the presser he had to survive *Rusalka* in the royal box. The referendum was in two days. Nya would leave him.

424

He wasn't ready for anything.

He nodded and adjusted his bow tie.

"Looking good, Jo-Jo!" That was Krebs, of course. Johan pointed at him. Winked. Tried to feel as carefree as he was acting.

"This will be quick because the opera waits for no one, and Johan believes the arts are integral to society. We will begin by addressing the allegations that appeared in the daily papers today," Greta said. "It has been alleged that Johan has been engaging in shady business practices, running a shell company to hide his funds from the taxpayers and increase his own wealth."

"Are the allegations true?" someone called out.

"Of course, they're not true," Johan said with a calm he didn't feel one bit. He flashed a charming smile. "Okay, press conference over."

A ripple of laughter passed through the assembled journalists.

"The reports are completely false and I am open to an independent investigation to prove so. Thank you."

"The latest polls show that the public has lost significant confidence in the von Braustein name, and that your recent actions may have cemented the end of the monarchy." Well, the guy from the *Looking*

Glass was getting right to it. "What are your thoughts?"

"Thoughts? If I'm solely responsible for the downfall of a kingdom that is hundreds of years old, I hope they at least use a good selfie of me in the history books."

More laughter. Good.

Another journalist raised their hand. "Do you have any explanation as to why you were hiding monetary transactions using a shell company?"

"I *wasn't* hiding them," Johan said. "I wasn't publicizing them, but most people don't. And I had good reason for that."

He smiled, even though he thought he might be sick. Johan had always been okay with the performances he'd had to put on. They'd never been *him.* But with Nya, and now with this, he was having to reveal parts of himself that he'd wanted to keep hidden. Personal things. The only things that separated Johan from Jo-Jo.

At this point, he wished he *had* been engaging in criminal activity.

"The accounts and the secrecy are connected to something private and unrelated to the royal family, which is why I didn't feel a need to share them."

"A trust fund for your secret children?" another reporter called out, and Greta had

had enough.

She leaned toward her mic. "Charity. That is what the funds are used for."

Johan looked around at the reporters, taking in the disappointment clear on some of their faces as silence filled the room. He pulled the mic back over to himself. "It's a network of charities I've been funding that I didn't want linked with me or my more unsavory undertakings," he added. "Many of you here have reported on me for years, so you understand that my name isn't exactly associated with respectability."

"Are you serious, man?" Krebs asked. "Like, helping kids and stuff?"

"Yes. Greta has posted all the necessary disclosures on my website and will be providing you with the link. Everything you need will be there. *Merci!*"

He stood, ignoring as they clamored for more information.

He'd almost made it to the door when Phillipe's voice rang out, breaking with emotion. "Are you saying that you've secretly been carrying on your mother's legacy?"

A hush fell over the assembled journalists. Mentioning his mother to him had been verboten, an unspoken rule, but one that most of the journalists who knew him had respected. Anyone who didn't immediately lost access to him.

Johan didn't force a smile — it was enough not to grimace. "Thank you, everyone. Any further questions will be answered in my memoirs, set to be published fifty years after I die."

He winked, though it was a lackluster one, and walked casually out of the room, even though he badly wanted to run.

He tried not to think as he strode past the security guards and down the hallway that led back to a private wing of the palace.

He could vaguely make out the shapes of people around him, but all of his attention was focused on the riot of emotion inside of him. His heartbeat filled his ears, but he heard Lukas's voice from the parlor, where he'd left him with his tutor.

"It looks like you charmed them as usual," his brother called out. "Social media is blowing up with news of how wonderful you are."

Johan gritted his teeth and kept walking. He hated this. Everyone talking about his good deeds. Everyone making him out to be some kind of saint, like his mother had been. He had wanted to keep that small part of her, that most important aspect of her legacy, to himself, and now it would be splashed everywhere for people to speculate on. The charities would fall under scrutiny, and their statuses might be affected.

But he had to be okay because none of this was Nya's fault, and he was about to take her to the opera.

He stopped. Took a deep breath. Thought of how awful Nya's night would be if he allowed himself to freak out.

That was the thing with emotions — they were like gremlins. You let one cute harmless one in, nurtured it, and soon a bunch of uninvited ones hatched, making a mess of things.

"How did it go?"

Johan inhaled deeply, schooled his face to a neutral expression, and turned to Nya's voice. For a moment, all his anxiety and turmoil were pushed to the background because he could think of nothing but her.

"You look . . ."

" 'Damn girl'?" she said, holding up her hands with a grin. "I know."

A beautiful floral African print top with matching bottom. Off the shoulders. Frills. BARE STOMACH. THIGH SLIT. Johan's brain rapidly cataloged these things, but mostly he looked at her radiant smile and forgot his worries. They would be there when Nya was gone.

Soon.

He helped her into her coat, his fingertips brushing her bare shoulders.

"I saw the press conference," she said. "Maybe we can go in through the opera's back entrance. Your father told me there's a special one that leads straight to the royal box."

"Are you sure? If ever you wanted to shock the world" — he looked down at her outfit before helping her button her coat — "tonight would be a good time to do it."

"I've been thinking about that," she said as they walked out to the SUV that would take them to the theater. "I don't think I want to live to shock people. Like you said before, I can't hurt my father without hurting myself, really. I can only do what I think will make me happy. And tonight, that's being with you, whether anyone sees it or not."

Johan let her words cascade over him. She equated him with happiness. There was no way to suppress that joy. There was no room for his fears when he knew she'd pushed hers aside for him. Worry would always be there — always — but for just a few hours maybe he could manage to enjoy his time with Nya.

"I think I'll try this 'being happy' you speak of," he said, slipping into the backseat

430

after handing her in.

They made their way to the theater's side entrance for the royal box, with Nya showing delighted surprise at the long hallway decorated with framed photos of famous performers who'd graced the stage. They passed through the foyer, a parlor with a bar and bartender, grabbing a few snacks before making their way to their seats. The box wasn't huge, because the theater wasn't huge, but it was much bigger than the others.

All eyes turned upward when they stepped into the box with its plush red carpeting and gold gilded seats, and Johan felt the atmosphere in the theater change. He'd been focusing on being happy, on having Nya close, but then he remembered why he hated being on display in the opera house, and why he'd resisted when Greta had mentioned the show.

"By the way." He leaned over once they'd taken their seats. "I love *Rusalka*. But it always makes me cry, so I hate seeing it in public. If I run off during certain portions, don't mind me."

He expected her to laugh and shake her head, but her gaze softened. "Why does it make you cry?"

"The sense of loss in the music. The idea

of being so close to happiness and losing it all." He shrugged.

"My shoulders are bare, but if you want to cry, these frills are very absorbent," she said, plucking at her top. "You can pretend you're being outrageous, and no one but me will know. But if you don't want to hide, I don't think anyone would judge you for that."

"Crying is not very Bad Boy Jo-Jo," he said, adjusting his bow tie.

"Well, I'm not with Bad Boy Jo-Jo, am I? And I don't want to be. I'm with Johan, who sleeps with an evil-looking teddy bear and cries at the opera."

She knew about Bulgom? And she hadn't said anything?

She rested her hand on his leg and gave it a squeeze. "I don't think Dvořák created this music so that men would run out of the theater instead of allowing themselves to feel it."

Something in Johan's chest loosened, and he grabbed her hand and kissed it. "I don't think I'm ready to give these people that part of myself. But" — Johan's heart beat faster — "I would give it to you."

Nya reached up and brushed his hair behind his ear, happiness in her eyes, and then someone shouted "Kiss!" from the seats below and he remembered that hundreds of people were staring at them.

He scowled toward the audience, but Nya kissed his cheek softly, which drew some hoots and applause from the usually staid opera crowd, and then the lights dimmed and they took their seats. Nya held his hand, and didn't let it go through the first act, and though Johan's heart felt full to bursting with emotion, he wasn't sure if it was from the music or from her.

When the curtain closed for the intermission, everyone began to stand, but then the star of the show stepped onto the stage, microphone in hand.

"Hello, everyone. I know this is a bit unorthodox, but we just had to make sure that we got to give a very special thank-you to someone."

Johan froze in his seat because he had one of his bad feelings.

"This evening, a list of private charities funded by Prince Jo-Jo was released."

Oh god, no.

"And one of those charities is the Liechtienbourg Fund for the Musical Arts, which allows young people from lower income backgrounds to train with the masters of their art. I am one of the beneficiaries of that program, and I just needed to say thank you. Thank you for caring, and your mother would be *so* proud of you."

The audience broke into applause. They stood in their seats and turned to him — and all of those gazes, all of the clapping, reminded him that his secret had been revealed. It was only a matter of time before people found out everything about the charities, before the image he had worked so hard to cultivate was trampled.

Johan had lost the reins of his own image; he had lost the one thing he had control over in his life. Worse, now people would bring up his mother all the time. It would be okay, they would rationalize, because they were saying nice things. Now every good thing he did would be a reason to bring her up and if he did anything scandalous . . . when he lost Nya . . .

He stood and grinned and waved as inside of him he screamed at the unfairness of a life that would let you hold nothing sacred, no matter how much you offered in its stead.

"I'll be back," he whispered smoothly to Nya when the ovation was finally over. "You don't have to come with me."

He marched into the foyer, closing the door soundly.

"Would you like a drink?" the bartender asked.

"Actually, just some privacy." He gave the man a rakish look.

"Got it." The man winked and quickly left the room, and Johan locked the door behind him. He stalked over to the bar and grabbed a bottle of whiskey, but didn't twist off the cap.

So many worries swirled in his head, he wasn't even sure why he was upset. But he was. And he needed to pull himself together. He'd promised Nya one night of happiness and he couldn't even give her that, it seemed.

He laughed darkly as he realized that he'd taken the fairy-tale bait, convinced himself it wouldn't be so very bad, and this was the beginning of the despair. The thought of what else was to come had him still clutching the bar, even as the orchestra tuned up.

He'd go back out once he collected his thoughts. He was always able to pull himself together, to hide all those vulnerabilities that he'd been told made him weak. He'd go back to Nya after a few minutes more, smiling and pretending everything was fine.

CHAPTER 23

The maiden had watched the fox god for many a moon, watched as he changed into jewelry and fine clothing and sturdy walking sticks. One day she'd had enough and brought him the meal she was supposed to save for her father because no one had ever thought of what the fox desired, and that broke her heart. She'd been punished, but she'd gone to bed happy because that night the bowl had been found on the back step, filled with small yellow flowers.

— From Phokojoe the Trickster God

Nya's worry grew as the opera resumed and Johan's seat remained empty. She couldn't focus on the beautiful set design, or the singer's haunting voice. She kept seeing that awful look in his eyes before he excused himself; it was the same look he'd worn in the photo she'd accidentally taken of him.

Only a few people in other boxes would be able to see her slip away. She didn't really care about them, but she did care about the performers who might look up and notice the box was empty. She waited until the audience was applauding the end of the second act's first song, then made her move.

When she opened the door to the foyer, the bartender was gone, and Johan stood with his back to her, hands clenching the smooth carved walnut edge of the bar.

"Are you all right?" Nya asked, closing the door from the royal box. The opening strains of the next song were beginning outside the door.

"I think I had some bad *kuddlefleck* before the press conference," he said lightly, gripping the bar hard. "Nothing to worry about here. You can go back to the box and I'll be there in a minute."

"Phoko. Don't talk to me in that voice."

"What voice?"

She wrung her hands together. "The one you hide behind. It's me. Nya."

He turned smoothly, walking slowly over to her. When she started backing up he kept walking, and when her back pressed against the wall he placed his palms flat on either side of her head.

"You finally did a wall slam," she said, try-

437

ing to make him laugh. To drive away the pain in his eyes as he stared down at her. "Now you've checked off everything on our fake relationship list."

"Why did you follow me in here?" he asked. He didn't seem angry, not with her at least, though his gaze was intense.

"Because I felt like you needed me." She lifted her hands to the knot of his bow tie, loosening it. "Why are you upset? They were saying good things about you."

"Because I give these people everything," he said in a low voice. "Everything. I smile, and I flirt, and I entertain. And it wasn't enough. It's never enough."

She undid the top button of his shirt, tugging at his collar so that he didn't feel restricted. "Go on."

"The charity work was the one thing I could do for myself. Without commentary or public opinion or PR spin. And now it's just more fodder for the tabloids. And they won't even focus on the right thing! Those organizations are full of people working hard, devoting their lives to helping, and now they'll be known for being the pet project of a playboy."

She nodded.

"You're right to be upset. Whoever released this information took away something very special to you. It's not fair and . . . it must have been painful, the way they brought up your mother."

"Life is pain," he muttered, a hint of self-deprecation in his tone that let her know he was still able to joke despite his upset.

" 'Anyone who says otherwise is selling something.' Yes, I've seen that film, too. Many times. Did you forget the ending?"

He lifted his head to examine her face, then shook his head. "Happily-ever-afters aren't real."

"You're very selective about what lessons you take from classic romance films," she said, lifting herself on tiptoe and kissing his chin. "I have a solution to this problem, Phoko."

"What's that?" his voice was rough, low.

"Don't think about anyone else. Or anything," she said. "Just focus on me. Us."

She kissed his jaw, the corner of his mouth, his stubbled cheek. Her body pressed away from the wall and into his, and she grabbed on to his lapels to steady herself.

He leaned his head away from her.

"You don't have to kiss it better, Nya. I'm a man. I can deal with my emotions on my own."

That stung, but slightly less because she

439

knew that, in reality, he was mad at himself because he couldn't.

"Why would you want to do that?" She combed his hair away from his face with her fingers. "I thought we were friends. And I thought . . . I thought you liked our debauchery."

"I do. But I don't want you to do something to make me feel better because you're used to making people feel better."

She let go of his lapels, leaned back against the wall, and looked up at him.

"I was doing it to make you feel *good,* not better." She shook her head in frustration. "Don't speak to me as if I act without thinking, like I'm some windup girl programmed by my father. I'm not as experienced, but —"

"You keep saying that," Johan interrupted, leaning his head closer to hers, "but you're incorrect. I'm definitely not a virgin, but I don't have experience with *this.*"

Nya felt that stubborn dream in her heart perk up its ears.

"What is *this* for you?" Her hands came to his face both to calm him and to hold his gaze to hers. He nuzzled into her hand and sighed, laughing with a resignation that might have hurt her if she didn't have an inkling of what he was resigning himself to, and why he found it so difficult.

"It's . . ."

Nya was glad she was holding him, because he did seem to be considering running out of the room rather than answering.

"It's caring, Nya. It's caring when I told myself I never would. It's caring when I know what will happen."

"You don't know what will happen," she said gently. "If you do, we should go play the lottery. I still haven't found a job."

"Exactly." He frowned. "Some things are inevitable. One way or another, you will leave me."

Outside the door, she heard the singer's voice rise and fall while holding a mournful note.

"Like your mother did?"

"I guess I have some issues I haven't quite worked through," he said ruefully. "More reason for you to turn and run."

"What if I don't want to run?" she asked.

"When I think of losing you . . ." His eyes squeezed shut and he shook his head.

"Oh, my sweet Phoko." Her own eyes were warm and close to overflowing, and her thumbs brushed his cheekbones as if wiping away the tears he refused to shed. "You know what to do if you don't want me to leave."

He dropped his forehead to hers, and there was a hint of mischief in his eyes now. "Trick you so that I can spirit you away to my underground lair?"

She laughed softly. "No. All you have to do is ask."

"Like your father did?" She knew he didn't say it to hurt her, but because he was always thinking of the ways people could be made to do what others wanted.

She brushed her mouth against his. "He never asked — he demanded. And he prioritized his pain over my wishes. If you're trying to compare yourself to him to drive me away, be accurate."

He exhaled, ragged and harsh.

"Stay," he said suddenly, desperately, the need so apparent in that one low word that her own throat went rough with emotion. "Please? Stay."

She nodded, her forehead rubbing against his. If he was taking chances with his feelings, she would, too. She was going to keep being brave. "I won't promise happily-ever-after, because you don't seem to believe in that. I'm giving you right now. Because I love you."

"Nya." Johan squeezed his eyes shut again before finally taking her in his arms. "Thank you."

"It's a very basic truth. No need for thanks."

He chuckled. "I love you, too. I've been worried this would happen since I first saw you in Thabiso's apartment."

Nya froze as his words sank in. "But . . . you couldn't even remember my name on the plane."

"I'm a very good liar. And I'm not nice."

She looked at him for a long while, then shook her head. "You put on an elaborate act of not knowing who I was . . . why?"

He raised his brows, an she read the fear and confusion in his flashing blue eyes. "To push you away because I was afraid of what would happen if I didn't. Because I was afraid of this. That's normal, right?"

She shook her head. "You are so weird."

He didn't seem to notice the affection in her words, so she didn't leave him hanging. "Well, then. I guess you really do love me if you were willing to go to that much trouble."

His head tilted to the side and angled down, the motion so fast that she barely saw the way his mouth curved into a grin before he moved in toward her. His lips were soft and he still tasted faintly of the sweet tamarind candy she'd passed him just after they'd taken their seats.

443

His kiss was hungry — more wolf than fox, despite the nickname she'd given him. His body pressed her against the wall with the slightest pressure as he kissed her, as if making sure she really would stay but ready to release her if she wished. Then he covered her lips with his own and his tongue sought out hers.

His hands smoothed over her braids, caressed her neck, planed down her bare shoulders, and Nya was almost overcome by the harsh reverence in his touch. There was so much *care* in the balance between delicate and demanding. He kissed her like that for what felt like forever, and she held on to him, their sighs and licks and nibbles writing a new chapter in their shared story, one that had nothing to do with pain and loss and fear.

When her mouth was plump and sensitive from Johan's kisses, he dropped to his knees in one smooth motion, one hand making use of the slit in her skirt to skim up her glutes and cup her ass. He looked up at her, his own mouth slick and swollen, his eyes flashing with desire.

"You got your wall slam, but I haven't checked off *everything* on my list. On the plane, I told you that if you came to bed, I'd eat you up. We don't need a bed for that, though."

He licked his lips, and Nya's knees went a little weak because she knew what that tongue could do to the most innocuous patches of skin. Now he wanted to taste her . . . there?

She leaned her shoulders back against the satin-lined wall for support, bracing herself, then splayed her fingers through Johan's silky auburn strands. She tightened her grip, loving the way his eyes went an intense stormy blue as he looked up at her. She'd been practicing her dirty talk, but this was going to be easy.

"Eat me up," she ordered. Three simple words to describe an act that she'd thought she was prepared for. She was wrong.

Johan's big hands moved away from her ass, gripping the fabric of her skirt, parting the slit, and pushing it up. His mouth was already dragging up her thighs from her knee, pressing hard kisses into the soft skin. Pleasure didn't make a gradual appearance — it slammed into her, pressing her body back into the wall, and that was before he pushed her underwear to the side and slid his tongue roughly over her clit.

Johan had always taken things torturously slowly, but not tonight.

"Oh my goddess," she gasped. "Holy . . ."

He shifted forward on his knees, nuzzling up into her as he swirled his tongue over her nub relentlessly. The lascivious sound of him licking her — savoring her — was an accompaniment to the aria being sung on the stage, along with the soft cries she couldn't swallow.

Her whole body vibrated with pleasure, like the delight she'd felt as the first loud attack of the orchestra filled the auditorium, but condensed so that it was barely contained in her body. His tongue curled between her folds relentlessly, like he was trying to unlock the secret of Tootsie Pops. Her knees shook, and she wasn't sure how much more she could stand — or how much longer.

It's too much! She thought one moment and then, *It's not enough!* She tried not to tug at his hair, but he must have felt her fingers tighten and he took her direction.

His hand gripped her ass to hold her steady, and then he pressed his mouth firmly over her clit and sucked. Nya went boneless at the sharp shock of pleasure. She could barely hold herself up as he increased the pressure of his tongue and the suction of his mouth swirled over her nub. Johan didn't stop, didn't break rhythm as he held her up — his dedication to giving her pleasure couldn't be called into question.

"Fuck. Fuck. *Fuck!*"

Nya pressed her fist into her mouth, unable to stop the cries that his tongue wrung from her, and when the peak of her orgasm finally hit her legs gave out and she slid to the floor where he caught her and pulled her on top of him as he lay back on the carpet.

"Ça geet et?" he asked smugly, his arms wrapped around her and his hand rubbing the exposed skin of her back. His answer was in her ragged breath in his ear and how her body still trembled from his touch. But even though her legs felt like jelly and they were sprawled on the ground, she wanted more.

"I could be better," she replied, sitting up so that her knees pressed into the carpet and she straddled him. She reached between them to unbuckle his belt and undo the button of his pants, kissing him as she pulled his cock free from his boxer briefs, and he was hard and hot in her hands. "I think we could both be better."

"Sugar . . ."

"Do you have a condom?" She asked in a firm tone because if he didn't want to be with her that was one thing, but she wouldn't be second-guessed based on some

447

notion of not knowing her own mind. Not in this.

He looked at her for a long moment, his gaze taking in her face, and then he smiled, leaning forward to kiss her roughly. He reached into the inner pocket of his tuxedo jacket and pulled out a square foil-wrapped object.

"The tuxedo came stocked with these." He leaned in to kiss her again, and this kiss was light and playful, then he pulled away to rip open the packet. "It's not like I've been carrying these around praying to all the deities that we might . . ." He shook his head. "I want you so badly, Nya. So fucking badly. In every way."

Nya felt an ache in her chest, and she knew what it was.

"I'm already yours," she said tenderly. Then she ran her hands down his lapels and tugged. "But I am really horny right now, soooo . . ."

She looked meaningfully down at the condom.

"You —" He shook his head with a low laugh, then rolled on his condom with practiced finesse, a nerve on his forehead jumping when Nya stroked him after it was on. "You really are something."

"Something?" she asked, stroking him,

wanting him inside of her but not wanting to pull her gaze from his.

"Something. Everything. Every damn thing." He looked at her like she could extinguish suns and ignite supervolcanoes. Then he was pushing up her skirt, running his hands worshipfully over her thighs, and —

"Oh goddess," Nya cried as he ripped her lacy underwear.

"Sorry," he said, grinning wickedly. "That's part of the debauchery package."

"Not sorry," she said, levering herself up with her knees. "That was hot, Phoko."

She should have been nervous, but she couldn't be, with Johan looking up at her like she was the most beautiful woman in the world, with him brushing her body with possessive but gentle caresses. He wanted her so badly that he was shaking with need, and that gave Nya all the bravery she needed to sink down onto his shaft.

"Oh!" She gasped at the unfamiliar thickness filling her.

Johan squeezed his eyes shut, his face flushed and his teeth clenched. He was absolutely still as she lifted herself up and down, up and down, taking him more deeply each time — except for his fingers gripping her waist, helping guide her.

"Johan. This is much better than I expected," she gasped, and he opened one eye. "I'm — You're —"

She sucked in a breath as the friction inside of her made her whole body shake with potent pleasure.

"We haven't even gotten started yet, Sugar Bubble."

Then he began to move his hips, slowly, slowly, but filling her more deeply than she'd thought possible. Nya felt a brief flash of pain, and whimpered, but it was gone as quickly as it had come and then there was only pleasure.

Johan sat up, still thrusting, kissing her mouth, her eyes, her face, his lips baptizing her with his affection. "I love you, Nya."

His words filled her with as much pleasure as the sweet, tender ache building in her core. The pain was gone now, and there was only the delicious friction of Johan's girth, and then of the fingers of one of his hands coming between them to tease her already sensitive clit.

Maybe it was the surprise that sent her over the edge — surprise that one man could give her so much pleasure while kissing her like he needed her breath to live. Her inner walls clamped around his cock and she threw her arms around him as she met his thrusts, a sobbing shudder racking her as her climax shook her.

"I love you, too," she cried as she came, which wasn't dirty talk but the only words her mouth could form when her brain temporarily stopped working.

"Oh god — Nya —" He hugged her tightly, too, then thrust at a slower, sharper rhythm as he whispered things that were alternately filthy and tender, words that pushed her so that Nya was caught in the riptide of another orgasm before he'd even finished his.

He collapsed back onto the carpet, still holding her close. From outside the door, the audience broke into raucous applause.

"Do you think they heard us?" she whispered, and Johan laughed, the sound loud and devious, and the vibration of it enough to make her toes curl. He rubbed his hand over her back.

"Maybe, though if you're louder than a professional opera singer and full orchestra you might have superhuman lungs."

"Superhuman lungs? We can test that once we get back to the castle." She kissed his jaw then nipped his earlobe, wondering how it was possible that she was already eager to take him again. And again.

"I will happily be your test subject in the

superhuman lungs experiment. Let's go." He glanced at the door. "I do feel bad about leaving before the show is over."

"They'll live," Nya said, hauling him to his feet. She leaned closer to his ear. "I'm not sure I will if you aren't inside me again soon."

Johan wasn't the only one who knew how to manipulate.

His nostrils flared and his gaze went hot. "I can't argue with that. I'll leave a note saying I had to go save my fiancée. I'm sure they'll understand."

Nya almost asked what it meant, that he'd said he loved her and called her his fiancée still. Their feelings weren't fake but their relationship was . . .

Then Johan grabbed her around the waist and kissed her, and the music played loudly outside the door, and she let herself fall into that kiss instead of worrying.

CHAPTER 24

The humans didn't know that Phokojoe's
ears were large and heard all. They didn't
know that he now spent much of his time
listening for the voice of the girl who
brought him sustenance and asked for
nothing in return. So when the girl's father
demanded she tell Phokojoe she desired
a coffer of gold, the trickster fox heard. An
old witch woman had told the father how
to take the Phokojoe's gift and keep it, so
that he would be rich and the fox god
would exist no more.

— From Phokojoe the Trickster God

Johan awoke with Nya in his arms, with her
hair pressed into his shoulder, her forehead
pressed into his neck, and her leg slung over
his thighs.

He waited for fear and anxiety to assail
him — he'd been too busy for those emotions after they left the opera the previous

night, losing himself in the touch of Nya, the taste of her, and the sound of her cries echoing from the high ceilings of his room. He'd told her he loved her, for god's sake — he should have been curled up in the fetal position somewhere, or online searching for safety helmets and whatever other objects could protect her from harm.

He took a deep breath, inhaling her scent as he did.

No.

No.

Nya didn't need or want his overprotection. He could do this. He was aware enough of his own problems, and he'd deal with them as he urged the people he cared about to deal with their own.

Portia had been sending him therapy referrals at least once every two months. Maybe he'd look into it. Yes.

There was a knock at his door and he slipped away from Nya reluctantly. The referendum voting was still happening the next day, and there was much to be done, like search out his brother who was returning from school to make an appearance at the castle before the polls opened the next day. He needed to find some way to make things right with Lukas, too, no matter how the referendum turned out.

He slipped on his pants and tiptoed over to the door, cracking it slightly. Greta stood at the threshold, expression tight. She held the daily paper in her hand.

"Have you seen this?"

Johan grinned. "Well, no, I was busy."

Greta unfurled the front page and revealed the huge picture. He had no idea when it had been taken. It was him, shrouded in darkness, touching the ring that he'd worn around his neck until he'd slipped it onto Nya's finger, with Bulgom Pamplemousse glaring out from beneath him. It was *him*. Not Prince Jo-Jo. His expression was somber and completely unguarded, blown up on the front page. And he was holding a *teddy bear*.

Christ.

"The Lonely Prince," the headline read. He scanned the article, and it was mostly nonsense but a bit too close to home — some story about Johan's never-ending pain, how he slept with his teddy bear close to his heart because he was so frightened of being alone.

All of the anger that had been pushed away by his night with Nya returned, having doubled in size. It muddied his thinking, and he crushed the paper in his hand. It was as he crushed it that he remembered

Nya's flash going off in the bedroom of the airplane.

No.

"Jo-Jo. I wanted to tell you yesterday that I saw a disturbing text on Nya's phone as I was holding it. Something about getting rid of outdated royal institutions. Very conspiratorial-like." Greta floundered. "Have you considered that most of this started when she arrived?"

That was true, wasn't it? The reports in the papers, the news that had somehow started to leak from Thesolo linking them together.

"And her father was attempting to destabilize their kingdom," Greta added.

"Hmm," Johan said.

I come from a family of politicians, Johan, and my father was a criminal one at that. You're not the only one who knows about manipulation.

It made sense, as far as schemes went. It was a good long con, all the coincidences that had driven them together that seemingly had no explanations. Now she was in his bed, and the reputation he had painstakingly built at the expense of his true self was in shreds.

"And . . . I rechecked the IP addresses of the latest posts on that forum, and whomever it was used *our* IP address. The comments were coming from inside the house, so to speak."

Johan tousled his hair, rolled his neck from side to side.

"Thanks. I'll talk to you later."

He closed the door and stalked back toward the bed. Toward the woman he'd told he'd loved, who he'd finally let his defenses down around.

She seemed to sense him coming, rolling onto her back as her eyes fluttered open. She smiled, and the anger suffocating Johan loosened.

He was being ridiculous. Wasn't he?

"Nya."

"I need coffee," she said, and then stretched. "And a massage. No one ever told me sex uses so many muscles!"

He tried to smile, but it was halfhearted, and when she noticed, her own faded.

"What's wrong?" she asked.

He held up the newspaper, watching her reaction as she took in the image. She sat bolt upright in the bed, grabbing the paper from his hands. "This is the picture I took on the plane."

"Yes. And somehow it's on the front page of the tabloids."

"Someone must have taken it from my

phone!"

She looked at him. "I'm sorry. I should have deleted it afterward. I didn't think I was important enough to have my phone hacked before, and then I was so caught up in . . . well, in you."

"You're sure you didn't send it to anyone? Not to any friends?" He hated even asking, because that awful, needy part of him told him that it didn't matter what she did. He didn't want to lose her, and especially not like this.

"My only friends are Ledi and Portia, who would never betray our trust, and I didn't send it, even to them."

He nodded and sighed.

Her only friends.

"If you have no other friends, who was the person you were texting with?" he asked. "I saw a message from him, you told me he was a nice person, and Greta saw something disturbing when she held your phone. Something about overthrowing governments."

He watched with dread to see if she cringed or balked or looked away from him, but instead she giggled and shook her head.

"Oh that! I told you it was a game. I can show you."

Relief flowed through him, pooling in the

458

cracks of his hardened anger, as she slipped out of bed to take her phone from the charger. He hadn't truly believed she would betray him, and he was glad he had asked instead of making assumptions. Now she would show him and everything would be fine.

"Here is my friend," she said, voice playful.

She handed over the phone and he saw . . . himself. A two-bit cartoon version of himself, with a silly, sly smile plastered on its face.

"What is this?" he asked, though something told him he really didn't want to know.

"It's *One True Prince,*" she said, taking the phone and scrolling. "It's an immersive virtual dating game and —"

"And that's me. You were dating a video game version of me?"

She paused, her head tilted with uncertainty. "No. I was playing a romance game. It's not *dating.*"

He remembered her laughing when he'd given her love advice during their adventure capturing a goat. She'd been laughing *at* him.

"And when I asked you about this love interest of yours, several times, you didn't think it wise to tell me about this game you were playing?"

He'd been ready to forgive her being some type of spy, meddling with his country's affairs. This? This drained all the relief from him and replaced it with an amorphous hurt.

She rubbed one hand up her biceps. "It seemed kind of awkward to bring up. And it's just a game."

"If it was just a game, why didn't you tell me?" he pressed.

She folded her arms over her chest now. "I did tell you. In this very room. When you asked me who I was getting messages from."

"Just a game where you were dating some silly version of *me*. I see."

"Why are you so upset?" she asked, and it seemed to be a genuine question. "The fact that someone stole a photo from my phone, and who knows what other information, is more pressing right now."

He didn't know why he was so upset. It *was* a game.

But he felt tricked, foolish. Nya had never seemed like she was particularly interested in his playboy persona. But she'd been playing that game, with the frivolous version of him, and she'd kept playing it, even after they'd agreed to the fake engagement. Even after he'd kissed her and thought he was going to burst from his heart being so full.

It seemed that needy part of him wasn't satisfied with love alone. It needed Nya to love him for himself, and not because she was obsessed with some fake version of him. That was the thing with need — it was multifaceted and once acknowledged, just the tip of an iceberg of unknown size. If anyone had ever told him that he'd actually let himself fall this hard for a woman and then doubt her because of some video game, he would have laughed. And yet there he was, blindsided by a seemingly trifling blow that would leave a hell of a bruise.

"I don't know." He got up and began to pace. "I know this is ridiculous. Trust me, it's the last thing I thought we'd argue about, but it's not great feeling like all of this was just some game to you."

IIis ability to speak so calmly surprised him; inside he was furious, mostly with himself. He thought he could read people so clearly, but he'd created his own fairy tale with Nya, one in which she'd seen behind his masks and somehow intrinsically understood who he was. But she'd clearly liked those masks and facades if she'd devoted so much time to the game version of him. She said she wanted him, Johan, but maybe she was just a Jo-Jo fan in sheep's clothing.

"It *was* some game to me," she said, her voice cool with anger. "I don't know where this righteousness is coming from. You ignored me for almost two years. You pretended you didn't know that I existed, or even my name. And I was supposed to just tell you everything? You're not the only one who gets to protect yourself, Johan."

He turned toward her, his movements carefully careless.

"And how was pretending that you had some lover desperately texting you protecting yourself?" he asked. His voice was harsh but he was unable to control it. He'd felt pure, undiluted jealousy about those messages. "I think that's just called lying."

"I didn't pretend anything!" She was standing now, wrapping his sheet around those curves that had been under his hands all night. "You assumed. And you know what? I could have told you it was a game, but you were the first person who'd ever even assumed that anyone would take interest in me in that way!" Tears filled her eyes and her anger made her accent clip her words. "I was embarrassed, okay? I didn't want to be silly, boring Nya, only able to find love in a video game. Especially not to you, who had looked through me for so long and could have anyone he wanted. I do apologize — for trying to save myself one more humiliation."

Scheisse de merde, he was being an asshole. He was being completely, indisputably ridiculous after everything that had passed between them the night before. But he also couldn't seem to get past this hurt *because* of everything that had happened the night before. He'd opened himself to her completely, thought he'd finally found the person who would see him as he was, love him as he was, and maybe all it boiled down to for her was a romp with a celebrity prince.

"If you want to talk about humiliation, imagine having to wonder if your . . . person cares about you or a fake version of you." He ran a hand through his hair in frustration, leaving his hand tangled in the strands, and exhaled harshly. "This is absurd."

"You told me you loved me," she said, her eyes wide with hurt and anger. "I think it was you playing games. Because you went from ignoring me, to being everywhere I was, to charming me, to offering this fake engagement, to taking me into your bed. And now that you've gotten what you wanted, and the referendum is tomorrow, you conveniently find some reason to take a small error and turn it into an unforgivable one. I know this playbook. Maybe I was wrong to think you weren't like my father."

Johan dropped his head, shaking it. "No. I didn't use you any more than you did me."

"But you *did* use me, at the beginning. Because you wanted me, and you couldn't admit that, so when you saw the opportunity to have me without actually doing the work of a relationship, you took it."

He wished she was less perceptive.

"I didn't think that far ahead," he said. "It was an impulse."

She made a sharp sound of frustration, one that was almost a sob.

"It's not fair if you're allowed impulses but I have to think ahead and predict how things will hurt you." She swallowed hard, pausing for a moment to collect herself. "You know, I understand why you're upset, but what am I supposed to make of this when you've already admitted to spending so much time trying to push me away? Will you always be looking for a reason?"

Johan didn't answer.

Just end this now, he thought. *Tell her you don't care and that this is over.*

But that was a lie — he could feel the anxiety at the thought of losing her pressing at his chest, squeezing. And today at least, he would not lie to Nya, or to himself. She'd been lied to her entire life. Her father had used love against her and Johan could do the same, quite easily. Manipulation was his job. He could tell her that she had misunderstood the way he held her, the look in his eye, and the emotion in his kisses. He could tell her he didn't actually love her. And she would believe him, eventually, because he could make people believe anything. But he wouldn't do that to her, even if he paid for it later. And he wouldn't do it to himself, because he deserved honesty, too. Just this once.

"I pushed you away because my interest in you was dangerous," he forced the words out. "Love comes with loss, and I didn't want to lose anyone ever again. I wasn't lying when I said I love you, but I don't know how not to be scared that I'll lose you. I don't know how not to be consumed by that fear. I was only just managing with Lukas and I messed that up, too."

She walked up to him, and her expression was so distraught that he felt it all through his body, the pain he was causing her.

"You like being the conductor, making sure each instrument in the orchestra surrounding you plays just so in order to protect your emotions. I'm not your instrument, Phoko, just as you aren't my weapon. I can't have my happiness dependent on your fears. I will never live like that again."

She's leaving.

He reached for her through a haze of panic. "Look. Let's just —"

Nya's phone chimed then, a snippet of an upbeat pop song, and he glanced at it. "Is it me, interrupting me?" he asked, trying to sound cheerful.

Maybe he could turn this around. He would just pretend that everything would be all right, and then it would be. He could pave over this hurt, inconsequential compared to most. He could ignore his fears. If this was the despair he'd been waiting on, it wasn't so bad.

Nya had picked up her phone and was speaking quietly in Thesotho. Her expression had already been tense, but it went slack as tears slipped down her cheeks. Johan went to her and pulled her into his lap. Even if his feelings were hurt, even if they were in the middle of this strange argument, he wouldn't let her cry alone.

She leaned against him and he could feel her shaking. "Okay. Okay. I will. Yes, *Nkhono.*"

She hung up and accepted the tissue he'd

reached over and grabbed from the bedside table.

"My father has been moved to the prison hospital," she said. "He really is ill, it seems. They're worried he won't make it."

Johan rubbed her shoulders. "What will you do?"

"I should go to him," she said.

"Do you want to?" The thought of her leaving before they could finish their discussion made his chest go tight, selfish as it was.

"No. And yes. But I can't live with the regret of what would happen if I don't."

He nodded, forced himself to loosen his hold on her as she stood.

Nya started walking toward the door to her room and then paused, a shuddering tremble going through her. When she held out her hand, he stared at her, then slowly held out his own. The thin silver band she dropped into his palm was still warm.

Her expression was so close to crumpling, but she lifted her chin. "As you said, this isn't a game. I'd rather return it now, because . . . because . . ." She shrugged, and he read everything contained in that small motion. Because she didn't need to worry over two men who let their fears control them. Because he hadn't truly meant for her to be his wife when he'd given it to her.

Because she had no reason to come back.

Johan held himself still around the pain that opened up inside of him, around his hopes for them collapsing like the walls of gingerbread houses.

"Okay." He clutched the ring. "Well. It was fun, right?"

"It was a good adventure," she said softly. Then she leaned down to kiss him on the head. "Good luck, Phoko."

"I can arrange the flights and take you to the airport," he said, trying to inject casual cheer into his voice. "I know you made fun of my car but —"

Nya shook her head. "My grandparents have arranged the flights. And I can get to the airport myself. You have to go meet your family and deal with the referendum. Make sure you talk to your sibling, okay? And listen, too. Lukas needs you right now."

She turned and walked through the door, bedsheet trailing behind her, and she didn't look back.

Johan wanted to call out her name, to throw himself at her feet, but he just sat there in numb shock. *This* was the despair. Seeing Nya walk away from him and not being sure if she would, or should, walk back.

It was better this way. If he lost her now, he wouldn't lose her later. He drew his feelings back into the vault where he'd kept them, though somehow that vault could no longer contain them. So he did what he supposed most people in the world did; he got up, carrying his hurt like a weight that he tried not to stumble under, and prepared to face the day — alone.

CHAPTER 25

Today I found Johan upset again. He asked me why the mothers in fairy tales always had to die. He said it wasn't fair. I didn't know what to say because he already knew the answer. My sweet boy threw his arms around me and begged me to promise him that I would never die. I came so close to lying to him, to both of us. But I told him that I would die one day, as all things must, and that it would be painful for him. I told him I hoped that before I did, I got to see him grow into the beautiful man I know he'll become. I told him I hoped I would see him fall in love. I told him that if I didn't live to see those things, I would still be there with him. Every time he felt deeply: every time he laughed or cried or raged. Because feeling deeply is something he got from me, if it's not too egotistical to say so. It is my

470

gift to him. I hope he always remembers that.

— From the journal of
Queen Laetitia von Braustein,
Private Collection of the
Castle von Braustein Library

After standing in the shower staring blankly at the tiled walls, he'd gone to Nya's room only to find it empty. She'd packed at record speed, it seemed, the quicker to get away from him.

He'd gone to the parlor, the first to arrive after the serving staff had laid out their breakfast, and Googled *One True Prince* as he waited. It was clearly a popular game, and there were hundreds of screenshots and dozens of videos of playthroughs.

He watched through a video showing the game if you were in a romance with the character that was based on him, a frown on his face at the ways in which the character was similar and different from him. His character was trying to overthrow the systems of monarchies, which he found a bitter irony in, given how much he'd done to put Liechtienbourg's in a good light, despite his disdain. The character Hanjo did it by collecting information about his fellow princes and giving it to the press, by committing small acts of vandalism like spray painting "Down with the monarchy!" and —

Johan sat up straight in his chair, brushing his hair out of his eyes as he stared at the screen. So many of the things this Hanjo character said in screenshots echoed what he'd read in the "vote no" forum, particularly from the commenter FloupGelee.

He remembered what Greta had said that morning — the IP addresses used had been at the palace . . . and at Lukas's school. In focusing on Nya, he'd missed a rather important connection. One that he couldn't bring himself to believe, but . . .

The door to the parlor opened and King Linus and Prince Lukas walked in. Linus sat and slapped his hands on his knees, his expression tense. Lukas sulked into a seat and sucked at the plastic tube of frozen yogurt that had been his favorite comfort food since he was a child, the Floup brand name emblazoned on the side of it.

"FloupGelee," Johan said blankly, and watched as Lukas froze.

"What?" Linus asked, looking back and forth between them.

"Why?" Johan asked. "For years I've —" He stopped, remembering what Nya had explained about her father, how he'd used his loving care of her to beat her down with.

He softened his tone. "Why are you under-mining the referendum?"

Lukas's eyes narrowed in anger, but then he frowned and his eyes welled with tears.

"Please," Johan said gently. "We can figure this out, but I need to know why before we can do that. I love you, and I won't do anything to hurt you. I won't get mad."

That wasn't a lie. Something must have driven Lukas to try to destroy his own future. Something he'd been too scared to tell Johan.

Make sure you talk to your sibling, okay? And listen, too. Lukas needs you right now.

Johan started to get an idea of what was going on, memory after memory slotting into place: Lukas's distaste for the preppy look; Johan telling Lukas to stay out of their mother's makeup; Lukas asking why some things were for girls and some were for boys, and the upset Johan's answer of *"Because that's how things are"* had caused. The fight they'd had just before Johan had left for Thesolo.

"I always pressured you to act a certain way, to project a certain image. Did you just get tired of that?"

Lukas put down the empty sleeve of yogurt and nodded jerkily.

"You always taught me what to do to be

473

the perfect prince. To hide everything important to me and always show everyone what they wanted to see," he said, his voice sounding so much like it had when he was small that Johan's own throat roughened. Lukas's clear blue eyes met Johan's. "What *you* wanted to see. Football, and riding, and being popular with the boys. Whenever I talked about what I wanted you told me it was something people would make fun of me for."

God, he really had messed it up. He'd thought he was helping, thought he was saving Lukas pain, but he'd overcorrected and began to push instead of guide. He'd always wondered why Mamm had let him act in ways that led to bullying and now he had his answer — she'd let him be himself. Johan had made Lukas think he should be someone else.

"I want to hide everything, which isn't entirely healthy, and I think I didn't make clear that you could do things differently," Johan said, trying to find the words to begin fixing this. "I didn't think that through, and I'm sorry. If this is about sexuality, you do know I'm not straight, right? I'll be the last person to judge you on that."

"Really?" Linus's eyebrows were raised high. The king was having quite the morning, it seemed.

"Thanks. But it would be hard for me not to know when you're literally famous for your . . . exploits," Lukas said with an eye roll. "I know you kind of hide that, or lots of people look past it, but what if the most important thing to me right now is something it hurts to hide? What if . . . I'm not a prince?"

"Are you a princess, then?" King Linus asked carefully. "That's fine! People love princesses!"

Johan shot Linus a gently quelling look. "Let Lukas talk, Papp. Please."

Linus's eyes went wide, but he nodded. "Go on, s— ah, child."

"I'm neither," Lukas said, then inhaled sharply. "I've always hated the idea of being a prince, and having to act how princes are supposed to act all the time. And though I do sometimes want to wear a dress and I like pretty makeup, I'm not a princess. It seemed like I could only choose between those two things! I mean . . . there isn't even any other option. I felt so trapped and then the referendum came up and I saw a way to get out of this without hurting anyone, or having you hate me for being difficult and —"

"Lukas." Johan walked over and knelt

475

beside his sibling, running his fingers through Lukas's soft hair like their mamm had done to him and Lukas both. "I would never hate you. *Never.* You understand?"

Lukas hesitated, then nodded.

He thought of Lukas's outrageous behavior, and Nya's assessment.

No one tries this hard to get a reaction out of someone they don't want to talk to.

"Even when you told me to sit and spin. I was mad, but hate was never even an option and never will be."

"Even though Nya left because of me?" Lukas asked pitifully. "I took the picture from her phone because everyone was starting to say they were going to vote yes. I didn't think you'd send her away! I'm sorry, *bruder.*"

Johan sighed. "I'm not okay with you violating her privacy, but that's not why she left. She had to go see her father, who is ill."

"She wasn't wearing her ring." Lukas was observant. "I like her. She figured out what I was upset about and made me feel better. And she was right — she told me you wouldn't be mad at me."

Of course. Because Nya had always assumed the best of Johan, when no one else did. She was kind enough to search for goodness in him, even when he'd tried to hide it.

"Lukas . . . do you still want me to call you that?" Linus asked. "I've seen reports about this on the news but I'll admit I don't entirely understand."

Lukas explained preferred pronouns to their father, and though Linus was clearly confused, he took notes and stayed quiet apart from encouraging his child.

"Let's think about your options," Johan said. "We're about to do a press conference. There was going to be a lot of talk about the referendum and blah blah blah. But you have something that you don't want to hide anymore and we'll have a captive audience waiting to have their opinions molded. We'll tell them what you need and make it clear that giving you what you need is the only logical response."

" 'If you fall, make it seem like the only thing that could have happened was you falling.' You do have some good advice tucked in with the lying and faking," Lukas said. For the first time since Johan had returned to Liechtienbourg, his sibling smiled at him instead of scowling. "Sorry I told you to fuck off."

"I deserved it." This wasn't about Johan's own feeling, but when he thought about

477

how long Lukas had been hurting in silence a band of guilt tightened around his chest. How much pain had Lukas been in that "sabotage the referendum" had seemed like the best course of action? "I'm sorry I put so much pressure on you to hide yourself away. I'm sorry I didn't *see* you."

Lukas shrugged, but their eyes were bright. They leaned back in their chair. "Well. Can you see me now?"

"Vividly."

"Good." Lukas grinned. "Just . . . please don't go all cool brother now, sending me dresses and stuff like that?"

"Let's go over what you want to do at this press conference. You don't have to give them everything."

He heard a sniffle and then glanced over at Linus, who was stalwartly holding back tears. "I have more questions, I'll admit. And, Lukas, we'll have a *stern* talk about undermining the monarchy. But . . . you two, right now? Laetitia would be so proud."

It still hurt Johan that Mamm wasn't there to give Lukas her own advice, but not as much as it usually did. And yes, she *would* be proud of her two children plotting to change the course of the kingdom's history — if the monarchy survived the referendum.

■ ■ ■ ■

Approximately an hour later, after discussing what Lukas needed from family and kingdom to be comfortable, Johan, Linus, and Lukas took their seats before the royal press pool. Lukas had added a thin strip of pink to their hair for luck, and wore a sparkly lip gloss Nya had given to them without asking questions and without judgment. Johan didn't wonder why she hadn't told him anything — she hadn't wanted to take that decision away from Lukas.

"I know that usually Johan and I handle the press, but today we are going to let Lukas speak," Linus said to the gathered journalists, who began to clamor at that.

Johan's body vibrated with nerves. He'd tried to shield Lukas for so long, and watching them step in front of a crowd of reporters to discuss something that would surely make international news and create a whirlwind of unnecessary speculation, was like having to sit still as fire ants marched over his body. He wanted to make a naughty joke. He wanted to stand up and rip off his shirt and sing an aria.

He sat still, except for the smile he directed at his stepfather. Linus had said Laetitia would be proud, but that meant he was proud, too, didn't it? Johan had been thinking a lot about how his trying to prevent his own hurt could hurt others. He placed a hand on Linus's shoulder and squeezed, and got a pleased smile from Linus in return.

Linus leaned in toward Johan's ear. "You called me Papp earlier."

"Don't get a big head," Johan whispered back. "It's just a word for a man who raises you and who you happen to love."

Linus made a gruff noise, still trying his damndest to maintain the von Braustein stiff upper lip.

"Hallo," Lukas said quietly into the microphone. Lukas glanced at Johan, who gave his sibling a firm nod and threw in a wink to remind them that they had nothing to fear. Lukas turned back to the crowd. "It's been noted that my behavior has been a bit strange lately. And this is true. I was acting out because . . . I'd decided that I didn't want to grow up to be a king. I didn't want to be a prince either. I've never been one, really."

The journalists buzzed and camera flashes went off and Johan saw the instant Lukas's expression shifted to something slightly vulnerable and slightly cunning. They were their own person, and would deal with the press as they wished, but they hadn't thrown out everything Johan had taught them.

"Let me explain this. First, I'm nonbinary. Our language and our culture are very much focused on masculine and feminine, but I'm neither. I prefer that the pronouns they/them be used when talking about me in any future publications, starting with the reporting on this press conference," Lukas said firmly. "This shouldn't be very difficult for a group of intelligent journalists like yourselves. It should be even easier when writing about royalty because we already have the royal *we*. The royal *they* isn't very different, is it?"

Lukas looked out at the crowd, smiling a bit when most of the reporters shook their heads. "If you happen to slip up, I won't banish you or even get angry. I just ask that you try to remember for next time. I will not be explaining this aspect further because all of you possess access to the internet, which is free in our great nation, and you can look it up."

There were murmurs among the reporters, but Johan shot warning glares at anyone who seemed likely to shout something out.

"As you can imagine, this has been a confusing time for me. Not figuring out my identity — I've known that for some time. But figuring out how to fulfill my royal duties and stay true to myself." They paused. "We are a kingdom with a long and storied history, a kingdom built on solid traditions, and I wondered if being myself would somehow disappoint people. But no. I'm still me. I'm still the same person who was born to serve and protect my people. And I hope everyone else feels the same."

Johan tried not to look like he was about to fall out of his seat from a mixture of pride and anxiety. He looked into the audience to find Krebs wiping away a tear before readjusting his camera to snap a photo.

"As I stated, my preferred pronouns are *they* and *them.* In addition to that I will no longer be referred to as *Prince* Lukas."

They looked at Johan, who held up a large photo of Lukas making a thumbs-down sign with one hand and frowning. The word *PRINCE* was written in large letters, meme-style, and crossed out with a thick red line.

"I will heretofore, if the monarchy exists after the referendum, be referred to as Prinxe Lukas."

Johan held up an image of Lukas giving a thumbs-up and grinning, with *PRINXE* in large letters along the bottom.

"King will likewise be *Xing,* though I

hopefully have some time before I have to worry about that one. Now, if there are any questions that aren't questions about pronoun usage or how to replace a *c* or a *k* with an *x,* I'll be happy to answer them."

The reporter from the *Looking Glass Daily* raised his hand. Lukas called on him.

"How does your brother feel about this?"

Johan rolled his eyes and leaned forward toward his mic. "My opinion is irrelevant, but since you asked, I feel glad that Lukas trusts the people of our kingdom to respect their announcement. I love them as much as it's possible to love anyone, and I couldn't be any prouder of them."

Lukas's eyes softened and their cheeks went rosy. Between the von Braustein stiff upper lip and Johan's obsessive desire to keep his emotions to himself, love had been shown more through actions than words in the castle. But sometimes people needed to hear how important they were, and maybe that was something else that could change moving forward.

Nya had told him she loved him, and it had been like being freed from a tower. Johan didn't think he could change entirely, but he could stop hoarding his most precious emotions.

The rest of the press conference was

Lukas ignoring people who hadn't respected their directive about questioning, and answering those who asked about their vision for the future of Liechtienbourg.

Johan knew there would be some people who responded with ignorance when the word spread, but they would handle it together as a family. And when he thought of family, he also thought of Nya, no matter that their engagement hadn't been real. His feelings for her were. He'd told her, but his actions hadn't backed it up, and he was going to fix that.

He'd gone over all the grandiose public gestures he could make — his specialty really — but none of them felt right. After the press conference, and making sure it was okay with Lukas and Linus, Johan made a call to Greta as he packed a suitcase. He paused to rummage around in his costume trunk, where he kept his captain's hat and mermaid tail, among other things.

"Clear my schedule for the next few days. I'll be heading to Thesolo."

"But what about the referendum?"

"Honestly? The referendum isn't my priority right now. I can retain my title of Tabloid Prince with or without a monarchy, and I don't really think I want that crown anymore."

Greta made a sound of consideration. "I see. Well, good luck, Johan. I hope you get what you need."

"We'll see."

CHAPTER 26

Phokojoe knew to expect the maiden. He knew what she would ask of him. He should have swallowed her whole before she opened her mouth, but he had come to love the maiden. He would give her anything she requested, even his own life.

"Phokojoe, I have nothing to offer you," she said when she stood before him, her skin lustrous like a dark pearl under the moonlight.

"You have treated me well and I will never forget that. What is it you most desire, lovely maiden?" he asked.

She bowed her head, so close to him that her floral scent filled his nose, and whispered her wildest dream into his ear.

— From Phokojoe the Trickster God

Nya stood in the waiting room of Thesolo's only prison, which was surprisingly nice given the ones she'd seen on American crime shows. It was decorated with plush couches and stocked with drinks and snacks. Like the orphanage where Nya had worked, the goal was to make it an environment conducive to growth, and — as with this waiting area — to not make people feel like castoffs in their time of need. Having a loved one in prison was hard enough, was the prevailing thought. Why make visiting them a hardship as well?

Nya's nerves jangled as she waited to be escorted to the hospital wing of the prison, where her father had been taken after collapsing. Ledi and Thabiso had offered to join her, but she needed to do this alone. Her grandparents had been forced into deciding whether to see the son they'd raised — or to forgive the man who had almost killed them — and were at a stalemate.

She still wasn't sure what she would say to him. She wanted to tell him how he'd stolen her dreams for so many years, had kept her trapped in a cage instead of letting her fly free and return of her own will. How he'd made her sick, threatening her health, had lied and manipulated and gaslit her so that she hadn't known what normal was or how to achieve it.

She'd thought she'd spend the flight from

Liechtienbourg figuring out her script, but her worries had been so overwhelming that she'd simply fallen asleep, as if her body had simply said *not today, Satan* and gone into hibernation mode.

Or perhaps she'd been exhausted from her night with Johan, followed by her fight with Johan. Her ring finger felt odd without the silver band she'd grown used to in such a brief period of time, and she kept thinking of what Johan would do with it, when the obvious answer was give it to someone else, eventually.

She had no reason to go back to him. The referendum was currently being tallied, she imagined, and whatever had passed between her and Johan had been meant to be temporary. She didn't fool herself into thinking that just because they'd been silly enough to fall in love it would change anything. People who'd loved each other deeply and earnestly for years sometimes parted ways; she couldn't expect a relationship that had lasted a few weeks and was based on lies to stand the test of time, no matter how much she wanted it to.

The prison nurse came out then, clad in his white uniform and looking uncertainly at Nya, and she braced herself for bad news.

"Ms. Jerami?" he asked, beckoning when

she nodded. "Right this way."

"Is he stable?" she asked. "My grandparents were told that his organs were starting to shut down from lack of food, and that he'd collapsed."

The nurse's steps slowed, and he glanced at her out of the corner of his eye. "Who told them this?"

"They received a call from the prison doctor yesterday."

The man's brow wrinkled. "It appears there has been some miscommunication. Your father is in here."

He opened the door to the room and the sorrow Nya had been bracing for was replaced by shock.

Alehk Jerami lay on the bed in the clean infirmary room with his legs crossed comfortably at the ankles, his eyes trained on the comedy show playing on the large TV hanging on the wall. He chuckled and bit into the apple he held in one hand.

He looked . . . well, he looked great. He'd grown a short gray beard and though he had lost weight, it wasn't from starvation. It had been replaced with muscle, as if he'd been hitting the gym. And then his head turned toward the door.

His did a double take and then quickly tucked the apple under his pillow, swallowing audibly. His expression began to droop and his shoulders hunched, and his languid repose morphed into one stiff with agony. When he spoke, his voice was weak and pathetic.

"Ah, my daughter, my child. You have finally listened to the will of Ingoka and returned to the path of obedience." He held out his arms as if expecting a hug. "I am so glad I will get to see you in what may be my final days."

"Um." The nurse glanced at Nya in confusion.

"It is okay," she said. She wasn't even angry. She knew what her father was like, and still she had come. Still she'd thought that maybe she would detail the pain he'd caused her, and he'd repent, and, like a pumpkin turning into a carriage, would transform into a father who was good and kind and loved his daughter without trying to break her. She remembered what Johan had said.

I don't know if you can ever really hurt a man like that.

He'd been right. He'd also been right that, sometimes, happily-ever-afters don't exist. She thought of how Johan had envied her openness and her ability to say what she felt. She thought that maybe he'd learned from her, even if they weren't meant to be together. Well, she'd learned from him, too. She'd learned that sometimes a lie was what would protect you from being crushed by the weight of your pain. She'd learned that lying was another tool picked up on a quest, and this tool could help her vanquish this final monster.

"Hello, Father," she said softly, inclining her head to show respect. "I am so sorry that I strayed from the path you have tried to guide me on for so long. But I am here now."

"It is okay, my child," Alehk said, eyes gleaming as he took in his victory.

"It is not okay, Father. As you said in your letter, I have dishonored both you and Mother with my actions." She glanced up at him from beneath her lashes.

He took her by both hands, what should have been a loving gesture seeming like manacles closing around her. She resisted the initial urge to tug her hands away.

"Well, now you are home and everything will be all right. And I have spoken with some people, those who still respect me, and they can get you an apartment close to the prison. That way you can come visit me every day, as a good child would."

"Yes, Father," she said, the grip of his

hands and the knot in her throat making her feel like the frail woman who had always given in to his will.

How had she lived her life this way for so long? How had she swallowed her hopes and desires to appease this man's ego, which would never be satisfied?

"And that way, I will know you are safe," he said, squeezing her hands more tightly. Nya's throat muscles worked. She still loved him, as much as she detested him, and she remembered long, long ago when hand-holding and praise from her father had been her world.

"Yes. I need your guidance, Father," she said meekly. "You were right about how awful it would be out in the world. I was so naive. I was deceived by so many people. I hate to tell you this, but . . ." Nya took a deep breath. "I lost all of my money. I had to sell everything in our home."

"What?" Alehk said, his grip on her hands loosened and she slipped them away, wiping them on her dress before pressing them together in supplication.

"Oh yes. I wish you hadn't done wicked things and been sent to prison. Now I have nothing. *You* have nothing."

"Why would you do such a foolish thing, girl?" His voice was no longer an agonized whisper. It was harsh with disbelief.

"Why, Father, you know that I am silly and weak and can't do anything on my own. You've told me this my whole life." She glanced up at him with wide eyes, watching him mentally scramble. "I don't understand why you would get locked away in prison and leave me alone if you knew that. It's almost like you wanted me to suffer. Is that what you wanted?"

Alehk grimaced. "Only Ingoka decides who suffers and who doesn't. If you are suffering it is because *you* have caused her offense."

"Is that why you are in prison, Father?" she asked. "Because you have offended Ingoka?"

"No," he said vehemently. "It is because my enemies have conspired against me. But Ingoka also rewards suffering."

Nya tilted her head. "Father, are you saying that if I behave wickedly, and suffer for it, I will be rewarded?"

"Ah! My heart!" Alehk clutched his chest, his face suddenly pinched with agony. It took everything in Nya not to give in to panic.

He's lying. He wants to hurt you.

Her father panted. "I have such a short amount of time left, you know. The doctors told me that I could die any day now."

There was the pivot, once he'd tied himself into hypocitical, nonsensical knots.

"The same doctor who told Grandmother about your collapse?" she asked sweetly. "I'd like to talk to this person."

"He is on vacation now, my child." He sighed. "I have money so don't worry too much about what you have lost."

"Hidden money?" Her stomach lurched as she remembered all the things he had refused to reveal to the authorities.

"Yes. The information is in the chest with your mother's wedding dress," he said in a low voice, as if he hadn't defiled his wife's memory by using that dress as a cache for his traitorous profits.

"Oh no. I sold that chest, Father."

Alehk Jermami shot up to a seated position. "What?"

"I sold it. I told you I sold all of our things. I am sorry."

Now that her father was visibly upset, a hand at his head, Nya wished she hadn't lied at all. She didn't enjoy causing him pain. The only thing she wanted from him was an apology, and a love that didn't suffocate her — she would never have those things.

"Actually wait, Father. I think I didn't sell

that chest." She watched as he sagged back down onto the bed, thinking she would keep his secret when anyone with common sense would expect her to tell Ledi and Thabiso about it. "I have to go now."

"Will you come visit me tomorrow?" he asked, his heart pain and shock completely forgotten.

"Yes," she lied.

"And you won't leave me again?"

"No," she lied, blinking back tears. There was no pleasure in these lies, so she gave him one truth. "I love you, Father."

She kissed him on his forehead, then turned and left before he could see her tears.

As she walked through the gates of the prison, it was her turn to clutch her chest. She doubled over, trying to breathe deeply like Portia had once taught her. How could someone so unworthy of her love still cause her so much pain?

It seemed love didn't differentiate between worthiness and unworthiness. Some monsters couldn't be defeated — they would always have their claws in you. She could understand why Johan had been so adamant about avoiding the emotion. She had lost him and her father both, in different ways, and it was awful. Terrifying. But she wouldn't shy away from love. She would likely be hurt, again and again, but if she closed herself off from that, wouldn't it be just as her father had wished?

She stood, breathing under control, and got into the car with a driver from the palace that had been waiting for her in the parking lot. She stared out the window as it pulled away, staring at the less familiar sights surrounding the prison, and the bustle of the city center, without truly seeing them.

She tried to imagine remaking a life in Thesolo, going to these shops again and walking these streets, but the same feeling of being trapped descended on her again. She loved her country, but she couldn't shake the feeling of constriction that had marked so much of her life there. The door to her birdcage was open, but it still felt too small.

"Here we are, Ms. Jerami," the driver said as they pulled up in front of the palace after passing through the security at the entrance gates.

"Thank you," she murmured, sliding out as a member of the palace staff opened her door. She walked toward the gardens instead of going inside to see her friends and family. She was tired and she was lonely, and she didn't want to talk about her father yet.

She also didn't want to talk about Johan and have to reveal her lie to her grandparents and the rest of the kingdom.

She passed Lineo, the palace guard who had witnessed so many of her embarrassing moments, and nodded. The woman didn't smile, but she nodded in return before touching her ear and turning away from Nya. Tears warmed Nya's eyes as she imagined Lineo and everyone else realizing they had been right — Nya had been silly to think things could work with Johan. Everyone would know he had pitied her.

No. He loved you. However it had turned out, that was one true thing in a lifetime of lies. She wouldn't let anyone take that away from her.

She exhaled deeply, walking toward her gazebo. She considered not going in to avoid memories of Johan but those were unavoidable, and maybe it would help to immerse herself in it. She didn't want to hide from pain — she didn't want lost love to warp her, as it had warped her father.

She was almost inside the structure when she heard a strange yipping noise.

She paused, looking around, then entered under the curtain of flowers and found . . .

"Phokojoe," she said, stopping up short. A man with a fox's head stood in the gazebo, leaning against one of its posts. The fox god sported a fine blue vest over a white shirt with the sleeves rolled up to the elbows.

"Lovely maiden," the fox god said in a slightly muffled voice tinged with a Liechtienbourgish accent.

Her heart began to beat fast, too fast. There was a pain in her chest, one she felt more deeply than she had in front of the prison but that filled her with gladness instead of sorrow.

It seemed Johan had done some reading.

"Phokojoe, I have nothing to offer you," she said in a trembling voice, responding with the appropriate line from the fairy tale.

The fox god took a step forward. "You have treated me well and I will never forget that. What is it you most desire, lovely maiden?"

"A job?" Nya joked, deviating from the script, because she wanted to make Johan laugh and because she still wasn't quite sure she could trust the happiness threatening her.

The fox head mask tilted. "Hmm. Employment isn't my domain, though I know some gods who could help with that."

"Great," she said. Then closed her eyes and pressed her palms against them, unable to contain the emotion swelling in her. *Joy.*

Fear. Hope. Love.

She hiccupped out a sob and then heard the sound of the fox god's designer shoes on the wood floor of the gazebo, moving toward her. When she peeked through her fingers she could see the blue of his pants and the dusting of auburn hair on his forearm as he stood before her.

"Is there . . . is there anything else you desire?"

The mask couldn't muffle the vulnerability in his tone, and she dropped her hands and looked up at him with wet eyes. He was within arms' length now and she reached out, running her hands up his chest before gripping the bottom of the mask and pulling it up and peeling it back. She laughed when it got stuck on his nose, forcing her to yank it to get him out of it.

Johan's auburn hair was plastered to his head with sweat and his face was flushed, but his eyes were so bright and hopeful as he looked down at her.

"I know this is a bit presumptuous," he said, and then that slow grin spread across his face.

"Yes. The story ends in Phokojoe's favor." She slipped her arms around his waist and looked up at him. "Imagine his luck, meeting a woman whose greatest desire is . . . him."

His hands were sliding up her back now, rubbing at the tension beneath her shoulder blades.

"I'll have you know that I'm a scholar of fairy tales," he said. "I have a different reading of that ending. He wasn't her greatest wish. She was *his.*"

They just stared at each other for a while, Nya enjoying the familiar solid bulk of Johan against her, even if he was sweaty and smelled like rubber.

"Why were we fighting again?" she asked eventually.

"Because we're human, and have baggage that love doesn't make disappear into thin air?"

Nya made a shocked face and pretended to pull away from him. "Eh! I thought you were a fox god! What trickery is this?"

Johan held her tight. "No trickery. I love you. And I know love is just the beginning of what it takes to make things work, but maybe we can try that? Making things work?"

His gaze was so earnest and so intense that she had to look away to think clearly. She rested her forehead on his shoulder. "I just came from seeing my father."

His hold on her tightened. "Are you okay?"

She sighed, leaning into him a bit more. "He wasn't really sick. And I was so mad that I–I lied to him. I told him I had lost all of his money."

"That's not so bad," Johan said.

"I told him I would go see him again, but I won't." She pressed her forehead harder into his shoulder and one of his hands came up to stroke the back of her neck. "I'm cruel, aren't I?"

"I think on the cruelty scale, using your possible death to make your daughter bend to your will is slightly higher."

She let him hold her for a long time, let all of her emotions swirl inside her and then begin to settle.

"I'm sorry for making you feel awkward with the game thing," she said, hugging him tightly. "I would have also been upset if I found out you were playing a game in which you date a bumbling girl from Thesolo."

He pulled back to look at her, brows raised with interest. "Is there a game like that on the market?"

He was grinning, and she grinned, too. "You're looking at it. Real-life three-dimensional dating simulation N.Y.A. — naughty young antelope."

He laughed then, and even though she hadn't been away from him for long, his laughter seeped into the parts of her that had become cracked under the knowledge that she might never see him again, filling those fractures.

She took a deep breath and met his gaze. "I want to be with you."

"When?" he asked.

"Now."

"Where?"

"Do you still have a kingdom?" she asked, remembering the referendum through her haze of happiness.

He glanced up and to the side. "Actually, I'm not sure. They were still tallying the votes when I left. But you are welcome to come back with me, even if it's no longer a kingdom when we return. I have my own apartment, you know. It has a huge bathtub and several large mirrors."

Nya's cheeks warmed.

"I think we have a lot of details to work out, but the basics are you love me and I love you and we want to be together. Is this accurate?"

"Ouay," Nya drawled.

Johan's laughter was light, more carefree than she'd ever heard it. "We'll figure this out. Together."

"You should kiss me now," she murmured, pushing up on her toes.

"Comme tu willst."

His lips pressed against hers as a sudden rain shower drummed along the roof of the gazebo. When their mouths were bruised and their hearts were full, Nya held Johan tightly, like any person would hold on to their wildest dreams. He held her back, like he would never let her go.

EPILOGUE

Ten months later

Nya stopped into the coffee shop near Castle von Braustein as she had every morning for the last two months, having discovered that she enjoyed their pastries more than those served at the castle, where they spent a good chunk of their time since Lukas was heading off to California and their first year of college soon. The referendum had gone in the von Brausteins' favor, and Lukas's panicked attempt to manipulate it had resulted in better communication and new ideas of tradition — and intensive family therapy.

Nya had been going to therapy on her own and with Johan, and though they both sometimes struggled not to fling their baggage at one another, most of their time was spent, well, happily ever after.

Nya hovered in front of the café's glass refrigerator, struggling over which pastry to choose as the barista made her caffeine-free mocha latte.

The coffee shop was down the street from the office space Johan had rented to house his newly rebranded nonprofit organization six months ago, and where Nya had been hired as director of education and youth programs. It was nepotism, sure, but she was also well qualified for the position and took her job very seriously.

She had coworkers who respected her decisions, and her own desk where she could sit and carry out important work. Johan was in and out of the office but tried not to give her too much attention. They'd both decided it would be unprofessional for him to give her suggestive glances across the office and, well, Johan had a hard time not showing exactly what he was feeling when he looked at her. It had grown even harder, lately, but she didn't mind when he popped into her private office to kiss her cheek or rub her shoulders.

She finally settled on getting a box with a variety of muffins, tarts, and pastries for her coworkers and began the walk into work.

Yes, her back ached a little as she walked and she missed her family, but she was happy.

It all felt so . . . perfect. She'd thought she

needed to go to a big city to find herself or return home ashamed. She'd thought she had to be boring and frumpy, or all-out glamorous.

Now she spent her days at a job she loved and her nights with the semi-prince she was planning a wedding with. She got to travel the world, sometimes staying at the finest hotels and sometimes in remote outposts, sometimes just for fun and other times helping to garner humanitarian attention and aide.

She'd thought her dreams were too big, but she'd been wrong — they'd been just right. All that had been missing, for her, was the person she could share them with.

She was almost back to the office when she heard a car come to a stop on the cobblestone street next to her.

She looked to her side to see one of the palace's black SUVs. The back window rolled down to reveal the face of the man who was still absolutely smitten with her, who still held her every night, but made sure to always give her space to fly free.

"Ca geet et?" she called out.

"I'm good. Need a ride?" he asked, raising one brow. His seductive gaze morphed into one of annoyance as Lukas's hand pushed his face back into the seat. Their smiling face popped up in the window; their hair was no longer pink, simply grown out long and worn down around their shoulders today.

"How do you tolerate him? Honestly. We have to go meet with some business leaders from France and all he could ask was, 'I wonder if they'll bring *macarons*? Nya loves *macarons*.' Sickening, honestly."

"Oh, you know you think it's cute," Nya said, opening the box of pastries and sticking it through the window. "Take a couple for the road. I'm going to be late for work."

Lukas grabbed a scone and Johan ducked his head to kiss the back of Nya's hand instead. Then he took an éclair with a wink. "See you tonight, Sugar Bubble. I'll be a little late because I had to reschedule my appointment with Dr. Freudsbard."

"Okay, see you tonight! Have fun haggling with the French!"

She watched the car pull away, then immediately screech to a halt.

Johan jumped out, ran up to her, and kissed her with the same passion he had the first time he'd debauched her, even as his hand slipped over her stomach and rested on the bump that could barely be discerned yet.

Both of her hands were full, so she kissed

him even harder since she couldn't slide her hand atop his to reassure him.

"Go to your meeting, Phoko," she said gently before giving him a final peck. He was smiling his nervous smile so she knew what was coming.

"You sure you're feeling okay? Does that have caffeine in it? Maybe you shouldn't be walking?"

She gave him the most loving glare she could muster. "Johan."

"Sorry! Working on it, working on it. I really just wanted a kiss." He snuck in another quick brush of his mouth over hers. "I love you."

"I love you, too!" she called out with a grin as he jogged back to the car. He opened the door, turning to stand on the sideboard and blow her a kiss as the car pulled away, because he still opted for the dramatic route every time. Lukas tugged him into the car by the lapels, and she continued on her way to work as they drove off.

You dream too big, girl.

She did. And she would never stop, if she could help it.

ABOUT THE AUTHOR

Alyssa Cole is a science editor and romance junkie who lives in the Caribbean. She founded the Jefferson Market Library Romance Book Club and has contributed romance-related articles to publications including *RT Book Reviews, Heroes and Heartbreakers, Romance at Random,* and *The Toast.*

The employees of Thorndike Press hope you have enjoyed this Large Print book. All our Thorndike, Wheeler, and Kennebec Large Print titles are designed for easy reading, and all our books are made to last. Other Thorndike Press Large Print books are available at your library, through selected bookstores, or directly from us.

For information about titles, please call:
(800) 223-1244

or visit our website at:
gale.com/thorndike

To share your comments, please write:
Publisher
Thorndike Press
10 Water St., Suite 310
Waterville, ME 04901